***

Visit exciting new worlds in three tales of space opera adventure, thrilling romance, and unusual pets by USA TODAY bestselling author Carol Van Natta.

In **Pet Trade**, after military cyborg Axur ends up with a cargo of designer pets, he enlists the reluctant aid of a veterinarian who can help him care for them. He terrifies her, but Bethnee can't say no to helping animals with her minder talent for healing them. When greedy mercenaries come raiding, can the cyborg and the veterinarian overcome their limitations, with help from their unusual pets, and save the day?

In **Cats of War**, tarnished military Subcaptain Kedron counts the days until he can leave his post as liaison to the government's quasi-prison system, even if it means leaving the one person who makes him want to stay. Factory repair tech Ferra tries to keep her head down while she finishes her restitution sentence, but the local shark wants her to steal for him, and she's running out of excuses. Everything changes when they rescue two genetically modified cats. When trouble erupts in the factory, it might just be the cats who save them.

In **Galactic Search and Rescue**, when an earthquake shakes up a nearby world, can two star-crossed rescuers save an entire community... and each other? Rescuer and telekinetic Taz hides her wounded heart and her unwise attraction to her new teammate. Animal telepath Rylando can't let his own growing attraction to Taz distract them both from the dangerous rescue mission. Can love—and a clever crew of animals—guide the couple out of the rubble and into a future together?

The Galactic Pets Collection is your ticket to science fiction action and romance — grab your copy today!

ALSO BY CAROL VAN NATTA

Space Opera - Central Galactic Concordance Series

- Last Ship Off Polaris-G (Novella)
- Overload Flux (Book 1)
- Minder Rising (Book 2)
- Zero Flux (Novella)
- Pico's Crush (Book 3)
- Pet Trade (Novella)
- Jumper's Hope (Book 4)
- Cats of War (Novella)
- Galactic Search and Rescue (Novella)
- Escape from Nova Nine (Novella)
- Spark Transform (Book 5)

Retro Science Fiction Comedy

- Hooray for Holopticon

Paranormal Romance

- Shifter Mate Magic (Ice Age Shifters #1)
- Shift of Destiny (Ice Age Shifters #2)
- Heart of a Dire Wolf (Ice Age Shifters #3)
- Dire Wolf Wanted (Ice Age Shifters #4)
- Shifter's Storm (Ice Age Shifters #5)
- In Graves Below (Magic, New Mexico)

GALACTIC PETS

THREE SPACE OPERA ROMANCES WITH ADVENTURE & PETS

CAROL VAN NATTA

CHAVANCH PRESS

PET TRADE

An injured veterinarian and a cyborg with unusual pets must join forces to save their town.

The vast Central Galactic Concordance strictly prohibits genetic experimentation and alteration of humans on any of its 500 member planets. Animals aren't so lucky.

On a frontier planet, veterinarian **Bethnee Bakonin** made a home for herself in the frozen north. Her minder talent for healing all kinds of animals would ordinarily assure her success, but her unwilling stint in the shady pet trade industry left her damaged and scared. She works around her limitations as best she can, and rescues pet trade castoffs.

"Volunteered" for a black-box research project, elite forces Jumper **Axur Tragon** now has dangerous experimental tech in his cybernetic limbs. He escaped and crash-landed a stolen freighter in the northern mountains of a frontier planet, only to discover a secret shipment of designer pets was part of the cargo. Determined to do right by them, he enlists reluctant Bethnee's aid in caring for them—a definite challenge, considering Bethnee is terrified of him.

When greedy mercenaries come raiding, can Axur and Bethnee work together to overcome their limitations, with help from their unusual pets, and save the day?

1

V eterinary medic Bethnee Bakonin limped toward the cage slowly. The huge dire wolf inside stood and eyed her with wary interest, but not fear or anger. The wolf's bright blue, intelligent eyes contrasted beautifully against her thick coat of charcoal grey and black fur. Bethnee reached out with another thread of her talent to get a sense of the designer animal's health. "Where did she come from?"

A capricious, chilly wind blew a dust devil into the center of the paddock, then let it go. Fall always arrived early in the foothills of the northernmost mountains on Del'Arche.

"A boutique alpaca ranch down south. New client." Nuñez frowned and crossed her arms. "Idiots thought a top-of-the-line, protector-class dire wolf would make a great herd dog." She made a disgusted sound. "They were going to shoot her because she wouldn't let the herd out of the barn. I convinced them to sign her over to me."

Bethnee eyed Nuñez. "How much did she cost?" Designer

animals from reputable pet-trade dealers weren't cheap. Recreating extinct mammals from Earth's Pleistocene period was perennially popular, because it avoided the Central Galactic Concordance government's multiple prohibitions against altering cornerstone species like wolves and coyotes. Bethnee had been saving her hard credits to buy her own flitter, instead of constantly having to borrow Nuñez's, but the rescued dire wolf took priority.

Nuñez shook her head. "Zero. They bought her cheap with a flatlined ID chip, so she's probably stolen. I told them I'd take care of the problem for free, and that it'd be our little secret." Knowing Nuñez, she'd pushed them with her low-level empath talent, so they'd be afraid of getting caught, and happy to be rid of the evidence. Nuñez had no compunction against using her minder talent to manipulate humans who hurt animals, which was one of several reasons why she and Bethnee got along so well.

Bethnee focused on sensing the wolf's mind. The fleeting thoughts were complex, with deep memories. The wolf had known and felt pack love for other humans, but hadn't seen them for a long time. The ranchers had beaten her to get her into the cage, and she didn't know what she'd done wrong.

Bethnee contained her talent and her anger, then told Nuñez what she'd found. "She's also got tracers in every major joint. Can I use your small surgical suite this afternoon?" The portable unit contained micro surgical tools with an AI-assist built in, and would make quick work of the excisions.

"Sure." Nuñez tilted her head toward the doors of the vetmed clinic behind her. "Let's get her inside."

"Does she respond to a name?"

"Didn't come up." Nuñez looked at the clock. "I'll make you a deal. After I put the flitter away, you help me feed and water the yaks, and I'll help you with the tracers."

"It'll snow tonight." Nuñez lifted the last bulky bag of feed and unsealed it. At age one hundred and nine, the woman looked like a plump rural grandmother who printed heritage quilts and baked cookies, but she was strong and smart, and could control a herd of fifty large buffalo with her minder talent.

Bethnee took the bag. "The weather AI doesn't think so." She angled her hip so she didn't stress her bad leg, then reached high to pour the bag's contents into the hopper.

"The yaks say otherwise." Nuñez took the empty bag. "They're huddling in the corner of the pen near the barn. Weather AI says it'll be a bad winter." She gave Bethnee a meaningful look. "You could move back to the clinic."

"We've been..." Bethnee began, then sighed. "I'm fine where I am. It suits me."

Nuñez continued as if she hadn't heard. "Still plenty of room in the clinic. You could live next door, because that hateful Raloff family abandoned the property to move deeper into the mountains." She headed for the sink to wash her hands. "If we shared the clinic again, you could actually leave town for more than a few hours and know your animals were safe, and maybe have your leg fixed. You're too young to be a hermit. You're homesteaded now, and the town would be happy to have you."

"No, they wouldn't." Bethnee followed Nuñez to the sink. "Too many people considered my animals a nuisance." She pointed her chin toward the big cage. "The first goat or child that went missing, they'd accuse the dire wolf. Or Jynx." Unusual snow leopards, no matter how well behaved, scared people who didn't know them.

As Bethnee washed her hands, Nuñez turned on the mini-solardry. "It was only the Raloffs and Administrator Pranteaux who complained, and he complains about everything." They both rubbed their hands vigorously in the warm, forced air. "Come on. Let's take care of your new wolf."

Bethnee was grateful that her friend hadn't gotten into the real reasons Bethnee couldn't move back. A lot of frontier settlers like the

Raloffs had moved away from the Central Galactic Concordance member planets to get away from minders, and everyone knew she was one, because she used her talents as well as her training to treat pets. Word got around.

More importantly, even though she'd escaped her former life in the pet trade three years ago, she still couldn't get within five meters of any man without taking the chance she'd be shaking like a leaf from mind-numbing fear. When she'd first arrived, she couldn't even be in the same building. She'd gotten better with time, but it was bad for business when she couldn't deal with nearly half the population of customers.

Nuñez claimed it was post-trauma stress, and just like her leg, it could be treated by competent medics and minders. Even if that were true, it would cost hard credit, and she needed every decimal she had to provide for her animal family. They didn't care that she was too scared and too damaged to live among humans.

2

Axur Tragon fought the rising wind to land the old runabout as gently as he could on the Tanimai community airpad. He retracted the canopy and climbed out, then stepped around back to open the hatch and untie the two covered carriers. "Almost there," he crooned.

He slung the straps on each of his shoulders, then walked to Tanimai's vetmed clinic. His cybernetic legs weren't pretty, but they gave him a long, smooth gait, even when carrying a thirty-kilo load.

He'd only been in town a dozen times since he'd landed three hundred local days ago on the frontier planet of Del'Arche. Crashed, really, but his former Jumper Corps flight instructor said as long as the pilot and passengers crawled away, it counted as a landing.

He hoped the veterinary medic wouldn't turn him away. Between his intimidating height, his long, shaggy hair, and his bizarre and heavy metallic poncho, he looked like a disaster refugee with mental issues. Throw in the scars and the visible cybernetics, and he probably scared birds from the sky.

The shallow lobby was open, but deserted. He stepped up to the wallcomp. "Hello?"

An older woman's face appeared on the display. "Be there in a minute. Set the carriers on the table."

He complied, after first testing the table to make sure it would hold.

Moments later, the interior sliding doors opened and revealed the woman he'd spoken to. She had black hair streaked with silver, and a pleasant smile. "I'm Aniashalaman Nuñez, the VMD. Call me Nuñez." She looked up at him from her considerably shorter height. "You must be the ex-Jumper, Axur Tragon. You're as tall as everyone says." Despite her Islander complexion and facial features, her accent was pure Standard English.

He returned her smile. "I'm actually short, for a Jumper."

Nuñez laughed and shaded her eyes as she looked up. "From down here, you all look like trees to me." She tilted her head toward the table. "What can I help you with?"

"I have some, uh, pets, and these are sick, I think." He shoved his hands in his pockets under his heavy poncho. "To be honest, I kind of inherited them, and don't know much about their care, except what I read in reference manuals. They all did okay in the spring and summer, but lately, these aren't."

"How many pets do you have?" Nuñez crossed to the table and lifted the cover on the first cage. "Ah, birds of paradise. Three females and a male. Are they mated?"

"No clue. To answer your first question, seven if you count species, and twelve animals total. I think they're all designer, rather than domestic." He tilted his head toward the second cage. "I don't even know what some of them are."

Nuñez lifted the cover of the second carrier. "Great balls of chaos, what a…" Nuñez pulled the cover off completely. "…chimera."

Axur suspected she'd censored a less diplomatic description. He couldn't blame her. Kivo was German shepherd-sized, but the resemblance ended there. He had black and brown stripes in his short, sleek fur, and six legs with clawed paws for running and catching. Gigantic, bat-style swivel ears sat on his broad, flat head. He had two tails with tufts of black fur on the ends. He was a prime example of what the anti-pet-trade activists railed against: tinkering with Terran genetics to create whimsical animals that would have never survived in the wild, much less natural selection. Kivo might be a genetic mess, but he was also the sweetest, most laid-back beast Axur had ever met, and was patient with all the animals, even the miniature dinosaur that often mistook Kivo's tails as something edible. "Kivo's usually interested in everything, and eats anything, but not for the past week. The birds just huddle in the bottom of their cage and won't go out."

Nuñez made a face. "I might be able to help with the birds, but Kivo is about as far off my chart as you can get. My patients are large herd animals and the occasional terrier or tabby. You need a specialist." She glanced up at him and sighed. "As it happens, I know one of the best in the galaxy, but she's not..."

A cacophony of goose honking from somewhere in the building interrupted. Nuñez glanced toward the back and frowned. "Sit a minute." She pointed to a lobby chair, then strode through the doors she'd come through and vanished. The doors slid quickly closed behind her.

He dragged the chair closer to the table and sat, putting his face closer to Kivo's cage. The chimera rolled back in the cage and exposed his striped stomach. "Sorry, buddy, no belly rubs until they give me permission to let you out."

Axur looked up when the clinic's outside doors opened to admit a tall, willowy woman with shoulder-length, deep blue-black hair and Asian features. She carried several bags and a box, and walked with a pronounced limp. She glanced at him, startled. "Does Nuñez know..." She trailed off as her attention riveted on Kivo.

After a long moment, Axur answered her unfinished question. "Nuñez asked me to wait here."

She darted a look to his face and awkwardly backed up several steps, dropping one of the bags. "Oh."

He started to stand and reach out to help her, but froze in mid-rise when her eyes widened in unmistakable fear. Her hand visibly trembled as she awkwardly scooped up the bag, then fled through the doors to the back.

He sat down again with a sigh. It never paid to play the shoulda-coulda-woulda game, but starting a year ago, it was hard not to wish for a different star lane for his life. He'd never been nova-hot beautiful like some in his squad, but he'd never lacked for companionship and bed partners for his twelve years in the CPS Jumper Corps. Then, unbeknownst to him, he'd been secretly selected for a CPS "special project" that changed him forever, including adding valuable experimental tech to his cybernetics.

Now he was an ugly mass of biometal and hardware that made him a walking, talking satellite uplink. Only the heavy poncho he'd kludged together from salvaged supplies kept him from constantly broadcasting his unique comm signature to the frontier planet's various satellites, and from there to the Central Galactic Concordance's intergalactic communications network. If he uncloaked, his days of freedom remaining would be measured by how fast a CPS ship could get to Del'Arche to hunt him down.

Kivo whined. Axur stuck his fingers into the cage again and tried to shake off his melancholy. He'd lived, and so had Kivo and the others, and life was hope.

Ten minutes later, Nuñez strode back into the lobby, looking harried. "Thanks for waiting." She put her fists on her hips. "I have an emergency, so I'll cut to the chase. I can't treat your pets, but Bethnee Bakonin can. She's the woman who just came in. She's already seen you, and that's usually a deal-killer for her, but if you keep your distance and don't make sudden movements, she'll look at your animals." Her chin jutted out pugnaciously. "She's a pet-trade expert, but she's also a pan-phyla animal-affinity talent, so if you dislike minders, you can jet right now, 'cause I'm one, too."

Axur put his hands flat on his thighs. "Minders are just people. I don't care if she uses dark energy magic, if she can help Kivo and the birds." He pointed a thumb toward the front doors. "I could wait outside."

Nuñez shook her head. "No, she'll need information from you. Just move your chair away and stay seated." She glanced at his stained pants and worn combat boots. "I'll assume you're not offering hard credit. What are you trading?"

"Fall harvest gourds, berries, and leafy greens. If it's more than that, we can negotiate." In the planet's official financial transaction records, the town's economy was barely a blip, but it did a thriving business in trade. From what he'd gathered, the settlement company took a percentage of all financial transactions, but hadn't found a way to close the trading loophole, so they often conducted unannounced audits, trying to catch the town breaking the rules so they could levy hard-credit fines. They took a percentage of those transactions, too.

Nuñez nodded. "Fair enough." She gave him a considering look. "Bakonin is like most high-level animal-affinity talents, better with animals than people, and like a lot of us here in Tanimai,"—she looked pointedly at the visible scars on his neck and jaw leading up to his disabled skulljack—"she's had a hard life. Be respectful, and she'll do right by you and the animals. Scare her, and you'll never see her again."

Axur didn't miss the unspoken warning that he'd never trade in town again if he did anything to make Bakonin bolt. "Understood."

He carried the chair to the far corner and sat, then hunched over to rest his elbows on his knees. It was as short as he could make himself.

Nuñez left. The doors stayed open long enough for Bakonin to limp in. She glanced at him briefly as she made her way to the table. Her shuttered expression changed to interest when she got to the birds.

Axur watched as she opened the cage with the four birds and

deftly pulled the brightly colored male out and turned him upside down to look at his chest and feet. "Yes, yes," she said soothingly. Her voice had a warm, husky timbre. She did the same with the others, then closed the cage door.

She took a deep breath, let it out slowly, then turned to look at him. "Nuñez said you've only had the animals for about nine months, and that you've got more at home. Were they in your ship when you crashed?"

Axur looked up at her, startled. "How did you know about the ship?"

One corner of her mouth twitched. "Hard to miss a streaking fireball that left a kilometer-long gouge at the north end of Park Plateau. No one knew anyone had survived until you came into town two weeks later offering exotic trade goods. People talk." She pointed skyward. "You're lucky the weather satellites were malfing again, or the company auditors would have levied a huge fine for terraform destruction, confiscated anything you had of value, then expatriated you to the nearest Concordance lockup for illegal trespass and occupation."

He ducked his head, embarrassed that it hadn't occurred to him that others might have seen his ungraceful entry into Del'Arche's atmosphere. "I didn't know about the animals until the hard landing ripped open the freighter's smuggling hold. I've tried to care for those that lived. The ship's library has good reference files."

Bakonin nodded. "Pet-trade dealers often ship on the sly to get around inspections and quarantines, and to deter thieves. It's a ruthless business." She pointed to the cage. "Your birds are healthy, but cold intolerant. If you don't give them a warm habitat and a diet of insects and fruit, they'll die. They're fertile, so if you do have a habitat, you'll have fledglings by the spring."

"Okay." He could work around the diet problem, but had no idea how he'd create a warm space out of the ship's wreckage, miscellaneous cargo, and the deadfall trees he'd hauled in for building materials. The possibility of offspring hadn't even crossed his mind.

Like everyone else in the Concordance, he'd gotten a birth control implant at the first hint of puberty, so reproduction took a deliberate decision between two people.

She turned to the chimera. Kivo exhibited intense curiosity, his leaf-shaped nose working and his ears swiveling forward. He stood, briefly, but his two back sets of legs shook, and he half sat. She opened the cage door. Kivo oozed out and crouched. She approached slowly, then gently ran her hands over his ribs, shoulder joints, and sharply articulated spine. Kivo leaned into her as she crooned nonsense words while she examined his ears, eyes, and wicked-looking teeth. He was soon rolling onto his back, stretching his six legs out, begging for attention. She smiled and rubbed his belly, and even laughed when he sloppily licked her nose when she got close enough. "Does he have a name?"

Axur was so mesmerized by her obvious skill and the glimpse of beauty in her smile that it took him a moment to realize she was talking to him. "Kivo."

She kept one hand on Kivo's broad head and stroked his ear muscles with her thumb. "I'm guessing you fed him fresh meat and produce from your garden, which is the best thing you could have done, because it's kept him alive. The dealer was probably returning him to the research company's designers as a failure." Sadness stole across her face. "Even if we eradicate the blood parasite and tailor some nutritional chems to counter the anemia it caused, which is his current issue, other problems are coming. He's already got early-onset arthritis, especially in his double hips and flexible spine, and his fine-motor control is degrading."

It sounded like Kivo had the chimera equivalent of waster's disease, a pernicious problem that plagued Jumper veterans across the galaxy. The CPS researchers conducting the "special project" claimed to have cured him of it as compensation for taking his arm. Last he'd heard, that was impossible, so he really hoped that wasn't another one of their lies. His tried not to focus on his resentment and turned his attention back to Kivo. "Why did they create him at all?"

She shrugged. "Pretend alien fauna for the wealthy, maybe? It's a fad." She stroked the large hump of Kivo's middle shoulder joints. "The bio-engineers actually got the six legs to work, but the rest of him is a fantasy hodgepodge." She snorted disdainfully. "Two tails." She rested her hip against the table and eased the weight off her stiffer leg.

"He follows me everywhere. He keeps the peace among the other animals, too." He tilted his head. "Can animals be empaths? I think he tries to cheer me up sometimes." It sounded daft after he said it out loud, so he was grateful she didn't laugh.

"Maybe?" She shrugged. "Human medical scientists still don't know what combination of DNA and subtrans amino arrays make the difference between human minders and non-minders, or even predict the gender expression continuum. Who's to say that animals aren't evolving along with us?"

"Makes sense to me. What's the treatment protocol for him?"

"A tailored antibiotic to kill the parasite and immune boosters. If we can't trade with the local chems and alterants shop, we might have to use hard credit at the human med clinic down in Asgorth."

"I've got some reserve freighter stock to trade." He sat up straight and immediately regretted it, because it caused Bakonin to catch her breath and step back. "Sorry." He hunched over again.

Bakonin's lips thinned, and she shook her head. "I just hadn't realized how tall you are. Ex-Jumper?"

Axur gave her a humorless smile and held up his left hand, where exposed biometal gleamed at his knuckles. "My cybernetic arm and legs didn't give it away?" Most people preferred flesh and bone.

"Cybernetics are fine." She took a deep breath and let it out. "I'm phobic around men, sometimes, which is my problem, not yours."

Kivo's ears swiveled toward the sliding doors, and he rolled to a sitting position. A moment later, Nuñez appeared, the front of her tunic covered in blood. "I need your help."

3

After Bethnee hosed down the instruments of the large-animal surgical suite with steaming hot water, she stood next to the floor drain and turned the hose on her unlovely but waterproof, tear-resistant work tunic.

Axur, as he'd asked them to call him, had proven to be more than just a pretty face. Nuñez dragooned him into helping extricate a buffalo cow from a tangled coil of spikewire. Nuñez used her minder talent to control the cow while Axur used the superior strength of his cybernetic hand to stop the wire from springing out when Bethnee cut it. As long as she stayed on the other side of the cow and focused on using her talent to heal the cow's deepest lacerations, she'd managed to keep her mind clear and her stupid shaking to a minimum. Nevertheless, she felt like she'd hiked to the top of towering Mount Taruka and back.

Axur hadn't flinched at the blood or injuries. When Nuñez commented on it, he'd admitted he'd been a trained field medic in the Jumper Corps.

Nuñez had laughed. "What the hell are you doing trying to make a homestead the hard way? The townspeople would be thrilled to build you a clinic, like they did mine."

Axur had looked away and mumbled something about it being complicated. Bethnee sympathized. She lived that every day.

Axur turned out to have another invaluable skill. The rattled, panicky owner of the cow only spoke halting English, but Axur figured out the woman spoke Korean, and served as their translator. He admitted to speaking eight languages fluently, and could get by in a lot more. Bethnee knew Nuñez was adding it to her arsenal of arguments of why he should move to town. Under her bluff and blunt exterior, Nuñez had a heart the size of the Andromeda galaxy, and didn't believe in complications.

It fell to Bethnee, with Axur's translation help, to negotiate a complex trade for their cow-saving services that resulted in Axur getting the drugs he needed for his chimera using a credit the rancher had at the chems shop, in exchange for Axur giving his food-trade goods to Nuñez, who would share them with Bethnee so she could make further trades for the ingredients for nutritional supplements for her animals and Kivo.

Bethnee found Nuñez and Axur in the holding pen outside. Unexpectedly, the chimera and the dire wolf also roamed the pen, pretending disinterest in one another. Bethnee sent a thread of her talent out to both animals, and found that Kivo considered the wolf a new friend, and the wolf was considering everyone in the pen, including Bethnee, as potential pack mates that needed guarding from the dangerous, grunting yaks in the neighboring paddock.

Axur laughed at something Nuñez said. Despite his untamed hair and the peculiar cloak he refused to remove, he was a surprisingly handsome man, especially when he smiled. And such was the irrational tangle of her phobia that she could admire a tall, good-natured man from afar, then be too scared to get close enough to see the color of his eyes.

"I'm going to remove the tracers from the wolf," she said loudly. "Want me to do the same for Kivo while I'm at it?"

Axur gave her a puzzled look. "Tracers?"

When Nuñez explained about the pet-trade practice of implanting active tracers that broadcast a valuable animal's location to the net, and passive tracers that showed up on bio scanners, Axur readily agreed.

With Nuñez's help and the portable surgical suite's micro instruments, Bethnee finished with both animals in thirty minutes. Nuñez planned to trade the active tracers to a client who could use them for tracking goats.

In the lobby, Kivo sidled up to the tolerant wolf and licked at her muzzle. Bethnee could well believe that Kivo was the peacekeeper among Axur's menagerie.

Nuñez entered and crossed to Axur to hand him a cup of hot coffee.

He smiled as he closed his eyes and smelled it, then sipped it with obvious enjoyment. "Stars, but I've missed this."

Nuñez grinned and sipped from her own cup. "I trade for it whenever I can." She pointed a thumb toward Bethnee. "Don't ever let Bethnee make it for you, unless you have a biometal stomach."

Bethnee shrugged. It tasted like burned acid to her, so how was she to know what was too strong? A thigh muscle in her bad leg spasmed. She needed to soak in her single luxury, the geothermal pool. She should just go home and...

"Dammit," she said. "I can't take the wolf with me today. I only have the glide board, and no den big enough for her." She caught Nuñez's eye. "Can she stay a few days?"

"Sure, but she'll be alone except for the geese and the yaks, and she'll hate it."

"I know you don't know me or my setup," said Axur, "but I could take her for as long as you need. My barn is big, and she wouldn't lack for company."

Bethnee looked at him in surprise.

Axur splayed his hands. "I have an ulterior motive. I was hoping you'd come out to my place and look at the rest of my pets. Tell me what they are, and how to care for them."

Nuñez nodded. "You can borrow the flitter."

The idea of going alone to a man's homestead spiked Bethnee's anxiety, but Axur had scrupulously accommodated her by keeping his distance, and it was a good solution for the new wolf. If she didn't like what she saw, she could jet. Besides, she had to admit she wanted to see the exotic animals Axur had told them about.

"Okay."

Axur looked pleased.

Nuñez blinked and raised her eyebrows. "You trust him?"

Bethnee pointed to the chimera, draped across Axur's sturdy cybernetic knees like a lapdog, and the wolf, who was licking Axur's hand.

"I trust them."

4

If Bethnee hadn't been following Axur's runabout, she wouldn't have found his high-country homestead. Which, she surmised, was as deliberate as his choice to stay away from town, as well as his choice to wear his awkward heavy cloak.

She landed the flitter in a clearing about a hundred meters southwest of the edge of his loosely fenced perimeter. She wished she'd thought to bring her glide board, to save her leg from the uphill hike while carrying her vetmed bag. Fortunately, the dire wolf stayed near with very little coaxing via her talent.

Axur backed up as she approached, staying well out of her discomfort range. "Sorry, I didn't think about the distance." Behind him rose two buildings fashioned out of starship freighter sections. The taller one had wide doors made from an airlock. "It's windy up here, so I want to give you an earwire so we can talk without shouting. It'll take me a few minutes to program."

"Okay." The wolf remained by her side, nose working overtime as she checked out her new surroundings. Bethnee reached out with her talent to do the same.

Axur cleared his throat. "Some of the animals are in the barn." He pointed toward wide, open doors. "I'll knock on the wall when I'm ready with the earwire."

Forty minutes later, Bethnee sat on a rough-hewn bench at the worktable inside the barn, packing her equipment back into her bag and talking via the earwire to Axur, who was in his living quarters area. She didn't subvocalize; animals didn't care if she spoke out loud. "You've got a fortune in stolen and illegal pet-trade animals."

"Stolen?" The earwire made his rich baritone sound thin and distant.

"Your e-dog, for one. 'E' for enhanced. He's military-trained, and his sensory implants and command processor are still active. If you knew the passcode and comm band, you could program a percomp to give him complex sets of orders to follow, and get a feed through his implants."

"That makes sense. I named him Trouble because that's what he gets into unless I give him jobs to do. Just like some Jumpers I know."

"Your three cats are illegal because the designer spliced in a few primate genes to give them those long, flexible toes and a broader diet, and left them fertile. Any CGC health inspector would destroy them on sight, in case the splice bred true. Feed them meat and dairy, and any fruits or vegetables they'll eat. You could trade with Nuñez for some yak milk. They'll probably go into their first estrus cycle in the spring."

"Lucky they're all female. Can you or Nuñez fix their playgrounds so I don't have kittens on my hands if some equally fertile male comes looking for love?"

The big dire wolf warily poked her head into the barn's entrance.

The boldest of the young cats had already left a stinging wound across her nose leather.

Bethnee laughed. "Fix their playgrounds? Yeah, we can neuter them. What did you name them?"

She held out her hand, and the wolf trotted over. She sent another thread of healing to the wound, but couldn't repair the wolf's injured dignity.

"Alpha, Bravo, and Delta. There were four, but one of them died the first day." He was silent for a long moment. *"I never liked cremation duty."*

"Me, neither." She ran her fingers through the wolf's rough coat and sighed for all the beloved animals she'd lost over the years. "Your two ravens are a non-fertile mated pair and bred to be pets, but they're about half again the standard size, and their wings are intact, so they'd be destroyed for unfair ecosystem advantage. They'll tolerate the cold, but they need clean water and bone-in meat every day, or they'll starve. There won't be enough winter carrion at this elevation. That huge aviary you built them is good, but give them more branches to sit on."

"I traded for extra cases of dog food this summer. What else do they need?"

"Grains, leftovers, especially any real meat, maybe some rotting fruit. They'll eat almost anything. You might make them some toys and puzzles with food rewards. Train them to do new tasks. Keeps their busy brains active instead of destructive."

"I named them Shade and Shadow, after that tri-D serial about thieves. I recover an amazing amount of stuff every time I clean out their bowls and baths."

She chuckled at how disgruntled he sounded. "Your foo dog, Shiza, is legal, probably stolen. They're designed to look like little curly-haired lions from pre-flight Chinese legends, but underneath, they're mostly dog, so you can feed him whatever you feed Trouble. Don't let Shiza bite you out of anger or fear. Foo dogs are designed to protect children, and his teeth can inject a nasty toxin. I can use Nuñez's lab to tailor vaccines for you and the others, as well as Nuñez and me, but it'll take a ten-day or so."

The big wolf sat on her haunches and rested her head on Bethnee's shoulder. She stroked the wolf's broad head. "Long day, huh?"

"I'm sorry, I've taken up a lot of your time."

"No, I was talking to the dire wolf. Her life is in flux at the moment, and she's in here with me, wanting affection and reassurance."

Axur mumbled something in a language she didn't recognize. Her minimal education hadn't included anything but Standard English, and whatever rude words she could pick up on the streets. *"What about the miniature dinosaur? I think it's supposed to be a stegosaurus. Its name is Ankle Biter."*

She shook her head. "I don't do reptiles, amphibians, or fish. Can't feel them at all. Your reference manuals are your best bet. It might need to stay inside for the winter."

"Can I ask how you know so much about the pet trade? You don't seem like the type."

Ordinarily, she zeroed personal questions, but he was trusting her with the animals he loved. More tellingly, they all cared for him and trusted him without reservation.

She considered what she wanted to say. Jumpers willingly volunteered to work for the Citizen Protection Service's elite military force. The CPS hadn't done nearly as well by her, though to be fair, the huge agency had multiple missions, and it had been just the one corrupt woman.

"Never mind, it's none of my business."

"No, it's okay, it's just..." She couldn't come up with the right word. Talking about her past brought on a sour stomach and leg spasms, which was part of why she didn't do it often. "In the mandatory age-seventeen testing for minder talents, I scored high for animal-affinity minder talent. The CPS Testing Center agent *said* she got me a full scholarship at the CPS Minder Institute. Thrilled my parents, because I'd get the education they never had and couldn't afford for me. I didn't care, as long as I got to train my talent and work with animals."

"That's not what happened, I take it."

"She chemmed me, gave me an illegal chimera implant to change my DNA's biometric signature, and sent me as a counterfeit indenture to her cousin, a pet-trade dealer on a space station. She told my parents I died in a tragic interstellar passenger liner accident. Even sent them a memory diamond with my original DNA and a death payment. My bondholder made sure I knew that if I ever escaped and went home, they'd have to give back everything, which would bankrupt them."

She didn't understand Axur's reply, but the words were unmistakably curses. She envied his vocabulary.

"The first bondholder was okay. He got me training and promised I'd be a contract employee as soon as he could afford it, if I kept quiet how he got me. Three years after that, a bigger company destroyed his business and bought all his assets for a fraction. Instead of freeing me, Breitenbahn imprisoned me on an interstellar research ship. He only cared about results. I was the only 'employee' who couldn't leave, couldn't complain, couldn't fight back. And after all, I was just an indentured, subbin' minder."

Usually, she'd be shaking uncontrollably at this point, but now, she just felt queasy. Maybe it was different because Axur was just a sympathetic voice in her ear, and she was hanging on to a warm, hundred-kilo dire wolf who could sever a man's leg with a single bite.

"Breitenbahn finally made them stop abusing me when the animals started dying because I was too damaged to care for them or help the designers."

"How did you escape? I'm assuming they didn't suddenly find their lost ethics and let you go. You're far too valuable."

"Shipped myself in a container of comatose bovines bound for a remote frontier planet. It was dangerous, but Breitenbahn hired this new guard from the indenture system who wouldn't take 'no' for an answer. He shot me with an equine tranq and…" She shied away from the hideous memory. "Anyway, Nuñez was inspecting the shipment and found me. She believed my unbelievable story and took me home with her. Fed me, gave me animals to care for, made me a part of her vet business, and didn't judge. That was three years ago. I owe her more than I can ever repay."

"If I was still a Jumper, I'd invite some of my squad mates for a little vacation that just happened to coincide with the destruction of that ship."

"Thank you. I think." She smiled. "I probably shouldn't condone personal vengeance missions by elite special forces with access to really big guns and explosives."

"What can I say? We're trained to take the initiative. Lowlifes like Breitenbahn are obviously a threat to the galactic peace."

"Well, if you ever get the chance, I hope you'll let me save as many of the animals as I can. They didn't ask to be there, either."

"I'll add it to the mission parameters."

She couldn't tell if he was teasing or serious. A vigorous gust of wind rattled the doors of the barn and blew in a cloud of pine needles. "Nuñez's yaks say it'll snow tonight. Do you have someplace warm for the birds of paradise?"

"Her yaks talk? Never mind. I figured I'd bring their cage into my bunk area until I can fix up the barn."

She looked up at the roof of the chilly barn and watched the dust swirl. "I could keep them for the winter, if you like. I have geothermal heating."

"Feeding them will add to your costs. I don't want to impose."

"You aren't imposing. I offered." She gently pushed the wolf aside. "You can keep my dire wolf in trade. Give her a name. She'll love guarding you, and having the run of the valley when it snows. She's built for the cold. She'll eat a lot more than four birds, though. I'll trade removing the tracers from the rest of your animals, and a barrel of nutritional pellets that would be good for all your canines, to make it even."

In the ensuing silence, she got to her feet and brushed off her butt.

"Okay, we have a deal."

5

Three months after meeting Bethnee, Axur pedaled the stationary generator cycle in his barn to give his anxiety a better outlet than churning his gut. Kivo had suddenly taken ill, and Bethnee had insisted on borrowing Nuñez's flitter and coming in person, despite a howling snowstorm. Axur had sequestered himself in the barn so as not to distract her. She'd grown more tolerant of his physical proximity in their various interactions since they'd first met, but Kivo needed her full concentration.

The earwire idea had worked so well that first day that he'd created a better, customized version for her and convinced her to wear it everywhere. It helped make up for the lost camaraderie of his fellow Jumpers, and Bethnee seemed to enjoy having someone to talk to as well. She'd dubbed it the Axur-net.

They discussed the animals, and laughed about how unprepared each of them had been to find themselves homesteading on a frontier planet. He'd at least had extensive Jumper survival training to fall back on. She grew up on city streets and had spent the last eight years in space.

Jumpers weren't good at waiting and wondering. They climbed into planetfall mech suits and kicked ass. He pedaled.

Two hours later found him adding worrying to the list of things he wasn't good at. Kivo had crashed twice, and each time, Bethnee had pulled him back from the brink. The last time she'd talked to him through the earwire, she'd sounded exhausted and distant, and she hadn't responded at all for the past ten minutes.

She was competent and smart, but something Nuñez had said one day, about a migraine headache being blowback from overusing her minder talent, had Axur thinking Bethnee might be in trouble. He wasn't trained to treat minders, because they weren't allowed in the Jumper Corps, but he was trained to treat humans. Despite what some ignorant zero-heads still thought, all minders were human. After five more minutes of plaguing himself with visions of calamity, he went back to his living quarters.

Kivo lay quietly where Axur had left him. Bethnee lay behind him, eyes closed, one arm and one knee draped loosely over him like a lover's. Kivo's breathing was steady. The tufted tip of one of his tails moved, and he swiveled one large ear toward Axur as he stepped closer.

Bethnee didn't so much as twitch, and looked pale and sweaty. If she'd been awake, she'd already be edging away.

He called her name softly, then louder, but got no response. He couldn't use his salvaged autodoc, because he didn't know how Bethnee would react to waking up in an enclosed cylinder little bigger than a cremation tube. That left his bed, which easily held him and various pets, so it wouldn't make her claustrophobic.

He gently extracted her from around Kivo and carried her toward the back room. She felt warmly female in his arms. He felt guilty even thinking it, because it would terrify her. He had no business wanting a woman who'd been treated as a subhuman, and beaten or worse to force compliance. Hell, the thoughts terrified him.

He was the opposite of attractive, and had enough baggage of his own to open a tourist shop at the spaceport. He couldn't see how it would end well for either of them.

She began to convulse just as he got her to the bedroom door. He let her legs drop so she could throw up without hurting herself, but he couldn't catch enough of the mess with his cybernetic hand to keep it from soaking her shirt and pants. The stomach-churning smell assaulted his nose, but as a former battlefield medic and current household servant to nine pets, he was used to dealing with all sorts of unpleasant odors and substances.

By the time he got her into the fresher, she was barely responsive.

He sprayed her off as best he could, but she wasn't wearing her waterproof work tunic, and was soon soaked and shivering.

Telling himself he was looking but not seeing, he removed everything but her underwear, then draped her with one of his blankets and carried her to his bed. He quickly found her veterinary scanner and used it on her.

And since he was already being unethical by examining her without her permission, he evaluated her bad left leg, with its deep, ugly scars and distorted tendons and muscles. He swore in several languages as he dressed her in one of his tunics, then covered her up with more blankets. Since she had been a Concordance citizen, her kidnappers—he refused to call them bondholders—could have had her injury fixed for free anywhere in the Concordance. They'd purposefully left her untreated for years.

He couldn't ever return to the Jumpers again, and he was in no position to organize a mission against Bethnee's captors, but he did send a fervent prayer out to the constant stars to exact the justice he couldn't.

6

Bethnee woke to unfamiliar... everything. The soft glowlight on the wall, the cat purring on her chest, the furry body at her side, the too-long sleeve of her shirt. Not to mention, a room that looked like the shell of an interstellar ship's stateroom.

The bed shifted, and a golden furry face appeared above hers.

"Hello, Trouble." Her voice sounded raspy and her throat hurt. The dog licked at her cheek, then pushed off from the bed and left.

The furry warmth at her side stirred. Shiza, the square-jawed foo dog with the perpetual cute grimace and drooling habit, scrambled to his feet and shook himself, leaving a drifting cloud of curly golden fur.

Bethnee cautiously reached out with her talent to Delta, the cat on her chest, just to make sure she could. She'd exhausted all her reserves to save Kivo because she knew how much Axur loved the beast. She didn't even know if she'd succeeded. Or what time it was. Or how she came to be mostly naked in Axur's big bed. That realization made her feel aware, but not wary. She put the thought aside for later.

She sat up and discovered a veterinary fluids pump attached to the back of her hand. She was still staring at it stupidly when Axur appeared at the bedroom door.

"How do you feel?" He touched a control on the wall to make the lights brighter.

"Like hammered horse shi... " She trailed off as she got a good look at Axur. She'd never seen him without winter clothes and his heavy cloak, and now there he stood, damp and naked except for the towel around his trim waist and defined abdominals. He'd tied back the coiled strands of his long, frizzy hair, revealing a well-muscled chest that was a blend of warm brown skin, a few scars to give it character, and a smooth transition to his cybernetic arm, with its mismatched synthskin patches and exposed biometal. "You're stunning."

He blinked, clearly nonplussed.

"Sorry." She couldn't stop staring. Didn't want to, in fact. "From the way you talk, I'd thought you looked like a corroded, spare-parts cyborg from the serial sagas." That was probably the lamest thing she'd ever said. "Sorry. I'll shut up now."

He started to speak, but stopped himself. He seemed not to know what to do with his hands. "I'm not standing too close?"

"No." She tried to puzzle it out. Humans usually felt like phantoms to her, like she was listening to the wrong frequency. "Maybe I'm still being affected by talent blowback sickness, but right now, you're not a ghost, you're solid. Like one of Nuñez's yaks."

He laughed out loud.

She shrugged, embarrassed. "Sorry."

"I'm flattered. Truly." His warm smile made her believe it. "Back to my original question. Your color is much better, and your temperature stabilized a while ago. How are you?"

"I'll live. How's Kivo?"

"See for yourself." He turned aside, and Kivo stepped forward, looking as healthy as she'd ever seen him. Relief flooded through her. He launched himself toward her to put his first set of paws on the bed and joyfully lick her face.

"Yes, all right." She rubbed his ears. "I'm happy to see you're alive, too." The aches in all her joints and the post-fever lethargy melted away at the affection Kivo was broadcasting. In that moment, she could readily believe Axur's theory that Kivo was an empath, just like Nuñez.

"I cleaned your clothes. Your earwire and percomp are on the table."

She had a hazy memory of a brightly lit room, and throwing up. "What time is it?"

"Eleven thirteen. Should be light out, but you can barely tell through the nonstop snow." At their latitude and a ten-day from the winter solstice, they got less than five hours of sun per day.

She was loath to leave the soft comfort of Axur's loving pets and his big bed, but she'd already kept him from it for ten hours, and she had to return Nuñez's flitter and get home. "Could I impose on you for the use of your fresher and something to eat?"

"Please don't kill me, but while you were unconscious, I examined your bad leg." Axur sat at the other end of his small couch and sipped coffee from a large mug.

A flare of unease spiked, but she smothered it. Nothing had happened. Axur was her kind, funny friend who talked to her every day. He wasn't a brutal man who drugged her and inflicted degradation and pain. Axur was a warm, strong, stolid yak. "And?"

"Completely repairable in any medical center with tissue-cloning facilities."

"And completely unaffordable. Homesteaders like me have to pay hard credit. Even settlers like Nuñez have to co-pay. This isn't the Concordance, yet." The swirling snow outside the window made her feel cold. She wasn't used to windows. "I have a better chance of winning the galactic lottery. Or I would, if I had enough hard credit to buy a ticket."

"I know, so I have a deal for you. You give me Serena permanently, and come every ten-day to check on my pets and help me with two-person jobs. In exchange, I'll design a procedure my autodoc can handle to reattach the torn ligament and repair the lateral quadriceps muscle that gives you the most grief. You'd have to stay off it for the day and eat a lot to compensate for the rapid-heal, but it should improve your mobility and strength."

Her jaw dropped. "You have an *autodoc*?"

"Yeah, it came with the freighter. Running low on basic chems and anesthetics, though. I'll need more afterward."

"Holy hells. Do you have any idea what a working autodoc is worth? And with your medic training and language skills? Nuñez was right. You don't have to hide up here. Move into town, and they'd build you the clinic of your dreams. The settlement company couldn't stop them or even take a cut."

A grim look settled on his face. "I can't." The conviction in his tone left no room for argument.

She would have liked to point out that he was obviously lonely, based on how often he pinged her just to chat, but he knew what he could and couldn't do. She disliked it when Nuñez pushed her, so she wasn't going to do that to her only other friend on the planet.

"You'll need your autodoc supplies for yourself, so no deal on that. I'll take the rest of the trade, though—Serena for the extra pair of hands and veterinary care." The wolf in question was out in the blizzard, frolicking like she was a spring-loaded mountain goat instead of a dignified guardian. "Your place is better for her than mine."

He frowned and reached for his cup, but stopped to examine the exposed biometal knuckles of his cybernetic hand.

She moved Shiza, the warmth-seeking foo dog, off her lap, then stood and stepped into her boots. Alpha, the darkest cat, helped by batting at the decorative lacings. Beta jumped her, Delta jumped Beta, and a battle royale ensued. It was a wonder Axur's living quarters weren't a constant shamble.

She glanced at Axur, expecting to see him smiling at his silly cats, but he was looking up at her pensively.

"Ever heard of a Citizen Protection Service black-box project?"

"Er, maybe?" She dredged up the memory. "Something about secret weapons?"

"I am one."

She had no idea what he was talking about, but his bleak expression made her want to comfort him. "Because of your cybernetics? Lots of Jumpers have those, don't they? You can't all be weapons."

"Because of what's *in* my cybernetics. The CPS secretly 'volunteered' me for a research group's project that turned me into a continually broadcasting comm unit. I could probably uplink directly to the high-orbit galactic comms buoy from here."

"I'm sorry, I'm not following." She touched the earwire he'd given her and convinced her to wear, even when sleeping. "Is that how you made the Axur-net?"

He stood and turned to her, shoving his hands in his pockets. If she took one step closer, she could almost touch him. It was the closest she'd been to him without the fear taking over her motor control to make her tremble with the imperative to run, to hide. She gave herself a mental shake to refocus on what Axur was saying.

"...first in my squad to try out the new, better battery in my cybernetic legs. I woke up in a space station in a high-security research clinic, with a new cybernetic arm that I didn't need, and a satellite uplink built into me. The assholes stole me and altered the records to make it look like I'd voluntarily signed on for their research project. They told me their goal was to improve field communications for Jumpers, but I soon figured out the real purpose was to intercept, decrypt, and twist enemy comms."

Her sluggish brain finally put together a piece of the puzzle.

"Your cloak. It blocks your broadcast." She looked around at Axur's quarters, made out of the pieces of an interstellar ship. "This is incalloy, for transit space. That's why you don't have to cover up in here."

"Yeah. I added a countervalent grid, powered by the ship's thousand-year batteries. It scatters my signal."

"Why do you need to?"

"Because ten months ago, I stole this freighter and escaped. The CPS wants me back, and not to return me to my squad." He held up his cybernetic hand and made a fist. "I'm still tuned up to enhanced Jumper speed and strength, which is illegal outside the Corps. I really am a cyborg. Point is, my cybernetics have enough experimental nanotech to buy Del'Arche's entire settlement debt. I'm the only survivor of ten other 'volunteers.'" He rocked on his heels. "When my signal pings any official comm system, the system records my unique comm signature. If that got back to the main Concordance net, it would likely trigger a galaxy-wide detain-and-restrain order on me that says I'm dangerously delusional, and offers a juicy reward to keep me iced until the fastest CPS cruiser can get here."

"I'm sorry, Axur. That farkin' flatlines." She didn't know what else to say. No minder talent in the universe could change the past, and she didn't know any minder forecasters who could advise him on how to improve his future. She limped to her vet bag on the table to check that it was sealed tight.

Axur grabbed his coat and step into his combat-style boots. "I'll clear the path again and warm up the flitter."

She eyed his everyday work pants. "Do your legs feel cold?"

"No, they're internally heated to normal body temperature. My processor interface tells me what the external temperature is." He smiled ruefully. "My ass and dangly bits get cold, though."

She laughed at his phrasing. He had the oddest euphemisms for genitalia.

He bunched his hair on top of his head so he could slip on his fancy transparent snow hood. "Some Jumpers choose to have the full input-to-nerve mapping done, to make the synthskin and cybernetics feel as real as possible, but I know the endocrine system isn't there, and I didn't want to be distracted by phantom sensations." He flexed his cybernetic hand. "The researchers did it for my arm without asking what I wanted. After I landed, I had to hack into my own processor to make it quit telling me about the burns. Even though I have the key, it took me days because of the evolving cryptogon."

He lifted his heavy cloak and pushed his head through the round opening, then sealed it. "I'll be on earwire."

He slid open the door to reveal a snow-covered wolf, who danced back in excitement when she realized Axur was coming outside.

His tone signaled in her earwire. *"Feel free to raid the cabinets or cold box if you're still hungry. You had a stressful night."* Heavy breaths of exertion punctuated his words.

"I'm good. I've been looking at your decor. Very mad techno. Did they teach you that in Jumper school?"

"Some. I learn languages more quickly when I busy my hands. The CPS researchers gave me comm specialist courses, and started training me to use the new tech I'm carrying. Even trained me how to repair my cybernetics. When they gave me control during testing and forgot to turn it off over lunch, I cracked their internal security and read everything, not just the sanitized version they gave me, which is how I found out about the nine other test-subject fatalities. I sure as hell didn't want to be number ten."

"I'm glad you escaped." As she said the words, she realized her life would be immeasurably less interesting without Axur in it. Because he wasn't there in front of her, it was easier to ask the question that had been bothering her. "Are you staying away from Tanimai because you're afraid someone in town would betray you to the CPS?" Someone like Nuñez, or her.

"No. If and when the CPS captures me, they wouldn't care who they else hurt, including anyone they thought I'd shared secrets with. Out here, they only catch me, and leave the town alone."

The implications of his story sank in. "You're just like Kivo.

You're a failed experiment they want to dissect." She took his silence to mean he'd already thought of that. "Why did you tell me all this now?"

The answer was a long time in coming.

"Because if you come up here someday and I'm gone, I wanted you to know that it wasn't my choice."

The thought of losing him to that fate terrified her worse than the fear response when the man got too close. And if that wasn't a complete contradiction, she didn't know what was. She felt like she ought to say something. "I would take care of your animals."

"Thank you. They're my family."

"Don't you have any of your own?" Not that he could go home while he was still a fugitive, but maybe he could see them again someday. People lived to a hundred and seventy and more with modern medicine.

"Dead. Con-Kella Pandemic of 3215. I was raised in group homes. The Jumper Corps became my family after that. What about you?"

"Only child, or at least I was. My parents worked long hours and left me home a lot. I made friends with every stray animal in the neighborhood, and figured I'd work at a rescue shelter." She gave a self-deprecatory laugh. "And look at me now, on top of the world."

"I'm at the barn. I'll send Serena to walk you down to the flitter."

"Okay." She took a deep breath and spoke before she lost her nerve. "You could come with me."

"Why, are you feeling sick?"

"No, it's just... I don't... You should..." The unexpected rise of emotion tangled her tongue. "My place is hard to find and well protected. If I show you where it is, and you need somewhere to hide, you could go there."

The silence stretched. She wished she could see his face, because maybe he wasn't interested, or thought the idea was lame.

"Okay."

An hour later, she landed the flitter on the snow-dusted gravel of her homestead's landing pad. Nuñez had told her to keep the flitter until the next day. The storm had finally stopped, but left deep snow behind.

Bethnee checked her security system's activity monitor, then opened the flitter doors. She collected her kit, locked the doors, and caught Axur's eye. "Stay on my trail so you don't get lost."

She led the way up the path to her home. Under the obscuring snow, it looked like ramshackle stacks of logs between a cluster of tall boulders. Kivo whined excitedly as she opened her front door and led him and Axur-the-yak inside. He was only her second human visitor. She'd have never believed she'd ever allow a man into her house if she hadn't been living it at that moment.

She turned on the lights, then pointed to the hooks by the door. "Hang your stuff there."

She'd already sent her talent out to her animals to tell them she was coming, and warn them about the stranger. Axur's tribe comprised extraordinary, valuable pets. Hers were civilization's discards, like her.

After Axur wrestled off his coat while leaving his shielding cloak in place, he stepped into the cabin's common area to look around. She'd purposefully left this part of her home looking primitive and half-dilapidated to fool any would-be intruders. She saw on his face the moment he started noticing the little features that would make an uninvited guest's life miserable.

"Impressive." He gave her a sly smile. "I'm glad I'm not your enemy."

"There's more outside. I'll show you before dark. I add to them when I get a new idea. I need a place to feel safe."

"Copy that." He tilted his head toward the back, hidden in shadows. "That where you really live?"

"Yeah, come on back."

7

Axur decided that calling Bethnee's place a cave was like calling Kivo a pet—true as far as it went, but a wholly inadequate description. The log cabin front concealed the sealed entrance to an extensive cave system. Its main feature was a subterranean hot spring that she'd taken full advantage of to create habitats for herself and her animals. He especially envied the temperature-regulated pool she'd built by shaping a natural depression in the cave and installing a series of pumps and pipes.

Until he saw her relaxed in her own environment, he never realized how effectively she hid her vibrancy and unconventional beauty. She'd even come within centimeters of him a couple of times without flinching. A strong desire to touch her and be touched back arced through him. He locked his knees and shoved his fists in his pockets under his poncho. It wasn't just general lust, because he didn't want physical affection from the other women he'd interacted with in town, and males didn't flux his drive. He shouldn't have agreed to come, but loneliness and longing overrode his reservations.

He shoved his conflict into the frustratingly large box of things he couldn't control and focused on something he could. "So, I've met everyone except Jynx."

Bethnee grinned. "I saved her for last, because you'll like her best."

"It'll be hard to top a white weasel trained to steal." He pointed toward her indoor garden, which she'd created by widening a natural cave cathedral and piping in circulating hot water and air. "Not to mention, an indoor bamboo forest to keep a half-blind red panda happy."

"Come see."

She took him through a narrow, curving corridor that led to a noticeably cooler part of the cave. The near-frosty air was a shock after the heat of the garden. Kivo's attention was riveted on the tall rows of stacked crates along the wall.

From between an opening in the stacks, a fully-grown snow leopard padded in. She glanced once at him and Kivo in seeming boredom as she gracefully jumped up onto the battered table. She sat and curled her long tail around her, watching Bethnee.

He started to speak, but froze when he was interrupted by a low, rusty-sounding half-growl from Jynx. "Uhm, is she torqued?"

Bethnee laughed as she stretched a hand out and moved closer to sink her fingers into the thick fur on the cat's neck. "No, that's just her 'hello.' It's called chuffing. You can come closer. It's a dirty little secret in the planet terraform industry that the last of the snow leopards died in a zoo long before First Flight, and that all the 'naturals' are actually recreations. She's designer, not feral. I've let her know that you and Kivo are my friends."

He edged closer, trying not to stress Bethnee but wanting a better look at the big cat's left front leg. "I've never seen an animal with cybernetics." The cat's distinctive spotted fur ended with a ragged transition to the raw, articulated biometal model of a cat's leg. The toes on the wide paw had lethal biometal claws. If she'd ever had synthskin—synthfur?—it was gone now.

"And you probably won't see another. Animal brains usually reject the motile processor input, even with complete nerve mapping and fluid sync. She's unique, and worth a fortune." Jynx chuffed again, showing her sharp carnivore's teeth. "Nuñez found her at the spaceport, wrapped like a mummy, half-dead, in a secret compartment of a large-animal container." Bethnee chuckled. "The yaks get nervous just smelling her, so Nuñez gave her to me. Besides, her visible biometal makes her a theft magnet. I can't let her go out very often."

Following instinct, Axur held out both his human and cybernetic hands for Jynx to smell. He smiled when she rubbed her head on both, marking him with her scent. "Cats are cats."

"Yep." She leaned her hip against the table. "I had a devious reason for inviting you here."

He grinned at her. "You're the least devious person I know."

She snorted. "I'm the least *tactful* person you know. There's a difference." She pushed a stray lock of dark hair behind her ear. His fingers tingled with the desire to find out if it felt as silky as it looked. "I was hoping you'd look at Jynx's cybernetic biometal-to-bone interface and tell me what needs fixing. When she jumps down from more than a few meters, her shoulder collapses, and now she's afraid of going up high." She pointed to mountain of crates. "I had to move her den down to floor level, and that makes her nervous."

"I'm willing," he said dubiously, "but I know absolute zero about leopard anatomy. We'd have to take her back to my place for the tools and computers. And even then, her cybernetics might be a whole different design."

"If we pool our skills and talents, I'd sure like to try." She rubbed Jynx's ear. "Humans have treated her so badly. She deserves the best life I can give her."

He'd have given anything to take Bethnee's sadness away, but he'd used up his lifetime quota of miracles when he'd escaped the CPS researchers. He shoved his hands in his pockets. "Whenever you're ready."

Four days later, Axur quickly carried forty kilos of chemmed snow leopard to the temporary exam table he'd rigged in his workroom. Jynx had made a bad jump the day before and was in constant pain.

Bethnee looked everywhere but him. "Did this room used to be the nav pod?" Her hands trembled when she wasn't focused on the leopard.

"Yes." He hunched over to lay Jynx on her side on the folded blankets. He maneuvered around to the other side of the table. "The landing drilled the freighter halfway into the mountain, so I took advantage of it and dug in more." He smiled. "I didn't win the hot-spring lottery like you did."

He pulled the big tech scanner down close to the leopard's leg. "We're in luck. She's got a hidden jackwire port at the shoulder interface." He pulled one of his longwires from the tray and held it out to Bethnee. "I'll show you where, if you'll insert it. When I run a diagnostic, tell me if it hurts her."

She bent close and inserted the wire with a steady hand. "Go."

He touched a control and watched the readout. "Standard processor, zero security. They must not have expected to lose her." He frowned. "Battery is old-*old* style, and running low." He looked at Bethnee. "I don't know how your talent works, but can you check the interface area for temperature? Her processor is conserving battery power by reducing the leg's internal heat generation. Probably feels like she's constantly cold." He put his human hand on Jynx's shoulder at the interface to see if he could feel the difference.

Bethnee's eyes lost focus, a sign she was using her talent. "It feels numb to her, but it always has. I thought that was normal." She frowned. "Damn, I think I missed a passive tracer, right at the interface. The cybernetics must have masked it."

He moved his hand aside so she could lean over and probe with delicate fingers.

"It's faint..." Her voice trailed off, and she straightened abruptly. "It's in *your* hand."

"What?" He held up his hand and flexed his fingers. "Frelling hell. I removed the standard Jumper tracers and the extras in my cybernetics. I never thought to look elsewhere."

"You might have missed them, anyway. It's pet grade. Tiny." She shook her head. "I don't know why, but ever since I healed Kivo, you've felt real to me, not like a ghost. I think I could tell you where the tracers are, if I get close enough." She blew out a loud breath and looked at her shaking hands. "And if I don't flatline." She crossed her arms and shoved her hands under her armpits.

Just great. The woman he most wanted to get close to was terrified at the thought of even touching him. "Let's deal with Jynx first."

The fix was easy to describe—replace Jynx's failing battery with one of his spares—and hard to achieve. What would have been a ten-minute procedure in a Jumper med center turned into three hours of guesswork and improvisation using repurposed equipment in his temporary lab. The trickiest part had been helping Jynx interpret and accept the full input from her cybernetic processor.

Axur triggered two mealpacks as Bethnee encouraged the leopard to walk in circles around the couch.

He eyed the weather through his only window. "We could take Jynx outside after lunch."

"Good." Bethnee smiled. "She's just humoring me, walking around in here. Thanks for giving up one of your batteries. At full strength, she's amazing."

"It's a good cause." He wanted to tell Bethnee she was amazing, with her courage to fight through debilitating post-trauma stress to help her pets and his, but didn't think she'd like the reminder. He pushed the heated tray across the counter toward her. "I'm glad the freighter had enough mealpacks for a decade, but I'm looking forward to growing season again. I was lucky the freighter was shipping seed starts and had a superb library in the shipcomp."

"I want to create a hydroponic garden." She crossed to the counter and pulled out the mealpack's utensils. "If it works for starships, it should work for the cave."

"I can print small flexible parts for you, like nozzles and connectors, if you can trade for lexo substrate."

She nearly choked. "You have a working *printer*?" She set her fork down and stared at him. "The only other printer within a hundred kilometers is owned by the settlement company, and they only take hard credit. You could trade for anything you wanted. *Anything*."

"I had no idea." Once again, he was surprised at all the things he'd taken for granted in his former life.

She frowned. "Actually, you might want to keep quiet until you read the settlement contract's sections on salvage rights. Nuñez sent you a copy, didn't she?"

He nodded. "Yes." He'd only read the part about homesteading, which said if he could improve a perimeter-marked plot of land for two years, it became his, and conferred legal resident status with it. If the company caught him before that, they'd haul him into the Concordance and charge him with trespass. And that was only if the relentless CPS didn't find him first.

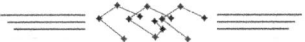

Axur would bet hard credit that he and Bethnee were the only two people in the galaxy who had ever seen a cybernetic snow leopard and a formidable dire wolf play tag in the deep snow.

Bethnee laughed when Jynx made an astonishing six-meter leap onto a boulder to avoid Serena's lunge. He snuck a glance at Bethnee, enjoying her happiness. "Are you helping them get along?" He tapped his temple, to indicate her enviable minder talent.

"A little. Mostly Jynx, because this isn't her territory."

He checked his internal chrono. "We better start collecting your gear, and I need to check the barn." He pointed a thumb toward Jynx. "I'll send Trouble out to keep an eye on these two." Axur had yet to be able to crack the encryption on the e-dog's command processor that Bethnee had told him about, but he kept trying.

Back in his living quarters, he found Bethnee leaning against the kitchen counter, holding her small veterinary surgical suite. "I'd like to try removing your tracers."

He blinked in surprise. "Now? Are you sure?"

"Hell, no, but it'll be worse if I give myself time to think about it." She searched his face. "Unless you don't trust me?"

"I trust you with anything except making coffee. Where do you want me?"

"Chair, I guess."

He hesitated, then pulled off his shirt and sat. "Let's try this first." Jumpers gave up caring about nudity in the first ten-day of training, but she might not be so comfortable, especially considering his gender. He held out his hand.

She opened the suite, exposing the instrumented interior, then swallowed visibly and took slow steps toward him. "Talk to me. Tell me how you escaped the shitheads who put tracers in you like you were a lab animal." She rested trembling, cool fingertips on the back of his hand. "I like the sound of your voice."

He described how he made off with hoarded supplies, including extra batteries and tools, and hijacked the freighter. A lucky torpedo right before he went transit forced him to reprogram the navcomp on the fly to exit at Del'Arche, where he skidded in on a failing system drive and scorched, cracked atmosphere wings. He used the debris to build his shelter.

She trembled the whole time, but she found and excised the tracers in his wrist, upper arm, and both of his shoulder blades. The surgical suite made it quick and nearly painless. The tracers under his collarbones were harder for both of them. Tremors wracked her, but she stuck to her task. He closed his eyes, but the butterfly touch of her cool fingers and the warm female scent of her saturated his senses. He could no more prevent his erection than he could prevent his satellite uplink from broadcasting. He prayed to the constant stars she wouldn't notice, or he'd never see her again.

When the suite sounded its completion chime, she pulled it off and lurched toward the front door to slide it open. She panted like she'd been running low on oxygen in her space exosuit.

After a moment of indecision, Axur climbed to his feet and pulled on his shirt, letting it hang loose over the front of his pants.

She turned back to him, looking pale and exhausted. "Sorry. I'm a warped mess." She brushed a strand of hair behind her ear. "You've got four more." A tear fell. She brushed it away absently.

"That's enough for today. If the CPS is close enough to ping-trace the rest of them, I'm as good as iced, anyway." He picked up the crate with the rest of her supplies. "No need to apologize for negative stress feedback. I've had it, and it's no less debilitating because it's just in your mind. Jumpers are lucky enough to get quick support and professional treatment from top-level minders and medics."

She gave him a watery smile. "I thought you said Jumpers ate pain for breakfast."

"We do. But we acknowledge the pain for each other, so no one has to carry it alone." He took a deep breath and let it out slowly, hoping to drain off the anger he felt at what he'd lost, what they'd both lost. "We look out for each other, because no one else will."

8

A hard fall off her glide board onto her bad leg left Bethnee barely hobbling as she let herself into her cabin. The added weight of her vetmed kit brought clawing pain with every step as she re-armed the security systems and checked the logs and the analog telltales. No one had bothered her in the two years she'd lived there, but carelessness was no longer in her nature.

She made halting progress to the cave's kitchen, escorted by her pets. She couldn't afford to be disabled, or she and the animals would go hungry. She wished Axur hadn't suggested they try to heal her leg with the autodoc, because she was tempted to take him up on the offer.

It had been five days since she and Axur had fixed Jynx—and since Bethnee had failed to finish removing the tracers from Axur. He pinged her that night and since, as if nothing had changed. Maybe it hadn't for him, but her world had tilted on its axis.

She'd willingly touched a warm, half-naked man. Her dark, horrific memories had lost some of their power. Maybe it was time and distance, but more likely, it was the healing balm of Axur. Handsome, resilient, clever, caring Axur, who resurrected memories of her younger days when sex was sweet and teenage dreams brimmed with passion and romance. Those memories used to belong to a forgotten stranger, but she could almost believe they were hers again.

Most of her reaction when she'd removed the tracers had been fighting the impulse to touch him, like a lover. It scared and exhilarated her. And the realization that he'd been sexually aroused by skinny, scarred her had made her almost forget to breathe. She'd let him think she was still afraid because he was a man with the power to break her body, when the truth was, she was newly terrified that he had the power to shatter her heart.

She could remain silent and maintain the friendly status quo, but could she live with herself if she did? She wasn't Jumper brave, but she'd worked so hard not to let fear rule her. It wasn't fair to either of them for her to stand in the doorway like a cat, neither going all the way out or in. She didn't know what he wanted, but she'd never find out if she didn't ask. She tapped her Axur-net earwire and waited for his response.

"Hey. I'm glad you pinged. I have an idea for fixing my broadcasting comms problem, but I need your help."

His voice sounded like he was right next to her, whispering into her ear, making her stomach flutter.

"Sure." She took a deep, steadying breath. "What do you want in trade to use your autodoc to fix my leg?"

The weak winter sun turned the snow glossy as Bethnee looked out the window of Axur's home. She hated being a patient, but knew she'd be just as attentive if Nuñez or Axur got hurt, so she accepted his coddling. In moderation.

"I thought I told you to stay off the leg," said Axur.

She turned to watch as he rolled in a cart filled with tools and equipment. "I hopped."

He rolled his eyes. "You're worse than a combat Jumper." He pointed to the chair and footrest he'd rigged for her. "Sit."

She hopped back and eased herself down. "It's boring."

"Yeah, well, that's why you're going to help me crack my second processor." He pushed the cart next to her chair, then put his stool next to it. "You need to eat like a Jumper today. Are you hungry yet?"

"No. Shaky, though."

"Am I too close?" He started to move the stool, but she put her hand on it.

"No." She pointed to the space just in front of her. "Sit and tell me what you want me to do." When he hesitated, she added, "You're still a yak."

He sat, watching her carefully as he did. She sent out a thread of talent to him, letting the solid strength of him fill her senses. Her new strategy had worked so far, even when she'd been pantsless in front of him and needed his help to lift her badly bruised leg into the autodoc. Admittedly, she'd had to reach for the minds of the trusting animals to remind her brain how to stay calm, but she still put it in the win column.

"Yesterday, I finally cracked Trouble's command module security. Mine looks similar." He held up a small hexagon-shaped percomp and a longwire. "I'm going to jack in, but if I trip the kill switch the researchers contantly threatened me with, I'll need you to reinitialize me. I'll show you how."

"It's sweet of you to not see me as a technological flatliner, but we both know the truth." She stifled an impulse to reach out and stroke his arm.

"That's why I'm going to show you. I stayed up last night and built some routines to try if the normal sequence fails." He opened a flat display and pointed to a long list. "They're in order of what I think you should try first, but I added notes about what they do, so you can use your judgment."

"You did all this last night?" She knew he was a get-it-done kind of person—probably all Jumpers were—but this seemed excessive. "Why the rush?"

He looked away from her, then back. "It's like you said. I'm hiding up here. Letting my limitations imprison me as much as the researchers did. I only see you and Nuñez, and a few townspeople for trades. I was good at being a Jumper, but that's gone, so I need a new career."

The thought of losing him burned like a beamer through her heart, but she couldn't begrudge him his freedom, any more than she could begrudge Jynx enjoying her recovered strength and agility. Axur's premium skills and valuable ship contents meant he could move to a warm southern city. After what the Citizen Protection Service had done to him, he deserved more than a quirky little town of misfits and a damaged, graceless woman who thought of him as a yak.

"Okay," she said. "Show me what to do."

"I'm in! My uplink controller isn't just similar to Trouble's, it's the exact same model, just customized."

It had taken Axur over forty minutes to explain all the contingencies he'd come up with, and less than ten minutes to crack his system on the first try. His whoop startled the cats and made Kivo dance in excitement.

"Congratulations." She couldn't help but smile in response to his delight. "Once I extract your other tracers, you can be truly free." Her bad leg was pins and needles, like she'd run into a cactus, but she'd take that over weak and numb. She slid her leg off the footrest and ignored the wave of wooziness that washed over her when she sat up too fast. "Fresher first, though."

"I'll get your crutches." He stood and gave her a stern look. "Stay put."

The natural light from the window made a bronze halo of his frizzy hair, which he'd grown to make him less recognizable. His short, darker beard highlighted his strong jaw. His thin knit shirt stretched across his wide shoulders and muscled chest, giving her the urge to snuggle against his warmth. She smiled up at him. "You're an impossibly gorgeous man."

He gave her an assessing look. "I think you're reacting abnormally to the recovery chems."

"Maybe," she conceded. "Normal and I have rarely been on speaking terms." A warm sensation flushed through her and pooled in her pelvis. "I think I could kiss you right now, and not even twitch." She lifted her rock-steady hand up to him in invitation and smiled. "Want to experiment? It'd be for science."

"No," he said firmly. "Not that I don't want to kiss you, because I do, more than you know, but you are nowhere near capable of consent right now." He backed away and shoved his hands in his pockets, making his shoulders and pectoral muscles flex deliciously. "If you still want to kiss me tomorrow, we'll talk about it."

The afternoon passed in a blur as she alternately ate snacks and dozed on the couch. She was soon victimized by small animals that wanted a warm body to sleep on or next to. She dreamily watched him solving the mysteries of his uplink, thinking him brilliant and sexy, wishing she weren't too impaired to savor the holiday from her responsibilities and her fears.

She finally woke and sat up around the time he was serving dinner. "Am I allowed to try walking now?" She massaged her thigh gently. "I have more sensation in the lateral muscle than I've had in years."

"That depends. Are you still dizzy?" He gave her a sardonic smile. "Do you still want to kiss me?"

She met his query with a steady gaze. "No, and yes."

He drew a surprised breath, then shook his head. "Use the crutches. Your brain isn't exactly green-go right now."

She sighed, knowing he was probably right. Even if the weird chems reaction temporarily freed her to act on her desire to invite herself into his bed for a hot connect, it wouldn't be pleasant for either of them when her old fears came back online the next morning.

She levered herself up onto the crutches and made her way to the fresher, where they'd put her overnight bag to keep it safe from critters. When she returned, she put a package in front of him. "Happy Solstice Day." She triggered her mealpack's heater.

He blinked in surprise, darting his glance between her and the package. His smile grew as he untied the twine and opened it. "Real coffee!" He held the cloth bag to his nose and took in the scent appreciatively. He held up the other gift. "What's on the longwire?"

"Common and relic language courses." She pulled out the utensils from her mealpack. "You said you don't have anyone to practice with. I only know Standard English and one city's street slang, and Nuñez has mostly forgotten her family's Tagalog, so I traded for the courses whenever I treated pets. You can help me expand my horizons. I need more swear words."

He smiled as he put the longwire in his shirt pocket and patted it. "Thank you."

Seeing how much the simple gifts pleased him, she vowed to give him as many as she could before he left for wider, warmer pastures. She must still be farked by the chems, because the thought made her want to hug him tight and cry on his broad shoulder.

He triggered the heater on his mealpack. "I have presents for you and Nuñez, too." Something on his cart beeped, and he grinned. "Excuse me a minute."

Axur returned with a small percomp strapped to his cybernetic wrist, and removed a disgruntled cat from his chair so he could sit. Beta promptly jumped into Bethnee's lap and settled.

"Okay," she said. "Remember that I'm tech illiterate, and explain to me what you've been doing. I think I'm finally awake enough to keep it straight."

"I downloaded copies of my processor and controller software, so I could test things on the comp instead of me." He pointed a thumb to his equipment cart. "Luckily, I exited the CPS research program earlier than they planned, so my tech's code isn't encrypted. The downside is, not everything works right, and they'd only just started training me on how to use it. I'll need time to reverse-engineer it and figure out what I can do."

He talked between bites. "I turned off the uplink. I'll be glad to retire my poncho. Then I purged my unique comm signature from the dozens of dataspaces they squirreled it away."

She nodded. "Sounds like the tech equivalent of the tracers."

"Yeah, that's me, valuable research animal." He finished the entrée portion of his meal in three shoveling bites. "I just finished a prog that'll let me uplink with whatever signature I want and control it with the cybernetic interface in my ocular implant. Next, I have to figure out how to twist the planetary geomarkers."

"Twist them?" She frowned. "Won't that mess up navigation around here?"

"No, not the geomarkers themselves, just the ping refs that go with my signal. Most comms satellites record signal origination data along with the unique ID. It'd be suspicious if a flurry of new IDs all came from outside one tiny mountain town, or with no refs at all. At the very least, it'd trigger a settlement company audit, which would *not* make me popular in Tanimai. I don't want my activities to trace back to anyone here."

"Why? What are you going to do?"

"Download every hypercube of data and AI analysis from the orbiting weather system. Technically, it belongs to the Del'Arche government." He scooped up the empty mealpack trays. "You said the satellite network was malfing at the time, but I want to look for evidence of my unexpected planetfall."

She chuckled. "Is that what Jumpers call a crash landing?"

A corner of his mouth twitched in humor. "Dull mission reports mean no unwanted attention from High Command." He glanced at her crutches on the floor. "Want to try walking?"

She took a deep breath. "Yeah, but first, I want to take advantage of what the recovery drugs have done to me, so I can finish getting the tracers out of you."

9

"**N**ow?" It would mean getting naked for her. His hormones were instantly on board, which was exactly why it was a bad idea. His unavoidable erection and obvious desire would likely traumatize her, recovery-drug high or not. If he ever hoped to take their relationship to a deeper level, she needed time.

He took a breath, held it, and let it out. "I think we should let Nuñez do it."

"I'm not..." She trailed off. "Okay." She looked away and dropped her head.

He knew he'd hurt her feelings, but didn't know how to fix it.

She stood up slowly, using the back of the chair for support. She rocked from side to side, as if testing her balance. "Feels weird. Strong, but weird." She started to take a step, then looked down at her feet with a frown. "I think I'm going to have to learn how to walk again."

"When they fit Jumpers with cybernetics, the physical terrorists tell us not to think about the mechanics, just focus on the intent to get somewhere."

"The whats?" She laughed. "Oh. Therapists." She turned. "I'll walk in here."

"Good." He watched Bethnee limp her way around the couch several times. "Are you limping because you have to, or out of habit?"

She stopped and looked at her legs. "Beats me." She shrugged. "I'll let you know tomorrow morning when we walk down to the flitter."

The satellite data he downloaded overnight was good, bad, and interesting. The network had indeed been offline for maintenance and hadn't captured his entry from orbit, but anyone skilled in reading surveillance images—including the weather AI, if it was programmed to look—would recognize the landing furrow.

The interesting data came from the settlement company. His query had inadvertently exploited a security weakness and garnered him the company's backup hypercube of corporate data and correspondence. A younger version of himself might've hesitated to read it, but being made into a research project had scoured the shine off his idealism.

He woke Bethnee. She sat up and pushed her hair back from her face. "What time is it?"

"Zero six hundred. Sorry, but we need to talk." He pointed to the table, where he'd set out a pitcher of water, cups, and two mealpacks. "Breakfast."

She stood and stretched again, and he looked away. The one glimpse of her mid-thigh-length sleeping tunic that clung to her high breasts, flared hips, and flat stomach threatened to derail his rational thoughts. He waited until he heard her moving, then turned back to watch her limp toward the fresher door because she drew him like a magnet. She was definitely walking more easily than before.

When she returned, she looked more alert. "My leg is feeling good. Want to scan it?"

"Later. Are you awake enough to think deep thoughts?"

She sat. "Depends on the subject. I can't solve the time-versus-distance paradox in interstellar transit physics before breakfast." She triggered the mealpack's heater.

He laughed as he sat and triggered his own. "I'll tell the Concordance Science Achievement Award Committee to stand down, then."

She pointed to the display he'd left for her on the table. "What's this?"

"Background reading." He reached across the table to turn it on. "It's why the wakeup call."

She nodded, then took a bite and started reading the highlights he'd hastily put together. He saw on her face the moment she got to the part that had caused him to wake her so early.

"Holy hells. We have to warn the town. Daylight is only five hours from now." She stabbed her fork toward the display. "And what the hell kind of audit takes a team of eleven to conduct one for a town of a hundred?"

"This is going to sound paranoid, but I think the audit is a cover for something else. A raid, a theft..."

Bethnee's eyes widened. "A hunt for a CPS fugitive." She stood abruptly. "You can't stay here."

He shook his head. "I have to." He crossed his arms. "It could be legit. The settlement company might be making a zero-tolerance example of Tanimai for cheating. If I get caught, the company could fine the town hard credits for not detaining and reporting an unregistered settler. If I'm the target, I don't want CPS hunters anywhere near the town. I won't go back willingly, and they wouldn't care about collateral damage. Which is why I want you to take the animals to the safety of your cave."

She stared at him for a long moment, and he braced himself for an argument. Her expression of fear and worry morphed into resignation. "Okay." She shoved her hands in her pockets. "You know what you can and can't do. I hate leaving you here alone, but I'm worthless in a fight, and I don't want the animals to be casualties, or hostages for your cooperation."

He let out the breath he didn't realized he'd been holding. "Thank you." Her trust humbled him. He resolved to be worthy of it.

Bethnee made it look easy to load a menagerie of animals into the close confines of the flitter. He'd probably still be trying to catch one of the cats.

He handed Bethnee an earwire. "A spare for our private net."

She put it in the top pocket of her coat. "Okay."

He handed her a slender length of rounded incalloy, with padding at one end and a bulge of fine wire net at the other. "Homemade shockstick." He showed her how to operate it. "It's Nuñez's Solstice Day gift, because that asshole at the spaceport transfer dock confiscated hers."

Bethnee nodded. "It's a great gift, and she'll love it. Thank you."

He handed her a small, flat box tied with a tiny strand of fiber cable, looped in a bow. "Your Solstice Day gift. Open it when you're safe."

She rewarded him with a shy smile as she slid it into her lower pocket. "I'll ping you when I get home."

He fought a strong urge to fold her into an embrace, because her departure felt too much like goodbye. He stiffened his spine and stepped back.

She opened the flitter's pilot-side door, then hesitated and turned back. "Do you think I'm still warped by the recovery chems?"

"I doubt it. They usually metabolize in six or eight hours, tops."

"Okay." She stepped up and in, then turned to face him. "Then I think you should know, I still want to kiss you. Be safe, Axur Tragon."

She closed the door and lifted off ninety seconds later, by his internal chrono.

He buried his roiling emotions under the activities of dowsing the glow lights and resetting the various analog security measures as he went back to his house. He prayed to the constant stars that the audit was just an audit, and that he'd be seeing Bethnee again soon, because he sure as hell wanted to be kissed by her, and return the favor.

10

Bethnee sent a short message from the air to Nuñez, but she had her hands full with flying and keeping threads of talent on eleven animals. Twice she nearly turned around when she remembered the look of longing on Axur's face when she'd impulsively told him she wanted to kiss him.

She pinged him the moment after she got the animals settled in the cave, and put out fresh water and food. Nuñez pinged a moment later. Bethnee told her what Axur had said about the audit timed for sunrise, and his suspicion about a hidden agenda.

"Farking settlement company assholes," Nuñez said vehemently. *"I'll get the local comm net going, in case the settlement company is monitoring the uplink, too."*

"I'll return your flitter to the clinic, and go home on my glide board."

"Okay. I'll open the gate for the yaks."

Bethnee disconnected, then took a minute to send images to

Axur's animals so they'd know the cave's layout and how to operate the pet doors. She wanted them to always have an escape route.

She grabbed her glide board, set the security system, and walked as fast as she could to the flitter, feeling time slipping away. It wasn't until after she was in the air that she realized she'd limped very little on the snowy path.

After delivering the flitter and Nuñez's present, Bethnee rode her board out of town. Just as she passed the last building, Nuñez pinged. Bethnee started to answer, but her friend was already talking.

"...he won't hurt you if you stay still. What are you two doing in my paddock? Back up, Upolu." Upolu was a large yak bull, with wickedly curled, sharp horns and a dislike for strangers. Nuñez's conversation continued after a moment. *"Well, there's nothing to see back here but yak shit. I'll need to see your IDs and verify them with settlement compa–"*

The connection cut off.

Everyone in Tanimai knew about the yaks and the geese, so the interlopers had to be the auditors, come early. The "inadvertent" comm was Nuñez's way of warning her. Bethnee grounded the glide board and sent a quick warning to Nuñez's spouse, then pinged Axur with the news.

"Where are you?"

"Edge of town. I'm–" An ear-splitting, chest-rumbling whump made her instinctively duck her head like a turtle. "I just heard a crash, but I can't see anything. I'll check the animals in the area." She sent threads of her talent out to all the animals she could find, both domestic and wild, and took advantage of their superior hearing and night vision to glean information. "I think it came from the Administrative Center. The building is collapsed inward."

"Isn't that where the satellite uplink is? Check your local comms."

She tried her percomp and the extra comm bracelet. "They're down."

"The best thing you can do is go home."

"I can't leave Nuñez."

"She has thick walls and neighbors and attack geese. You're alone on a glide board. You're brave as hell, and I can't tell you what to do, but I will tell you that the hardest lesson a Jumper learns is when to retreat."

She blew out a frustrated breath. He was right. "Okay, here's my offer. I'll go home, if you'll use your fancy tech to figure out what's going on, and get help for Nuñez and the town if needed."

"Deal. Stay safe, Bethnee Bakonin."

She launched into the air again and hunkered down behind the board's wedge front to reduce wind drag. Guilt gave her second, third, and tenth thoughts about her decision. It felt like she was abandoning the truly good and generous woman who had saved her life and helped her learn how to live on her own. Bethnee would never forgive herself if Nuñez got hurt, but she'd also never forgive herself if she became the lever to bend Nuñez to their will.

11

Bethnee was so distracted with visions of calamity that she almost didn't notice the first sign that someone had breached her perimeter. The gossamer lengths of fiberet cable trailed down to the ground instead of invisibly spanning between the trees. An air vehicle had flown through and broken them, triggering the chemical reaction that made them faintly glow.

She veered off north into the trees and turned off the board's light, flying by terrain sensors alone. She slowed to almost a hover, a meter above the forest floor, maneuvering around the trees and boulders.

She heard voices. A man and a woman.

"What the hell is this sticky stuff?" The man sounded outraged.

"Move slow. Grab my hand." The woman sounded like she was suppressing laughter.

Bethnee grounded her board quietly behind a tree and buried it in the snow, fighting hard against instincts compelling her to run. The animals needed her to stay.

She sent threads of her talent to her animals and Axur's to tell them all to hide in the caves.

She heard squelching sounds as the intruder walked through her moat that had a mix of yak dung, mineral salts, and scrap glass road glue, kept warm by a geothermally heated grid at the bottom. Once he got out, cold air would turn the thick coating on his clothes glass-hard.

Bethnee took a deep breath and let it out slowly, then peeked around the tree trunk. Two figures in one-piece blue snowsuits and transparent snow hoods trudged through the snow, away from the moat. The taller figure scraped the orange gunk off his butt as he walked. She opened her talent senses, but as usual, the humans felt like ghosts. She extended further and felt two more ghosts, clustered near the front of her cabin. That was more than a third of the auditor team.

She limped as fast as she dared to the edge of the trees. The interlopers were using both flying and hand lights. They'd see her if she tried crossing the main path.

She coaxed a nearby wild owl into looking at the front yard and borrowed the owl's superb hearing. Three men and a woman, all in one-piece snowsuits, stood at her front door.

"...haven't got all day," the woman groused. "Let's get the power-ram to breach that door and look, then get the hell out of here. I don't like being restricted to stunners and tranqs." She sounded irritated.

"That's 'cause you'll shoot anything that moves." A wide-shouldered man opened a display.

The man who'd been in the moat looked down as he stomped his legs. "Fucking mud is freezing, even through my suit."

"Like you're any better," snapped the woman. She pointed to the display. "What does the tech scanner say?"

"House has powered security, but nothing outside... No, wait. One double-tech signature. That way, and close." The owl's vision showed her an image of a man pointing into the woods.

Ice flooded Bethnee's veins as she frantically powered down her earwire and comms bracelet, berating herself for stupidity.

"Signal died." He tapped the display on the heel of his hand a couple of times.

The woman focused on the main path. "If it's the vet, she can just let us in. Keeps us on schedule."

They must have figured out where she lived from homestead records. They hadn't asked permission to land, but it didn't pay to piss off auditors, if that's what they were. Especially auditors with weapons.

Her only hope was to lure them into the woods and into her various security measures. None of them were fatal, just strong deterrents for the uninvited. She switched her battery-powered wrist light to low-power green and risked brief flashes to tell her where to step over rocks and duck under the branches. Learning every meter of her property in light and dark had helped her feel safe. She skirted around the fifteen-meter clearing. On the far side, she switched her comms bracelet on and off, mimicking an intermittent signal.

Two interlopers came through the trees, their lights marking their progress. She backed further into the shadows. They plunged into the virgin snow of the clearing. A faint whipping sound whistled in the air.

"Son of a bitch!"

"Who the hell leaves coiled spikewire in the middle of farking nowhere?"

Bethnee took advantage of their noise to make her way down the hill. An empty flitter occupied her gravel landing pad. She limped behind it and down into trees and rocks to the southeast. Adrenaline jacked up her tension and turned her stomach sour. Her thigh spasmed.

The sound of another approaching flitter echoed against the mountainside.

She scrambled under nearby shrubs and let the disturbed snow cover her. A smaller flitter landed behind the first. Two people exited and walked toward her house.

"...enforcers are coming to investigate." A woman's voice with a Mandarin accent. "Trummler wants us out by local dawn."

"I thought the auditor was supposed to intercept any calls from the area. We paid her enough." A man's voice, muffled by a high collar.

"Call came from an ex-Jumper, so the dispatcher took it seriously." The woman didn't sound happy.

Bethnee would have smiled if she weren't so scared. Clever Axur had found help.

Their words confirmed they weren't auditors, which meant they were after something or someone else. She didn't know what to do besides distract them so they'd leave her house alone, and delay them long enough so they'd run out of time and leave.

She'd never imagined she'd be wishing for a speedy visit by the Del'Arche Planetary Enforcers.

Bethnee had crammed herself into a rock hollow, wracking her brain for ideas. She was exhausted, and out of options, because dawn was coming.

The intruders failed to breach her house's physical and tech security, and had grown increasingly irritated about not catching her. Especially after two of them fell down a steep hill and the others had to deploy ropes to help them up the loose debris underfoot. They'd grown more wary of her traps after that.

She reached out once again to the animals to make sure they were safe. To her dismay, she discovered Trouble, the e-dog, was outside the cave and headed toward her. His fleeting thoughts listened to the controller in his head with Axur's order to find Bethnee and protect her. She refused to put any of the animals in jeopardy for her.

"Got her!" said a male voice. "It's faint, but the scanner says she's twenty-three meters south, and moving closer. I'll send lights."

Trouble's controller was permanently on, meaning the intruders were keying on him. She'd promised Axur she'd keep his animals safe.

With trembling fingers, she powered on both her higher-powered comms bracelets and her earwire, then pinged Axur. She subvocalized as she slid out of the hollow and stood. "I hope you hear this soon. Six people are at my place. They can't get into my house. They've been chasing me. I'm going to let them catch me, or they'll hurt Trouble. Send the enforcers here if you can."

She limped her way out from under the trees. She didn't have to go far before lights flew close and a black-haired man and a blonde woman, both with blood spots on their pant legs, came toward her at a fast walk. She turned and ran away, exaggerating her limp so it looked like her top speed.

"Get her!" shouted the man.

The blonde woman ran, then launched herself at Bethnee to take them both tumbling down into the snow. The blonde woman rose to her knees and roughly pulled off Bethnee's comm bracelets and earwire and threw them away. "You won't be needing these." She grinned like a shark. "I heard something bad happened to the town's satellite uplink." She grabbed Bethnee's arm and hauled her to her feet, then jabbed Bethnee's shoulder with an unpowered shockstick. "Where is it? Where's the shipment?"

"Wait," said the black-haired man. "The boss will want to hear this. Bring her to the cabin." He tilted his head toward her house.

The woman clamped a strong hand on Bethnee's arm and pulled her along. Bethnee limped as slowly as she dared, using the time trudging through the thigh-high snow to touch the strong, trusting minds of her animal family to keep herself from falling into a fog of fear. Her thigh muscle cramped once, then quieted. A small victory.

Three more people stood near her front door, all wearing the same new-looking blue snowsuits. They must have sent the man with the ruined one back to the flitter to stay warm. An Asian woman stood and watched, arms crossed and fingers drumming, as a dark-skinned man with an upright crest of flame-red hair folded and pocketed a scanner. The third, a noticeably shorter man, pulled down his collar and stepped closer. He stared at her legs, then looked intently at her face. "Well, well, the God of the Gaps has finally answered my prayers. It's Indenturee Bakonin."

She knew that face and voice from her worst nightmares. Kanaway, the guard with chems and perversions. The pieces fell into place. They weren't a freelance theft crew raiding the town, or CPS operatives looking for Axur. They were mercenaries after the bounty for a lost shipment of valuable designer pets. The shaking started, and coherent thought began to disintegrate. She desperately sent her talent out to every animal she could reach with the imperative to stay hidden. She forced herself to focus on the Asian woman's combat boots, counting toe taps. The animals depended on her to buy time for whoever was responding to Axur's call for help.

"What's wrong with her?" asked the black-haired man.

Kanaway grinned. "Oh, the little subbin' bitch wants me so bad she's trembling. Did you miss me?"

She shuddered, but somehow found the courage to look at him straight in the eye. "I hope Breitenbahn liked the record of what you did." She glanced down at his crotch. "Cured your soft and tiny problem yet?"

The blonde woman guffawed loud and long.

Rage flared in Kanaway's eyes as he slapped Bethnee. "That fake vid got me blacklisted from the trade." He slapped her again, harder. She staggered with the impact. She straightened up and watched him warily. At least her time in Breitenbahn's cruel circus had taught her how to take a hit.

The Asian woman gave Kanaway a hard look. "Enough." She turned and gave Bethnee a plastic smile. "We're looking for a pet-trade shipment." Her tone turned cajoling. "Help us, and we'll give you a percentage of the reward."

Bethnee spat blood on the snowy ground near Kanaway's boots and said nothing.

The Asian woman sighed and gestured toward the man with the red mohawk. "Domaki, find out where the shipment is and let's go." She cast an annoyed look at Kanaway. "Move, Kanaway."

Kanaway's thin lips curled in hatred, but he stepped back. In Bethnee's jagged memories, he was big and impossibly strong, but seeing him now made her realize he was actually shorter than her.

The red-haired man moved closer. "She's hard to read." He took off his glove. "I need to touch her."

The blonde woman grabbed Bethnee's arm, stripped off her glove, and forced her to hold out her hand. Domaki grabbed Bethnee's trembling, ice-cold fingers.

Bethnee felt the man's telepathic talent questing for her mind and memories. She plunged her mind into Jynx's and focused on the snow leopard's alien thoughts.

Distantly, she heard words with her ears and in her mind, but Bethnee-the-leopard ignored them as unimportant.

Domaki pushed a succession of images of pet-trade animals at her. She didn't recognize any of them until he got to a foo dog and six-legged chimera with two tails. She pulled out of Jynx's mind, because snow leopards didn't know how to lie. Bethnee shot Domaki a memory of when she'd treated Kivo for the near-fatal illness and his breathing had stopped. *Dead.*

All of them? demanded Domaki.

She felt him nibbling away at the corners of her mind, trying to access other memories. She called up image after image of animals she'd raised on Breitenbahn's ship, and let Domaki feel her deep sadness for each one she'd lost.

How do you know Kanaway?

The question took her by surprise, leaving her vulnerable to Domaki's probe into her darker memories. When he touched the worst of them, she felt the first wave of the familiar deep, seizure-like tremors.

Frelling hell! Domaki apparently didn't like her memories any more than she did.

She spitefully sent him the indelible image of how she'd looked after Kanaway finished, with a swollen face, and bruises and blood everywhere. How he'd shoved her half-conscious naked body into a ship's autodoc to heal away evidence of the assault, unaware that the ship's security monitors recorded his actions.

Domaki hastily withdrew from Bethnee's mind. She collapsed to her knees, heart racing, gasping for breath, unable to control her shudders.

Domaki backed away. "The research chimera died some time back. She hasn't seen any of the other animals."

"Bullshit," snarled Kanaway. His hands curled into fists. "She's the only small-animal vet on the planet. She's a stubborn, lying bitch."

Domaki gave Kanaway a disgusted look. "Don't tell me how to do my job, you warped little twist." Domaki pulled on his glove. "It's been eleven months since the bounty was posted for that shipment, and the active tracers are in a herd of mountain goats, not high-end pets. She doesn't know anything." He looked to the orange-tinged horizon. "If we leave now, we can meet Blue team at Point Exeter before it gets light."

"She'll have animals in her house." Kanaway could sound very reasonable when he wanted to. "If any of them are valuable, we can at least show a profit."

Domaki shoved his hands under his armpits and shook his head. "Ain't gonna be me that compels her to let us in." He cast another disgusted look at Kanaway. "Too many bad memories."

"Give me five minutes with her," said Kanaway, his tone persuasive. "I bet I can get her to talk."

The Asian woman hesitated, then shook her head. "No more fishing. We're out of time. Trummler okayed this mission because Kanaway's intel pointed to Del'Arche for where the high-value shipment ended up, and it'd be a quick in-and-out to question the only two veterinarians. This is a bust." She waved a hand to encompass everyone. "Flitters airborne in five. Let's go." She pointed to Domaki. "Ride with Kanaway."

With the Asian woman leading, they walked purposefully down the path toward the flitters. Bethnee pivoted on her knees to watch them go. She tried to follow them with her talent, but it was like trying to follow phantoms.

She waited until the last of them vanished up the path, then sent her talent out to search for Trouble. He was appallingly close, under a tree, and would have been an easy target if one of the mercs had seen him. She collapsed onto her heels and let the muddy yellow dog come to her, even though it wouldn't be truly safe until the flitters took off.

Trouble allowed her to put an arm around him and hug him close. She wished the blonde woman hadn't stripped her Axur-net earwire, so she could hear his voice again.

Inexplicably, Trouble pulled away and stared intently at the path, growling softly.

"Come on, Domaki." Kanaway's voice. "The sooner we find my pet-tracer scanner, the sooner we get off this ice ball."

Bethnee sent a panicked imperative to Trouble to run, but it was too late. Kanaway and Domaki strode into view, their flying lights illuminating her and Trouble.

Kanaway looked triumphant. "This really is my lucky day." He pulled a stunner out of his pocket and casually shot Domaki twice. Domaki's body jolted like he'd been struck by lightning, then crumpled.

Kanaway aimed the stunner at her. "You're worth ten times the bounty of that old research shipment." Avarice lit his face. "And I know just the buyer. He's been looking for you for three years."

12

A xur landed the runabout on the flat rocks above Bethnee's cave just as the sun crept over the mountaintops, burnishing their white tops with gold. She'd pointed out the path the first day he'd been there to meet Jynx. He loaded his gear and started down the steep trail. He sped up when he overheard one of the mercs say he'd forgotten a scanner and would catch up to the others soon. Merc companies weren't usually that disorganized.

Bethnee was likely paying the price for his mistakes, not the least of which was forgetting that the experimental tech in his cybernetics wasn't the only thing of value in the frozen north. He'd already been loading his runabout when he'd received her ping that she was planning to protect Trouble by letting the mercs catch her. He should have taken into account her willingness to sacrifice herself to protect the animals she loved. Her pet-trade captors had taught her she had no value, and he hadn't found the right time or words to tell her how much she meant to him.

At least the Del'Arche Planetary Enforcers were on their way.

He'd lucked into an ex-Jumper answering his ping, and she'd believed him and agreed to send help. Then he'd used his experimental tech to crack the raiders' temporary comms net.

They were a mercenary company specializing in freelance bounty hunts. While a southern squad went after a trio of brothers whose capture would bring a big payday back in the Concordance, a smaller northern squad went north for a stolen shipment of designer pets with a high reward, and anything else they could steal while they were at it. They considered a small frontier town as easy reaping.

They'd only intended to disable the town's satellite uplink, but the cheaply made building had collapsed. The three culprits had joined their two teammates at Nuñez's vet clinic, where they'd been attacked by pissed-off geese and nearly been gored by an enraged yak. That team beat a hasty retreat to rendezvous with the main squad to the south. The remaining six went after veterinarian Bethnee because they knew the coordinates of her homestead.

The same homestead to which he, like the flatliner he was, had sent her and his animals, thinking to keep them out of harm's way. He was only slightly relieved when the merc company's few comms after that told him they weren't finding her to be easy reaping, either.

From the trees near her cabin, he heard a man's voice but couldn't make out the words, and he couldn't tell where it was coming from. He wished he had hearing like a dog's... but he did, sort of. He quickly tuned his experimental tech to Trouble's command processor, and pulled the auditory feeds.

"...the door right now, your filthy dog dies in front of you." A man's baritone but nasal voice, full of menace. *"And you know I'll do it, too."*

"It's open." Bethnee's ordinarily expressive voice sounded flat and defeated. Axur clenched his jaw.

"You first. No surprises."

Axur crept closer.

"Are you going to leave Domaki down on the path? He'll freeze." Her tone said she didn't care if he did.

"That's his problem. Slimy, subbin' minder. He was going to tell

Na Ming lies about me, just like you did with that fake surveillance vid you sent Breitenbahn. He blamed me for your escape."

Axur eased westward, close enough to see a red-haired man down, blocking the path to the flitter pad. He quickly stripped the unconscious man's weapons, percomp, and earwire, then zip-tied his wrists and ankles and rolled him off the path into the ditch full of snow. The heated snowsuit would protect him from the cold for a while.

"Turn on the lights," said the man with Bethnee and Trouble. *"Where are the other animals?"*

Axur ran down the path to the flitter, which they'd obligingly left unlocked. He pried open the control panel and used his homemade high-powered shockstick to good effect.

"I only have one other. This house is too small for him. Axur mostly lives in his den up the mountain, but he's closer today."

Axur smiled and let relief take some of his tension as he exited the flitter. Bethnee knew he was there, and was buying time. He sobered quickly, because she was playing a dangerous game.

"Pet trade?"

Axur ran up the path toward Bethnee's house.

"No."

"Liar. Make him come to you."

Axur used his cybernetic strength to jump to the top of the big three-meter-high rock in Bethnee's front yard, which made him less immediately noticeable if her captor happened to look outside. The sun was already over the trees, and would soon be curving higher.

"I can't get around his controller. He's not pet trade, he's a military-enhanced experimental."

Axur heard the unmistakable sound of a slap.

"Call him, or I'll stun the dog and you both. Maybe have some naked playtime with you. Find out if you still like it rough and dirty."

Axur unslung his flechette gun and extended the guide for distance shots. His freighter had been sadly lacking in powered beamers, blasters, or railguns, so he'd made some analog weapons of his own, and practiced with them.

The mercenary comms band flared to life in his ear with an abrupt tone. *"Kanaway, Domaki, what's the holdup?"* The Mandarin-accented voice of the team leader sounded exasperated.

"Uh, Domaki tripped on something in the vet's yard and got stunned. I'm rigging something to carry him on." Axur rolled his eyes at Kanaway's unbelievably thin story.

"Quit fucking around, Kanaway, or I'll term you." The team leader disconnected without waiting for Kanaway's reply.

Kanaway's ugly laugh rang out. *"Stupid pig doesn't know what and who you are. I'll take you by myself, and make Breitenbahn bleed mega credits to get you back. His business isn't so good since you left."*

Axur found a quasi-prone position on the rock and aimed his gun with its homemade flechettes loaded with quick-acting dormo. All he needed was a clear shot at Kanaway's bare skin.

"Call the animal. Now."

"We have to go outside, and leave the dog in here, or Axur won't come at all."

"Bullshit."

"Shoot me, then. Good luck carrying me all the way to your flitter and taking off before your crew comes looking. No grav carts around here like on Breitenbahn's ship."

Stunner fire sounded, and Trouble yelped loudly in pain. Axur forced himself to let it roll off him, or he wouldn't be calm enough to make the shot.

"Outside!"

After a long, tense moment, Bethnee limped slowly through the doorway, then stumbled forward when the man shoved her. "Call him!"

She winced with every step as she limped haltingly toward the center of the little yard and stopped. Kanaway followed too close to her for Axur to shoot him. She bowed her head for a long moment, then turned to her right and looked expectantly toward the trees.

Kanaway clamped one cruel hand on her neck and with his other, pointed the stunner toward the trees. A large raven landed in the tree and screeched loudly, making Kanaway twitch.

A flicker of movement on Axur's right tugged at his attention. He risked a quick glance and caught a glimpse of a large, black-furred shadow stalking through the snow.

Axur winced at the loud tone in his merc comms earwire.

"Kanaway, we're coming for you and Domaki. Trummler's order." The team leader sounded disgruntled.

Kanaway let go of Bethnee's neck just long enough to touch his own earwire. "I'm already in the air." He spoke aloud rather than subvocalizing.

"Your flitter's tracer is reporting itself as damaged and stolen. We'll meet you in Tanimai."

Kanaway swore but said he'd be there, then touched the earwire. He stomped his foot in frustration and grabbed Bethnee's neck again and forcibly turned her toward the path. "Let's go."

She took one step, then stumbled sideways and landed on one knee. Kanaway let go as he struggled to keep his balance.

A black blur shot out from the trees to the west. Kanaway saw the movement, but too late to avoid being knocked down by a determined dire wolf. Kanaway's stunner sailed into the air and landed on the snowy gravel.

The man rolled sideways and up to his hands and knees. He crawled fast toward the fallen weapon, but had to duck and cover his face to avoid the attack of a huge black raven, cawing noisily, diving straight for him with talons outstretched. He threw himself toward the stunner, but not in time to stop the other black raven from stealing it in a flurry of flight.

Axur kept his gun trained on Kanaway, but couldn't get a clear angle without shooting Serena, who stood between Kanaway and Bethnee, shoulder fur fluffed stiff, growling menacingly.

Kanaway scrambled to his feet and spun to face the new threat. He held a phase knife in the stance of an experienced fighter. He touched his earwire and spoke aloud instead of subvocalizing. "Hey, Na Ming. Bring the big flitter back to the vet's house and get the tranq guns ready. She's got a fortune in stolen pets, starting with a trained dire wolf."

After a long moment, the Mandarin-accented woman's voice answered. *"Okay, but you better be on the level."* Na Ming sounded supremely testy. *"We're fifteen minutes out."*

"See you soon." Kanaway touched his earwire again. His eyes hadn't once left the wolf. "Company's coming. Give us the pets, or I'll tell them what you are and what you're worth."

Bethnee stayed on her knees and said nothing.

Kanaway sidestepped toward the open door of Bethnee's house. "Since you were so anxious to get me out of your house, the others must be in there."

Axur wished he could talk to Bethnee, but since he couldn't, he reviewed his mission parameters. Protecting her was top priority, but she now had reinforcements from his animals, and probably hers. His secondary objective called for protecting them all from the mercenaries, which was a better use of his skills and resources, but it meant he'd have to leave Bethnee with a monster.

Axur fucking hated the hard choices of war.

13

Bethnee felt like she was floating. Adrenaline still soured her stomach and made her shake, but she'd apparently hit her limit on fear, and had no more to give.

Kanaway sneered. "Hey, Bakonin. How much does a dire wolf bring at auction?"

The man was trying to keep her afraid, not thinking. She'd had enough of that to last a lifetime. "I don't know. How much do you think I can trade for Domaki?" She'd seen through the raven's eyes when Axur had pushed the telepath into the snowdrift. "Wonder what he'll tell your bosses?"

Kanaway huffed. "They won't believe him. They know minders are all liars."

She sent a thread of talent to cue preciously cute, plump Shiza, the little foo dog with the fierce heart of a lion. He waddled out into the weak midday sun and barked.

Kanaway turned. A slow, greedy smile formed. "See? Liars."

She asked Shiza to step closer to the man, but stay out of his reach. "Don't pick him up," she warned.

"What's he going to do, drool on me?" Kanaway laughed derisively.

Bethnee took a nervous breath, then sent Shiza instructions. He barked once, then turned to go back inside the house.

Kanaway glanced at the dire wolf, then focused on the foo dog. "Come here, you expensive little shit." His tone was baby-talk sweet as he patted his thigh.

Shiza slowed and turned to look up. Lightning fast, Kanaway dropped his phase knife to grab Shiza by the curly mane with both hands and drag him closer.

Enraged, Shiza twisted and bit down on Kanaway's exposed wrist.

Kanaway screamed and shook his arm, then rocked back a step back and kicked Shiza's ribs. The foo dog didn't let go. If Kanaway noticed a white weasel dart in and steal the phase knife, it didn't register.

Kanaway dropped to his knees, yelling, trying to roll Shiza onto his side. The foo dog planted his feet and used his strong neck and broad shoulder muscles to stay upright.

Bethnee climbed unsteadily to her feet and moved to stand by Serena.

"Get it off me!" He punched the dog's head, which caused Shiza to clamp down again even harder.

"Shiza," said Bethnee. She used her talent to help the foo dog realize he'd won. Shiza gave the man's crushed, bloody arm a tearing shake, then opened his wide, square jaws and scrabbled backward.

Kanaway lifted his good hand toward his face, but froze when Shiza keened and bared his sharp, bloody teeth.

Bethnee realized he'd been reaching for his earwire. She couldn't let him call for help. Before she could talk herself out of it, she pivoted in and stripped it off his face, then pivoted back. Her torn fingernail left a welt along his jaw. Blood welled immediately.

He swung a slow, sloppy punch at her. His venomous look would have once quelled her. He lifted his knee to put one foot on the ground. "You're fucking dead."

"No, but you are." She invited Shiza to come closer to her. The little dog limped a little as he moved to lean against her knee. "Foo dog poison is neuro-hemorrhagic, designed to kill quick, and you got two full injections. I told you not to pick him up."

"Bullshi'..." He shook his head as if trying to clear it. "They're sold to children... Prob'ly fast dormo or somethin'." His words slurred as he absently wiped red-stained drool off his chin with his good hand. The injured arm drooped listlessly at his side, gushing a pool of bright red blood onto the snow-whitened gravel. "You're gonn' be my ticket back..."

He slumped forward over his knee, then toppled sideways. He shuddered, then lay still.

Bethnee thought she should have felt something, watching the horror of her nightmares draw his last two wet, gurgling breaths, but nothing came. She had no more time to worry about it. Four greedy mercenaries with tranq guns were about to land on her doorstep.

She sent her talent out to check on the animals, but she was on her last reserves. Coordinating dire wolves, ravens, weasels, and foo dogs to defeat Kanaway had been like running a marathon. She asked bruised Shiza to go inside to protect injured, still dazed Trouble.

She wished she were a telepath like Domaki, so she could communicate with Axur, instead of just sensing his general location. She absently shoved the earwire she'd stripped from Kanaway into her chest pocket, only to find the one Axur had given her already there. Kicking herself for forgetting, she put it on and subvocalized a message. "Kanaway is dead in my front yard. I'm resetting the cabin's security. Tell me what I can do."

He came online almost immediately. *"Are you okay? Are you hurt? I've moved some of your traps to arrange welcome surprises for the mercs. They're running late. With luck, the enforcers will catch them here."*

She hadn't realized how much she'd needed to hear the sound of his voice until that moment.

"Tired. A bruise or two. Shiza and Trouble need treatment."

"I don't suppose you'd go back inside the cave and stay there?"

"Not a chance. It's my farking homestead. Can Serena and I come down the path?"

"Yes, I'll meet you. It's going to get crowded around here soon, and I want us all to be ready when it does."

14

Axur hung up his poncho, then sat with Bethnee on the small couch in her chilly cabin and watched the two planetary enforcers standing near the front door. Their orders were to keep an eye him and Bethnee, but they were more interested in friendly Kivo.

The other enforcers who'd landed took custody of the mercs. With Bethnee and the animals acting as lookout, Axur had lured the mercs into Bethnee's traps, then shot them with one of their own tranq guns. Because one merc was dead, the enforcers insisted on waiting for their commander to arrive with Pranteaux, the Tanimai town administrator.

Axur stole glances at Bethnee. She looked bruised, tired, and pale, but not flatlined. He admired the hell out of her.

Shiza the foo dog now sat across her lap and partly into his, contentedly drooling a wet spot on both their pant legs. Bethnee finger-combed his curly mane. She surprised Axur by sliding her hand into his and mouthing the words "thank you." He squeezed her hand gently in acknowledgment.

A few minutes later, a tall, muscular woman in uniform and flexin armor, and a short, rotund man in a puffy-collared, plaid long coat entered the cabin.

The short man blinked and squinted as he looked around with disdain. His eyes widened when he saw Kivo, then narrowed when his gaze landed on Bethnee and Axur. He drew breath to speak, but the woman beat him to it.

"I'm Commander Cherkogin, and I'm sure you know Administrator Pranteaux." She took in her surroundings with darting glances, then focused on Axur. "Tragon?"

"Yes, sir." He stifled the urge to salute.

Cherkogin turned her gaze to Bethnee. "You must be Vetmed Bakonin."

Pranteaux cleared his throat loudly. "She's the landed homesteader." He made it sound like an infectious disease. "I'll bet he's the illegal settler who's been trading in town." He pointed a curling, accusing finger at Axur.

Cherkogin frowned. "First things first, Administrator." She tilted her head toward Bethnee's front yard. "How did the merc die?"

"Foo dog poison," said Bethnee, patting Shiza's shoulder. She explained the events in terse sentences. By the time she was done, Pranteaux was staring at the sleepy foo dog in horror.

Cherkogin looked at Axur. "We intercepted the rest of the merc company where you said they'd be." She hooked her thumbs in her utility belt. "The DPE takes a dim view of kidnapping Del'Arche settlers or stealing from homesteaders." She turned to Pranteaux with a sly smile. "And an equally dim view of destroying valuable protection animals like foo dogs."

Pranteaux's mouth gaped like a fish. "But it *killed* a man!" He looked back and forth between the foo dog and Cherkogin's unyielding expression. He blew out a frustrated breath, then glared at

Bethnee and pointed at Axur again. "He's still illegal. He's been skulking around for months. I've been trying to catch him."

A fleeting look of distaste crossed Cherkogin's face as she turned away from Pranteaux to meet Axur's gaze. "What's your status?"

Axur had known this moment was inevitable ever since he'd chosen to meet the enforcers, so he could be there to protect Bethnee when they questioned her. He let go of her hand so he could stand, but she held him fast.

"He's my plus one."

Axur hoped he kept his confusion off his face. Cherkogin raised an eyebrow.

Pranteaux gawped, then recovered. "He can't be. You're not a paid settler. You can't tell me he lives in this pile of logs with you." His mouth twisted in disdain as he looked her up and down. "You hate men."

"I don't hate men." Bethnee let go of Axur's hand, then gently urged Shiza to jump down and got to her feet. "I'm afraid of men who want to hurt me. There's a difference."

Axur stood and stayed next to her. Whatever her play was, he was in.

Bethnee pushed her hair behind her ear. "I looked it up. The settlement contract says homesteaders get one 'plus one,' as long as he agrees to reside on my homestead for a GDAT standard year." Bethnee wove her fingers through his and held up their joined hands. "I'm declaring Axur as my plus one."

Cherkogin smiled. "I'll be your official witness." She raised her arm to tap her percomp gauntlet. Her smile turned sharper. "I'll even register the declaration for you, since the town's satellite uplink building got destroyed by the greedy mercs that your 'plus one' helped stop." She directed her next words to Pranteaux with a pointed look. "He single-handedly saved your town from an armed invasion and wholesale theft of its valuable animals."

Axur tilted his head toward Bethnee. "She delayed this team so you could catch them."

Pranteaux clamped his jaw and looked away with a frown. His eyes widened, and his expression morphed into sly challenge. "Clause 624.308.T.51." He looked at Bethnee. "You'll have to cohab or marry your 'plus one.'" He gave Axur an insulting smile. "Can't have Slick Slims taking advantage of the gullible and stealing their homesteads." He looked around at the furniture and sneered. "Not that this dump is worth stealing."

Cherkogin shook her head. "The council rescinded that stupid clause two years ago. You can't force people into domestic contracts."

Pranteaux jutted out his jaw, clearly intending to continue the fight.

Cherkogin was having none of it. "Quarks and quasars, man, I brought you here to confirm Bakonin's identity as the homesteader and remand the mercs if needed, not meddle in people's private lives." She shot quick glances to her patiently waiting enforcers. "The administrator's work here is done. Escort him back to the flitter."

Pranteaux gave everyone in the room one last, sweeping glare and stomped through the door that commander had already opened. The enforcers left with him.

"Bureaucrats," muttered Cherkogin. She kept the door open and turned to Bethnee. "Would you mind stepping outside and, uh, getting your dire wolf guardian to stand down?"

Bethnee snorted. "You could have just said you want to talk to Axur alone." She sealed the coat she hadn't yet taken off and limped to the door. She left without a backward glance. The door closed behind her.

"Sorry," said Cherkogin, with a shrug. "I tank at diplomacy."

"Apologize to her, not me." He tilted his head, finally able to place her familiar-sounding voice. "You were the ex-Jumper dispatcher this morning."

She nodded. "Yep. We're really short-handed. How'd you like a job with the Del'Arche Planetary Enforcers?"

Bethnee's head pounded and her joints ached from the fever she'd brought on herself by healing both Trouble and Shiza. Her talent felt thin and wispy as she extended a thread of invitation to Serena, who was sitting in the middle of her front yard, keeping herself between Bethnee and the waiting enforcers. Serena stood and trotted toward her.

Snapping at the commander hadn't been her finest moment. She heard Cherkogin's job offer right as the door closed. It was ideal for Axur. He'd have purpose again and make new friends, because Axur was very likeable. He'd have a team of enforcers to protect him if the CPS ever came calling.

Bethnee sat on a flat rock and buried her hands in Serena's thick winter fur. Daylight was more than half gone.

From the trees, Jynx chuffed twice, loudly. The enforcers looked around uneasily.

Serena's ears pricked forward. Bethnee chuckled. "Yes, she definitely taunted you. Go play."

The dignified dire wolf unexpectedly turned and licked Bethnee's face, then bounded off into the woods after the snow leopard.

She stuck her hands in her coat pockets and dropped her head to stretch her neck for a moment. She listened to breezy gusts stirring branches, and drifted for a bit, pretending the sun was warm. In her first few months on the planet, any weather at all had disconcerted her, after years living in controlled space environments. Now the wind through the trees sounded like freedom.

The door to her cabin opened, and Cherkogin strode out. Axur and Kivo emerged a moment later, but angled toward Bethnee instead of following the commander. Cherkogin turned to look at Axur, then gave Bethnee a respectful nod. "We're clearing out. Thank you for your help, homesteaders. And congratulations, by the way." She turned and made an upward spiral motion to her enforcers, and walked down the path with them following.

Axur stood, fists on his hips, watching them go. Kivo sidled up to her and put his head on her knees. When the last, low thrum of high-low flitters finally faded, Axur held out a hand to her. "Could we go inside now? My dangly bits are getting cold."

She smiled and took his hand, and let him help pull her up. "Can't have that. You might need them."

The front cabin was finally warm again. She didn't want to go back to the cave until Axur's comms band monitoring confirmed that the enforcers had rounded up all the mercs and were on their way south.

She poured boiling water into the teapot. Axur sat at the kitchen-area counter she'd built to be comfortable for her height. Even though his face still sported streaks of dirt, and mud caked his long hair and beard, he was still plasma hot. She probably looked and smelled like something her weasel had dragged in. Felt like it, too.

Axur idly folded a thin towel into various shapes while they waited for the tea to steep. "I keep meaning to read the settlement contract, but legalese puts me to sleep. Tell me about this 'plus one' clause."

"It's complicated. Paying settlers can sponsor as many people as they like, and it confers homesteader rights to those people after a year, as long as they live on the settler's property. Those people can't do the same unless they wait another a year and buy or build their own homestead. Nonpaying but landed homesteaders like me can sponsor one person at a time."

Axur smiled. "Thank you." He gave her a speculative look. "What's Pranteaux's friction with you? Is it because you're a minder? 'Cause if that's the case, it's bullshit."

"No, he's a minder, too, a general filer who remembers everything. Nuñez says he's a control freak who overcompensates with his need for respect." She shrugged one shoulder. "I just think he's an asshole. Probably didn't help that I told him so to his face."

Axur laughed. She was going to miss the sound of it.

She poured tea into both the waiting cups. "Congratulations on the new job, by the way. Will you have to move to the spaceport?" She pushed one cup and a sugar stick across the counter toward him.

"I didn't take it." He dipped the stick into the tea and stirred once.

"Why?" Maybe he felt like he owed her. "This is just your legal residence for the year. You don't have to actually live here. You could be with Jumpers again, and it'd be a good use of your abilities. You like people. You liked Cherkogin." She pointed to his hanging poncho. "You're free."

"All valid points, and I'd have said yes if they'd offered when I first landed." He stroked Kivo's broad head, which was resting on his thigh. "But everything changed when I discovered the pets." He looked around at her tiny cabin. "I never had my own home before. Being a planetary enforcer would take me away from home a lot." He swirled the sugar stick in his tea. "I liked being a Jumper. They help people in trouble, and look after their own. But I volunteered for the medic training and kept up my language skills because they're often more effective than guns." He gave her a lopsided smile. "Don't tell any Jumpers I said that."

"Your secret's safe with me." She couldn't hold her answering smile for long. "You have a lot of assets. You could move to a bigger city and be a medic and rent your printer."

He stilled. "Do you want me to go?"

"No, I want you to stay, because I think I'm in love with you." She wrapped her arms around her ribs. "But it's not about me. I want what's right for you."

A slow smile stole across his face. "All the cities are in the south, and Serena would be miserable in the heat." He stood and eased his way around the end of the counter. "I know you'd take her, but Trouble wouldn't have anyone to watch over, so I'd have to leave him and the others with you, too. Kivo's a theft magnet, like Jynx, so I'd have to leave him, as well." He edged toward her, close enough to touch her. "And that means everyone I love would be here."

She looked up at his strong, kind face. "You could have anyone you want. Someone who can promise not to be scared with you. Someone who's normal."

"Normal is boring." He touched the scarred side of his neck with his cybernetic hand. "I'm no prize." She hadn't seen that vulnerable look on his face before.

"Because you're a cyborg?" She reached out to slip her hand into his. She stroked a thumb over the exposed biometal knuckle. "Cybernetics are a part of you, but they're not you. The man I know is caring, smart... beautiful." Her eyes welled with tears. "Anyone would be lucky to have you."

"What if the only one I want is a nova-hot veterinarian who loves animals?" He slid his other hand up her arm slowly and rested it on her shoulder.

Bethnee smiled. "Nuñez would be happy to hear it." She put a hand on Axur's waist. "She and her wife think you're sexy. They like to share a handsome man on special occasions."

Axur shook his head. "The only woman I want also has a cybernetic leopard and a hot-spring pool." He put his other hand on the side of her face, and wove his fingers into her hair.

She leaned into his touch. "As it so happens, the only man I want is tall and strong, and loves animals."

He lowered his head to hers, stopping just before their lips touched. "Do you still want to kiss me?"

She raised her hand to his face to caress his cheek. "More than anything. Do you want to be kissed?"

"More than anything." He met her halfway to join his lips with hers.

He tasted cool and sweet. Heat pooled in her abdomen and warmed her core. She pulled herself closer, wanting to share the heat with him. He left her mouth and trailed kisses to the side of her face. She gasped in a mix of pleasure and pain as he brushed by her sore jaw.

He pulled back to look at her face. "Sorry, I didn't think." He touched delicate fingers to her cheek. "I've just wanted you for so long. I love you."

She gave up fighting the tears and let them fall. "I love you, too, but I'm a mess. Could we maybe talk about this in my geothermal pool?"

He gave her a lascivious grin. "*Naked* in your geothermal pool?"

She chuckled. "Yeah, naked." She boldly slid a hand around to cup his muscular ass. "I'm worried about your cold dangly bits."

15

They didn't make it to the pool as fast as Axur had hoped. Security systems needed arming after he'd moved his runabout down to her landing pad and brought all his gear into her marvelous cave. Animals variously needed calling in, drying off, reassuring, feeding and watering, and cleaning up after. He and Bethnee needed food, too. Using his enhanced speed and strength burned through calories like dry kindling, and he didn't have Jumper nutrient rebalancer concentrates to compensate. Bethnee had pushed her talent limit to the edge, too.

Finally, she led him to the geothermal pool. She turned and kissed him. "Hello, new homesteader."

"Hey, yourself." He could drown in the depths of her eyes. "Can we get naked now?"

She laughed. "Yes." She started to pull her tunic up with trembling hands, but he stopped her. "I want to make love with you more than my next breath, but I don't want to scare you. We don't have to do this now." He slid a hand up to her shoulder. "I'm not a telepath or an empath, I'm just a flux-to-the-max Jumper. You have to tell me what's too much, or too fast, or too close."

"I'll try. Sometimes, it takes me by surprise, and I just have to ride it out." She held up shaking fingers. "This isn't from fear, it's from wanting you." She flattened her palm on his chest. "I haven't had a lover since I was seventeen, and that was sex in the back of prepaid autocabs. You'll have to tell me what's going on with you, too. I love your strength, but I can't read you. I tank at communicating with humans."

"As it happens, I have built-in capacity for comms." She snorted in amusement. He captured her fingers and kissed them. "We'll figure it out together."

They explored each other in the warm pool. He loved finding the places where he could make her gasp and moan, and helping her find the spots on him that sent fire through his every synapse. He carried her naked to her bed, and only had to evict four furry occupants before joining with her to give them both the pleasure they'd been seeking. Their bodies seemed to fit together, like they'd been made for each other.

When he awoke and turned the lights up a bit, he discovered the bed had been invaded by three cats, a ferwinkle, a foo dog, and a six-legged chimera. He had a feeling their bed would never be cold or empty.

Bethnee stirred and rolled to the side, eliciting a muffled meow of protest from Delta the cat. Bethnee sighed and rolled back to drape herself on Axur. He loved the feel of her skin on his, the scent of her, the weight of her on him.

"What time is it?" she asked.

He checked his chrono implant. "A little after zero one hundred."

She slid her hand up to caress his jaw with her thumb. "Can't sleep in a strange bed?" She tweaked his earlobe. "Or with a strange woman?"

"You're not strange, you're unconventional." She made a rude sound, and he laughed. "Cyborgs love unconventional women who live in caves." He wrapped his arm around her waist.

"Good," she said. "I love cyborgs who have their own freighters. And printers. And autodocs. And runabouts." She kissed him between each item she listed.

He laughed. "It's too far for my potential patients and customers, though. I like your idea of looking at the abandoned house next to Nuñez's to see if we can make it into a medical clinic." He kissed her hairline. "According to a forecaster friend of Cherkogin's, trouble is brewing in the Concordance, and frontier planets should expect an influx of refugees. Something to do with Ayorinn's Legacy. You know, those nonsensical poems that predict a radical vector change for civilization." He shook his head. "The CPS dismisses them as a hoax, but I don't trust the CPS much anymore."

She sat up slowly and stretched. "I'm going to the fresher and check on Trouble. Want some water?"

"Yes, please."

He watched her because he could, enjoying the sleek curve and sway of her slender hips as she walked. She hardly limped at all. As soon as he could afford it, he planned to take her on a trip south for full repairs and healing. He sat up and rearranged pillows, blankets, and animals so she'd have a place to sit when she came back.

She returned carrying a glass of water and the wrapped Solstice Day present he'd given her. Trouble the dog walked in behind her, less energetic than usual, but looking alert. She handed him the water, then helped Trouble up onto the bed next to Kivo.

She kneeled on the bed and stroked Trouble's head. "I'm not sorry Kanaway died."

"Me, either." Axur took a deep, steadying breath to keep the anger at bay. He wanted to resurrect the sick twist, just so he could kill him himself, more slowly.

She crawled toward him to sit next to him against the pillows, holding the present. "Can I open this now?"

"Sure." He watched her face as she unwrapped and opened the box.

After a moment, recognition dawned. She stroked the heart-shaped piece of fur and looked up at him with a smile. "You printed this?"

"Yes." He loved her quick mind. "I've been working on a formula for synthskin patches for me, so I thought I'd experiment with synthfur for Jynx's leg. She deserves to be free to go outside whenever she wants."

She put the fur back in the box and put it on the nearby ledge, then kissed his shoulder. "It's a perfect gift." She slid herself under his arm. "I've been thinking. Even if nothing comes of the forecaster's prediction, it wouldn't hurt to plan for an influx of new people, anyway. Once word gets around you're a trained medic with an autodoc and willing to take trade, more people will visit Tanimai, and some will stay."

"I guess I'm the first of the influx, then." He picked up her hand and kissed her fingers. "Lucky for me, I fell madly in love with a woman with a homestead and built-in pet family."

"We're the lucky ones." She kissed his chest. "I think you should talk to Cherkogin again. Offer to be on reserve, train with them monthly. You'd learn things you can't find out from just listening to their comms. Then we could prepare better, if we do get more refugees."

"You wouldn't mind?" His two potentially serious relationships while in the military had foundered when their assignments had taken one or both of them away for ten-days at a time. "I have to admit I was tempted, but you're more important to me."

"I appreciate that, but you've got skills you should be using." With a somewhat awkward move, she straddled his thighs and faced him. "Strength. Comms. Languages. Making friends. Blowing things up." She rested her hands on his shoulders and gave him a crafty smile. "Make them pay you in hard credit."

He laughed. "Now the truth comes out."

"Yep," she said. "We have to finish more of the cave so your animals can be comfortable when we're here." They'd decided to spend time at both her place and his, to maintain his homestead claim. "That takes renting the rock laser, and that takes hard credit."

He glided his hands up to her waist and leaned forward to give her a long, sensual kiss, with a promise of more. "I love a nova-hot woman who knows how to make a good trade."

CATS OF WAR

***

A tarnished military subcaptain, a repair technician hiding from her past, and two genetically engineered cats must join forces to save an important factory.

*Military Subcaptain **Kedron Tauceti** counts the days until he can leave the rare metals factory and his current duty station as the liaison to the galactic government's Criminal Restitution and Indenture Obligation system. The post was protection—and punishment—for exposing a theft ring during his previous assignment. He's more than ready to get his career back on track on a new base halfway across the galaxy, even if it means leaving behind the one person who makes him want to stay. Not that he's told her, because technically, he's her warden.*

*Former financial specialist and current indenturee **Ferra Barray**, hiding from her past, only has three months to go on her restitution sentence. She's lucked into a tech repair job. If she keeps her head down, she'll soon be free to figure out her future. Unfortunately, the local shark behind every illegal scheme in the facility wants her to steal for him, and she's running out of excuses. And now the heroically handsome Tauceti, who she hoped could help, is transferring out.*

Everything changes when Ferra discovers two genetically modified cats. Saving them takes incredible risks. She doesn't know what she'll do if she can't convince Tauceti to rescue the cats and keep them until she's free to come for them.

But when trouble erupts at the factory, it might just be the cats who save them.

1

* ARGINT D'APA METALS PROCESSING FACILITY, PLANET OLAZA OKOMVELO * GDAT 3242.201 *

High Command Ground Division Subcaptain Kedron Tauceti longed to open the window in his office just once before leaving.

Not that he wanted more insects in everything, but even fresh air that smelled like a swamp would alleviate his office's stuffiness. The Central Galactic Concordance government section of the building that housed him, the CRIO staff, and the lone Citizen Protection Service representative was a later addition to the metals filtering and processing facility. The retrofit ducting did little to improve the inadequate ventilation and air handling. He'd been through three portable fans in his two-year tour of duty, and the fourth died an hour ago.

At least he wouldn't have to put up with the upcoming sweltering summer heat. He'd be on his way to his new post in four ten-days, six single days, and twenty hours. He didn't even pretend he hadn't started a countdown clock.

Serving as second-in-command for the small military base on Merganukhan, a backwater planet if ever there was one, probably wasn't most people's idea of a plum assignment. Unless their previous stint was the military liaison to the CGC's Criminal Restitution and Indenture Obligation system at a rare metals processing facility in the middle of a gigantic, insect-ridden, moss-laden swamp.

His current, soon-to-be-former, assignment was partly protection and partly punishment. He'd expected consequences from exposing a theft ring, because it tarnished the name of a military family as fabled as his own. From almost his first day as logistics chief on the huge, multi-divisional military base on Parlayan Six, Commodore Salah Chuma M'tendere had singled him out for much more than professional attention.

He hadn't known her long enough to be interested in a personal relationship, much less intimacy. When he'd figured out the real attraction had been his access to physical storage and quartermaster systems to enable sophisticated thievery, he'd gathered evidence and given it to High Command.

Unfortunately, the fallout made the entire chain of command look incompetent and lazy. That was only partly true, because the theft ring had been as clever as they were bold. Only complacency and rising greed got them caught. Most of them, anyway.

He wondered if the military investigators ever found the rumored treasure ship that M'Tendere reportedly hid before her high-profile court-martial at headquarters on Concordance Prime. By that time, High Command had appointed him to the CRIO post on Olaza Okomvelo "for his safety," instead of subcaptain of a mech division, for which he'd trained and positioned himself. His stint at the Argint d'Apa plant had put him out of sight—and conveniently unavailable to journalists—for the last two years.

He fervently hoped the long-awaited reassignment notice meant High Command had finally forgiven him for his good deed. It would take a decade to get his career back on track.

The clock display of his wallcomp declared the time to be midday, but the farking thing was only right for about an hour after a manual reset. The military-issue percomp on his wrist said it was actually close to the start of evening meal service, and his stomach agreed. Once the technology repair specialist came by, he'd be free to go eat, meet with the security chief, and take his customary evening walk before hitting the military gym.

He'd considered canceling the tech appointment, since he'd be gone soon, but he'd kept it on principle. He'd been submitting unanswered trouble reports for two years. The overworked and chronically understaffed facility's tech repair lab was finally getting around to checking out all his perennially malfunctioning office systems. At least he could leave everything in working order for his successor.

Kedron knew he shouldn't complain. The local CRIO installation was well run and passed audits with all green flags. He'd heard horror stories from the CRIO staff about notorious hellhole installations and rumors of secret installations that were even worse. It would have been just his luck to be assigned to one of those.

At Argint d'Apa, military veterans were few and far between, so the liaison job left him with a great deal of free time. The murky local chain of command meant few orders and little oversight from above. He submitted status reports and assessments for military indenturees, studied and took online training courses in things that interested him and might further his career, and kept himself in shape by visiting the gym a lot. He had yet to convince himself he'd been doing important work for High Command or the galactic government.

The biggest local issue he'd seen was the facility's chronic and currently resurgent problem with recreational chems. They were forbidden for all indenturees, but not for staff. When he'd asked about the policy or reported potential trouble, the facility manager had firmly and repeatedly told him to mind his own jurisdiction.

The other reason he didn't cancel the repair appointment was the technician who'd made the appointment, Indenturee Ferra Barray. In a facility full of restive, resentful, or resigned people—including him, sometimes—her cheery demeanor and lively sense of humor were a breath of fresh air.

He would've had no occasion to interact with her at all, except her records mistakenly identified her as ex-military, so he'd conducted her intake orientation four months ago. The regular CRIO staff was short-handed and overworked, so he'd kept Barray on his assignment list.

He'd had regular check-ins and several more random interactions with her since, including being stuck for a day in a shelter lockdown for a hurricane event. She'd made friends with everyone and kept the nervous indenturees occupied by teaching them an elaborate, convoluted logic game that Kedron was half-convinced she'd invented on the spot.

He secretly wanted to get to know her better, and maybe become friends. That, however, was a no-go, full-warn, all-red stop. He refused to go within a thousand kilometers of striking up a personal relationship with an indenturee. Thanks to his last post, he knew exactly what coercion felt like. How the pressure left a sick, sour stomach and constant anxiety.

He would rather let himself be savaged by the big hellhound escapee-retriever dogs that the plant security guards kept than do that to someone else. Bored guards sometimes caught unlucky wild animals and threw them to the dogs for "training," which also happened to involve betting. Kedron hated that he couldn't stop them. The only thing he or the CRIO staff could do was make sure it stayed on the civilian side of the compound.

Right on time, Barray knocked on the sliding door frame, then entered. She carried a bag slung over her shoulder. "Greetings, Subcaptain."

"Indenturee Barray." He nodded. "Thank you for coming."

She looked around and smiled when she saw the clock display. "Wallcomp troubles?"

Disgruntlement drove him to his feet. "*Everything* troubles. The only reliable tech in here is my percomp." He raised his arm to show the military gauntlet. "The wallcomp, the deskcomp, the light and enviro controls, the door lock, you name it, they're all glitchy." He pointed his chin toward the dead fan. "Even that sparked out an hour ago."

Her eyebrow raised. "And you're just reporting all this now?"

"What do you mean, now?" He took a deep breath to control his temper. "I have been submitting trouble reports for the last two years."

"That's odd." Skepticism crossed her face. "The records show two complaints from two years ago, a replacement fan a year ago, then nothing else until yesterday." She unfolded a battered tablet and brought up a holo display that showed four entries.

"Nonsense." He reached for his deskcomp, hesitated, then used his own percomp instead. It only took a moment to find and display the twenty-seven complaints. "These are what I submitted." He was glad he'd thought to keep copies.

"That's, uh, quite a list." She held out her plant-issued tablet. "Can you send those to me? I'll check when I get back to the repair lab."

He found the tablet's signal and transferred the list. "Done."

She put the tablet in her thigh pocket and looked around again. "Let's try for a quick win and fix the door lock first. That's security and safety, so it has priority." She took a tech scanner and a multitool out of her bag and turned to the door.

Rather than be a nuisance, he made himself sit and bring up the deskcomp display, so she wouldn't feel scrutinized. Her running commentary as she removed the panel amused him.

"Oh, no, I won't hurt you. Just a little probe." She pulled a datawire out of her bag and inserted it into the exposed connector. "There's a good module. Tell me all your troubles."

"Do you always talk to tech?" he asked.

"I talk to everything." She chuckled. "Blame my childhood on a space station. We couldn't afford pets." She turned to him. "I'll keep it in my head."

He raised his eyebrows. "You have a tech skulljack?" He resisted the impulse to touch his, hidden behind his ear. It had been quiet for two years, but soon, it would again enable him to interface with the AI of an assault tank or a three-story-tall military spider mech.

Laughter bubbled up out of her. "No, I meant I'll be quiet." She shook her head. "Even if I did have one, CRIO would have forcibly flatlined it. Thank chaos I flunked the minder tests, or the Citizen Protection Service would have put me on disruptor drugs, too." Her mouth twisted in scorn. "I guess CRIO and the CPS think all indentures are threats to the galactic peace."

He agreed with her acerbic contempt, but it wasn't politic to say so. He shrugged a shoulder. "You don't have to be quiet for my sake." He pointed to his display filled with flat photos and holos. "I'm just familiarizing myself with the native flora and fauna near my new post."

"Oh? Where is it?" She frowned. "Or is that crypto?"

"It's not secret at all. I'll be second-in-command of the combined military base on Merganukhan."

She chuckled. "Gotta be a Fourth Wave terraform. All the good member planet names were taken by then."

Her humor was infectious. "Third Wave, but the name is made up. When the colonists finally paid off the settlement company debt, the CGC High Council wouldn't let them rename the planet to 'Suck Flux, RSI.'"

Laughter burst out of her. "Too bad. I'd go out of my way to visit a planet with that name." She waved fingers in a sketch of a military salute. "Congratulations on the new post, Subcaptain, and good luck." She turned back to the door lock.

He knew others found him to be too focused and intense, which is why he had few friends. Being shy and slow to open up didn't help. He'd tried to change that in his liaison position but hadn't gotten very far. He lived on the compound and disliked most of the guards. He had little in common with the CRIO staff or the regular company employees. He preferred to avoid the CPS representative, and was an ocean away from the planet's only military base.

It was a sad commentary on his life that the only person in the facility to wish him well was an indenturee repaying a hefty restitution debt for destruction of CGC military property.

Ferra's day had started badly, then gone downhill and off a cliff from there.

Once again, dreams of flitter crashes and hunting for something lost, with two voices calling her, woke her more than once. She was short on sleep and long on clumsiness.

She'd flatlined the controls in the plant manager's expensive solardry unit. She'd barely escaped being cornered in the indenturee recreation hall by one of Lambru's recruiters. After the midday meal, a guard stopped and scanned her for contraband, all because she'd been carrying an empty crate. The same guard who passively watched her carrying crates full of equipment through that same central hallway every day.

She'd been looking forward to spending a few minutes with Subcaptain Tauceti. He was the only person in the entire facility who treated her with respect.

All right, that wasn't quite fair. The repair lab supervisor appreciated that she'd reduced his backlog of tech service requests, but to him, she was a replaceable commodity. The guards weren't outright abusive, but they were bored enough to let trouble among the indenturees play out for the entertainment value, as long as it didn't affect the regular staff or impact plant productivity. The less said about the guards who handled the dogs, the better.

Most of the indenturees kept to themselves and tracked their restitution balances like they were winning lottery numbers. The few that perpetrated inside scams and schemes were a pain in the ass and definitely to be avoided.

Tauceti had been her hidden ace, the one person she hoped she could go to if, despite her precautions, bad trouble found her. And now he was leaving. Frellin' hell.

The door lock was an easy fix, once she removed the underpowered spinwire scaffold some previous tech had made instead of simply replacing the failed C6 dot. Experience had taught her to carry several in her bag. She was careful not to disturb the security connectors. None of her business that the company monitored the High Command military liaison's office door.

She tested the wall control several times, then turned to face him. "The door should work now. Try it from your desk."

He touched the controls. The door obligingly opened, closed, or locked each time. He smiled. "Yes, thank you."

She stepped over to the wallcomp. "Yeah, I see you, looking all innocent."

He chuckled. "Sly troublemakers, are they?"

She nodded. "Oh, yeah. Either that, or they have swamp allergies, like us humans."

"Mold or spores, perhaps. The scientists complain about them." He glanced at his percomp, then went back to reading. A faint rumble came from the direction of his stomach.

He was probably hungry. It likely took a lot of concentrated protein and nutrients to keep his muscular body in such great condition. He made even the boring daily uniform look heroic. With his strong jaw and piercing blue eyes, he belonged in military recruiting holos. The bold geometric designs cut into the sides of his short brown hair offset his reserved demeanor, giving him an air of danger.

Dangerous to her, anyway. Apparently, being tired and cranky made her vulnerable to nova-hot men. She would never have acted on her secret fantasy of pouncing on him, because it would have ruined their relationship and compromised them both. Besides, he seemed completely oblivious to even blatant sexual flirtation from women or men, at least from what she'd seen.

Perhaps he needed an emotional connection with someone before becoming interested in getting physical. In which case, it was just as well he was leaving, before their friendly professional relationship had a chance to grow into anything personal. Loneliness made people do stupid things.

The wallcomp's small access door refused to open. She tried to pop off its decorative faceplate, but it clung to the bezel for dear life. When she finally pried it off, it slipped out of her fingers and landed on top of her foot, then bounced on the floor. "Ow!" She picked it up. "Sorry."

"Are you all right?" His concern seemed genuine.

"Fine." She fought off a blush. "I'm a certified non-adept. If this is the worst that happens, it'll be a good day." She gave him a self-deprecating smile. "Swamp allergies are giving me weird flying dreams and waking me up, so I'm sleep-deprived, too. I've got a medic appointment in the morning." And she was babbling to the pretty man. She gave herself a mental shake as she leaned the faceplate against the wall. "If it's okay with you, I'll assess all your tech now, then come back with the right parts."

He nodded. "As of now, my schedule is clear for the next ten-day."

His expression said he didn't know how he felt about that. He was a decent man with a sense of humor hiding under his contained personality. She'd felt bad about lying to him during the intake interview, because he seemed like an ethical man, too.

Oh, stop, she ordered herself.

Tauceti probably fluxed her drives because she missed her ordinary life, when she'd had friends, and one or two more-than-friends for physical affection and comfort. That was before everything blew up, thanks to her no-good, dead-to-her, may-he-slowly-rot-in-transit-space twin brother.

Those thoughts were a deeply-rutted, rocky path. "Move on, Barray," she muttered to herself. She picked up the scanner and focused on the wallcomp.

Twenty minutes later had her wishing she'd taken a backbreaking processing plant job instead of demonstrating a little tech experience during the skills assessment for restitution job placement.

Every single tech device in Tauceti's office, from his wallcomp, to his clock display, to his frelling portable fan, was infested with surveillance tech. Redundant, overlapping, interfering surveillance tech, some of which had been installed by rank amateurs.

Telling him would reveal her expertise, which was far deeper than her official records hinted at. She should know, because she'd written them herself. Deactivating the tech would bring the same result.

Also, if she'd misread Tauceti, and he deserved to be that tightly monitored, taking any action would expose the investigation.

Despite what the crime and conviction record said that had gotten her to Argint d'Apa, she was not anti-social. She'd been keeping a low profile for safety and working off her self-imposed sentence for being mind-bogglingly trusting and desperately stupid.

She needed more information on Tauceti before she could decide what to do. Her job meant she'd been in enough of the Argint d'Apa systems to know she could do some investigating of her own and not get caught. Her former specialty had been multi-node fractal meshes for financial systems, not processing plants that collected rare metals from the runoff that filtered through the swamp, but they had remarkably similar principles.

In the meantime, the people at the other end of the surveillance feed might find it suspicious if she didn't at least make a token attempt at her job. "Could I borrow your guest chair again? I've got time to fix your clock before I go."

"Of course." He watched as she carried it over and stepped up onto it, then went back to his deskcomp display.

Knowing the various spy eyes were watching, she fumbled around in the clock systems, as if improvising. Which she would have been, when she first arrived. Luckily, she knew how to read schematics and she'd learned quickly. Once she paid her debt, she'd need a new career, but it wouldn't be a repair tech. Her experience in Argint d'Apa proved they only saw grumpy people.

Surreptitiously, she overpowered her multi-tool, then touched it to the offending, power-grabbing module that contained a spy eye and who knew what else. She jumped when it actually sparked. *Frelling amateurs.* "Sorry, little clock."

"Are you okay?" he asked.

"Fine." She isolated the fried module but left it in place. "Just a bad connector." She traced the other connectors to make sure no other vampire tech was stealing power. "I think I've got it fixed."

She stepped off the chair and carried it back to its place.

Just as she picked up the handles to her bag, his office door opened to admit a knee-high cleaning bot. It raced into the room, zoomed by her feet, and banged itself into the south wall. It backed up and did it twice more.

On the third run, Ferra intercepted it. "Come here, you." She grunted as she lifted the heavy bot and turned it on its side. Tri-treads spun in place, like a turtle trying to right itself. She opened the concealed access plate and used the handle of her multitool to kill the power. "Does this happen to you a lot?"

"Are you talking to the bot or me?" Tauceti was suddenly close and looking down at her.

She covered her surprise with a laugh. "Both. You go first."

"No. Bots don't usually go berserk in my office." A twinkle in his eye belied his serious expression.

"Wonder why it's out in daytime." She patted its shell. "If it's still here when I come back tomorrow, I'll find out—"

"What are you doing to that bot?"

A woman stood in the doorway, arms crossed. Her digital name tag proclaimed her to be E. Calderosh, Facility Maintenance, and tailored work clothes confirmed her to be regular staff, not an indenturee. She looked mid-thirties, but could have been five times that old if she'd had regular maintenance or a full-body makeover. A crown of frizzy gold and silver braids kept her hair in place. Her expression made Ferra feel like a teenage miscreant.

"The bot malfunctioned," said Tauceti firmly. "Barray turned it off."

Calderosh's suspicious look cleared. "Oh, well, that's all right, then. I'll take it." She left for a moment, then came back in the room with a gravcart that had the sorry remains of another cleaning bot on it. She looked at Tauceti. "You haven't seen any other bots, have you? Some of these big ones and a bunch of the smaller ones are missing." She shaped her hands as if to hold something the size of a sports ball.

He shook his head. "No." Even standing casually, he looked like a vid star. No wrinkles, no dust, not a hair out of place.

Ferra stood and moved away from the bot, only to stumble over her own equipment bag and land on her ass. Her multitool went flying and bounced off the bot, then off Tauceti's shin.

"Sorry." She picked herself and the multitool up off the floor. She hid her embarrassment by bending over to seal and pick up her bag, allowing her loose, wavy hair to hide her face.

Clearly, she was a menace. For safety, she sould go straight to her room and stay there until the bad-luck chaos cloud moved on, except she still had things to do.

He glanced at her. "No harm done."

"At least the damn dogs didn't try to eat this one." Calderosh lifted the bot onto the cart with ease. "I have a feeling some of the bots got past the outer fence and are trying to clean the swamp." She rolled her eyes. "My boss will probably want me to go out and retrieve them."

Ferra laughed. "Because they'll smell so good when you get them back."

"Exactly," said Calderosh. "If you find any, turn them in. The plant manager posted a restitution bounty for them."

Surprised at the woman's friendliness, Ferra smiled. "Good to know."

Tauceti raised an eyebrow. "Has anyone tried turning the same one in multiple times?"

Calderosh chuckled. "A few of usual chiselers tried, but I hid asset tracers in the returned bots."

A lock of hair fell in Ferra's face. When she went to brush it back, the pass-tracker cuff on her wrist suddenly fell off and bounced on the floor in two pieces. She must have hit it when she fell. She scooped up the two pieces with a sigh. Her supervisor would probably charge her for printing a new one, since it would be her third.

Calderosh dug into one of the bellows pockets in her vest. "Here. Glue it with this until you can get it fixed." She produced a tube and held it out with a smile. "Locktight water sealer. Handiest stuff on the base."

Ferra shook her head. "Sorry, I don't know how to use it."

Calderosh pointed to the blue end. "Put the paste on the broken ends, hold them together, then zap it with the microcharger on the top. Hardens in seconds."

The bracelet-style percomp around Calderosh's wrist began blinking. She touched her earwire and subvocalized. As she listened, her expression transitioned into annoyance.

She blew out a noisy breath and grabbed the gravcart's control bar. "An indenturee named Healey sabotaged the kennel doors before her unauthorized departure, so of course, I'm the only non-indenturee in the whole facility who can let the damn hellhounds out." She handed the tube to Ferra. "Leave it with the subcaptain when you're done."

Calderosh stomped out with the gravcart trailing her like a child's wagon.

Ferra looked at the tube, then put it on Tauceti's desk. "I'll leave this with you right now. Considering the day I'm having, I'd probably seal my fingers together."

His expression softened as he glanced at the broken pieces in her hand. "Want me to try?"

"Sure." She put them on the desk, then backed away. "I'll just stand over here, in case clumsiness is communicable."

He deftly applied dabs of paste on each broken piece. "You're not clumsy." Pushing the ends together right the first time, he held the cuff together with one hand and touched the microcharger tip to the joins. "You're just tired." He leaned over his desk to examine the joins under the bright lamp.

"Yeah, that too." A violent, wet sneeze took her by surprise. She barely had time to cover her face with her elbow. "And allergic."

Good thing she wasn't trying to impress Tauceti, because otherwise, she'd be thoroughly mortified by the whole visit and have to avoid him for at least a ten-day.

"The medics have chems for that." He handed her the repaired pass-tracker.

Ferra laughed. "I'm pretty sure no chems in the galaxy will cure clumsiness." She slipped the tracker onto her wrist. "Besides, I avoid any drugs if at all possible. If there's an obscure side-effect that's worse than the disease, I'm guaranteed to get it." She hitched the bag's strap higher on her shoulder. "I'll get out of your orbit so you can go eat."

He nodded and glanced at his percomp. "What time will you be here tomorrow?"

"Assuming no front-office emergencies, nine-hundred-ish. Maybe earlier if the medic clears me fast."

"I'll be here." He went back behind his desk. "Get some rest."

She felt like she ought to salute or yes-sir him, even though she wasn't military. "Uh, thanks for fixing my cuff."

"No problem." He sat and turned on his deskcomp display.

For a moment, she thought he looked lonely, sitting in his perfect uniform, in his perfect office that had nothing personal to relieve the generic sterility.

She shook her head as she left his office. *Move on, Barray.*

3

Kedron had unexpected free time after his quick cafeteria dinner. Argint d'Apa's security chief had canceled their regular meeting, likely because the guards hadn't yet recaptured Healey, even after deploying the genetically modified hellhounds. The shady pet trade had originally designed them as status symbols for the wealthy; the military found them useful and expropriated the patents. Argint d'Apa security got them as part of their deal with CRIO. The dense biomass of the swamp and the types of metals in the mountain runoff water made ordinary tracers and trackers next to worthless outside the plant compound's perimeter.

While Kedron wouldn't miss the Argint d'Apa facility, he would miss the swamp. He'd disliked it at first, the same way most staffers still did, but it had grown on him. He'd spent time studying its ecology and gone with the biodiversity scientists on a few sample-collection expeditions. Living so close to untamed nature made it easier to understand how everything, from the majestic giant trees to annoying clouds of gnats, had a place. Maybe he did, too, even if he couldn't see it.

He put away his uniform and decided to walk laps on the campus's wide perimeter walkway, rather than spend another evening alone in the gym. Regulations restricted it to military personnel, and he'd never seen the CPS representative use it.

As much as possible, he kept his interactions with her in virtual space. As a mid-level telepath, she could read thoughts, and as a low-level sifter, she could affect brain chemicals, detect lies, and sense the use of active minder talents. Military personnel caught with minder talents earned an immediate, permanent transfer to the CPS's Minder Corps.

Kedron's minder talent wasn't much, just an ability to use seemingly unrelated information to find things of interest, but he'd rather direct traffic for a city of half a billion or be an indenturee than work for the Minder Corps. Too many private family stories warned of how badly the Minder Corps treated its personnel. He'd learned to hide his talent well enough to beat the CPS Testing Center for mandatory age twelve and seventeen tests, and random ones since, but some sifters were better than the testing equipment. Fortunately, minder talents in the patterner class were hard for even high-level sifters to detect.

He pulled on pants and a specially treated long-sleeved top to ward off biting insects. Last, he stepped into one of his few indulgences—custom-tailored, waterproof, adaptive boots. Even with myriad modern transportation options, Ground Div gunnin, from the lowest ranker to High Command commodores, spent a lot of time walking, running, and marching. Good boots made all the difference.

He looked out the north-facing window of his quarters to check the weather and the path. Non-essential indenturees were on lockdown, and half the staff was busy, so he wasn't surprised to see it deserted. The tall perimeter fence's horizontal power lines beyond the road-glass pathway glowed faintly as reminders of their presence. The overhead and glass path lights blinked on and off erratically, then stayed off. Twilight and mold sometimes messed with the sensors.

Shadowed movement caught his eye. Someone carrying a shallow, rectangular crate stepped off the path toward the exterior powered fence. The figure knelt right in front of the fence and set the crate down. After furtive looks left and right, the hunched figure slid something under the fence.

Instead of zapping the person into insensibility or setting off the alarm, the visible bottom three fence lines between the two posts raised like a curtain, leaving a torso-height gap. The figure quickly extended a pole to push the crate outside the fence as far as possible, until it butted up against the big rock outcropping. He or she retracted the pole and picked up the device from the dirt. The fence line sank and straightened to its usual position.

The lights flickered on briefly. The figure pulled on a hood and hunched forward, but he'd already recognized the face. Ferra Barray.

She stepped onto the path and headed west. The lights came on and stayed bright. He watched until she vanished.

Protocol said to report anything unusual to the security chief, but Kedron had repeatedly been told, politely but sternly, to stick to his own star lane.

He wished he could come up with a more probable theory than suspecting that Barray was dealing contraband. A non-indenturee confederate would likely pick up the goods. Chems, pilfered equipment or tech, and stolen raw metals were all likely candidates.

He wouldn't have tagged her for a thief. She'd been convicted of crashing a friend's air-racing yacht into a Central Galactic Concordance government launch hangar that housed military orbiters. When she couldn't pay the court-ordered restitution, the CGC arbiter remanded her to the CRIO system. The record implied she'd been chemmed to the gills.

That didn't sync with her comment earlier that day about avoiding drugs of any sort, but everyone did stupid things now and again.

He wanted Barray to be the person he thought she was, but his experience with the theft ring situation taught him not to be swayed by what he wished to be true, and to look at the actual facts. He needed to know what was in the crate.

Crossing to his closet, he pulled out a dark jacket and wrist lights, plus a bigger floating light.

On the way to the facility's main ground gate on the other side of the complex, he tried to think of a reason to be trudging around in the swamp after dark. He was a lousy liar, so it had to be plausible. The best he could come up with was that he'd seen a potential problem with the perimeter fence but wanted to confirm it before reporting it.

The gate guards checked his credential and biometric, then waved him on through without so much as a curious glance.

He saw no one on the inside lighted walkway as he made his way carefully around the outside from the south. The compacted dirt had deteriorated into mud holes in some spots but was mostly intact. The glass-over-rock base would protect the facility for a while, but he had no doubt the swamp would eventually win, if left unchecked.

Chilly water soaked the bottom half of his pants by the time he found the crate. He crouched beside it and checked his surroundings, then turned on his lights to examine it for traps or trouble. Finally, he opened the lid.

Inside, a mother muskrat and three tiny, furry brown babies nestled in a bed of wilting water vines and rusting lettuce leaves.

Relief flooded him as he quickly closed the lid. Ferra wasn't dealing, she was rescuing. He'd once accidentally discovered her vomiting after seeing the guards throw a stray animal to the hellhounds. He'd brought her towels and a water pouch and felt guilty because all he could do was help her clean up the mess.

Since he was already muddy, he carried the crate farther into the swamp. He set it on a hillock near the water. The young muskrat had bred very early in the season, so her babies might not survive anyway, but at least now they'd have a fighting chance.

He opened the lid and encouraged the little family to get out. The mother squealed in evident distress. He hated to take the crate, but its garish yellow color and plant logo would attract attention if a patrolling guard saw it. He left the bedding and the lettuce on the hillock, then collapsed the crate flat and carried it back.

Once again, the guards asked no questions, just pointed him to the cleaning jets and solardry so he wouldn't track muddy footprints through the halls.

By the time he stepped into the hot shower in his private fresher, his satisfaction at discovering the benevolent nature of Ferra's secret had morphed into curiosity about a new mystery. How had she breached the fence?

4

Ferra's bone-deep exhaustion made her wonder if she wasn't actually just dreaming about waiting her turn to pay in the slow-moving cafeteria line.

After finishing her shift, eating late, and sneaking the young mother muskrat and her babies out of the compound, Ferra had gone straight to bed.

Unfortunately, the dreams were more vivid than ever, with two distinct thought patterns in her head. One was lonely and worried, and the other was in pain and cried for help. It didn't take a certified therapy telepath to figure out her subconscious was manifesting her fears the only way it knew how. If the medics couldn't counter the allergen affecting her, maybe they'd give her a dormo patch. Seven uninterrupted hours of sleep would be worth losing bonus money for being on call after-hours.

She pushed her tray forward in the track, debating on splurging on fresh sweetfruit and caffeine to supplement her usual cheap mealpack and water pouch. No such thing as a free breakfast for indenturees.

A hissed argument and commotion behind her made her and everyone else turn to look.

Too late, she realized it was a setup. Indenturee Lambru cut in line in front of her with his tray full of expensive, freshly made hot dishes and premium real coffee. She'd trained herself to track and avoid his various confederates, who she thought of as remora, but in her fog of exhaustion, she'd forgotten to track the head shark himself.

He might be wearing the same indenturee uniform as everyone else, but the details painted the image of an intersex who presented male and had a taste for stylish shoes, resilk undershirts, and pearlescent cosmetics.

His mild and meek air belied his involvement with every illegal activity in Argint d'Apa, both indenturee and staff. His official story was that he'd been a low-level employee for a pharma blackmarketer. However, his current restitution debt was an order of magnitude higher than hers, despite five years in the CRIO system. Luckily, a departing indenturee had warned her early on, or she might have been unwittingly reeled into his schemes.

He gave her a pleasant smile. "Hello, Barray."

She nodded, allowing her eyelids to droop a little, as if barely functional and pre-verbal. Not far from the truth, actually.

His expression transitioned into almost shy diffidence. "I wonder if I might ask a favor?"

She gave him credit for his acting ability and for getting straight to the point. Ever since her first month in the tech department, his intermediaries had been looking for a lever to get to her. Thanks to having had to bail her brother out of trouble dozens of times, she knew the type, and knew how to play dumb or avoid them.

She yawned to cover her glance toward the guard who was chatting up one of the food servers. No help there.

Lambru smiled as he pushed his tray forward. "Up too early, or up too late?"

She shrugged. No one moved into the gap in line behind her, so no help there, either.

He pushed his tray forward, then grabbed hers and pulled it next to his fast enough to make its contents slide to the edge. "I'm so sorry." He lifted the meal pack and pouch with exaggerated care and returned them to the center of her tray.

She wasn't surprised to see her tray now sported a hand-printed list peeking out from under the mealpack. Indenturees weren't allowed personal percomps or unmonitored net access, forcing them back to the pre-flight Stone Age for communications.

She knew how this went. If she accepted the list, she was on the hook. If she tore up the list or reported it, he'd make an example of her. Delay was her only option. She shoved her hands in her vest pockets and looked up, then back to him.

His oily smile smacked of used flitter sales. "I'm sure we can come to a trade arrangement that benefits everyone." His tone took on an unctuous quality. "You will find it very worth your..." He trailed off with a frown and a sniff. "Is something burning?"

She waited until he noticed her mealpack's heater had set the whole pack on fire.

"Shit," she said loudly. She pulled the water pouch off the tray, then fumbled to open it.

The paper list under the mealpack caught fire and emitted dark smoke.

She grunted with effort. Just as she got the pouch open, the overhead fire suppression system opened up and doused the fire, plus everything in a four-meter radius, with orange foam.

Indenturees sputtered in dismay and outrage. Lambru backed up. He lost his footing and cracked his elbow hard on a nearby chair.

A food server and two guards converged on their position, with more on the way.

Between the acrid smell of the burned tray, the carbonized smell of burned food, and the cloying citrus scent in the foam, Ferra's stomach threatened revolt.

"What happened?" demanded a guard.

Ferra pointed to the mess on the tray. "Mealpack heater overload."

The suppression foam made a soupy gelatin on the hot tray. Everywhere else, it turned to powder, causing several people to sneeze.

"Third fail this month," groused the food server. His thick Islander accent gave a musical cadence to his words. He opened a yellow collapsible crate to collect the mess.

A guard peered at Ferra. "You look pale."

"I just need something to eat." She pointed her chin toward the blackened tray. "Preferably not overcooked."

The food server chuckled. "I bring you one different. No charge." He raised his voice and addressed the rest of the people with ruined food. "If you no pay, go back to kitchen. They fix again." He repeated it in Mandarin, which was better than his English.

Ferra sipped water from the pouch she was still holding. Her stomach gurgled.

"What if we already paid?" whined an indenturee.

The food server pointed to the woman just striding in from the office area. "Ask manager."

Ferra stayed with the guards when the affected indenturees headed toward the kitchen. Lambru's irritated expression could have been for her or the mess, but he followed the others.

She stood quietly aside while the guard subvocalized a quick report to the shift supervisor. The food server brought her a new mealpack with a different logo on it. She nodded her thanks, then turned to the guard.

"Permission to take this with me for later?" She brushed orange powder off the front of her and didn't want to think about what her hair looked like. "I have a medic appointment in fifteen minutes, and a CPS re-test after that."

The guard shrugged. "Yeah, go ahead. Just don't leave it for the swamp rats or the birds to find."

Ferra ducked out the cafeteria's side door and made a quick stop in her cell to stash the mealpack. She knew from experience that anything but water and maybe a little bread would make her nausea worse.

At the clinic, the medic's blood tests said no allergies, toxins, molds, or weird spores. She'd described her dreams as vivid but not scary, and didn't mention the nausea, which would go away on its own. They gave her generic advice and one mild dormo patch, then asked if she knew how to fix autodocs. The facility had six of them, to compensate for the distance to a full medical center, and one or another of them was always acting up. She had to profess ignorance and told the medics to contact the tech repair manager.

The CPS representative apologized for the need for a re-test, but she'd discovered the equipment had been miscalibrated in the previous test. At least she didn't ask for a free repair job.

Ferra didn't even bother to complain about this being the fourth time she'd been called in, each for a different excuse. It happened with all the indenturees, so she didn't feel singled out. She dutifully submitted to the measurements and tests, which again failed to discover any minder talent.

Non-minder indenturees assumed the rep was either padding her expense report or got a bonus for the number of tests. The fifteen or so minder indenturees got scut jobs and lived in segregated, higher-security cells. Plus, they had to take mandatory disruptor drugs to dull their talents. No one wanted to be identified as a minder.

In the tech repair office, she arrived just in time to be sent to the CRIO offices for an emergency call. Someone had breached their security to steal one of their deskcomps and smash the others. She salvaged what she could and replaced the rest with loaners. By the time she got back to Subcaptain Tauceti's office, she had to apologize for it being mid-afternoon, and six hours after she'd promised.

"Quite all right," he said. "How are you feeling?"

She smiled, once again charmed by his thoughtfulness. "According to the medics, my immune system is 'within acceptable parameters.'" She rolled her eyes. "They prescribed less stress, more exercise, and more sleep."

He smiled, and she felt like she'd won a gold star. Honestly, the man was dangerous.

She pointed to her bag. "I have parts for your wallcomp." Mindful of the multiple surveillance monitors, she frowned. "I have to put together a cart to bring the equipment I'll need to figure out all the things wrong with your deskcomp. The lab manager has to approve me taking it out. And parts printers are chained to the lab."

"Why don't I bring the deskcomp to your lab?"

"Are you sure? Argint d'Apa rules say you military people can't let your government tech out of custody. You'd have to stay." She could even quote the policy to him because she'd written it at lunchtime and inserted it into the lab's manual that no one had accessed in the last three years. *Come on, Tauceti, take the bait.*

He tapped his wrist gauntlet and looked at a display. "How about right after you finish with the wallcomp?"

"Sorry, I'm jammed until eighteen hundred." She tilted her head. "How about after the evening meal? I'm on call, but only for emergencies. Fewer interruptions." She gave him a lopsided smile. "Unless the chief scientist ditches his prized sample collection bot into a sinkhole again."

He frowned at the deskcomp and rubbed behind his ear, then glanced at the clock display.

She waved apologetically. "Never mind. You shouldn't have to give up your free evening just to get your tech working."

She put her bag down and popped the faceplate off the wallcomp. Maybe she could come up with some other way to lure Tauceti away from his fishbowl of an office.

She wanted to rip out the whole wallcomp and start over, but that was just frustration talking. It hadn't asked to be crippled by at least four different surveillance devices that tracked the sound, movement, power usage, and, previously, captured a video feed. "Poor little comp, you were just trying to do your job, weren't you?"

She used her company tablet to bring up a standard systems map for the wallcomp. She made the display big and visible to whoever was watching. Just a low-skilled tech, doing her job, cleaning out the non-regulation clutter.

She slowly and carefully removed each of the sensors, and dropped them into a shielded parts recycling bag. The sound monitor was the worst. Whoever installed it and its high-charge battery had been lucky not to flatline all the connected wallcomps in that wing or start a fire.

Maybe she could ask Tauceti to come to the indenturee gym to teach her how to use the ancient analog exercise equipment. *Right, because that didn't sound like a sleazy invitation at all.*

She'd been avoiding looking at Tauceti, because he deserved not to be interrupted, and she'd be distracted by the sinfully handsome scenery, but now she turned to him. "Try vocal commands for the wallcomp."

He paused the scrolling display of whatever he was reading. "Ceiling lights to fifty percent."

The lights dimmed.

"Restore ceiling lights."

The lights obligingly brightened to the previous setting.

A smile his face. "I'll try the other controls later."

She pointed her chin toward his desk. "I still need to test the touch controls." By which she meant, clear the crap out of those systems, too. "Is now a good time to displace you for about thirty minutes, or do you want to set an appointment?"

He glanced at the clock display. "Do I have to stay?"

"Uhm, the manual didn't say." She wanted him there because he made her feel safe, but she needed to get used to him being gone. "It's up to you."

Belatedly, she realized she couldn't remember if she'd been talking to herself, as usual. She'd probably annoyed him.

He stood and pointed to his deskcomp. "The search for the pertinent policies would take longer than it's going to take you to fix it. I'll stay." He moved his deskcomp to the high, narrow counter that ran the length of the office's far wall. "Use my chair if you'd like."

Twenty minutes later, she packed up her gear, including the three extra "bad parts" to be recycled. "Once I get the cart sorted, I'll ping you for an appointment to work on your deskcomp."

He cleared his throat. "I could bring it this evening."

She couldn't help but grin. "That's great. Nineteen hundred?" That should give her plenty of time to eat and clear the decks.

"Yes." He looked so serious that she wanted to ask what was wrong. *Get a grip, Barray.* Even if he told her, what could she do about it? She'd always been a soft touch for people in need, a trait her brother had exploited repeatedly until she finally wised up the hard way.

She settled for nodding and striding out of his office. In her experience, messengers didn't fare well when delivering bad news, and she imagined he wasn't going to like what she had to tell him at all. She imagined he wouldn't like this messenger much, after tonight.

5

K edron's quest to recover his usual decisiveness failed. He hadn't found it in the military gym, the cafeteria, or his office.

He'd accepted Barray's invitation in a moment of weakness. Canceling was the right thing to do, but he couldn't make himself do it. The idea of spending more time alone with her felt too damn good, even if it was just watching her fix his benighted swamp slug of a deskcomp.

On the other hand, he could return her rescue crate and tell her to be more careful.

On the third hand, now that he was leaving, it didn't really matter if the deskcomp got fixed or not. His successor would probably get a new one anyway.

On the fourth hand—

Enough, he commanded himself. He scooped up the crate with the deskcomp and its accessories, ordered his office lights to twenty-five percent, and marched himself to the tech repair depot.

Ferra met him at the secure entryway and led him through an

oddly-shaped suite with a maze of counters and shelves full of crates overflowing with parts-printer substrates. Their destination was a long, skinny room with windows all along one wall and a dizzying array of equipment crowded on every available surface. Some looked at least twenty years old. She had him put the yellow crate on a small gravcart.

"We're also the chair graveyard, so test anything before you sit down." She pointed to a bench next to the windows. "That's safe."

She emptied the crate and set it on the floor. Her efficient fingers quickly stripped the deskcomp down to essentials and inserted four longwires. She'd called herself non-adept, but her sure movements didn't sync with that description.

She pointed her chin toward the door. "Shut that, would you? Stray signals mess with the diagnostics."

He leaned over to press the control, and the door irised closed.

She shoved her hands in her vest pockets. "We have about ten minutes. This lab is tech-suppressed to the rafters." She blew out a noisy breath. "You're not going to like what I have to say, and I'm sorry, but I think you're as vector-straight as your record says, and you need to know. Your office has more overlapping, multi-factor, duplicate surveillance tech than a corporate spy showroom, and it's all aimed at you."

He blinked. He started to tell her she was wrong, but his brain engaged at the last second and stopped him.

First, she obviously knew a lot more about tech than she let on, as evidenced by her trick with the perimeter fence. Second, she had nothing to gain from telling him, and had gone to the trouble of bringing him to a safe place to talk. Damn cleverly, too.

Lastly, he wouldn't put it past the military theft investigators to have installed the surveillance. More than one had doubted his innocence and ethics.

He tilted his head to look up at her. "How do you know what my record says?"

She raised an eyebrow and waved toward the whole wall full of percomps, deskcomps, and pieces of more comps, then put her hand back in her pocket.

Okay, it had been a stupid question. "Can you remove the surveillance?"

She leaned her hip on the counter. "Are you sure you want me to? It'll alert the watchers that you're aware of them." She glanced at the deskcomp on the cart. "Some of the tech looks old, some new. Maybe you have multiple watchers, which would explain the redundancies."

He tapped his fingers on his thigh. "The CRIO contract forbids Argint d'Apa's security from monitoring the government staff, but all that means is, 'don't get caught doing it.'"

She shook her head. "It's not standard company equipment. They monitor your office door, but that's likely emergency safety protocol."

"I wonder if I'm really the target. How far does it go? The CRIO or the CPS offices? My quarters? The whole government wing?"

She shrugged. "I didn't see anything in the CRIO deskcomps that got thrashed this morning, but I wasn't looking. Break something else, and I will." She snorted. "Better yet, break that stupid CPS testing equipment so what's-her-name doesn't keep re-testing the non-minder indentures every month."

"She does?" He shook his head. "Never mind." He considered the array of comps and tools on the long counter. "If I request a general tech assessment of the government wing in anticipation of an infrastructure upgrade, can you check for surveillance?"

"Sure, but my boss will probably assign one of the staff techs. I'm not allowed to do important stuff alone."

He thought a moment. "Do they work after hours? On call, like you?"

She laughed derisively. "You're kidding, right? Regular tech staff won't do shift work in the middle of a swamp. They all commute from Magloviti City. Even brilliant pay doesn't make up for the location. That's why Argint d'Apa applied for a CRIO partnership."

She pointed to the wide, fluorescent green stripe on her uniform that clearly identified her as an indenturee. "They get cheap labor who can't leave. The CGC buys the rare metals the plant filters out of the runoff so they can build more interstellar ships. And if the scientists patent something from the swamp, the company makes a killing." Her expression turned sheepish, and her hands fluttered. "Sorry, I'll get off the bandwidth now."

"You don't approve of the CRIO system?" He'd never given it much thought until he'd been assigned as liaison.

She shrugged. "It's better than being sent as slave labor on the stellar flux-particle collector stations, like the old Central League used to do, but CRIO is too much like pre-flight debtor's prison. 'Debt to society' should be more than numbers on a balance sheet." One of her eyebrows raised. "You don't see rich folk working for restitution fair wage or hunting for cleaning bots for the promise of a bounty."

"True enough." He happened to agree with her, but he needed to get back to the subject at hand. "I'll require the tech assessment to be done after hours."

"Better say 'preliminary' or something that sounds inconsequential. I'm not certified."

Steady beeping sounded. She turned and expanded a holo display on one of the counter deskcomps. "Show us what's ailin' ya', *leannan*." He didn't recognize the word, but her accent had a tinge of rural British Isles. Given her space-station origins, she probably picked up an eclectic vocabulary from all the major languages.

As she rotated the holo, he counted nine blinking red indicators. She brought up another holo and synced it with the first, so it rotated in tandem.

"Two of those"—she pointed to the blinking holo—"are simple soft-logic faults, but the rest are unauthorized add-ons, including a full data intercept. Which reminds me, your trouble reports never got seen or logged because they were marked as already completed. I think a previous staffer set up the routine to avoid the workload. If it makes you feel any better, yours weren't the only reports that got lost." She made a rude noise. "My boss is seriously torqued. You should see our queue now. Twenty months of backlog."

"Is my deskcomp worth cleaning up, or should I requisition a new one?"

"It's up to you." Her mouth twisted sideways. "The watcher obviously has free access to your office, so they may re-infect the deskcomp as soon as it comes back." She crossed her arms. "Yours has a military shell, but the internals are straight commercial. Our inventory says it came in with a previous liaison six years ago."

Guilt pinched him for not doing a security audit when he'd first been posted to Argint d'Apa. To be honest, he'd been going through the motions and feeling sorry for himself for two years, wondering what he could have done differently to save his career.

"Fix it for now. I'll tell the new liaison to order a replacement." An idea struck. He pointed to the military gauntlet on his arm. "Can you add tech that will alert my percomp if someone breaches the shell?"

"Maybe." Her eyes darted away. "Before this gig, I was just a hobbyist doing favors for friends."

He suspected that statement left out volumes of interesting truth, but he had no desire to interrogate or judge her. "It's okay. I'll just be happy to have tech that actually works."

"I sync that." She pointed out the window toward a battered workstation with a huge display. "If you want to kill time while I fix this, that has a direct uplink to the galactic net." Her irrepressible humor peeked through in her smile. "Leaves even the plant manager's pretty and pricey comp in the dust as far as speed."

He'd been planning to be suave and clever about returning the yellow crate to her, letting her figure out how he'd found it, but now it just seemed mean. She'd taken a huge chance, telling him about the surveillance, instead of turning a blind eye.

He cleared his throat. "Since we're in the place for delivering private news, I saw what you did at the fence last night." He waved toward the yellow crate. "I took the, er, contents farther away from the perimeter."

Her stricken look made him want to hug her. He shoved his hands under his thighs. "I only saw you because my window faces that direction, but it was a risky thing to do."

"I thought I'd be safe because of the lockdown." Tears welled in her eyes. "I'll find a different way, but I'm not leaving critters like that in the compound."

Even though he was just warning her, he felt like a heel. "Indenturee activities aren't my jurisdiction, and neither the plant nor the CRIO staff wants my input." He flicked his eyes toward the crate. "Rescue as many animals as you want."

"Thanks." She blinked her tears away. "Chaos, but I hate crying. Never does any good."

"If you don't mind telling me, how did you lift the fence?"

She pulled a multitool from her vest pocket. "I modified this to exploit a design flaw." She put the tool back. "Argint d'Apa and CRIO know about it, but they think no one else does, so they're in no hurry to spend the funds to replace it." Her mouth twisted. "Good thing Lambru and his sticky-fingered crew can't use it, or anything of value not fastened down would be on its way to every no-questions-asked market on the planet."

It was his day for surprises. "Marazzo Lambru? He's one of my current ex-military charges. I wouldn't have tagged him as a leader of anything."

Her expression hardened as she picked up a probe from the counter and bent over the guts of his deskcomp. "He's good at that. Likes to keep his hands clean."

While he waited on the bench, secretly entertained by the little conversations she had with parts of his deskcomp, he used his gauntlet percomp to look up Lambru's record. The high restitution debt resulting from his conviction as a blackmarket lab employee should have made him ineligible for a level-two facility like Argint d'Apa. However, the blackmarket pharma industry was awash with untraceable cashflow. It wouldn't be the first time that untraceable cashflow funds had changed hands to give an indenturee an easy-glide ride.

Kedron added Lambru to his private list of people who might want to know what he and the government staff were doing. He had the feeling it was going to be a depressingly long list.

Ferra wiped the mist off her face and handed certified technician Yolalo the R-685 module he'd asked for.

He placed it the socket, then used his tablet to tell the filter controller to connect to it. Before coming to Argint d'Apa, Ferra hadn't known water filters could be the size of a four-story building. A lucky quirk of geography meant the swamp collected runoff from the nearby mountains, where an ancient meteor strike had left exotic debris. By extracting the valuable rare metals, the plant made the swamp healthier, meaning downstream cities got more potable water.

Yolalo turned to Inzaya, the senior certified technician who watched the filter's readout. They both wore company-issue red rain slickers. Ferra only had her indenturee uniform. It felt like she was standing in a fog bank. If the water had been cascading down as usual, she'd have been drenched from the spray inside two minutes.

"I heard it was an interstellar escape pod." His accent hinted at Afro-French, and he affected an all-over gold skin tone, making him look like an illegally sentient android from a science-fiction serial. He collected sex partners the way some people collected novelty liquor bottles.

Inzaya, with her enviable dexterity and beautiful mahogany skin, shook her head. "Sensor is still flatlined. Try tracing the upline. I heard it was just a downed high-low flitter."

The whole compound buzzed with the news. The hunters and hellhounds hadn't yet found Healey, the escapee, but they had discovered wreckage and a body, the latter of which they'd managed to save from the icy spring runoff that flooded the swamp.

Yolalo opened a bigger panel, exposing more of the filter's tech systems. "Two longwires, gate class."

Ferra opened the tool cart's top drawer, found the correct compartment, and put the two longwires in Yolalo's waiting hand.

"Well, I saw what was left of the body after the swamp rats had been chewing on it for a week or two." He gave an exaggerated shudder. "You don't wear a space exosuit to fly a flitter."

Ferra dropped her head to hide her frustration. She was only supposed to have delivered the cart, not stand around and hand out parts like she was a pastry vendor.

Inzaya must have seen her. "Someplace else to be, *indenturee*?"

Ferra ordinarily would have kept her head down, but her work queue had doubled that morning.

Despite the dormo patch the night before, dreams of flying and being lost continued to plague her. During one of her waking periods, it occurred to her that she might be able to get a head start on Tauceti's project by combing through the newly unearthed trouble reports to look for tech failure patterns similar to those in his office. She couldn't work on the big plant equipment alone, but most of the trouble was in the staff and indenturee wings. The repair manager agreed to give her a restitution bonus for each backlog ticket she cleared.

"Yes, sir." Ferra gave her the military honorific. Inzaya had been in CGC Water Division decades ago and still used her former title from time to time. "The staff cafeteria payment kiosk, the security chief's receiving office, the staff immersion theatre, the military flitter stacker, the guard desk at the front gate, the—"

"All right, you've made your point," said Inzaya sourly. "Dismissed."

Ferra turned and walked quickly but carefully along the damp suspended walkway that led to the open-air lift to take her back to the ground floor. Good thing she'd never been afraid of heights, big turbines, or waterfalls of massive amounts of swamp water.

The pervasive humidity throughout the complex doomed her to perpetually frizzy hair for the duration of her indenture. The nearest body parlor or body shop was a hundred kilometers south, in Magloviti City. Indenturees were stuck with whatever mods they'd come in with, so she was glad her look was now all natural. None of her friends would recognize her. More importantly, none of her enemies would, either.

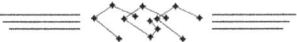

Of the first seven trouble spots on her list, one was a failed node, one was the result of a small bot trying to clean an electrical power bar, and five had the same surveillance tech infestation.

Someone had spent lavishly, but not wisely, and hired an incompetent person to install it. She made an executive decision to leave the tech in place unless it completely broke the system in which it was installed. No sense being the common denominator in the surveillance disruptions.

After Tauceti had gone away with his deskcomp, leaving the yellow crate with her, she'd spent the rest of her evening diving through Argint d'Apa data, which had surprisingly lax security. Maybe their physical isolation made them feel immune. No local company records mentioned the surveillance, or Tauceti by name.

The less accessible, but not totally crypto government records netted the same result, except the CRIO office copied Tauceti on every daily report, memo, and meeting recording they produced, regardless of how trivial. He dutifully copied them on every mind-numbing report and memo he produced. No wonder he looked forward to leaving.

As she restocked her bag and logged the completion of her last task for the shift, she decided to wait until morning to turn in the two small cleaning bots she'd found that day. She also contemplated skipping the evening meal and going straight to bed. Memories of her nightly dreams had invaded her thoughts all day, insinuating themselves into her idle moments.

Two distinct voices were scared and lonely, and desperately needed her help. She knew she had a weakness for being wanted and needed—her twisty brother had often taken advantage of that—but this felt different. And now that she finally had quiet time in the lab suitable for contemplation, it had a direction. South. And a persistent image to go with it, of posts, trees, and stacks of boxes.

Her job kept her busy all day, so she hadn't spent much time outside, but the trees in the image reminded her of the tall, droopy ones in the staff recreation yard, next to the tall fence that separated staff and indenturees. She'd heard complaints about them blocking the spring sunlight for the indenturee container gardens.

Despite her growing compulsion to go check, she couldn't just wander out to confirm her hallucination. She didn't know the area, so she'd be vulnerable if Lambru's remoras cornered her.

Too bad the gardens didn't have tech for her to fix, because they wouldn't bother her while she was on official business. She'd given them the impression that while on duty, a constant monitor listened to every word she said and tracked every location she visited. Both were true, but her work tablet did the listening, and the pass-tracker cuff got her past checkpoints and only actively reported her location when queried. As far as she knew, the repair lab manager hadn't looked at the logs in two months.

She put her tech bag on the shelf, then dimmed the lights to half. One of the two bots she'd found had been charred, and its warning light blinked. "Yes, poor thing. I don't know how you got up on that counter, but maintenance will fix you up in the morning." And she'd get the bounty for returning them both.

Inspiration struck. She'd be on official business if she tracked an errant bot that just happened to go to the southeastern corner of the indenturee yard, near the trees.

She raised the lights to full and pulled one of the heavy, disused mobile repair bots out of the cabinet. They didn't do well in water, so the techs couldn't use them in the filtration plant, and they were too big for the smaller jobs typically assigned to her.

She named it Oran Mòr, because of its stylish orange stripes, and directed it to stick to the indenturee side, avoid people, and go to the southeast corner of the perimeter fence. Remembering the trick the maintenance tech had used, she added an asset tag under the maintenance door so she could use an inventory scanner to track it, in the event it got lost or waylaid. Some enterprising indenturee might mistake it for a cleaning bot and kidnap it for the bounty.

From the cabinets, she pulled out the large company-logo backpack and snugged the bot into it. She about fell over when she put the backpack on and tried to stand up. Wilderness hikers carried heavier packs, which meant they were even more warped than she'd thought.

The bot's little climbing feet dug into her back as she trudged down the corridor to the indenturee dining hall. She had to show the backpack's contents to the guard to prove it wasn't contraband.

She paid for her mealpack, then took it out to the long, curving patio that overlooked the weedy indenturee courtyard. The landscaping looked half-finished to her, but what did she know? In space stations, plants grew in densely planned and orderly hydroponic gardens, and massive walls of moss supplemented the oxygen exchangers. Wherever she was going after her penance, it would be on a planet. She wasn't ever going back to living in space.

Luckily, none of Lambru's crew had followed her outside. Twilight brought chilly spring breezes. She put her mealpack on the farthest table, then set her backpack behind her on the ground, with the opening facing the grass. She put her tablet on the table, so she'd look busy, and dawdled over her meal of mixed meat and vegetable bits in a spicy sauce, covered in a layered pastry. She'd had worse growing up, but she'd since grown to love real food at real restaurants with happy people around her.

Through the windows, she kept an eye on the dining hall. The short-handed serving staff worked hard during meal service, because Argint d'Apa policy banned indenturees from kitchen-related jobs. She gathered it stemmed from an incident years before, when an indenturee got caught trading premium fresh food for sex. Indenturees were free to have as much consensual sex with each other as they wanted, but not with the staff. And apparently, the woman's preferred location for hot connects had been every available horizontal surface and wall in the pantry and prep area.

Ferra didn't miss sex as much as companionship and quality time friends who cared about her, and she wasn't likely get those in prison. All right, not prison, according to the CRIO system representatives, who assertively rejected any use of the word, but it sure felt like it to the indenturees. No other workplace she knew used plasma-powered fences, guards, and hellhounds to make the workers stay.

Her vest wasn't good protection from the chilly evening breeze. She used her tablet to check Oran Mòr's progress and found the bot was a good thirty meters from her.

Brushing off crumbs as she stood, she shouldered the now empty backpack, resisting the urge to turn and look behind her. She took her trash to the recycler, then slipped out the side door into the hallway for indenturee quarters. She walked past mostly closed doors to her own at the far north end, where she stopped long enough to put her warmest shirt on under her indenturee uniform tunic and utility vest. Back in the repair lab, she killed time by working on a solution for Tauceti to monitor his deskcomp.

The flaws in her plan became apparent after it took the bot a full hour to signal that it had reached the southeast corner. One, night had fallen, so she was going to need handlights and a shoulder torch to find her way, much less see if the frelling trees matched the persistent image in her head. Two, it was raining.

Now she couldn't leave Oran Mòr outside overnight, because of its vulnerability to water. She knew she shouldn't have named the little bot, because now she felt responsible for it. From the open office closet, she took out a red rain slicker and slipped into it, then pulled on the big backpack.

She tapped into her ever-simmering resentment at how Lambru got away with all manner of shit in the plant as she tromped down the main hall. The guards were more suspicious of happy indenturees.

The guard at the indenturee wing's south door made her walk through the metals detector and asked where she was going.

"Repair bot wandered off. Rain will ruin it." She brandished the inventory scanner. "This says it's outside by the container gardens, and I'm on call tonight."

"Better you than me." The guard waved her on through, then pointed to the hours-of-operation notice on the door. "If it's longer than fifteen minutes, you'll have to go around to the north entrance."

"Okay." She nodded her thanks as she pulled on her hood and switched on the high-lumen torch.

Every bench and shrub looked scarier in the dark. In the rain, the two moons did little to light the way. She walked carefully, wishing she had high-tech boots like Tauceti's. Her shoes had gripper soles for safety in the water-logged filtration plant environment, but the mesh uppers let in every drop of rain. Military people got all the best toys.

The standing white-legged boxes for the container gardens looked bigger than she remembered them from her first-day tour. Probably because she'd been surreptitiously eyeing the outrageously handsome Subcaptain instead of paying attention. She skirted around to the left, under the hanging tree branches. Slower, fatter raindrops drummed on her hood.

The closer she got to the corner of the fence, the more she became convinced she had visitors in her mind. Not telepaths, because they used words, and not empaths, because they were all about feelings. The two thought patterns were lost, and cold, and hurt. They'd called and called, and finally found someone to hear them.

Great, now she was dreaming while awake in the middle of a rainstorm.

She aimed the torch for the dark hulk that had to be the repair bot. Sure enough, there were Oran Mòr's orange stripes.

It turned its head, opened its eyes, and meowed softly.

You came.

Ferra nearly stumbled to her knees. The torch dropped to the ground and winked out.

A creature rose to its feet and shook water everywhere.

Help us.

A picture blossomed in her mind of another creature, waiting in the dark beyond the fence, unable to fly over it because of a broken wing.

She lit one of the small hand lights on her wrist. The creature in front of her stood knee-high at the shoulders and had the hint of an orange-striped bat-type wing folded flat along its side.

"You're real." It was all she could think to say.

The creature switched its long tail in annoyance.

Yes. Help us. Help him.

Once again, the image of the injured creature flashed in her mind.

Her wildest fantasies had never included sentient animals. It was too cold and damp to be a dream. And too cold and dangerous for an injured creature to be stuck outside.

She eyed the midnight-black creature. "If I raise the perimeter fence, can he crawl under?" She visualized the memory of lifting the fence to push the yellow crate outside.

Yes.

Edging closer to the inner fence, she considered her options. Somehow, she needed to get her multitool to the bottom of the fence line. Any human on the walkway would make the overhead lights come on. However, the motion sensors were trained to ignore animals, or the lights would be blinking on and off all night.

I can do it.

She looked down to see the creature sitting at her feet, looking up. The gold eyes mesmerized her for a moment. She got the impression the creature was female and anxious, and wanted comfort. Just like Ferra.

She gave herself a mental shake. Solve the problem. Deal with the mysteries later.

She fumbled under the rain slicker to find the vest pocket. She wrestled out the tool, selected the correct setting, and turned it on, then offered it to the creature.

We are not creatures. We are cats. Unmistakable pride accompanied the declaration.

"Of course you are," she whispered. "Everyone knows cats are telepaths and have wings."

The cat took the multitool in her mouth. *We are superior cats.*

The lithe cat oozed under the lower fence rail and streaked across the walkway, then dropped the multitool on the ground and batted it into place. The electrical fence lines warped upward in a semicircle.

Ferra took a deep breath for focus, then *pushed* through the multitool. She hadn't lied to Tauceti about how she lifted the fence, she'd just omitted the part about using telekinesis. She didn't trust anyone with *that* secret.

The cat crouched. The subtle light from the walkway's road glass reflected off her fur, making her hard to see, even though Ferra was only three meters away. In her mind, she heard the cat tell her mate to hurry. That's what he was, too, not just a companion.

A moment later, another winged cat, larger than the female, crawled through the opening. When the cat was all the way through, even his long, flat tail, Ferra released the fence. She sent an image to the female cat, asking her to bring back the tool.

The male cat limped across the walkway and slid under the inner fence rail. The female clawed the multitool away from the perimeter fence, then picked it up and trotted to where Ferra stood with the male.

Ferra crouched down to take the multitool. The male butted his wet head into her hand. The physical contact made the mental connection stronger. His wing and leg hurt. The breeze chilled him and his mate. The water was wet.

She smiled a little that his biggest gripe was about being wet. She sympathized. It had taken her several years of planet-side living to get used to water-based showers.

The cats couldn't stay out in the rain. Neither could the repair bot. She pictured her plan to the cats.

7

Ferra shut her cell door, dimmed her lights, then slid the fully expanded backpack off her shoulders and set it carefully on the floor. She held it open for the remarkably patient cats to crawl out.

The universe, or perhaps the pre-flight Egyptian god of cats, granted extraordinary luck that night. She'd missed the south door operation window, so she'd had to trudge through the rain with twenty kilos of superior cats in her pack and twenty-five kilos of rain-slick repair bot hugged to her chest. She must have looked enough like a drowned swamp rat that the guard pointed her straight to the solardry and volunteered a gravcart for the bot.

The foreign thoughts and feelings in her head distracted her, but they also comforted her. She wasn't warped, twisted, or fracturing from loneliness.

The cats crouched and slunk around the small room, smelling everything. "I've got to take the bot and the backpack to the lab and return the cart." She didn't know how much they understood, but she projected images as best she was able.

The small female looked at her. *We will hide.*

"Good." She opened the tiny closet and even tinier fresher. On impulse, she crouched down and held out her hands to the cats. The male ignored her hand and went straight for her knee. He rubbed his triangular-shaped face against her. She stroked his damp fur. The female cat licked her outstretched fingers.

For no reason she could name, tears threatened, and she wanted to gather the cats in her arms. She reluctantly stood and stepped back. She dimmed the lights further, then locked the door behind her.

In the lab, she put a drying mat on the shelf, then put Oran Mòr on top of it and left the cabinet open. "I'll check you tomorrow," she told it. If cats could be sentient, so could bots.

No emergency trouble reports meant she could close up the lab, so she returned the gravcart and walked back to her cell. Worry tried to hurry her feet, but she walked sedately, then closed and locked the door behind her, just like any other evening.

The bed looked inviting, but first, she had to look after the cats. Their presence was warm and comforting in her mind, even if she couldn't see them. She used the wallcomp to turn up the lights and darken her only window.

The female oozed out from under the bed, followed by the male.

Now that she saw them in better light, she didn't know what she was looking at. Wide, cat-like heads and ears, with narrower muzzles, and nose flaps. Mottled dark fur with a faint rosette pattern, and folded, bat-style wings with fine downy fur. No orange stripe on the female's wing, so that must have been a trick of the light. Their front paws had sharp-looking claws and opposable toes. Their tails were long and ovoid.

We are cats. That was the female.

We were made for war, thought the male.

Food? asked the female.

Ferra didn't know what to do with cats designed for war, since the Central Galactic Concordance government had kept the peace across the galaxy for the last two centuries, but she could do something about food.

Reaching up to the top shelf of her closet, she retrieved the mealpack she'd stashed there two days ago. She triggered the heater and put it on a narrow counter that served as the cell's desk and table to warm.

She gratefully sat on the bed and pulled off her clammy shoes and tossed them onto the drying mat by the door. "Do you have names?"

The female's tale twitched. *Yes.*

Ferra laughed. The cat was just like some AIs Ferra had known, unhelpfully literal and disdainful of imprecise questions. Ferra tried again, this time forming the words in her mind and projecting them to the female cat. *What is your name?*

My call sign is Novo Seventeen Alpha.

I am Bozlurian Four Delta, volunteered the male.

"I'll just call you Novo and Boz, if you don't mind." She stripped off her damp socks stepped into the fresher to hang them in front of the ventilation grate.

When she came back, the mealpack signaled it was done, so she opened the lid and set it on the floor. "Sorry. No plates. You'll have to share. I hope you like protein egg straws and vat-grown ham."

She felt Novo's insistence that Boz eat his fill.

As he bolted down bites, Ferra sensed his hunger pangs being eased, the same way she could feel the constant pain in his wing and shoulder. She made a mental note to use the net uplink to look up vet med treatment protocols for cats and bats. Boz said they'd been designed, so she decided to check out pet trade references, too.

Chaos, but she was tired. She needed to think where to hide the cats while Boz healed, but her brain wasn't cooperating. She'd have to deal with it in the morning.

She stripped off her clothes and hung them in the closet. Her nose told her she'd soon need to book an appointment at the communal clothes sanitizer, or people would smell her coming.

She pulled on her nightshirt, then arranged a nest of spare

blankets in the closet for the cats. If someone noticed it, they'd just assume she was a slob. She filled the licked-clean mealpack package with water from the fresher, told the cats goodnight, turned the light to low, and crawled into bed.

The next thing she knew, two furry bodies snuggled on either side of her, making rumbling noises in their throats. The cats projected comfort and relief, and the feeling of coming home again. She stroked their silky soft fur and cried for how scared and lonely they'd been.

For how lonely she'd been. Not just lately, but ever since she was thirteen and her parents abandoned her and her twin brother on the space station and never came back. Ever since realizing she'd have to cut all ties with her brother because he'd drag her down with him. Ever since learning he'd sold her to a vicious, violent crew to pay off a gambling debt.

She fell asleep in purry, furry warmth.

8

After the evening of unsettling revelations, as Kedron had come to think of the repair-lab meeting with Barray, he'd spent a sleepless night wrestling with his choices, past and present.

He'd finally concluded that he'd learned the wrong lesson from his disastrous last post. He'd spent the last two years doing only his duty and nothing more, hoping HQ would call him back to his career. He'd been afraid that if he upset the sky skimmer again, his next assignment would be a fifty-year exploration expedition to the Great Void between the galaxies.

What he should have learned was that if his life plans didn't work out the way he hoped, he needed new plans. Not every Tauceti had to be a field commodore by age fifty, like his father, or have a galaxy-famous strategy named after him, like his great-great grandmother, who'd only retired three years ago at age one hundred and sixty-two. He could be the Tauceti who used his skulljack to train military hardware AIs how to work with humans, or made a quiet civilian military base run smoothly, or who had a family to come home to every night.

Since he no longer worried about making waves, he'd spent the last three days investigating the mystery of the source of the surveillance. He used the cover story of creating a comprehensive procedure manual for his position, which had never had one.

He'd also re-enabled his skulljack and started wearing a high-powered communications wire again. When he'd first arrived, the constant barrage of trivial communication between the various AIs in the plant had just about driven him around the bend. Almost anywhere else in the civilized galaxy, nonessential equipment used specific, reserved bands, but Argint d'Apa hadn't bothered, not even for the government offices. The compound was small enough that he could hear every system in it.

He could have requisitioned a filtered comms wire, but at the time, it had felt more fitting to simply disable his skulljack. As a consequence, he was out of practice and was still learning to pick out individual systems from the constant sea of noise. AIs were a chatty lot. The annoyance would be worth it if it helped him identify the watchers.

He'd already begun making appointments with people he interacted with, starting with the CRIO coordinator. He'd easily convinced her to approve the after-hours tech infrastructure assessment request, once he'd told her he'd volunteer to escort the technician and contribute from the military liaison budget to help pay for upgrades. He'd also discovered that he had authority over the CPS office suite. The Citizen Protection Service only admitted to being part of the military when it suited them, but he far outranked the local CPS representative. He simply notified her of the assessment.

Fortunately, the tech repair supervisor had obligingly assigned Barray, who would be starting the assessment that evening after her dinner.

At the appointed time, he met her at the guard checkpoint and escorted her to the CRIO office suite, to which he'd been given full access. Mindful of possible surveillance tech, he sat in a guest chair and pretended to read on his percomp.

Even though he'd had plenty of human interaction recently, he had to admit he still liked Barray's company best. She wanted nothing from him, and she made him laugh. With the theft ring situation, he'd had no one on his side except his assigned military advocate. At least this time, he had someone to trust, though he worried he might be putting her in danger.

Barray worked quickly around the office, using a scanner and her tablet. She looked more rested than she had a few days ago. He wanted to ask, but interaction might alert potential watchers to their friendly relationship.

No, not relationship. There would be no relationship-having with indenturees. Temporary alliance, maybe.

He distracted himself by asking the perimeter fence if it had detected anything unusual the night Barray had rescued the muskrats. The fence had a lot to say about all the animals and people it cataloged as proximate threats, but nothing about faults or disruptions. Unsurprisingly, the front gate's AI refused to communicate without an access code—couldn't have clever indenturees convincing the gate to let them out.

The interior perimeter path and lights shared an AI that reported a litany of complaints about mold and mud interfering with its sensors and ignored all nonhuman signatures.

All in all, it wasn't how he would have configured the security systems, but as Argint d'Apa's security chief had reminded—

"Subcaptain?"

He looked up to find Barray in front of him. The look on her face said she'd been waiting for him to respond. The downside to listening to machines is that he forgot to listen to people. "Yes?"

"Permission to use that chair to stand on?" She pointed to the chair next to him.

"Of course."

As she leaned over to pull the chair out, she dropped a small piece of paper in his lap. A flick of her eyes told him she'd done it on purpose.

It appeared to be a random list of locations throughout the complex. He used his percomp to take a quick flat image, then held up the list. "I think you dropped this."

She smiled ruefully. "Yep." She crossed from the large wallcomp to take it from him. "Sorry." She stuffed it in her vest pocket, then went back to climb on the chair and open the wallcomp's service door.

"No problem." He hoped that sounded casual enough. He'd become hyper-aware of his actions, knowing he might be watched. With luck, his inherent stiffness would cover any gaffes.

On Barray's list, more than half had extra marks next to them. All had lines through them, except the bottom few, all in the CRIO office. The item at the top, his office, had the most extra marks. She'd said his office had a lot of surveillance tech. If she'd found more tech in the locations on the list, that meant that the majority of the company and government staff areas where tech could be found also had covert eyes and ears.

That gave a whole new dimension to his investigation. He'd been thinking small, like the company vice president negotiating the government contract renewal, or Lambru, who needed to know if the government had discovered his activities. Installing tech throughout the facility and having the time—or a sophisticated AI—to sift through the results, took considerably more resources. No fact had yet jumped out and tripped his finder sense as significant. He needed more data.

Barray pulled an instrument from her bag. "All right with you if I set up a tech suppressor for a few minutes?" She pointed toward his gauntlet. "You'll lose comms."

"Okay."

She touched the controls.

Silence reigned, except phantom echoes from his military-grade comms wire and the three office fans.

"Two minutes." She circled a finger. "Extras all around. Not like your office, but bad enough. This wallcomp is a mess." She smiled crookedly. "Even the portable fans have cameras."

"Any commonalities? The locations on your list seem random."

"Could be selection bias—I looked for trouble tickets like yours because I get a bonus for clearing them. The biggest commonality is the same model of camera. I've counted at least a dozen. The rest are incompatible and wrong-sized components, and they were spliced in wherever they'd fit. Whoever installed them knows even less about hardware tech than I do."

He frowned. "You are very knowledgeable."

"That's kind of you to say." She waved off his statement. "I know Argint d'Apa systems. I like reading, and taught myself the basics, because I didn't have anything better to do with my time and it kept me away from trouble." She pointed a thumb toward the wallcomp behind her. "Whoever did this is the kind of amateur you read about in the newstrends. 'Inventor Accidentally Flatlines Planetary Traffic Control System.'"

"Hmmm." Pesky facts didn't fit any of his theories.

"Since you didn't want me to remove the extras in your office, I've been fixing the trouble but leaving the tech in place, unless it caused the malfunction." She shook her head. "It still could be two different watchers, because some of the tech is done right."

She stepped off the chair to fish in her bag for a small multitool. "Before I kill the tech suppressor, this is for you." She slid it across the small conference table toward him. "Press the blue and red together twice and the light will blink if you're within a couple of meters of the surveillance cameras."

"Thank you." He pocketed it, touched by her thoughtfulness. On impulse, he added, "If you ever need help with a rescue, let me know." She was taking a lot of chances for him, so he could take one for her.

She blinked in surprise, then gave him a blinding smile. "I'll keep that in mind." She turned off the tech suppressor, closed up the wallcomp, and dragged the chair back into place. "I'm done in here. Where to next?"

It wasn't hard to pretend boredom as he followed her from room to room and finished up in the hallway. Barray hardly said a word, though her expressive face suggested she was still having running conversations with the tech she evaluated.

He hadn't allowed himself to watch Barray very much, because then he'd have wanted to talk to her. The woman in her written record didn't sync with the woman in person. Blame it on his finder talent, but he loved solving mysteries, and she definitely was an intriguing one. And, as he'd had to repeatedly remind himself, completely off-limits.

At the end of three hours, she slung her heavy tech bag over her shoulder. "My supervisor will send you the report."

"Any particular issues for upgrades?" That should be vague enough for the watchers.

He escorted her to the guard checkpoint.

She shrugged. "Humidity, mold, behind on maintenance. Like everything else in the plant." She snapped her fingers. "I forgot to mention, I found an old surplus fan, if the plant hasn't replaced yours."

"They haven't. I'll come get it tomorrow."

"I'll leave it in the lab with your name on it. If I'm not around, ask the tech no duty." She walked away, and he returned to the CRIO office to make sure he hadn't left a mess, then went to his quarters.

He wanted to try out the camera detector immediately, but he made himself wait until he could think of a way to disguise both it and his actions. The frustrating part was, even if it came up negative, that just meant no cameras. Barray had mentioned a half-dozen types of surveillance she'd found. Suddenly, sleeping in his military high-low flitter seemed very attractive.

Unless one of the watchers *was* the military, in which case, he may as well sleep in his comfortable bed.

9

Ferra hoped Tauceti got the message she'd sent, and more importantly, figured out the hidden meaning. Otherwise, loitering after hours in the hallway near the government wing would be a magnet for guard suspicion, even though she was on official business. She didn't want to be memorable or appear in anyone's report.

Her quiet indenturee routine had become significantly more exciting since she'd rescued Novo and Boz.

She'd fallen in love with the cats when they'd cuddled and comforted her that first night. In her twilight dreams, the cats told her how they'd arrived on her proverbial doorstep. Their handler had been the dead man from the downed ship in the swamp. They'd all been undercover with an interstellar jack crew. After a betrayal, they'd barely made it out in an escape pod. Knowing he was dying, the handler released the cats and sent them to look for someone who could hear and help them. They'd found Ferra.

They'd nearly scared the life out of her the next morning when she could feel them in her head but couldn't find them. They'd appeared before her eyes in the pile of blankets, by way of demonstrating that their amazing fur put chameleons to shame. They could blend in with practically anything. It took conscious effort to drop the camouflage.

She'd since learned more of what cats of war could do. For one, they'd figured out how to get into the air-handling ducts in the facility, and into the garages intended for the maintenance bots. After examining the controls, she made tiny tokens for them to wear so any bot garage door would open for them. With luck, the plant's bot technician, Calderosh, would never notice.

For another, they'd told her where more small bots could be found so she could turn them in for the bounty. She was both amused and concerned when she started hearing rumors of the facility being overrun with giant blood-sucking bats or invaded by carnivorous miniature dinosaurs. Human science might have expanded their reach throughout the galaxy, but superstition was still alive and well.

She'd worried about feeding the cats, because she couldn't keep buying extra mealpacks without causing comment. Fortunately, they'd discovered the kitchen on their own and had been helping themselves to meal scraps ever since, but now, she worried they'd be caught. The sneaky, stealthy cats of war were insulted by her worry.

Ferra lucked out in not having to hide or explain net searches for veterinary medicine. Argint d'Apa had an entire hypercube of regular and pet-trade reference material in the huge indenturee library. It was one of many topics in the "career rehabilitation" section.

The most astonishing discovery she made was that she might have another minder talent besides telekinesis. According to the reference, a lot of vet meds in the pet-trade business were animal-affinity minders. Most were genera- or species-specific, such as horses or dogs. The best of them could mentally connect with and heal anything in a given clade, such as mammals. A very useful talent, considering the ethically challenged pet trade bred pretty much any fantasy animal they could sell—miniature dragons, hellhounds, or flying cats. Novo and Boz were likely experimental, or special order.

Their creation was probably illegal, but she couldn't fault the military's actions, since it brought her the love of two superior cats.

The best news was that, while the Citizen Protection Service's Minder Corps aggressively recruited telepaths, telekinetics, healers, and sifters, they didn't have much use for animal-affinity minders. Not that she planned to march into the CPS office and ask to be tested. The Criminal Restitution and Indenture Obligation system reflected galactic society's suspicion of any minder, and enforced stricter security and separate, harsher justice for them.

Being an animal-affinity minder with a feline-family specialty explained why she could hear Novo and Boz so well, but had no connection to other animals, such as the genetically engineered hellhounds or natural young muskrats. It also explained why, when she touched Boz, she could sense the extent of his injury and his pain. Based on comparing anatomy images with what she could feel, he had sore and inflamed muscles, and maybe torn ligaments at the wing-shoulder joint. Easily repairable if she could sneak him into the veterinary medic autodoc in the dog kennel area and program it for a special cat, but she might as well wish for wings of her own.

The large clock display on the wall behind the guard station said Tauceti should be along soon. None of the clocks showed the whole planet, probably to avoid reminding indenturees and staff of anything outside Argint d'Apa. The paid staff turnover rate was almost on par with how often indenturees cycled in and out of the system.

The government wing door irised open to reveal Tauceti. She kept her expression bored, but she couldn't help but notice his body-skimming exercise clothes that fired her imagination. Nova hot didn't even begin to describe him. She didn't blame the guard for giving him a lingering, appreciative once-over.

Tauceti waved her through. "The force exerciser won't move at all."

The wing door irised closed behind them as they walked down the hall. She smiled a little at his explanation. Force exercisers weren't supposed to move. Credible lying wasn't in his skillset, apparently. A nice change from the indenturee company she currently kept, and her brother and his buddies.

Keeping her head down, she followed him into the military gym, where she set her bag on the force exerciser's seat.

The small gym had little surveillance tech, and at his request, she'd disabled all of it. She didn't blame him for wanting one safe place to himself. After checking the CRIO regulations, she'd done similar work in her cell, leaving only the emergency audio monitor in place. Argint d'Apa security couldn't very well ask the repair office to fix spy eyes that weren't supposed to be there in the first place.

He sat on a bench and looked up at her expectantly.

"I'll get straight to the point. I have a massive favor to ask."

Warmth drained from his expression as he stiffened. "What favor?"

She'd been so wrapped up in the needs of the cats that she'd forgotten her place, and his. Stupidity like that could destroy them both. "I'm sorry. Never mind."

She reached for the bag's strap. She'd find another—

"What favor?"

His bleak expression wasn't encouraging, but she'd already come this far. "I heard the military is sending you early to your new post, and that you're leaving in five days."

He looked startled, then shook his head. "I only got the orders this morning." Exasperation laced his tone.

"Once you notified the front office, everyone knew." It's what had given her the idea, in fact. "The favor is to take some animals away with you."

His eyes widened. "This is about a rescue? I suppose I could make a stop in the swamp on my flight out."

She shook her head. "No, I want you to take them with you to Merganukhan. You need to meet them to see why."

"I do?" Now he just looked perplexed.

She pulled her multitool out of her pocket and opened the

wallcomp. After a moment, she used telekinesis to slide open the air handling grid in the ceiling.

Turning, she looked up in time to see Novo poke her head out. Her fur had taken on the mottled dull brown of the duct tubing but was already turning beige to match the ceiling by the time Tauceti followed her gaze.

Novo oozed out like an extrusion, then jumped to the ground with barely a thud. Boz followed, landing less gracefully. Both cats eyed Tauceti with keen interest.

For his part, Tauceti froze, then began shaking his head. "No, slow down. Wait. One at a time."

Ferra's jaw dropped. She could feel the cats talking to Tauceti, but not with the mind speech they used with her. It felt weird.

Novo sat in front of Tauceti and stared unblinkingly into his eyes.

Boz limped over to Ferra and rubbed his head on her knee. *He is a military controller. Our controllers sync with him.*

She crouched to rub Boz's rounded, mobile ears, which he liked. *Controllers?* She'd gotten better at talking with her mind instead of her mouth.

The tech in our heads. Ask Novo. Boz padded over to sit in front of Tauceti.

Novo drifted by Ferra briefly, then began investigating the equipment in the room, looking and sniffing. *We have military computers in our brains. You do not. He does. We can report to him, but he can't feel us like you do.*

Ferra looked at Tauceti and remembered his question about a skulljack, and how he rubbed behind his left ear when thinking. It made sense that not all military personnel with skulljacks would wear tattoos that lit up and pointed to them, like elite forces Jumpers did.

Tauceti looked up to meet her gaze. "You bonded with them." His neutral tone gave nothing away as far as his feelings.

She shrugged. "They needed my help."

"Their former handler, Galagade, the pilot who died, worked for the Minder Corps as a covert operative. The cats' comps say they are stealth weapons and think I'm their new handler. The comps think I'm the animal-affinity minder who bonded with them. The cats say otherwise."

She appreciated that he'd avoided accusing her of being a minder, but it didn't solve the problem.

"I can't be a handler. I'm an indenturee. I've got another two or three months to go, depending on how many extra shifts and bounties I get." She made an exasperated noise. "They're not safe here, despite their chameleon fur and skulking skills. The guards would love to throw them to the hellhounds."

Novo circled back to rub against Ferra's leg. *We can fight.*

Ferra shied away from the image. She'd seen what the hellhounds could do. "You're their only hope for getting out of here, especially since you can hear them. I was hoping you could board them someplace on Merganukhan until I can come for them. I can pay."

He shook his head. "Pets are strictly forbidden on Space Div military transports." Boz, the petting junkie, had already wedged his muzzle into Tauceti's hand. "Besides, Minder Corps probably wants them returned."

Ferra shuddered. "I'll turn them loose in the swamp before I'll send them back there. Once they'd connected with Galagade, the researchers experimented on all three of them, trying to break the bond, and it hurt. They'd probably still be in the labs, except Galagade had family in high places. The CPS transferred him and the cats to the sneaky spying and theft division." She waved toward the cat currently perched on top of the free-weight stacker. "At least, that's my interpretation of Novo's story."

He shrugged a shoulder apologetically. "Even if I was a subgeneral instead of a subcaptain, Space Div wouldn't let me bring them on board."

"What if you were a courier for a top-secret project?" She shoved her hands in her pockets and rocked on her heels. "I can make it so in the records. I can say they're lethal or communicable, so no one wants to get within five meters of them."

He raised an eyebrow but said nothing.

Time to do what was right for the cats. "That's how I sent myself here."

His eyes widened. "You came here on *purpose*?"

"I needed to vanish, fast. I know it sounds crazy, but the CRIO system seemed the safer alternative at the time." She blew out a noisy sigh. "I'm a... I *was* a top-level financial systems integrator, working for one of the big galactic information exchanges. I refused to bail my brother out of trouble for the umpteenth last time. He lured me to a meeting, supposedly to say goodbye. Turned out he'd sold me like I was exotic fresh fruit to the big, powerful crew he owed a lot of money to." Chaos, but that final betrayal still hurt. "The crew needed someone with my skills to move their money and hide their trail. I convinced them I'd signed on willingly, so they didn't watch me like they should have. I escaped, but they were hot on my afterburner, so I couldn't go anywhere near my former life. I used my data manipulation skills to steal pieces of records to make a new identity, insert me into the CRIO system, and vanish." She blinked to keep the tears from falling. "I can do the same for the cats."

Novo jumped down to the floor, using her wings to keep her from making a thud.

"Why didn't you go to the planetary police, or the CGC military detectives?"

She sighed. "I panicked. I didn't know anyone in law enforcement—maybe the crew had them on payroll, too." She shook her head. "I deserved to do time for trusting my brother one more time, even though I'd told him to not even send me a fucking birthday message ever again." Honesty made her tell him the idea that had occurred to her yesterday. "It's possible they found me and paid someone to install the surveillance tech. To them, I'm like that runaway cleaning bot the other day—misbehaving property to retrieve and keep better track of this time."

He frowned as he continued to pet a loudly purring Boz. "I thought you said the tech has been around for at least a year. You've been here less than four months."

"Some is old, some is new. Still could be two sources." She made a frustrated sound. "I can't take the cats with me until I know it's safe."

Novo leaned against Ferra's legs. *We will teach you to hide.*

Ferra sat on the force exerciser's frame and leaned over to stroke Nova's downy fur. *Thank you. We'll think of something.*

Tauceti's expression turned bleak again. "I'm not safe, either." He frowned and looked away, a troubled expression on his face. The hand petting Boz stilled. "At my last post, I blew the whistle on a theft ring. The military sent me here for my safety, but some of the investigators suspected I was part of it. They refused to believe that I had absolute zero personal relationship with the commodore, despite her insistence we were lovers." He swallowed and looked down. "I'm not built that way. I don't make friends easily, so I had no one to tell when she pressured me. If I had slept with her, I don't know that I would have told them, anyway. I didn't want to be known as the Tauceti who used hot-connect sex to get promoted."

"Chaos, that tanks." She wanted to comfort him, but that was impossible. The past couldn't be changed. She shoved her free hand in her vest pocket and made a fist, wanting to deck whoever had hurt him so badly. No wonder her clumsy request for a favor had rocked him so hard.

"What I'm saying is that I'm no safer for the cats than you are. The surveillance could be the military investigators watching me, hoping I'll make a mistake." He put his hands flat on his thighs. "If they caught you tampering with my records, they'd send you to military prison for decades."

His defeated look matched the way she felt.

"I apologize for involving you in this." She stood and brushed a few hairs off the front of her uniform.

She aimed thoughts at Novo and Boz. *Let's go. I snagged a nice meaty mealpack for you tonight.*

She watched as they jumped to the top of the exercise equipment, then launched unerringly into the tube that looked too small. They were truly amazing creatures.

Superior cats, thought Novo.

Yes, you are, Ferra sent, as she slid the wallcomp door shut and again used her teke to close the ceiling grate.

She turned to Tauceti and tried to memorize his too-handsome face, his still-troubled face. She'd deal with the pain of losing him later. "I probably won't see you again before you leave. Best of luck at your new base on Merganukhan." She smiled briefly. "I'll always remember the planet's real name of 'Suck Flux, RSI.'"

She scooped up her tech bag and stood by the door until he stood and opened it with a wave of his hand. They walked silently down the corridor to the end of the hall, where the door irised open.

For the sake of their guard audience, she gave Tauceti a slightly peevish look. "Next time, try not to move the force exerciser. It's not built for it."

Tauceti nodded gravely but said nothing.

Ferra trudged off, feeling the weight of the world on her shoulders. Well, the weight of two light-boned cats, anyway.

10

"What I wouldn't give to be in your place." Soares, the CRIO coordinator, gave Kedron a wide, envious smile. "Getting off this stinking planet tomorrow and back to civilization again."

She'd invited herself to sit with Kedron at the midday meal. The Argint d'Apa security chief had invited him out to dinner that evening in Magloviti City. Odd how they only considered him worth talking to now that he was leaving.

His new policy of honesty with himself made him admit he could have engaged with them and the others when he'd first arrived, and perhaps made friends.

Kedron nodded and gave Soares a polite smile in return. "High Command could still change their minds again."

Soares laughed. "Good point. Don't jinx fortune by counting your cashflow chips before you have them in hand."

Kedron should have been as happy as Soares apparently assumed he was, but he'd spent the previous four days wishing he could stay longer. He'd come up with one idea for Barray's cats and sent it to her via the command processors in the cats' heads, for one of them to relay to her. But other than removing one obvious threat, he had no ideas on how to protect the woman herself.

Not that it was any of his business to do so, but he felt responsible. He'd involved her in his investigation into the surveillance source. The fact that he'd failed to find it left her vulnerable to whoever was behind it. She'd trusted him, and he'd let her down.

Soares finished the last swallow of coffee. "Any idea who's replacing you?"

"No," he said. "I'm lucky that High Command remembered to send me the updated transfer orders with the earlier departure date."

Soares laughed again. "That's the government for you." Her bracelet-style percomp blinked. "Gotta run. I'll see you tomorrow to say goodbye."

She took her tray and left him alone once more. He might have felt it more keenly, but the kitchen and dining hall AIs murmured in his head, something about canine treats for an audit. AIs usually knew about surprise inspections before any of their human counterparts. He'd used it to his advantage more than once in his career to avoid a red flag or two from overzealous inspectors.

After dropping his tray in the recycler, he headed toward the building's shipping section to check on his little-used military high-low flitter. Tomorrow, he'd fly it to the planet's only military base and space port, on the next continent to the west, and leave it for his successor.

He used the comms wire in his skulljack to direct the shipping pad's flitter stacker to release the flitter into the separate military hangar, which was little more than a garage. The AI complied, but warned him it couldn't accept it again until after the upcoming maintenance cycle that would put it and the traffic controller out of commission.

His finder sense flashed an alarm. He detoured to a nearby fresher and sealed the door, then queried the rest of the AIs in the complex. Suspicion confirmed, he closed his eyes and filtered through the hundreds of signals until he found the two he was looking for.

Novo, Boz. Find someplace to hide from an all-facility lockdown and inspection. It starts at 0930 hours. They're calling it a training exercise in the records, but they're actually looking for illegal chems, and they'll be using both the dogs and hellhounds in a room-by-room search. Warn Barray.

He hoped the cats got the message, because he didn't know how to make their controller wake them. He'd deliberately avoided getting to know the cats after their introduction, convincing himself it wouldn't be fair to them.

Now, he saw his behavior for what it was—his old, bad habit of avoiding the possibility of pain by pulling inside his turtle shell. One he needed to break.

He enjoyed solitude from time to time, but not all the time. He liked meeting extraordinary cats, and getting to know smart, laughing women, or at least one in particular. He'd be lying to himself again if he denied he already felt an emotional connection with her.

Their current circumstances weren't their lot in life, they were only temporary. The likelihood they would meet again by chance was incalculably remote, but he could change that, if he had the courage.

Remotely, he checked that his comms wire connected properly to the flitter, ensured its general status was green-go, and left it in the hangar for tomorrow. He walked briskly back to his office, stopping at the guard station along the way to borrow a gravcart. He filled the cart with all the portable tech from his office, even the replacement fan, then presented himself at the tech repair office secure entryway and pinged until someone answered.

A gold-skinned technician whose company name tag read "Yolalo" let him into the office. He frowned suspiciously at the gravcart's contents. "What's all that?"

"Tech from my office. I'm flying out tomorrow. *My* procedure says military government tech has to be secured for my successor."

Yolalo didn't need to know he'd learned from Barray's tactics and written the procedure himself just a few minutes ago. "*Your* policy says I have to bring it to you for chain of custody."

Yolalo grunted and turned toward the back. "Barray! Customer."

When no one answered, Yolalo muttered about no one ever being around to do their jobs. He unloaded the cart, recorded the asset tags, and locked them all in a sealed container.

Kedron used his wait time to query the repair depot's AI about the locations of all its self-directed mobile repair components, which was how it categorized the human repair technicians. He couldn't do so from outside the office because of all the shielding and tech suppressors.

Unsurprisingly, the technicians were scattered all over the building. Barray turned out to be in the filtration plant, on the top walkway above one of the gigantic filters.

His plan to accidentally run into her just in time for the lockdown would have to wait until she came back. Unless...

He headed toward the plant. As he walked, he called up the liaison manual on his military percomp to add a new procedure.

11

Ferra would have kicked herself for being so blazingly stupid as to get cornered by Lambru's remoras in the filtration plant, but she needed all her energy to avoid getting hurt or worse.

She'd been with Tech Inzaya on the bottom level, helping fix the lift controls. Inzaya sent Ferra to the top level, then got called away. Ferra had already tagged the presence of several of Lambru's crew working in other areas. The moment Inzaya left, they'd started to move toward Ferra's location. She'd be a fool to think it was just coincidence.

She'd need wings to get to the open side windows. The big powered lift couldn't move until the bottom-level control panel freed it. She could barricade herself in it, but "lift accident" made a pithy title for an injury report. So did "accidental fall," which was why she opened the cage for the emergency ladder. It was little more than rungs on a giant articulated chain, but it would get her down safely.

Except it was already in use by a well-muscled black-haired woman manually climbing up it. "Heyo, Indenturee Barray, what's the rush?" She sneered. "Too good for the likes of us who actually *work* for our restitution?"

Ferra held her hands up and backed up, putting the lift at her back. She didn't have long to wait.

Lambru himself arrived with the three other remoras. "Don't bother calling for help. The repair tech monitors can't hear you in here." He opened the front of his indenturee uniform to reveal a tech suppressor in his floral undershirt pocket. As was apparently his habit, he got right to the point. "You moved yourself from nonentity to competition when you stole my stash of cleaning bots."

"Bots?" She didn't have to pretend confusion. "I thought you wanted me to steal tech."

Lambru's eyes narrowed. "I hate liars." He pointed a curling finger at her. "You've been seen with *my* bots every day this past week." He pointed to her pass-tracker cuff. "Very crafty, using that to get by the guards to sell *my* product to the staff."

Ferra shook her head. "I hunted cleaning bots for the bounty that technician Calderosh told me about. I don't know shit about your product. I haven't sold anything to anyone."

"Hmmm. Let's pretend I believe you for the moment." He tapped pursed lips with a metallic-pink fingernail. "Your previous lack of cooperation represents lost-opportunity costs that require personal restitution." He pointed to her tech bag. "I'll take that, for starters."

We are coming. Boz was in her head.

No, she thought furiously. *They'll hurt you.*

She dipped her shoulder and let the bag slip down. It landed half on the catwalk grate, at the edge of the open lift. "It's all yours. Might be hard to explain at the checkpoint."

Lambru gave her an oily smile. "You let us worry about that. Your pass-tracker, too."

Suddenly, blue and red lights began flashing, accompanied by an ear-splitting alarm. An automated voice blared from everywhere.

"Attention, all personnel. This is an all-facility security lockdown.

Stay where you are until further notice. You may only move if your present location is unsafe. Motion detection commencing. Tracker location audit commencing. Filtration turbine shutdown commencing. Follow orders. Do not interfere with the guards or the dogs.”

"Fuck," said the black-haired woman. She looked to Lambru. Two of the crew ignored the announcement and took off at a run down the catwalk.

The blaring announcement repeated, making Ferra's ears ring.

The irises over the roof skylights began to close. The walkway darkened.

Behind Ferra, the lift suddenly jerked to life. When its safety gate encountered her tech bag, it sounded a loud, buzzing alarm. She eyed the gap.

Lambru lunged forward to grab Ferra's arm and kick the bag into the lift. The gate closed. The lift sank out of sight.

He grabbed the back of her neck hard, hauled her to the edge of the walkway, and forced her to look down at the waterfall. "If you cross me, you'll be taking a swim, just like indenturee Healey." He grabbed the flesh at her waist and gave it a hard, twisting pinch. "She didn't even make it past the filtration pump before she died."

He forced her down. His fingernails gouged into her skin. The walkway grate dug into her knees.

She reached out for the cats to tell them to stay with Tauceti. He was a good man. He would keep them safe.

Lambru turned to his three remaining remoras. "You two, go block the other two lifts on this side. Durga, block the ladder. We're up here to rescue Indenturee Barray, who got stranded up here in the lockdown." The crew trotted off to carry out his orders.

He tightened his grip cruelly until Ferra cried out in pain. "Stay." He shook her neck twice, then released her.

The chest-deep vibration of the gigantic turbine changed pitch. The waterfall of swamp water slowed. The shadows deepened as the skylights closed.

If Lambru was going to toss her over, he'd have to do it quickly.

Her heart raced, and she wanted to throw up. Just like when her brother abandoned her to the mercy of the jack crew. She didn't know how to talk her way out of this one.

You are not alone. Novo's thoughts flooded her with fierce anger and fiercer love.

Ferra's eyes ached with unshed tears. *Thank you for that.*

The walkway vibrated briefly. From her position looking down, she saw the lift start to rise from the ground level.

Lambru noticed, too. He warned Durga, who was standing at the emergency ladder, then turned a threatening glare on Ferra and made a "lips zipped" gesture across his mouth.

By the time the lift arrived, Lambru had turned off his tech suppressor and was the picture of fluttering, ineffectual concern. He needn't have bothered, because the lift's lights showed it had nothing in it, not even her tech bag.

Lambru swore and stomped to the railing and leaned over to peer down at the lift column's base.

The vibration of the turbine faded. The waterfall's volume decreased.

Durga cried out. "What was that?"

"What?" demanded Lambru, turning to look.

"Something flew by and pulled my hair." She moved closer to the uprights of the cage, looking fearfully upward into the shadows. "This is where the vampire bats live. They think it's night."

"There's no such—" He screamed and stumbled backward, holding his face. Blood seeped through his fingers.

Duck, ordered Novo.

Ferra sat on her heels and bent over to cover her head.

She peeked to see Boz climbing over the railing, his fur color rippling to match the shadows and crosshatch gray of the screening.

Durga screamed again and scrambled onto the emergency ladder and began climbing down. An eerie keening arose, causing Durga to whimper and descend faster.

Lambru fumbled with something inside his tunic. The deep claw marks on his face dripped red. The naked snarl on his face foretold violence.

Boz leapt onto the man's back, digging in with sharp claws and yowling with anger. Lambru howled. Ferra used her teke to nudge Lambru's stumbling feet. He tripped and fell to his hands and knees, which threw Boz off his back.

Boz opened his wings and flew upward, but she could feel his pain. He couldn't last.

Hide, Ferra told him.

The plant's automatic inside lighting finally snapped on.

Lambru pulled a small stunner out of his tunic and spun around, ready to shoot, but found no target. He aimed the stunner at Ferra. "What are those things?"

Ferra shook her head violently, letting him see her terror.

He used his sleeve to wipe the blood off his face.

Behind him, as if from nowhere, Subcaptain Tauceti climbed quickly and silently over the railing and onto the walkway.

Ferra concentrated her teke on Lambru's hand and pushed with everything she had. The stunner arced up and landed on the walkway.

Before Lambru finished his vicious oath, Tauceti jabbed him with a stick. Lambru stiffened, then crumpled like a deflated balloon.

Tauceti stepped over him to crouch close to Ferra. "Can you move?"

She sat up, feeling bilious, but that was better than feeling dead. "Yes. How did you get up here?"

He stepped back while she stood. "I hung on underneath the lift." He collapsed the stick and slipped it into his thigh pocket.

She edged away from Lambru's body. "What did you hit him with?"

"Military shockstick." He quick-stepped down the walkway to scoop up the fallen stunner and drop it in his uniform chest pocket. "The lockdown is still in force." He crossed back to search Lambru's body and confiscate two more weapons and the tech suppressor.

Her spirits sank. "Do I have to stay here, then?" She shoved her hands in her vest pockets to hide the trembling. Between the adrenaline aftermath and the blowback nausea from overusing her lightweight telekinetic talent, she was a mess.

"No." He invited her into the lift with a wave of his hand, then followed her in and closed the gate. The lift descended.

He looked at his feet. "To be honest, I was hoping to get stuck with you."

She squinted at him. That made no sense, so she focused on the more immediate problem. "What about Lambru?"

"He's being transferred." Tauceti's smile had a hint of predator. "I'm responsible for all military indenturees. I arranged a slot at a higher-level CRIO facility. At his present restitution rate, he'll need another eighty years to pay his debt. The CRIO system isn't meant to be a lifelong career."

She touched her neck and winced, then looked at the blood on her fingers. Her stomach churned.

Tauceti's smile faded. "I've just decided Lambru will be leaving tomorrow, with me. He's not safe here."

"He's, uhm, hurt." She mimed a cat's claw down the side of her face. She couldn't think of anything in that part of the plant that could plausibly cause those injuries. Lambru would scream about being attacked by something, even if he hadn't seen it.

Tauceti nodded. "I'll make sure he gets treated in the big autodoc before we go. Twilight drugs sometimes give patients vivid dreams."

The lift arrived at the ground floor. When they stepped out, two guards with a leashed hellhound approached them. "Lockdown means everyone, *amigo.*"

Tauceti pointed upward. "Call the medics and bring a gravcart. There is an injured person on the top walkway."

Ferra had never seen the command side of Tauceti. She wasn't surprised the guards looked at him with careful regard.

The guard not holding the hellhound leash touched her earwire and subvocalized. After a brief conversation, she nodded, then turned to Tauceti. "The Sec Chief respectfully asks you to confine yourself to the military area until we've concluded the search."

Tauceti nodded. "Very well. Barray will be with me."

"Indenturees aren't..." The guard trailed off.

Tauceti's forbidding expression would have stopped a squad of Jumpers in their tracks.

"Okay, then," said the guard. She nudged her partner. "May as well start up top."

On impulse, Ferra reached out with her newfound animal-affinity talent to see if she could sense the hellhound. She thought she felt its presence as an entity, but nothing of its thoughts or emotions. She needed practice.

They are drooling puppies, said Novo in her head. The image of a hellhound baying at the two moons accompanied the disdainful thought.

Ferra dropped her head to hide her smile. *Says the superior cat who chases her own tail.*

12

K edron showed Barray where he'd stashed her tech bag, then led the way through the main plant doors. Instead of going down the long hall to the government wing, he turned left, into the shipping area and out onto the flitter pad. He led her into the small hangar and sealed the door behind them. Technically, it was a military area.

The high-low flitter took up most of the room. He opened the flitter's side door, then gestured inside. "It's the only place to sit."

She walked up the shallow ramp and stepped inside, only to be nearly tripped by two spotted, winged cats twining about her legs. She laughed as she waded through cats to get to the bench on the far side. The moment she dropped her bag and sat, Boz draped himself across her lap like a rug. Novo put her front paws on Barray's knees and presented her chin to be rubbed. "You are both treasures."

Kedron was glad he'd remotely retracted the hangar's roof and opened the flitter's skylight for the cats. He leaned against the entryway and watched the reunion. Barray's happiness made him smile, too.

Her earlier fear had cut him like a knife. Her injuries were partly his fault. He should have removed Lambru the first day he'd thought of the way to do it, not waited for the CRIO system to respond to the order.

"Thank you for what you did. You and the wee beasties." Nova dropped to all fours and licked her own leg.

"They felt your distress and alerted me. I'm glad we got to you in time."

"Me, too." She smiled up at him. "You even look heroic just standing there. You should be in military recruiting posters throughout the galaxy." She blushed and looked away. "Sorry, that was inappropriate."

His face burned with a blush of his own. "I was, actually. When I was a sixteen-year-old cadet. I hated it."

Her eyes widened in surprise. After a moment, she nodded once. "The other cadets teased you mercilessly, didn't they?"

Novo's attention focused on something outside the flitter. In a flash, she launched herself past Kedron's legs. He turned to look, but the cat had vanished. No wonder their processors identified them as stealth weapons.

"They did." He'd had no idea what he'd been letting himself in for. Most people assumed it had been his ticket to fame. She was the first person he'd told who'd understood.

She smiled sympathetically. "When we were fourteen, my twin brother and I topped the local newstrends for a few months as the prize-winning holo image in an exposé about the secret world of abandoned children on space stations." She made a rude sound. "Secret, my ass. We were wards of the government, living in group dorms. I changed my look as soon as I could afford a body parlor, so I wouldn't be that kid anymore." She pulled out a strand of dark wavy hair. "I haven't looked like this in fifteen years."

He stepped further inside the flitter and watched her stroking Boz's shoulder and wing. "What did you think of my idea on what to do about your treasures?"

"Idea?"

"I sent them a message three days ago to relay to you."

She looked down at Boz, who swiveled an ear and twitched his tail. She frowned, then looked up again. "They won't tell me."

Kedron suspected they didn't want to leave her. He knew the feeling. "I could ship them to me via a commercial transport and mark the container as live scientific samples."

"From what I've read, that's how the pet trade used to smuggle their wares, so now, eco-inspectors open every container. That's why..."

She trailed off and her eyes widened.

Novo trotted past him carrying a small, struggling cleaning bot in her mouth. She dropped it at Barray's feet. When it righted itself and started to move, Novo stopped it with her paw.

Barray laughed as she gently urged Boz off her lap, then picked up the cleaning bot. "My restitution account thanks you."

Novo went back out the door. Boz stretched out on the end of the padded bench. His fur color rippled into a pattern that made him look like a carelessly wadded-up blanket. The cats truly were remarkable.

Kedron watched as Barray pulled out her multitool and opened the bot's service port. She touched something inside, and the bot stopped waving its rollers.

Second thoughts about his plan to talk to her about the future tied his tongue. He still had authority over her. Maybe she'd think he'd retaliate if he didn't like her answer. And once again, he was expecting her to take all the chances. "Is it too late to make me a courier?"

Ferra held up the little bot to the light and peered into its interior. "Hmmm?"

"What are you doing to my bot?"

Startled, Kedron turned to see Calderosh, the maintenance tech, standing in the entry of the flitter. He hadn't heard her approach. He hadn't even heard the door.

"Your bot?" Kedron asked.

Ferra put the bot back in her lap and closed its port.

Calderosh held out her hand. "I'll take it off your hands, if you'd like."

Ferra held the bot as she put her multitool in her pocket. "No, I'm good, thanks. I'll give it to my boss, so I get the bonus."

Calderosh produced a very lethal hand-beamer from her pocket. "I insist."

She edged in, covering both Ferra and Kedron. She couldn't miss at that distance. "Hand it over. Easy."

Ferra slowly leaned forward to put the bot in Calderosh's hand, then sat back down on the bench.

Calderosh curled her arm to hold the bot against her ribs. She waved the beamer toward Kedron. "So, what's this about treasure and a courier?"

He kept his face neutral and said nothing. He reached out to the cats. Once again, they couldn't go for help, so they'd have to *be* the help.

Calderosh hissed in annoyance. "I thought it was my lucky day when the famous Subcaptain Kedron Tau landed here and I found out about M'Tendere's missing treasure. All my data-broker contacts said you were her number-one boytoy. I thought you were just laying low, waiting until the meteor storm passed." She rolled her eyes. "But no. You are the most boring man on the planet. After two years of watching and waiting for you to leak significant information, I deserve a frickin' medal." She aimed the beamer at Barray's knees, the threat implicit as she glared at him. "So, tell me about the goddamn treasure."

Barray sighed loudly. "It's a pet-trade shipment. One of the scientists has a side gig, designing unlicensed hybrids for a pet-trade company." She pointed to the bot. "Just like your bots, indenturees are everywhere, and no one notices us. I overheard the arrangements for a live shipment for tomorrow." She frowned sourly and pointed a thumb in his direction. "Since Subcaptain Perfect is also leaving tomorrow, I was trying to convince him to intercept it and act as a courier, so I can pay off my restitution early."

Although he probably shouldn't have, Kedron admired her ability to weave a lot of little truths into one big lie.

Novo's controller requested orders on whether or not to kill Calderosh.

Disable only. They had enough trouble without explaining a dead body.

He suddenly noticed both women were looking at him. He frowned sternly and shook his head. "Pets are not allowed on military transports."

Calderosh's expression turned thoughtful. "What kind of pets? None of Lambru's spy eyes recorded any pets."

Barray shrugged. "Dunno. I know the shipment weighs twenty-two kilos. How did Lambru get surveillance tech in the government wing?"

Calderosh shrugged. "Hired people, probably. Lots of personnel turnover here, which is good business for me. My bots found the fresher where he hid the central data collection hub, so I modified the AI to delete anything with me and my bots. Which was a mistake, because it took me a while to figure out Lambru was stealing them to send them along the ducts with his crappy home-brew recreational chems. They're what killed that indenturee, Healey. Lambru dumped her body in the filtration plant and made it look like an escape." She shook her head. "I've got the proof, so I'm going to have to do something about him."

"No need," said Barray. "He got hurt in the plant at the start of the lockdown. Tauceti is taking him to the military base tomorrow. I heard he's being transferred."

Kedron nodded when Calderosh looked at him questioningly. "He will not be coming back." In the level-five facility where Lambru was going, he'd be a nurse shark in a sea of krakens.

"Good." Calderosh looked at her beamer, as if she'd forgotten she had it. After a moment, she slipped it into her pocket.

Barray eyed Calderosh speculatively. "Do you have any contacts you trust in the shipping business?"

Kedron hoped his face didn't give away his disapproval about Barray negotiating with a woman who'd been willing to shoot them with a beamer.

"Maybe." She squinted one eye. "This is about that pet-trade shipment, right? I deal in grey-market data, but I have friends. I'd have to see what's being shipped."

"Is now a good time?" Barray's expression was the picture of innocence.

"Sure." Calderosh's tone held a wealth of skepticism.

Barray smiled. "Look to your left."

Boz decloaked, his skin and fur rippling as it changed shape and color. He sat only a few centimeters away from Calderosh's leg. He hissed.

Calderosh jumped right and banged into the entryway hard enough to rock the whole flitter.

Novo hissed from the right, then decloaked. She unfurled a bit of wing, then folded it again.

Calderosh froze. "What the hell are they?"

"Cats," said Barray.

"Right," said Calderosh sarcastically. "Because all cats have wings."

Barray laughed. "Only superior cats have wings."

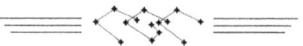

By the end of the lockdown two hours later, Calderosh left the flitter after agreeing to use her contacts to ship the cats to Merganukhan a week after he arrived. His job was to sell the cats to Barray's supposed pet-trade contact, then split the profit with Barray and Calderosh. He'd pay for the shipping, so he'd have less incentive to steal the cargo for himself. He wasn't sure how that was supposed to work, but it satisfied Calderosh.

He disliked the idea that anyone believed he'd be involved in such a transaction, but realistically, after his last post, people would always question his motives. Regulations and ethics didn't always intersect.

Mindful of Calderosh's ubiquitous bots, he turned on the tech suppressor he'd confiscated from Lambru, then sat next to Barray on the bench. "Can we trust Calderosh?"

"I think so. She's got a good gig here, collecting and selling unrelated data. She's probably a finder of some sort, so she can sense what's valuable." Barray smiled. "I'll bet half the fund managers in the financial industry are unregistered minders. Finders for the research, forecasters for trends, filers to remember everything they hear or see. The CPS can't expose them without crashing the galactic economy." She snorted. "Or without admitting they've been ignoring the patterner class of minders for the last century, because there are too many of them."

"I never thought of it like that. Maybe that's why the Ayorinn Legacy meme is so persistent. The promise of freedom and equal treatment for minders would definitely resonate if it affects half the galactic population." He tapped his fingers on his thigh. "That would also explain why the CPS is so obsessed with obliterating it, and why they keep failing." He smiled wryly. "Not that they'd admit that, either."

Boz jumped onto the bench and butted Barray's arm, then licked her cheek.

She laughed and pushed him away. "Yes, you poor starving creature. I'll buy each of you an extra mealpack for lunch."

A distant attention tone sounded three times, followed by unintelligible words. Kedron's earwire told him it was the all-clear for returning to regular operation. The bongs that signaled the midday meal service would be coming soon.

"If I'm out of line, please tell me, but I want to pay for shipping and boarding the cats until you can come for them." What he really wanted was to pay off her restitution debt, but then they'd be right back where they were now. "You're taking the risks."

Her eyes narrowed in thought. "I'll split the cost with you. I'll give you codes for an account for my half. But I'm paying Calderosh's commission on the 'sale,' since it was my idea." She leaned forward and rested her elbows on her knees. "I'll resolve the restitution in ninety, maybe a hundred days. After that, I have to clean up the mess I left behind. You okay with waiting six months, or even longer?"

"Yes. Take as much time as you need." He tilted his head toward the cats, where Novo was grooming Boz. "They can stay here tonight, if they want."

The lunch bongs sounded.

Barray rubbed her neck and winced, then stood and stretched, exposing red and bruising skin underneath her tunic. "Maybe the medic will give me a painkiller."

Maybe he could accidentally drop Lambru on his head a couple of times on his way to the military base. He turned away before his expression gave him away.

He pushed to his feet. "I'll be giving my full contact information to the CRIO office. I'll make sure they know about the policy that requires them to let military indentures send private communications to me until such time as my successor arrives."

She looked puzzled. "I don't remember reading that policy."

He scooped up the tech suppressor and put it in his pocket, then handed her tech bag to her.

"That's because I haven't written it yet."

She laughed and shook her head. "I think I'm a bad influence on you, Subcaptain Perfect."

He certainly hoped so.

EPILOGUE

As far as Ferra was concerned, the Merganukhan southern-continent spaceport was one of the best-kept secrets in the galaxy. Of all the transportation hubs she'd been to in her life, she'd never seen a more well-run facility.

Despite her attempt to keep herself iced, anticipation kept bubbling up and making her grin at the stupidest things, like the bright mid-afternoon summer sun streaming in through high, clerestory windows, or a small cleaning bot in the fresher.

Once her gravcart of luggage, her identification, and her person passed inspection, all she had to do was find the most handsome man on the planet. Fortunately, he'd pinged her with his location in the military section.

The easy part of her life after Tauceti left had been finishing her restitution. Lambru's sudden departure shattered his organization. After the cats left, she didn't have to worry about them being discovered. As a parting gift, they told her where Lambru had hidden his illegal chems laboratory. She told Calderosh, who got a company bonus for reporting it.

Ferra got bonuses for catching up on all the minor tech repairs.

They went a lot faster when she could just rip out the surveillance tech instead of dancing around it. As a goodwill gesture, she made sure some of the better equipment ended up in Calderosh's parts lockers instead of the recycling bins.

The hard part had been going home. Her brother hadn't just sold her to pay his debts, he'd sold everything of hers he could get his hands on, including her flat and her flitter. He'd even gone to the trouble of declaring her dead for the insurance payout. It hadn't done him any good. He'd met with a very messy, very public fatal accident three weeks after she'd arrived at Argint d'Apa.

She spent five days in a luxury hotel, pampering herself while she tied up loose ends. Last time, she'd left in panic, only knowing what she didn't want. This time, she knew what she wanted and hoped for, and took the time to set things in motion for the next phase of her life.

Her stomach fluttered as she stepped into the space station's military lobby, suddenly worried that maybe Kedron couldn't make it, or had changed his mind. Exchanging dozens of messages and a couple of expensive realtime vid calls wasn't the same as seeing him in person.

Relief flooded her when she saw him striding purposefully toward her. His relaxed, confident smile made her grin like a fool, but she didn't care. He wore civilian clothes, but he still looked like a hero to her.

He waved his arm wide. "Welcome to Suck Flux, RSI."

She laughed. "I'm very glad to be here." She stepped in a little closer. "Would it be all right if I hugged you?"

He opened his arms. She wrapped him in a tight, fierce embrace, then let him go, or she'd never stop. He smelled good and felt better. She'd been dreaming of that and more for four months, eight days, and sixteen hours. Not that she had been running a countdown clock or anything.

He looked at the gravcart behind her. "Where's the rest of your stuff? I brought the biggest flitter in the transportation pool, just in case."

She shrugged. "That's it. I'll tell you about it tonight. We're still on for dinner?"

"Yeah, about that. All the good restaurants are booked, so I hope you don't mind eating at my place." He pointed toward an exit. "This way."

He offered to take her backpack, and she let him, even though the gravcart had room.

"You have a place?" She couldn't resist teasing him a little. He'd admitted to not having lived off base for his entire military career.

"Yeah, the base is short on command-level housing. I pointed out the policy that said base leadership shouldn't be clustered together, and volunteered for off-base quarters." The twinkle in his eye belied his serious expression.

She smiled. "It wouldn't happen to be a brand new policy, would it?"

He laughed, a sound she loved to hear. "No, it's an old policy, just not used very often."

His place turned out to be an isolated, ranch-style quick-formed house that backed up to a marshy eco-preserve. He'd chosen it because he'd kept the cats.

Her reunion with them was every bit as joyous as she'd imagined. Even reserved Novo was all over her, sending love and jumbled thoughts, and purring loud enough to wake the neighbors, if they'd had any. Boz tried to nuzzle inside her shirt like he was a kitten rather than a stealthy, lethal weapon of war.

"Did have trouble keeping Novo and Boz?" The Ground Division military manual she'd read during the interstellar flight to Merganukhan had been very adamant about not allowing personal pets in military quarters.

Kedron took off his boots and put them on the dry mat by the front door. "I couldn't find a boarding facility I trusted, so I rented a tiny apartment for them until I got approved for off-base housing." He twitched a smile as he brushed cat fur off his pant leg. "My coworkers assumed I was overnighting with a lover who has pets."

Ferra laughed. "You should have heard Calderosh complain about cat fur in Argint d'Apa's air ducts." Boz nuzzled her hair. "You'd like her, I think. The only reason she pulled that beamer on us in the flitter was because she thought we were working with Lambru. She's funny and surprisingly ethical. She only sells financial-related data, and won't deal in personal relationship information at all."

He sat cross-legged on the floor with her. "Dinner will be takeout from the base mess hall, but it's good." He pointed toward the front of the house, where the big military flitter sat waiting outside. "Why so little stuff?" He looked down at his splayed hand on his thigh. "Not staying?"

Nudging Boz away, she slid closer to Kedron. She slipped her hand into his. "I'm staying." She squeezed his hand gently, then waited until he met her gaze. "I really like you a lot. I've been dreaming about this day, but I want to take the time to do it right, at a pace that works for you. You're worth it."

He squeezed her hand. "I like you a lot, too. You and the cats are a good influence on me. I never lived with pets before, and now I can't imagine living without them. They remind me not to withdraw into my shell. You make me not want to."

His words touched her. "To answer your question, I don't have much stuff because I'm starting a new life." She explained what her brother had done.

With the love from the cats thrumming in her mind—and holding hands with the man she was falling for so fast she felt like she'd jumped off a cliff—she finally realized her brother had never loved her the way she'd loved him. *Move on, Barray.*

Novo crawled into her lap and curled up. "The financial industry is high risk for me. I don't ever want to be a target like that again. I liquidated all the accounts my brother couldn't find and left my old life for good. I'm keeping my new identity and starting a new career."

He stroked the back of her hand with his thumb. "In what?"

"Veterinary medicine. I'm studying for a basic vet med certification now and plan to sign on with a local clinic to get hands-on experience." She hoped to find someone who could help her learn to use her minder talent, too. She didn't want to keep it secret from Kedron, but first, she needed to research military policy on whether he'd have to report it if she told him.

"I'll ask around for recommendations, if you'd like." He smiled. "It's a good excuse to talk to people, instead of just issuing orders."

"Yes, please. I'd like to stay near the base. Near you, if you're alright with that. You make me feel safe." She looked around in the open living space, where the decor leaned heavily toward climbable sculpture and high padded shelves. "Can the cats stay here while I look for someplace to live?"

Kedron took in a deep breath and let it out quickly. "I'd kind of hoped you'd want to stay here. I haven't taken you on the tour yet, but the house is divided for two. There's a separate kitchen and—"

"Yes." She couldn't keep the joyous grin off her face. "I'll take it. I don't care how much you want in rent. I'll take it."

"I don't need the money. I need you." His vulnerable, serious look melted her heart.

"Could I kiss you?" she asked. "If it's too soon, just say—"

"Yes," he said.

He shared with her the sweetest kiss she'd ever had, with the promise of a bright future.

Novo rubbed her head contentedly on Ferra's arm. *You should mate with him. He is warm at night and good at petting.*

Ferra smiled. *Working on it.*

GALACTIC SEARCH AND RESCUE

When an earthquake shakes up a nearby world, can two star-crossed rescuers save an entire community... and each other?

Experienced rescuer Subcaptain Taz Correa hides her wounded heart. A telekinetic tech-whiz recently transferred to the worst Galactic Search and Rescue unit in the galaxy, she'd hoped after her string of epically bad breakups she'd have a fresh start. But when she can't fight her feelings for her new teammate, she's terrified her secret affection will show and cost both their careers.

Subcaptain Rylando Dalroinn's telepathic connection to animals used to be everything. But he has no idea how to admit his growing attraction to Taz, especially as it's completely against the rules. And when they're sent as a team of two to help a devastated town, he knows he can't afford to let his heart's desire distract him from their dangerous mission.

As Taz works with Rylando and his unusual squad of trained animal helpers to free a desperate group of citizens, she puts her life on the line to protect her partner's beloved creatures. But when Rylando realizes the people he's rescuing are more than just innocent victims, he'll have to throw out the rulebook to save them both.

Can love—and a clever crew of animals—guide the couple out of the rubble and into a future together?

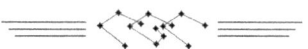

1

Perlarossa Orbital Space Station • GDAT 3242.333

S ubcaptain Taloszjaril "Taz" Correa stood, hands on her hips, surveying the storeroom. Nothing distinguished it from hundreds of others on the Perlarossa space station, except for Silver Team's name over its open doorway. And the farkin' disaster inside.

Swirling dust tickled her nose, and a burned chemical stench seemed to coat her tongue. She resisted the impulse to wipe the sweat from her face with the hem of what had been her cleanest undershirt. The sticky stains would probably give her a rash.

The only orderly thing was the room's exposed structural framework shaped sort of like a giant animal kennel. Precisely spaced holes marched up the verticals that curved upward on all sides. Dangling twists of metal gave mute evidence of the equipment that used to be hanging neatly from hooks. The jumbles of crates and uneven mountains of cables, gantries, chairs, and unidentifiable charred crap looked like the aftermath of a tornado.

That was what hasty shuttle launches did to carefully maintained storerooms when some asshole carelessly left the room's blast-proof doors wide open. Leaving her and the rest of Silver Team to clean up the mess.

Would it kill the universe—just once—to let her get an entire downtime shift's worth of sleep?

The sudden grating whine of a badly tuned skimmer engine assaulted her ears for a millisecond until her ear protection implants kicked in. To her right, the four-person, canopied air skimmer took up about a quarter of the room. More, now that it was half buried under a mound of debris.

In the far left corner, a giant brown-and-tan weasel sank his sharp teeth into the blackened corner of a piece of freight padding. The skimmer's whine didn't faze him at all.

Taz touched the earwire on the side of her face. "*Rylando? Is it okay if Lerox bites the burned bits?*"

"*Yeah, he's ace, as long as he doesn't eat them,*" said Subcaptain Rylando Delroinn, in her earwire. "*I asked him to investigate the damage. It's good practice for him to figure out how recently the burn happened.*"

Taz couldn't help but smile as the fearless beast wrestled with the two-meter-square padding like a puppy with a chewtoy. Technically, Lerox was a pet designer's idea of what a pre-flight, long-extinct prehistoric weasel called an "ekakeran" might have looked like. That was how the zero-ethics pet-trade industry got around legions of laws against genetically altering cornerstone species like badgers, tayras, or wolverines. Lerox's shoulders stood just above her knee. When he wasn't exploring or nibbling everything, he was sliding into a human lap to demand a belly rub. He lived on the other side of the universe from shy and stealthy.

Taz envied Rylando's easy camaraderie with all his animals. He trained them in rescue tasks, but his minder talent allowed him to sense their thoughts, guide their actions, and see and hear through their superior senses. The unit commander insultingly called them pet-trade rejects, but Taz knew better. They were a working team.

Very non-regulation, but better than most of the human teams in their bottom-of-the-barrel Galactic Search and Rescue unit. Central Galactic Concordance Foundation law dictated that the Citizen Protection Service had to operate GSAR, but the law didn't say how well.

Turning to the corner behind her that had escaped the worst of the tornado, she stepped up into the ship-loader's skeletal assist frame and connected to its interface. Bands wrapped around her calves, thighs, torso, and arms to secure her in place. The dented and scratched frame looked like cobbled-together bird cages salvaged from a scrap heap, but she'd tinkered with the tech so it operated smoothly and quietly.

She oriented the holo display as she cataloged the damage. After the cleanup, she planned to check the security vids. If she won the bet with herself that the careless asshole had been Franecki from Red Team, she'd reward herself with an extra thirty minutes of sleep. Lazy Franecki often raided Silver Team's working supplies. It'd be a cold night in the black void before she'd fix any more of Red Team's tech.

Five of the six Galactic Search and Rescue unit's teams were responding to a mass disaster on Uttara Phalgurni, one of the seven colonized planets their underfunded, understaffed first-responder unit was now assigned to cover. A catastrophic landing accident had torn up half of the only operational spaceport and set the other half on fire. To make matters worse, the disaster trapped thousands of injured people during that planet's peak travel season. Lucky for the citizens, their planet was only one interstellar transit day away from the GSAR unit's home station, so they got help fast.

Meanwhile, she and Rylando had to deal with the disaster at home base. GSAR's hand-me-down shuttles were held together with bootleg-printed parts and retrofitted salvage. A leaky system drive on one of them had acted like a giant wind-driven flame thrower, setting everything in the launch bay on fire and tumbling into the unprotected storeroom.

The engine noise stopped. Rylando climbed out of the

skimmer's control pod with the lithe, fluid grace of a swimmer. His GSAR yellow and red uniform complemented his tawny brown skin and short, thick brown hair. If he had any civilian downtime clothes, she'd never seen them.

"How's our transpo?" Taz righted a dented and blackened three-hundred-kilo crate that blocked the wide bay doors. With luck, the unknown contents survived the heat.

"The systems say the controls and engines are green go." He wiped his hands on his pants. "Good thing our airsled was still on Hatya's shuttle, or it would have toppled onto the skimmer." He gave her a crooked smile. "Then if they deployed us, we'd have to borrow glider boards from the local youth."

Taz snorted. "Thank the universe the animal autodoc is still in the repair bay. GSAR would never spring for a replacement."

One of the two nearly identical cats, probably Deimos, leapt to the skimmer's flat canopy and sat, supervising humans and animals alike. She and her brother Phobos were as tall and long-legged as Lerox, but lighter and thinner. With Siamese markings, silky fur, and stumpy tails, they had regal grace in abundance. Feline lovers melted when the friendly cats asked to be worshipped... er, petted. They were likely confiscated from a pet-trade dealer or smuggler. She'd deliberately avoided asking Rylando where he got any of his team. She didn't want to force him to lie to her.

With the assist frame taking care of the mass, lifting and carrying the heavy crate out of the storage room was a matter of angle and balance. And making sure no four-legged team members were in her path. Shen, the tan brindle-coated shepherd-retriever mix with energy to burn, sometimes believed humans needed, well, shepherding.

The two-story launch bay was an even worse disaster area than the storeroom. Everything that hadn't been fastened down looked like it tried to climb the back wall to get away from the heat. It reeked of burned chemicals. Good thing she'd eaten hours ago, or her stomach would be twisting itself in knots.

Unfortunately, since Silver Team was currently undeployable with only two rescuers and one assigned pilot, they'd likely get tasked with cleaning up the launch bay, too.

Taz made a command decision to start a new stack in front of the neighboring unmarked storage bay. She used her telekinetic talent to brush aside a couple of badly bent equipment stands before easing the crate down.

That talent was why she'd been moved from a regular military mech-maintenance unit to the Citizen Protection Service sixteen years ago. A handy talent in rescue situations, and in cleaning up messes. Not so handy when former military colleagues had learned she was a minder. They'd instantly treated her like she was a secret jack-crew spy who'd stolen the squad's party slush fund.

It hadn't mattered that she hadn't known about her talent either. None of the mandatory tests she'd been given when growing up or joining the military had even hinted that she might be a minder. No family history, either. Or none that they'd admit. They'd been horrified when she told them and quickly disavowed her existence.

Saving herself and two teammates from a runaway grav sled earned her an iridium-star commendation and pay bonus, followed by an immediate one-way transfer to the Citizen Protection Service's Minder Corps. Still military, but with many more mission areas and very different rules.

Her regular military experience with big equipment and her new talent made her a suitable candidate for the CPS's Galactic Search and Rescue division. She'd jumped at the chance. Helping people was why she'd joined the military in the first place.

At least the CPS valued her minder talent and taught her to use it. Of course, they'd also insisted she needed addictive enhancement drugs to make it reliable. That, she soon discovered, was the same story they gave all minders in the telepathic and telekinetic categories. The higher the level of talent, the more powerful the drugs they needed. She wasn't the only transferee who'd quickly decided that was a mech-load of manure.

To start with, drugs weren't required for everyone in the Minder Corps, just the so-called heavy talents like telepathy and telekinesis. Filers with perfect memories, and forecasters who could spot patterns in a sea of data and predict the future, were exempt. So were animal-affinity minders like Rylando.

He'd said he'd known he was a minder before the first round of testing at age twelve, so it hadn't been a shock. By joining the CPS GSAR division right after his age-seventeen test, he'd gotten nova-class veterinary-medic training for free and a well-paying career working with animals. On the other hand, he'd had to put up with people calling him subhuman and worse all his life. That had to have tanked.

Stop thinking about the sexy man you can't have, she told herself, *and get back to work.*

After she cleared three more heavy crates, she filled a flat cart with smaller items. Rylando helped, and so did the two dogs. Energetic Shen identified candidates for the pile, and Moyo, the larger and stronger dog, helped pull and carry them.

Moyo wasn't like any other hellhound Taz had ever met. The pet trade originally created them as terrifying fantasy-style guard dogs for the wealthy. The military liked them so well they confiscated the patent and bred them to seek, track, and kill.

As to Moyo, while most hellhounds were star-void black, she looked like she'd been in a glow-paint fight. Plus, she loved everyone, two- or four-footed. Rylando said it made her too trusting. He kept her away from the other teams and their working dogs. She suspected there'd been trouble in the past.

That wariness extended to Taz. Which kind of hurt, if she was honest. Granted, she was the noob, with only one hundred fifty-two days in the unit. He'd only recently begun letting her look after some of his animals while he was away. Maybe in time, he'd realize she would never, ever hurt an animal or take advantage of Moyo's good nature. If she stayed long enough to prove it to him.

With a flurry of wings, a small but very long-legged brown owl landed on the left shoulder of her assist frame. She froze in mid-lift so as not to frighten the bird. "Hello, Mariposa."

The owl ignored her in favor of staring intently at the far corner of the storeroom, beyond where Lerox had been wrestling with the padding.

She followed its gaze. "Rylando, did you put the insect habitat in the far-left cabinet like usual?"

The cabinet's doors had gone missing, and the contents of the shelves were heaped in front of it.

He turned to look. "Frelling hell." Exasperation sharpened his tone. "That's two weeks' worth of treats scurrying their way into everything."

Insects were a vital part of successful terraforming throughout the galaxy. They were also unstoppable stowaways in the human diaspora, even on military space stations. However, GSAR Unit Leader Bhayrip would use it as a new excuse to again pressure Rylando to decommission the non-standard animals that dined on insects. It irked the captain that CPS regulations protected animal-affinity minders from being ordered to get rid of their animals without extraordinary cause.

"Could Lerox help Mariposa find them?" She pointed to the big weasel, who was now trying to get his mouth around the arm of a fallen chair.

Rylando laughed. "I'll admit that Lerox will eat practically anything, alive or dead, but he draws the line at beetles and grasshoppers. Once we're done here, I'll lower the lights and see if Otak will help."

Otak was another non-standard rescue animal. According to Rylando, the giant pouched rat was a genius. Humans had bred thousands of generations of them to detect scents in the nano-parts-per-billion range. Each family line specialized in one particular scent, such as explosives or plant pests. Frontier planet settlers swore they were more reliable than the most sophisticated detection tech. And a lot cheaper, too, considering the outrageous markups that settlement companies charged for everything.

From what she gathered, the breeder sold Otak to Rylando for half price, thinking the rat's nose was defective. Rylando's talent told him that Otak's sense of smell was fine, he was just confused by the number of scents he could distinguish. So far, Rylando had trained him to alert on eleven distinct scents and was working on a twelfth. He'd named the rat for a famous polymath from the First Wave of human expansion into the galaxy.

A tone sounded in her earwire. *"Either of you free to bring me a mealpack? I missed morning food service, and the cupboard in Comms is bare again."* Jumper Captain Hatya Wa'ara exaggerated her musical Islander accent. *"If I have to gnaw on the upholstery, I'm claiming Lerox did it."*

Rylando tapped his earwire but spoke aloud rather than subvocalizing. *"I'll bring you three, just to be safe. Lerox is still on the stink-eye list for chewing holes in Soong's home-brew beer pouch."* A big head bumped into Rylando's hip hard enough to knock him sideways a step, making him chuckle. *"Moyo wants to come, too."*

Ordinarily, the job of monitoring status and answering staff pings fell to the unit's six comms techs, but they'd all deployed to the emergency with the rest of the teams. In the GSAR, comms techs were even rarer than rescuers, and transferred out even faster. Silver Team only had a designated pilot because Hatya was on loan from the CPS's elite-force Jumper Corps. Bhayrip would need half a dozen CPS approvals to get her officially reassigned to a different team.

Taz caught Rylando's eye. "Tell her I'll take a four-hour shift at twelve hundred after I grab a few hours of sleep. She'll listen to you. She's supposed to be training for her upcoming physical-fitness test, not stuck sitting on her ass in Comms because farkin' Red Team commandeered our whole bin of secure-net earwires."

Hatya was great with people and command, but she had the typical Jumper habit of thumping misbehaving equipment. Since everything in the GSAR section of the space station misbehaved, it got a lot of thumping.

In her random off-hours, Taz put her mech-maintenance experience to good use, repairing and improving Silver Team's tech. She spent too much of her own money on parts, but it gave her something better to do than brooding about the bed she'd made for herself.

"Good idea," said Rylando. "I'll take a shift after that."

He wove his way through the jumble and left, Moyo capering excitedly at his side. Most hellhounds lumbered.

Captain Bhayrip couldn't send Silver Team out until they got replacement rescuers. He skirted GSAR policy and temporarily lent her and Rylando to other teams. She'd just got back from a Blue Team response to a downed sky skimmer with mass casualties on Floris Delta. When Rylando wasn't deploying to disasters with his animals, he trained dogs and birds for the regular military.

It wasn't her business, but she worried that Rylando hadn't had a downtime shift in several ten-days, or even the opportunity to visit the CPS's post-trauma therapist. GSAR rescuers sometimes needed help dealing with horrific experiences, or the stress would eat them up inside. He'd worked five back-to-back disaster deployments and just got back from a dog-and-handler training session on Alyphorux, another one of the planets their unit covered. Captain Bhayrip seemed to think Rylando's training trips were a twisty scam he'd cooked up to get free vacation time.

Bhayrip wasn't the worst unit leader Taz ever had, but he was a close second. She avoided him as much as possible. One unfinished year at a CPS Minder Academy in his youth seventy years ago had apparently made him an expert on everything related to minders and talents. His idea of management was jumping in with gravity boots, causing chaos, then blaming everyone else when it blew up in his face. He couldn't be bothered to pay attention past the first thirty words of anything. Unfortunately for disaster victims everywhere, he was determined to stay on active duty and deploying for rescues until the mandatory retirement age of one hundred thirty.

Shen barked at her and nipped at a leg pocket flap on her loose uniform pants.

Taz laughed. "You're quite right, Shen. I'm supposed to be working, not star-gathering. You're a good dog to remind me." Unlike the other teams' dogs, Shen didn't appear to have a functioning controller in her head, so Taz had to speak to her in human language. Even if Shen's controller worked, Rylando probably wouldn't let Taz connect to it, any more than he'd let the other team members do so.

With a watchful eye for wandering weasels and shepherding dogs, she quickly cleared the rest of the large items that didn't belong to Silver Team and added them to the outside stack.

The rest of the storeroom mess wouldn't need the assist frame, so she marched it to the corner, disconnected, and stepped down to the floor.

Out of habit, she used the manual controls to power it down instead of her implanted headjack and controller. In rescues, having military-grade implants that could wirelessly interact with chatty military and civilian AIs was just as handy as her teke talent. They were legacies of her military days, but she'd only met one or two other CPS minders who had them. She'd styled her straight dark hair short over her forehead and long enough on the sides to cover the jack. Out of prudence, she avoided mentioning the implants, in case having them broke some obscure CPS regulation. Rylando knew, but no one else in the unit seemed to have noticed.

Both cats now sat on top of the skimmer's control pod canopy, as if surveying their empire and finding it wanting. Mariposa the owl was excavating the jumble in the corner, intent on eating every insect she uncovered. When Lerox lumbered over to nose through the pile, she screeched and flew up to the top of the cabinet. Lerox's pawing made a bigger mess but did cause more insects to move, making them easy prey for Mariposa to swoop in for the catch.

Taz couldn't tell if Lerox's actions were meant to help the little owl or coincidental. She'd have to ask Rylando. She'd often seen him encourage them to use their skills and superior senses to uncover hidden contamination and damage, so maybe that explained it.

Thankfully, he never used his minder talent to march them around like brain-wiped automatons, like she'd seen one previous team member do several years ago. Most animal-affinity minders were better with animals than people, but that miserable excuse for a rescuer had hated both the job and anything living. Rylando was the exact opposite.

And once again, her thoughts wandered without her permission to her teammate. Apparently, her stupid heart learned nothing from her epic record of failed relationships. Especially the last disaster that had caused her to request an immediate transfer, even though it meant agreeing to an extra year of CPS service. Her lover from regular military Space Division had turned out to be a cheating thief, and she hadn't seen it coming.

With this new assignment, she'd vowed to be professionally friendly with everyone but wear extra flexin armor around her heart. Easy enough with the rest of the misbegotten unit. She hadn't counted on Rylando being so sexy, funny, and clever. Or how much she enjoyed being around his animals.

She picked up the chair Lerox had been trying to eat and carried it to the wall where it belonged.

Null chance of anything happening between her and Rylando. Even if he hinted that he returned her interest—which he hadn't—they'd have to go stealth mode with their relationship. She wasn't doing that ever again.

Besides, it was unwritten but well-known GSAR policy to break up any such unions—even cohab contracts and marriages—by transferring the parties as far apart as possible. Just like GSAR to make a service-wide blanket policy instead of dealing with occasional individual problems. With her rotten luck, they'd assign her to her dysfunctional family's home planet, or even worse, back to the duty station she'd just escaped from.

Blowing out an exasperated sigh, she got back to work. Keeping busy was the best thing to keep her from the same spiral of thoughts she'd been spinning for the last hundred days. She cleared a path to the skimmer and made two piles, one for undamaged goods and one for potentially repairable items. GSAR units rarely threw anything away and weren't above trading or scavenging. Lately, new supplies from headquarters came just about as often as having the only winning numbers in the Hundred-Planet Lottery.

Shen sat and looked up expectantly, as if waiting for something to do. Taz tried one of the few commands she knew. "Shen, find the exit."

The moment Taz raised her hand, palm forward, Shen took off like a rocket around the bulk of the skimmer to the far-right end of the storeroom. Stymied by the jumble of bins blocking the door, she nosed and squeezed her way through them. Once she touched her nose to the door, she backed up, sat and barked twice, paused, then barked twice again.

The two cats watched Shen's actions like they were spectators at a grav-ball match, making Taz laugh.

"Good job, Shen!" Taz showed the dog her flat hand, then lowered it to her thigh. Shen trotted back to Taz's side and sat, looking up.

She crouched and stroked just under Shen's ear, praising her cleverness. Recently, when Rylando had been away for a couple of days with Moyo and left Shen behind, Taz had awakened to discover the smaller dog sleeping on the foot of her bed. Probably missing Rylando and wanting some company. Taz pretended to herself that she hadn't been feeling the same thing.

Shen licked Taz's chin, then stood, tail wagging.

Though it was probably silly, Taz had made a habit of explaining what she was doing to the animals when Rylando wasn't around. "We need to move more of this so the cleaning bots can do their job."

Taz turned a mock glare and a wagging finger toward the two cats. "And leave them alone, you delinquents."

Lerox, apparently bored with the pile of debris, jumped up on one of the few undamaged crates and started grooming his belly, hind leg in the air.

"Come on, Shen, let's clear more paths while we don't have a weasel underfoot." She snapped open a few crates for collecting the smaller items. Handing some of the items to Shen to carry was fun, and the smart dog quickly figured out which crate Taz pointed to. The sooner they made a dent in the cleanup, the sooner Taz could sneak off for a nap before taking the comms shift.

Not that anyone would thank her or Rylando for taking care of the mess. As near as she could tell, Unit 1051 had become the short-term detention pen for screw-ups and the permanent punishment post for unredeemable assholes. If only she'd known that when she'd looked for the unit with the most vacancies, presuming they'd take her immediately—which they had. She should have asked around for recommendations, but all she could think of at the time was getting away.

Her best guess as to why clever and highly competent Rylando stayed in the unit was his unusual team. He knew the regs backward and forward, and easily stymied Bhayrip's petty machinations. A more effective commander in a better unit might outmaneuver Rylando into giving up his animals.

At least she'd had the good instinct to let Bhayrip and the others think she was on punishment detail for a previous colossal clusterfuck she'd been ordered not to disclose. Much safer to be dismissed as just another fly-by fool than resented for being Ensign Excellent.

Thirty minutes later, just as she was closing the center cabinet, Rylando and Moyo strode into the storeroom.

He looked around with a grin. "This is ace. You've made impressive progress." Crossing to the now-accessible skimmer, he slid the crate he carried onto its floor. "Sorry I took so long. I had to clear the debris off the food-storage unit, and Hatya needed time with Moyo. The uncertainty about GSAR is stressing her, so when even a Jumper admits she needs comfort…" He shrugged apologetically.

"It's stressing everyone out." Taz made a disdainful noise. "Except Bhayrip, because he refuses to believe the CPS would disband us."

Rylando shook his head in disgust. "He thinks because Concordance Foundation law requires the CPS to provide search and rescue, GSAR is untouchable."

"He really thinks that?" She rolled her eyes. "I suppose I shouldn't mention the Minder Corps base consolidation, or the rumor that Minder Corps personnel are disappearing every day? Or anything about Ayorinn's Legacy?"

"Not unless you enjoy twenty-minute tirades." He fished in his thigh pocket and brought out a water pouch. "According to him, bases get realigned all the time. Desertion rumors are scurrilous attempts by anarchists to destabilize the government."

Taz hooked a thumb into her belt. "I'm almost afraid to ask what he thinks about Ayorinn's Legacy." Even hermits living on wandering asteroids had heard of the legendary forecast that would free all minders and change the course of human civilization to save it.

Rylando snorted. "No such thing, according to the Captain, Ayorinn wasn't a genius forecaster, he was a genius twist artist, and the CPS leaders fell for it."

"Oh, right, because *that* explains forty years of mysteriously published poetic quatrains. And resurging memes powerful enough to cause riots. And the fact that the CPS has failed at every attempt to stamp them out."

Even in her respected position as a skilled rescuer, Taz and everyone else in GSAR had faced raw, naked hate for using their mental talents to save lives. Sometimes, it felt like Ayorinn's legendary forecast was the only thing that gave minders hope of better days ahead.

"Unrelated and exaggerated, per the captain." He twitched a

shoulder toward the cabinets she'd just closed. "Did any of the bowls survive?" He leaned down to pet Shen's head. "She's thirsty."

"Oh, yes, one did. Sorry I didn't think of it." She turned quickly back to the cabinet to hide her embarrassment. She'd hoped the dog liked her company and was accepting her as a teammate. Instead, she'd just wanted water. Clearly, the sooner Taz transferred out of the unit, the better, even if it tacked on yet another year to her CPS contract.

She pulled out the bowl and crossed with it to where Rylando stood. "Before I forget, I think Red Team also took our last set of flying-camera eyes when they took our comms. You might want to inventory the rest of our gear to see what else they 'requisitioned.' I'm going offline for a nap."

"Wait," said Rylando. "Hatya said not to relieve her until fourteen hundred. She's still on light duty, so she said she may as well take advantage of the enforced rest. Her hip is acting up."

Only Jumper Command would regard urgent, high stress, dangerous search-and-rescue missions as "light duty." Hatya groused that her new cybernetic leg and hip hadn't worked right from the start, which was why GSAR and Silver Team had lucked into the temporary assignment of an expert-level pilot.

"Good for her." Taz was afraid it was something worse than slow healing. The whole galaxy had heard rumors of the pernicious waster's disease that afflicted too many retired Jumpers, but it wasn't something active-duty Jumpers ever talked about. "That'll give me time to finish recalibrating the animal autodoc. The other teams might need it if their dogs get hurt."

As Rylando crouched down to place the bowl on the floor, he looked up at her. "After all the repairs you've done for GSAR, you could get a job on any planet as a tech specialist once you term out of your contract."

Taz laughed. "Only if they don't care that I only follow the official instructions as a last resort."

Plans for a life after the military topped the list of favorite discussion topics in GSAR. Hardly anyone in the organization had a surviving relationship with partners or family, or even outside friends. A lot of retirement dreams centered around changing that.

A longing for rest pulled at her like high gravity. "I love the rescue mission, but most planetary response teams rely on volunteers. Sadly, grateful thank-yous from the rescued don't pay the rent." She tilted her head toward the ship-loader assist frame in the corner. "I'd have a better chance as a construction-equipment operator. Some companies like hiring telekinetics. What about you?"

His head dropped as he poured water in the bowl. "Haven't given it much thought, really. I'll see what presents itself when my contract terms out in three years."

Taz knew he was shading the truth, but she couldn't blame him for wanting to keep secrets. She had plenty of her own.

Not the least of which was that she was eligible for self-initiated transfer in six more days, which was coincidentally her thirty-ninth birthday, per standard Galactic Date and Time. If she stayed, he'd probably come to trust her more, but he'd break her heart. He'd be happier with another animal-affinity minder, not a people-loving tech-tinkerer with a historic record of epically bad relationships.

She planned to make the transfer a birthday present to herself, since no one else cared enough to celebrate it. Her heart wouldn't survive being crushed again.

He stood and rolled up the empty pouch. "Hatya thinks the CPS might invoke the 'extraordinary need' clause for the regular Minder Corps staff who are left to keep them past their contract termination dates. Show the galaxy that Ayorinn's Legacy isn't real." Turning, he tossed the pouch toward the recycling crate, but it overshot and landed on the floor. "Maybe they'll do that to us, too."

Since she was closer, she scooped up the pouch and dropped it in. "The Legacy always warps the CPS's judgment, but I can't believe they'd be that stupid." She shook her head. "Even a hydroponic moss plant would realize it'd cause even more Minder Corps staff to self-exit."

Shen, having made a splashy mess on the floor with her enthusiastic lapping, nudged Rylando's thigh with her wet muzzle. He absently caressed her ear. "Yeah, probably. How do you weigh duty versus family?"

"I'm glad I don't have to make that choice." She pointed to the totally innocent-looking cats, who were now sprawled across the flat top of the skimmer, grooming each other. "Don't let them kill any more cleaning bots. The station's civilian facility manager is starting to notice theirs are going missing."

The sound of his laughter followed her out the door. She was going to miss that man.

Halfway to her quarters, the alert tones sounded in her earwire and echoed throughout the GSAR section. Hatya's voice followed.

"Silver Team, report to Dock Bay Seven for emergency deployment to planet Perlarossa." Per protocol, the tones and announcement repeated twice more.

Taz touched her earwire as she launched into a run toward her quarters. *"Copy. Be there in ten."*

She allowed herself one moment of pining for her warm, soft bed, then started her deployment checklist. Uniform from her quarters, supplies from the lockup, gear from the storeroom, stay-awake chems from the clinic.

Questions could wait. Disasters never did.

2

Salamaray Township, Perlarossa • GDAT 3242.334

The close, familiar confines of Silver Team's box-like airsled gave Rylando the illusion of a cozy nest, if he discounted the smell of raw fuel and being surrounded by erratically blinking controls. The wide, wraparound windows of the control cab showed nothing but the shadowed and scarred shuttle wall. At least the fold-down jumpseat he'd strapped himself into gave his stiffening thighs and back a rest. He should have asked Taz to help get the animal crates into the airsled instead of doing it all himself.

He closed his eyes and took several deep, measured breaths and imagined he was breathing in the scents of summer on the dock in his favorite countryside lake. Those memories reminded him why he put up with crappy GSAR equipment and an even crappier GSAR boss. Three more standard years and he'd be free to settle there permanently instead of mostly seeing it on holos. Like most rescuers, he had a hefty amount of paid leave stacked up, but rarely got approval to use it. He'd had enough of constricting space stations and urban disaster zones to last a lifetime.

The airsled's insulation blocked the sounds but not the vibrations of atmosphere entry. Hatya's skill made the entry smoother than GSAR's regular pilots would have, but the oft-rebuilt, much-customized shuttle shook like a hellhound after a swim.

He raised his talent to connect with his animal team. Fortunately, they'd been through similar rides many times and considered them just part of their job. They'd been shaped by experience and his mental influence, but they were all unabashedly emotional creatures who operated on instinct. Part of his job was to manage his adrenaline and lead with calm.

Ordinarily, he wouldn't have brought the whole team without knowing more about the ground conditions. But he refused to leave his animals with clueless space station military staffers who couldn't tell a weasel from a wyvern. And the thought of Bhayrip finding them unguarded froze the air in his chest.

Hauling all the crates into the back made the airsled look like an overstuffed supply closet. However, it left more room in the shuttle's hold for Taz's GSAR mech suit and everything else of Silver Team's they'd crammed in. With only two human rescuers, they'd need all the extra tech they could carry to make up for their lack of staff. Too bad they'd been no room for their skimmer. Now that it was finally running right, thanks to hours of work by Taz and Hatya, Bhayrip would probably "borrow" it and Silver Team would never see it again.

"Ready for a sitrep, sir?" He didn't need the preceding identifying tone to recognize Taz's distinctive voice through the earwire. Even when she subvocalized, the low-register, sultry quality came through.

Though he and Taz held the same rank, he had seniority, making him Silver Team's nominal field commander. All that meant was his name went on reports. Taz didn't need orders from him to do her job. And not even Bhayrip was boneheaded enough to bark out orders to an active, cybernetic-enhanced Jumper who could throw him out the nearest airlock without bothering to open it.

He touched his earwire. "*Green go.*"

"*Salamaray—accent on the 'mar' part, by the way—is at the edge of a big mountain range. Southern hemisphere, early hot season. The town has maybe twenty-five thousand residents, tops, but it's the hub for the whole region of micro industries and original family compounds. The earthquake was a Geo-K 19. A strike-slip fault ripped the town in half around dawn, local time.*"

Hatya chimed in. "*Wait till you see the nav-sat images. The fault line tracks across twelve-hundred kilometers.*" Geology was one of her hobbies.

"*We'll be the first outsiders on scene,*" continued Taz. "*The planetary government's only emergency-response office is twenty thousand kilometers away, and they already used up their annual budget.*"

"*Funny, that,*" Hatya replied acerbically. "*Governments never want to spend funds on disaster prep. Then it costs 'em ten times as much when disasters actually happen.*"

"*All too true,*" said Taz. "*But to be fair, Perlarossa was settled and scammed by those RSI assholes. The High Court judgment canceled the debt, so now the planetary government has to reconstruct all the records just to know what they have. RSI sure as hell won't tell them.*"

Hatya growled. "*All settlement companies are lying, cheating manogi leaga. RSI was just greedy enough to get caught.*" Her tone made it clear that whatever she'd called them in her native language wasn't flattering.

"*Back to Salamaray,*" said Taz quickly, probably to avoid Hatya's favorite rabbit hole. "*Near as I can tell, we're being deployed because it's the hometown of High Council Leader Tsoh Yazhi Shua.*"

"*Betcha it's a twist,*" Hatya muttered darkly.

Realization dawned on Rylando. "*Hatya is right. It's a twist. Bhayrip's been lying to GSAR about the unit's staffing so they don't cut his budget allocation. GSAR thinks Silver Team has a full staff of nine because he counts my animals. High Command probably ordered the deployment to impress Leader Tsoh. Bhayrip had to comply or he'd get caught.*"

"*So that's why his orders kept harping on our advisory mission.*" Taz's disgust was plain in her tone. He could imagine the look on her expressive face.

"*Yep,*" he replied. "*And why he avoided giving us details about the rescue part.*" He snorted. "*Couldn't very well officially tell us to just pretend like we're helping.*"

Taz made a rude wet noise.

"*You two can't say it, but I can,*" said Hatya. "*My rock collection is smarter than your captain.*"

Rylando laughed. "*Thank you.*"

A minute later, Hatya's tone sounded. "*Sitrep update. Yanoshi, the ERC, gave us coordinates. You pet your sweet doggos while we ask the ERC where they want us to deploy. We're fifteen minutes from the landing zone.*"

Hatya's bluff good humor always made him smile. "*Acknowledged and confirmed.*"

With luck, the Emergency Response Commander had some background in actual emergencies. Not all did, especially in small towns.

Fortunately for Silver Team, Taz had a way with words that deflected grandstanding politicians and guided flailing leaders who were in over their heads. Diplomacy wasn't his ace.

The more he got to know Taz, the more he wondered whose tender tail she'd stepped on to land in their sorry unit. Silver Team's previous rescuers had been no loss when they'd moved on. Especially the violent asshole who'd hurt Moyo. Rylando had been doubly careful when Taz first arrived, afraid she'd be even worse.

Instead, she was everything he could hope for in a teammate. She did little things for him and the animals all the time without needing to be asked or expecting praise for it. Hatya liked her. Most importantly, his team liked her.

He used to think animals were all he'd ever need. He wasn't a top-level talent, but he could connect with just about any land animal in existence, though he preferred mammals and birds. In the last few years, however, he'd found himself longing for human companionship, too. Not just joyhouse visits for physical relief, but people he could talk to and laugh with. People he trusted to have his back. People he cared about and who cared about him.

Hatya's ready friendship had already broadened his horizons. Taz's engaging personality and easy acceptance of his animals—not to mention her sexy everything—had him dreaming of more.

But even if he miraculously dreamed up the right words to tell her, he would never speak them. A relationship would ruin both their careers. Taz took her military oath more seriously than he ever had. Besides, he had no idea if she returned his interest. Probably not, since she was a professional, unlike the rest of Unit 1051.

He selfishly wanted her to stay, but her minder talent and skills were too valuable. Whatever her previous sins, GSAR would soon forgive her. Which was why he hadn't told her that Shen had an implanted controller that—if he reactivated it—Taz could connect to using her own. He'd disabled Shen's to save her from being ordered around by the other team members, who too often treat their dogs like fur-covered animated toys. He'd guiltily come to realize Taz wouldn't do that, but told himself it was better that way. Shen would be devastated when Taz left her behind for a better post.

"*Hang on,*" said Hatya. "*Landing zone looks like a stacker fell off the building and dumped flitters everywhere. We'll have to improvise.*"

The slim white woman in a dusty russet tunic and shiny gold boots finished entering data on her tablet. "Eli! GSAR 1051 is here!" Her piercing voice made Moyo, who stood next to Rylando on the muddy, sodden grass, duck her head and rub an ear with her paw. He wished he could get away with doing the same. The hearing protection implant in his left ear was malfing, and he hadn't had time to get it fixed.

The structure behind the woman was an upside-down recycling container with a crudely cut doorway. They'd placed it on what looked like a softcrete children's playground area, which itself was surrounded by a two-meter-wide ring of permeable hardscape. Rylando gave the town extra points for a creative solution to the problem of no pop-up emergency-shelter domes.

The woman turned around and vanished inside, leaving Rylando, Taz, Moyo, and Shen standing in the hot noonday sun. Water shimmered everywhere. Apparently, the earthquake had ripped underground water pipes, which had flooded this part of town. The playground in front of them looked like a manufactured archipelago in a flat sea of soggy green.

Taz tilted her head to indicate the mountains that loomed to the northwest. The dust kicked up by the earthquake made them look foggy gray. "Planetary weather AI says the wind will pick up this afternoon. It's been a very dry year." She shook her head. "The last thing this town needs is a wildfire."

He agreed. Unfortunately, disasters didn't care what humans needed or didn't.

A booming deep voice came from inside the container. "...get someone to cut windows for the cross breeze. We're stifling in here."

A big, burly man with brown skin even darker than Hatya's and a wild shock of black and gold hair exited the doorway. He shaded his eyes from the sun, then strode toward them at the edge of the hardscape ring. "I'm Eli Yanoshi, Chief of Regional Law Enforcement. Your pilot said it's just you two and your service anim..." He glanced down at the dogs, then did a double-take at Moyo. Though she wore an official GSAR harness and vest, her party-colored fur often startled people. "We'll take all the help we can get."

Taz gave him a casual salute. "That's why we're here." She told him their names. "Are you still wanting us to check out the Citizen Activity Center?"

Yanoshi deftly tied his coils of hair in a knot on top of his head. "Yeah, like we said, we don't have high-power extraction equipment. "A sour look settled on his face. "The CAC is built like a frellin' fortress. Supposed to withstand anything up to a planet-buster bomb, but you saw the images. The two-story end collapsed like an exploration spacer on a chems binge. We hope to chaos that no one was in that part."

"How many people are likely to be in the main part of the building?" Rylando tilted his head toward their shuttle, about fifty meters back on a buckled plascrete ground-vehicle parking lot. "Our shuttle's scanners indicated seven or eight lifesigns, but the thick walls are interfering with the readings."

"Dunno." Yanoshi made a face. Behind him, the loud-voiced woman came back outside and headed their way. "The settlement company built it to be the town hall, but the government moved out decades ago. They lease some space for commercial use and run the rest like a commons. No one had reservations to use it today, but the private businesses have entry codes and can do what they want."

"Still no-go on the ground-based comms," said the woman as she approached, "but we've got satellite comms up. Pinging the outlying hubs now. Anything I should tell Planet Gov?"

"Yeah," said Yanoshi. "Tell them to evac the medical center first. RSI built that one, too. Chaos only knows what kinds of corners they cut there."

The woman nodded and went back inside.

Yanoshi brushed dust off the front of his tunic. "We've put out an area call for equipment. My husband is riding in on our farm's excavator, but it's a snail, and the roads are iffy. We can use it to start clearing some of the debris." His lips tightened briefly. "And recovering bodies."

"Are you doing okay?" asked Taz gently. "I'm guessing this kind of work isn't exactly what you signed up for."

Yanoshi blew out a gusty breath. "Yeah, I'm good. Family's okay. Our greenhouses are a total loss, but we've got savings and insurance. Good thing my husband is a plant-affinity minder, or we'd probably lose the business." He looked at Taz as if seeing her for the first time. "Thanks for asking."

She nodded respectfully, then lifted her arm to show him the rugged GSAR gauntlet-style percomp she wore. "It'd help if you share everything you can about the Citizen, uh, the CAC. Architecture specs, use plans, access codes, infrastructure, occupants, the works. We know Perlarossa construction regs, but it sounds like the settlement company built the facility before they were enacted."

Yanoshi lifted his arm to tap on his similarly styled gauntlet. "I'll send what we have now and more as we find it. Unfortunately, because the CAC was supposed to be our designated emergency-relocation facility, it also housed the regional hub for comms. Data access is slow as an ice flow until we stand up a replacement. A lot of little towns around here rely on us for comms, too. Planet Gov—that's Perlarossa government—is reallocating someone else's backup unit for us."

Rylando made a snap decision. "We have an extra standalone hub we won't need. It's old, but it's got extra capacity and range. You're welcome to borrow it."

"Yeah?" Yanoshi's eyes narrowed. "What's *that* gonna cost?" He blinked, then ducked his head. "Sorry, that was... It's just that GSAR is part of the Citizen Protection Service, and we haven't had... They don't usually, er, share unless there's something in it for them."

Taz waved his apology away. "It's okay. GSAR is outside the CPS's core chain of command. Some days, we're not fans of our agency, either. The hub is a spare. But we'll need it back when we leave." She twitched a smile at him. "Our boss gets a little salty when our tech doesn't come back with us."

"Deal," said Yanoshi. "We should only need it for twelve, maybe eighteen hours at the most. Planet Gov promised to deliver ours by the end of the day."

Shen bumped his knee. Rylando could feel her need to do something besides stand in the water and listen to humans chatter. "We thought we'd set up our temporary base on the Center's front courtyard. Does that work for you?"

Yanoshi cast a dubious glance toward the big shuttle. "The fault really tore up that section of town." He snorted. "This is supposed to be a geologically stable ancient lakebed, but we've already had two aftershocks."

"How about we take our airsled for a quick survey?" asked Taz. "That'll give you time to get the hub unloaded. Our Captain Wa'ara can sort it for you."

"Works for me," replied Yanoshi.

Thirty minutes later, Rylando sealed the entrance to the sturdy pop-up dome that was their new temporary command center. The lock was keyed to only GSAR Unit 1051 personnel, which thwarted would-be looters or overreaching local incident commanders. Only one small area near the target building was flat enough to set it up. The rest looked like a road glass recycling yard.

He'd already rigged the animal team with their working harnesses and collars, then slipped into his own red harness with light armor and tech. Taz wore her GSAR-issue, fully enclosed, armored, tech-powered assist frame, popularly known as a mech suit.

In the GSAR publicity vids, the gleaming, streamlined mech suit was obviously modeled after the Jumper combat version. It looked nothing like the real ones used in the field. Instead of shoulder-mounted hellrail guns, GSAR mech suits had grappling and construction tools, plus a variety of hooks and straps for holding more gear. Shiny coatings never lasted beyond the first few rescue deployments. Each user customized their suit according to their own preferences and skills. With Taz's enviable gift for tech and eye for decoration, hers was practically a work of art.

Rylando tapped his earwire. *"Did you find a place for the shuttle?"*

"About that," replied Hatya. *"I know you really need a third, but I have to fall out of line for this operation. I'd probably be the one needing rescue."*

Concern shot through him. Jumpers thought of themselves as invincible. That Hatya was taking herself off the front battle line meant she was seriously compromised. *"Your leg and hip again?"*

"Yeah. Too much sitting, I guess. Even if I used the cargo lift frame we brought, my new cybernetic controller might lock up. 'Improved version,' my ass."

He hated hearing the thread of guilt in her tone. *"We'll be fine. Just a quick in and out."* Or so he hoped.

Taz chimed in. *"Considering the town probably doesn't have many undamaged flitters right now, I bet they'd be grateful for use of the shuttle and your skills."*

"Okay, I'll ping Yanoshi and trade him volunteer time for a full tank of fresh water. Keep in touch."

"Copy that," Rylando replied. *"We're green-go here. See you soon."*

3

Salamaray Citizen Activity Center, Perlarossa • GDAT 3242.334

Taz noted with wry amusement that the CAC building looked no better close up than it did from a distance. Adding texture to utilitarian blocks made them look like construction-print rejects.

Because her armor was better protection than what the airsled offered Rylando and the animals, she led the way through the wide entrance. The building's AI answered her queries with variations on "please try later," so she ran every scan her suit could manage the moment she got inside the meter-thick walls. Being buried alive under a failing roof would absolutely ruin her day.

The architectural schematics labeled the long, cavernous space beyond the wide entrance as the Grand Foyer. It looked more like a retro transport depot. She took it as a good sign that all the interior lights still worked, not just the glowing emergency beacons. Functional life-support systems were always a bonus.

While connected to her suit, she didn't need to tap her earwire to talk to Rylando over their GSAR secure net. *"My scans say this end of the structure is sound. Lifesigns are clustered in an area leased to a business called Eye-Fire-Mind. The doorway in the northwest corner of this room should be a hallway that leads to it."*

She switched on her top torch and aimed it toward the hallway. Dust swirled in and out of the light beam, suggesting the ventilation system was still working.

"My scans say the same." The suit's superior tech made his voice sound like he stood right next to her. *"Let's proceed."*

Turning to her right, she crossed toward the target hallway. *"That's odd. In this part of the building, at least, my scans say the subfloor is made of incalloy."*

"Mine, too. Yanoshi did say it was built like a fortress."

Taz made a rude noise. *"Starships need incalloy for transit space. Space stations need it for the gravity layer. Terrestrial buildings in small towns don't need incalloy anything."* She made a scornful sound as she stepped over a pile of glass that might have once been a sculpture. *"Unless RSI installed it so they could run up the settlement debt."*

He laughed. *"You've been talking to Hatya."*

"She did send me... Oh, hell, the hallway's blocked." She read the scan results. *"Three interior wall units collapsed into the hall. At least it's wide enough to maneuver in. Ceiling is solid but tight for the sled. Floor is solid. I can clear the debris and you can follow, or we can look for another way in."* She couldn't resist teasing him. *"What are your orders, exalted Field Commander, sir?"*

"Clearing it will be faster." After a pause, he added, *"And I'm demoting you if you keep calling me that."*

She grinned at his grumpy tone. *"Yes, sir. I'll make a note, sir."*

Stepping into the hall, she extended her straight forks and slid them under the first large section of tilted wall. As she lifted it, she used her teke talent to clear material from the separation point to give it room to tilt inward, away from the passage. Thankfully, only one had cracked into several pieces. The rest of the wall units were modern and modular, rather than the monolithic, chisel-textured denscrete blocks that made up the exterior.

Mindful of the taller, wider airsled behind her, she monitored the scans to make sure her actions weren't causing unintended problems for her teammates, human or otherwise. The airsled had one bad propulsion coil and two marginal coils, so it wasn't as fast or maneuverable as it should be.

"*Architectural plan updates just came from the town.*"

She finished pushing aside debris. "*Anything new about our search target? The building's AI is still traumatized, I think.*" The technical term was "crisis fallback basic state," but to her, its disoriented responses sounded like humans who'd gone into tunnel-vision survival mode.

"*Yeah, the space used to belong to a financial firm. Looks like our lifesigns are together in what used to be a four-meter-square datavault. Multiple air vents. Used to have its own chiller, but that might be gone now.*"

"*Good shelter in an earthquake.*" She pulled in the updated schematics to look for herself. "*Left at the upcoming intersection, then forty meters west to the door.*"

"*Concur. Proceed.*"

One of the first things she'd noticed about Rylando was his similar respect for field safety and communication protocol without going overboard. It was a welcome pleasure to finally work with someone she synced with. And look at her, mooning over that someone instead of paying attention to her job.

Retracting her suit to as small a profile as possible, she stepped into the intersection and ran scans and visuals. "*One more downed wall. Ceiling's still stable. Just a cheap install job on the wall sections, I think.*"

"*Probably. Based on the number of overlays and changeouts on the plans, the interior has been reconfigured dozens of times since the local government moved out.*"

"*I wouldn't rent here even if it was free. Too depressing. No natural light at all, not even piped in.*" She lifted the wall up and tilted it out of the way. "*Clear.*"

"*Agree and proceed. Moyo smells recent human scents.*"

"*Good. Looks like the business has an external wallcomp for visitors. Want to try it, or barge right in?*"

"*Let's knock first.*" Humor laced his voice. "*One trauma per day for them is probably enough.*"

She moved farther down the hallway so Rylando could glide the airsled into position. He hovered in front of the wallcomp and pinged it. His amplified voice rang out. "Hello. Subcaptains Delroinn and Correa from Galactic Search and Rescue. Do you need assistance?"

The response came fast. "*Oh, hell yes, we need assistance. We're stuck in the storeroom and the door is jammed. We've been here for six hours, no comms.*"

The mid-pitched voice had a Spanish accent and sounded more peeved than panicked.

Taz guessed the current business converted the datavault into a storeroom.

Rylando spoke into the wallcomp. "How many people are with you, and is anyone hurt?"

"*We are six adults, one teenager, and one toddler,*" said a softer, higher voice with a Standard English accent and a businesslike tone. "*Instructor Nadryer broke her leg and cannot walk. Everyone else is well.*"

Rylando nodded. "We're outside your main entrance and are coming for you now. As a precaution, please get as far away from the storeroom door as you can."

Taz stayed where she was as Rylando backed up the airsled a few meters, then grounded it, got out, and pointed toward the door. "While you get us in, I'll get the med pack and team ready."

"Copy," she said, letting her suit amplify her voice. It had taken her years to remember that people couldn't see her nodding her head while she was encased in petroplas and metal.

Thanks to the GSAR rescuers' exclusive access to a vast collection of security-system emergency keys and overrides, it only took her a few moments to breach the business's front door and duck inside. Outside of the gallant hearts of the rescuers, those keys were probably GSAR's most valuable asset.

Other than the corner to Taz's right, which was occupied by a huge, grey denscrete block that looked like it had crashed through the ceiling, the rest of the room seemed inviting. Soothing colors, real springwood floors, mirrored walls. A scattering of shoes, plus upended tables with broken crockery under them and disarrayed cushions made it look like the aftermath of an exuberant pillow fight.

Shen, Moyo, and Rylando followed right after her. Moyo planted herself in front of what looked like a vault door to what was now the storeroom, nose to the seam where it met the floor. The hellhound loved meeting new people.

Shen made a lightning-fast run around the room and disappeared into what the plans said should be a kitchen, then returned to sit next to Rylando's foot and look up at him alertly. He smiled and patted her head. "Yes, Shen, people will soon need herding."

Taz laughed. "She loves having someone to look after, doesn't she?"

"Yes," Rylando agreed with amusement, "and telling them what to do."

Her suit flashed an alert. "My scans say the door is a standard internal pivot-hinge. The frame is bent at the upper left corner. I think I can straighten it enough to free the door."

He nodded. "Anything above us we should know about?"

She checked the plans as she focused deep scans upward. "Roof is solid denscrete and intact." She pointed to the block that had cratered a hole in the corner. "I don't know where that came from. Building headspace storage, maybe? Nothing on the plans." She stepped closer and extended her mech suit's vertical jacks. "Please ask Moyo to move for a minute."

Rylando and Shen stepped back into the middle of the room.

Moyo rose and crossed to stand beside them, but her attention remained on the door.

The jacks snugged into the doorframe, then slowly expanded to lift pressure off the frame. She kept an eye on the ceiling scans. At the bottom, the springwood buckled and splintered, but the plascrete subfloor held. The moment the readings said the frame evened out, she hammered the door once on the non-hinged side. It bounced open with a crash. Only her armored fist stopped it from unhelpfully banging closed again.

When she retracted the jacks, the frame sank, but held firm. The thick vault door would probably never close again. "Scans clear." She marched backward four long steps and stopped.

Before Rylando could move, a bronze-haired man came out of the storeroom. Once away from the door, he bent over, breathing deep. "*Grácias a Diós para aire fresco!*" Probably the source of the Spanish-accented voice from their first contact. Sweat rings dampened the armpits of his casual green tunic.

Taz knew the storeroom had plenty of fresh air, or they'd have all been unconscious, but the stress of the situation had probably made it seem stuffy.

Rylando moved closer to the opening. "I'm coming in with medical equipment. I have two trained rescue dogs with me. If it's okay, they'd like to make friends."

"Yes, of course," said a soft, feminine voice from within.

Taz stayed in her suit but retracted her helmet. Distressed people responded better to a human face than a hunk of metal, even though she'd printed flower designs on the outside.

Within a few minutes, five barefoot adults and one barefoot teenager carrying a clingy toddler stood in the main room. Taz's scans said none had major injuries, but she'd prefer to confirm that with the better medical scanner from Rylando's medical pack.

Shen ran through the group like they were an agility course, then vanished into the storeroom after Rylando. Cheerful, friendly Moyo circled the group slowly. When she caught someone's eye, she sidled closer. People found themselves smiling and petting the big, goofy head before they realized she'd suckered them into it.

Zero-heads like Captain Bhayrip thought any animals were a nuisance. In Taz's opinion, teams like Rylando's should be a part of every rescue involving people.

The soft-voiced, brown-skinned woman wearing a loose tunic and pants introduced herself as Vangelio, the co-instructor of a meditation class. Her serene nature seemed to be a good influence on the others, though it might also be her active empath talent.

Taz had no intention of asking. For one, the woman's talent helped the other victims as much as Moyo did, especially people like the claustrophobic man. For another, despite a decade's accumulation of Central Galactic Concordance anti-discrimination laws, experienced minders didn't announce their talents to strangers. Just like Taz had never admitted to anyone that she was more than just the telekinetic the CPS thought. She was also a sifter.

That talent had shown up several years after her teke, long after her CPS testing and training ended. Once she'd realized she wasn't warping toward delusional, she'd secretly researched how to use it. She'd gotten pretty good at telling when someone was lying or about to get violent, and could usually sense activated minder talents in others if she was close enough. However, she tanked at being able to affect the brain chemistry in anyone.

High-level sifters could dope people to insensible, or flood them with happy hormones like they'd taken la-la chems, or make them trusting and talkative during interrogations. She could barely sense brain receptors at all. Her trauma-medicine training hadn't addressed the nuances of neurotransmitters and hormone generation.

She didn't dare ask the CPS, either, or they'd put her on heavier minder drugs that required more stringent monitoring. Her current drug-evasion method of taking the drugs, getting tested, then dosing herself with a black-market reverse wouldn't work if they checked more frequently than once every hundred days.

Rylando's tone sounded in her earwire. *"Could you call in the floater? Casualty is a female, broken leg and dislocated hip. Tried to heal herself with her minder talent and nauseated herself.*"

"*Will do,*" Taz subvocalized. "*In the meantime, I'll get names for the records.*"

"*Good idea.*"

Sending detailed navigation instructions to the self-propelled emergency-medical capsule waiting outside only took a few seconds. Once she stepped out of her mech suit, she realized she had a rapt audience in the teenager, who'd handed the toddler off to what looked like the mother.

She grinned. "If we have time, I'll show you how it works."

The boy started to nod, then glanced toward this bronze-haired man and dropped his gaze.

"Is that a hellhound?" asked the woman now holding the toddler. A Spanish accent softened her consonants. "Such bright colors."

Taz chuckled. "I know, right? Subcaptain Delroinn says she's a teenager experimenting with her style." Rylando traded with the commercial body parlor on the space station to keep Moyo from looking like a nightmare menace. He said it hurt Moyo's feelings when people were scared of her.

The actual teenager in the room, whose hair and glittery surface skin art put dazzling interstellar spectra to shame, rolled his eyes.

Taz spoke to the group. "We've got a med capsule coming for Instructor Nadryer. In the meantime, can I send your names and ping refs to the town's Emergency Response Command?" She held up her gauntlet percomp and set it to record. "They'll get posted to the regional status hub so if anyone's looking for you, they'll know you're okay."

One by one, they spoke their information. Unsurprisingly, the bronze-haired man turned out to be the father of the teenager and the toddler and cohab to the toddler's mother.

Taz looked at their bare feet. "Stay there a second while I collect your shoes. The airsled can't carry you all, so a couple of you will have to walk, and the entrance area has a lot of broken glass."

The lavender-skinned intersex person in the group laughed sardonically. "I hope it's the remains of that ugly-ass monstrosity from RSI that was supposed to represent Perlarossa as a pink pearl in a cosmic clamshell."

"Yes," said the Russian-accented, green-haired woman in flowing, summery clothes that Taz envied. GSAR's distinctive yellow and red uniforms were flexin-armored and tough as incalloy. They weren't cool or comfortable. "But not as ugly as the company that would have stolen all our family compounds if it could."

Taz gathered all the footwear she could find and let the group sort them out. The toddler refused to wear hers and threatened a tantrum. A few moments after Vangelio activated her empath talent, the little girl settled down and let her brother help her.

For several seconds, the room lights flickered, and the subtle sounds from the air vents stuttered.

A shadow crossed Vangelio's expression. "That shouldn't have happened. This building has its own independent power source. It's one of the reasons we chose it."

Keeping her own concern off her face, Taz pointed to the business's wide-open front door. "We've already cleared the path, and we've got floodlights, even if the emergency lighting fails." She turned to the rest of the group. "Did any of you see anyone else in the building this morning before the earthquake?"

The adults shook their heads, but the teenager spoke up. "When I was in the hall with Hermanita, a girl in a big coat asked me where the lifts down to the commercial basement storage units are. I told her."

"What time was that?" asked Taz.

The boy shrugged. "Zero-five-fifteen? Hermanita quit fussing, so we went back inside."

Taz didn't know much about the boy, but she was impressed that he was up and awake at that hour. In her own youth, she'd needed at least ten hours of sleep, and mornings had been torture.

She used her controller implant to tell her suit to scan in the direction of the lifts. The architectural plans hadn't even hinted that the vague "basement storage" label actually meant individual units that could be rented or accessed any time.

Unfortunately, from her current location, the lifesign scans were inconclusive because of the denscrete construction and the damned incalloy. Turning her back on the group, she pinged Rylando and subvocalized what she'd learned.

"Trade places with me. I'll send the team out for a quick scouting mission while you get our wounded into the floater. I already asked Hatya to find out about the building's power situation."

Movement outside the entrance caught her eye. *"Floater just arrived. I'll bring it in now."*

The capsule was about the size of her mech suit, so it fit through the storeroom's doorway, but with little room to spare.

When Rylando stood and strode out, Shen hesitated at the entrance, head swinging back and forth, like she couldn't decide whether she should follow him or stay with the injured woman.

"Go on, Shen," Taz said quietly, pointing toward the door. "I won't let anything happen to her."

It was probably just coincidence that Shen barked as if in response, then took off to catch up with Rylando.

As Taz knelt, the woman caught her eye. "Sorry I'm such a stinking mess."

Someone had put a sweater under the woman's head for a pillow. The source of the smell stained the front of her cloud-patterned blue tunic.

"You're fine. A little vomit isn't too bad. The capsule will neutralize the smell." Taz smiled gently as she picked up the scanner that Rylando had left out by the medical pack. "I'm Subcaptain Correa, by the way. You're Instructor Nadryer?"

"Yes." Tears fell from the woman's eyes. "I'm a terrible example for my students."

"I'm pretty sure they'll understand." She checked the scanner's readings on her patient's injuries. "I can't lift you without causing you pain. I'd like to give you a quick-acting pain patch first."

Nadryer shook her head. "No, no, they don't work on me. My talent..." More tears fell. "I should never have tried to slow that block. Exhausted myself and tripped in the hole. No energy left to heal with, and now I'm blowback sick. I just wanted to save our really expensive floor. Stupid."

If the woman had been using her talents, Taz might have realized sooner that she must be a multi-talent minder. "You don't have to answer, but are you a sifter? I can use a neural pain block instead. Invasive because of the microneedles and takes a little longer, but no brain chems involved. You'll lose sensation below the waist."

"Yes, do it." replied Nadryer. "Is it against GSAR rules to use your sifter talent on me? I feel like I'm on a neuro thrill ride. It's making my pain worse, too."

Taz blinked at the woman's matter-of-fact request. "I'm sorry, I can't."

"Fucking CPS." Nadryer gave a watery sigh. "Why even hire minders if they won't let them work?"

Taz slipped her hand under Nadryer's back to center the neuro block over her cervical spine. Maybe because of the skin-to-skin contact, she thought she could sense the imbalanced neurotransmitters and the flailing receptors. Sort of like a subtle version of the haze of impending violence, but chaotic, like misfiring electrical nodes in a tech circuit.

On impulse, Taz leaned closer and lowered her voice. "I can't help because I don't know how. Besides, I'm low-level at best."

Nadryer's eyes widened for a moment. "Whoever told you that was full of shit." Her expression softened as she studied Taz's face. "Want a quick lesson? We advertise meditation classes, but what we really do is train minders. The CPS's methods don't work for everyone."

Taz had no idea there was such a thing as private minder tutoring. "Thank you, but not right now. You need all your energy for yourself."

A weak smile played on Nadryer's face. "I wouldn't be spending the energy, you would. Healers can sometimes work on themselves, but sifters can't. Like trying to tickle yourself." A moment later, she sighed again. More tears flowed. "Ah, that's better."

The relief on Nadryer's face told Taz the neuro block finally kicked in. She grounded and opened the capsule right next to Nadryer so it wouldn't skitter away like a cat that wanted to be admired but not touched.

Nadryer's forehead wrinkled. "Wonder what happened to my boots?"

"Instructor Vangelio has them." Taz slid a fat safety strap from the capsule under the woman's waist and hooked it around her. "I'm going to lift and slide you into the capsule, rather than roll you in. It'll help if you cross your arms tight and keep your back strong instead of saggy."

A corner of Nadryer's mouth lifted in amusement. "Saggy?"

"Technical term. Used by rescuers everywhere." Taz took a centering breath, then used her telekinetic talent to ease the woman into the capsule. It took concentration to keep her floppy legs in line with the rest of her body.

Nadryer lifted her hand to touch the top of the capsule.

Taz nudged the woman's hips in to center them. "Being in a capsule is like being in an autodoc that flies. I'll tell it about the neuro block and that you're, er, allergic to receptor-type painkillers. When I seal the door, it'll insert a billion microneedles, scan your injuries, and take you to the nearest accepting medic center. Any questions?"

"No." Unexpectedly, the woman grabbed Taz's hand. "Thank you. Get training for your sifter talent. It's at least as strong as your teke talent."

"I will," Taz agreed reflexively, then remembered the woman was another sifter who could detect half-truths. "I'll consider it." But not while she was still in the CPS, where a telepath could interrogate her anytime they wanted if they thought she was hiding something like that. As it was, she was alarmed the woman had sensed her unactivated sifter talent without even trying.

Taz extracted her hand, entered data into the capsule's controller, then sealed it up. Nadryer's face, visible through the viewport, relaxed to unconsciousness after a few seconds.

Just as she was guiding the capsule out the storeroom door and into the main area, the lights flickered again. Nearly ten seconds this time. Not a good sign.

Rylando crossed to her. "New lifesign near the lifts." His finger brushed his nose and chin, meaning the lifesign came via one of his animals, not tech. He started to speak, then appeared to think better of it. "Let's get this group safe, then check out the lifts."

"Apologies for interrupting, sirs," said Instructor Vangelio, "but we know the way out, and you said it's clear. Your skills are needed that way." She pointed in the direction of the lifts. "Someone is growing very fearful."

Rylando's gaze drifted and lost focus for a long moment. He turned toward the group with sudden energy. "We accept your offer. Watch the glass in the front foyer. Your flitters, if that's how you got here, are inaccessible right now. Head for the park about a kilometer east. Emergency Response Command will get you sorted." He squeezed past Taz to enter the storeroom.

As Vangelio herded her students out just as effectively as Shen would have, Rylando came back with the medical pack slung over his shoulder.

"Orders?" she asked.

"Suit up and follow me. A young human female is dangling from something thin at the bottom of an open lift shaft."

4

Salamaray Citizen Activity Center, Perlarossa • GDAT 3242.334

From hard-won experience, Rylando knew not to trust the airsled's self-navigation capability in an unknown structure. Taz and Hatya said the much-patched AI needed total reconstruction from its neural net on up. Considering GSAR's budget woes, there was a less than zero chance of that.

Unfortunately, it meant he couldn't both operate the airsled and keep in mental contact with his animal team. He trusted them not to create havoc, but sometimes they let their mission get in the way of their good sense.

He wasn't much better. Though she hid it well, he knew Taz disliked being underground. He'd instinctively wanted to save her from having to descend into a deep shaft by sending her with the group they'd freed. Not only was it against the regs—and common sense—to operate solo, but she'd have been deeply insulted. And rightly so.

It came down to trusting her to tell him if she couldn't handle something. And hoping she trusted him enough to admit it. The trouble was, considering how diligently he'd kept her at a distance, first out of wariness, then while fighting his fascination, he wasn't sure he'd earned that trust.

The wide hallway opened into a wider area that served as the lift lobby. At least the building plans proved accurate about the location of the lift shaft, but neglected to note the fact that it was at least three times larger than usual.

He slowed the airsled to a hover and triggered its scanners.

The lift's sliding doors should have been closed, not gaping open to expose the shaft below. To the left sat Shen and Moyo, both watching him and Taz for orders. A quick check with his talent told him the cats were around the corner in the far hallway, investigating an interesting smell.

On the walls, static directional displays showed maps and listed occupants in that section of the L-shaped building. A separate display advertised the storage business in the basement, listing the features and prices for their units and reminded existing customers to use their access token to operate the lift. Too bad the building AI wasn't speaking to Taz, or they could have queried it about the number of token uses that morning.

Pieces of the patterned ceiling littered the floor, especially near the dimly lit shaft.

Taz's tone sounded in his earwire. "*My scans say the decorative ceiling layer isn't stable, but it's thin. The denscrete above it is solid. I might be getting more lifesigns below ground to the west, but it could be echoes. The lift shaft is lined with more incalloy.*"

The airsled's results came back a moment later. "*My scans confirm.*" He was more inclined to agree with Taz's theory about the settlement company running up the planet's debt. It would have been cheaper to line the shaft with rainbow corundum crystals set in hand-wrought filigree.

He eased the airsled forward and grounded it. At his request,

Moyo and Shen trotted over and jumped in the open side door. The two cats agreed to think about it.

Taz crossed straight to the shaft opening, crouched, and extended her shoulder camera array and floodlight pointed down. "Hello! Subcaptains Correa and Delroinn from Galactic Search and Rescue. Do you need assistance?" Her suit-amplified words echoed on the hard walls.

"Yes! I'm stuck down here. You must help my father, too!" The faint German-accented voice sounded like it might come from the teenage girl he'd seen in Moyo's memory. He increased the sound detection on his console.

"Is your father with you?" asked Taz.

"No, he's in the storage section. I hope. When the earthquake hit, the frelling lift took me all the way below the basement and wouldn't move. When the wallcomp wouldn't wake up and I couldn't get comms on my percomp, I climbed to the top of the car and opened the service access. But I'm too short to reach the service ladder."

Taz's words echoed again. "Is anyone else with you? Are you hurt?"

Rylando brought up the holo image and readouts from Taz's cameras. No wonder the girl's voice had sounded faint. The shaft bottom, which should have only been five or six meters, was almost twenty meters deep.

A girl with intricately braided but dusty hair and light brown skin looked up. Her long-sleeved coat puffed out on all sides. He'd have thought it was too hot to wear for summer, but fashionable civilian clothing baffled him. In GSAR, he had a choice of formal military dress greys, rescuer yellow and red, or sleep pants. He wasn't ever off-duty long enough to make it worth owning anything else.

"Not really. I fell on my butt when my belt broke." She pointed to the bottom rung of the service ladder, well above her head, where a short length of strap still dangled. He gave her points for trying.

"Okay," replied Taz. "Let's get you free first. Then we'll go for your parent. What's your name?"

"Jhidelle Barallone. My father is Xolor Stramlo."

Taz's voice came through his earwire. "*The sled will fit in the shaft with plenty of room to spare. You could fly her up while I climb down a few meters to see if I can get better readings on the lifesigns.*"

"*Do it.*"

The lights flickered several times, then steadied. He couldn't tell if it affected what should have been always-on emergency lights in the lift shaft. Current construction codes required bright lights with independent thousand-year power sources. No telling what a flagrantly corner-cutting settlement company had used a century ago.

Hatya's tone pinged. "*Silver Team status check. I'm a glorified autocab. Just dropped off medics and supplies at the ERC.*"

As usual, thirty minutes went by fast in rescue situations. His percomp would have reminded him if Hatya hadn't initiated the check-in first. He touched his earwire. "*We're good so far. Cleared our initial target. Six and a half lifesigns headed for the ERC and one evac capsule headed for the medics. No recoveries needed.*"

"*That's good,*" replied Hatya. "*I hate cremation duty.*"

"*Sync that.*" Rylando hated attending memorial services for the dead, too. They made him feel guilty for not having saved them. "*We have detailed building scans to share with the ERC, too. Should help them with repairs.*"

"*Speaking of scans,*" said Taz, "*are you near enough to deep-scan from the shuttle? We think we might have multiple lifesigns in the basement, but it's denscrete and heavy metal construction. We're at the lift lobby now.*"

"*I'm already in the air. Be there in two,*" replied. Hatya. "*Meanwhile, I sent you as-built records and occupants for the building. No one can explain the power glitches.*"

Rylando confirmed the new data and pinged acknowledgement as he watched Phobos and Deimos stroll across the lobby and jump into the airsled.

"Baskets," he told his team, and reinforced it with the hand sign. They jumped into their respective crates without a fuss, though Phobos chose to stay with Deimos instead of going to his own. Rylando sent them all the mental equivalent of a quick pat of praise.

All the animals suddenly stood up. Phobos meowed and Lerox gave a low warning grunt. Mariposa, the little owl, woke and rocked side to side on her perch. Moments later, a low vibration rumbled beneath him. He leaned out the airsled's open door and shouted, "Aftershock!" then closed it.

Taz scuttled back from the shaft opening and maintained her crouch. The walls swayed. More pieces from the ceiling dropped onto the airsled's roof and the floor.

Six seconds later, the vibration and swaying faded to nothing.

Rylando sent reassuring thoughts to the rest of the team as he threaded his way past the equipment to the back. He opened Otak's crate and gently slid the tense rat into the low chest sling he wore under the harness. The other animals would be all right in a few minutes, but Otak needed warm physical contact to climb out of his spiral of panic.

Outside, he heard Taz's amplified voice. "Jhidelle, are you okay down there?" On the console's display, holographic Taz rose to her feet and stepped toward the shaft, though not as close as she'd been before.

The airsled's console amplified the reply. "*Ja, ja,* I'm fine. Just more dust."

Hatya pinged again. "*Confirming your lifesign readings. Three clustered about seventy-five meters west of the airsled. Never seen a whole community building of incalloy. What did the builders do, salvage a crash-landed interstellar freighter for construction materials?*"

Taz described their plan of action to the girl while Rylando lifted the airsled to glide slowly to the opening.

"*You go first.*" She pointed to the shaft. "*Don't scrape me off the service ladder on your way back up.*"

"*I won't.*"

Carefully easing into the shaft, he let the airsled sink slowly. He kept his scans running realtime in case the metal walls hid unexpected damage.

The shaft could have fit two more big sleds like his. Maybe the architect planned the lift to hold a hundred people at a time, to fulfill the CAC's alternate purpose as the town's emergency shelter.

He keyed the airsled's amplifier. "Jhidelle, I'll land at the far side. Please stay where you are near the ladder until I open the side door for you."

Keeping a steady pace, he glanced at his cameras to see Taz in her suit climbing down. She made it look so easy to adapt her human motive agility to the tech. The only time he'd tried on a mech suit, he'd tripped over his own two feet and done serious damage to the commander's favorite shuttle.

Landing on the roof of the lift car proved impossible. What he'd taken for a dusty solid surface was actually a warp mesh that couldn't handle the weight of the airsled and would snare the runners. He set the sled to a stable hover and opened the side door. Holding onto the sidebar with one hand, he leaned out and beckoned Jhidelle. "Come on." If the third power coil wasn't so bad, he wouldn't have had to yell so loud to be heard over their vibration.

She clutched her coat lapels with one hand and walked quickly toward the airsled. He gave her a hand up and pointed her toward the jump seat. "Pull that down and web in."

Moyo stood in her crate, tail wagging, making a soft snuffling noise. Jhidelle's head snapped to the back. Her eyes widened as they darted to each crate.

"They're our trained rescue team," he told her and pointed to each. "Moyo, Shen, Phobos, Deimos, Mariposa, and Lerox."

The animals were clearly as fascinated by her as she was them.

Taz's tone sounded in his earwire. "*I'm halfway down. I think this shaft is twisted five or six degrees, which is probably why the lift grounded itself. Some of the service ladder rungs have popped their*" anchors. *My scans agree with Hatya's on where the lifesigns are. The basement hallway seems clear, and it's big. Maybe the lifesigns are stuck in one of the storage units? Hatya's updated records say each unit has its own life-support system, but they depend on the building's independent power."*

"*Which is glitching,*" he subvocalized.

Waving to get Jhidelle's attention, he pointed to the side of the jump seat. "Web in. Safety rules. Sit sideways so there's room for your feet."

"*I recommend we get the others now,*" said Taz, "*rather than making a second trip.*"

After making sure Jhidelle hooked the web all the way, he squeezed by the tall equipment cases to stand at the front controls. "*With only two good coils instead of three, we might have to make a second trip anyway, if the lifesigns are heavy. As it is, we'll have to re-stack the crates, or hook one to the roof.*" The airsled's scans agreed with Taz's and Hatya's. "*Let's try it.*"

"*Copy that. Meet you in the hallway.*"

Since the girl was webbed in, he didn't bother closing the side door as he slowly raised the airsled up the shaft twelve meters, then eased it into the wide-open doors of the basement hallway. Simple hovering was easier on the coils than grounding and lift-off, so he floated in place a half meter off the floor.

Scans didn't stress the coils, either, so he ran the full array. A series of at least twenty or thirty light-ringed doors lined the hallway, each with the company's logo and a number, an impressive-looking lock, and a nearby wallcomp. Seen from this perspective, the building was a lot bigger than it had looked upstairs, and this was the short end of its L-shape.

Taz swung into Rylando's holo camera view a moment later, as if she'd used anti-gravity to get to the hallway entrance. Her floodlights turned off as she walked to stand next to the airsled's open door. All he could see out the door was her suit's knees to her shoulders.

He turned to look at his passenger. "Which storage unit will your father be in? And do you know who's with him?"

"I don't know," replied the girl, sounding miserable and worried.

In the sling on his chest, Otak abruptly turned around and stuck his head out toward the open door, nose quivering. Rylando lightly connected to the big rat's thought stream. The reason for Otak's alert was unsettling.

Turning back to the controls, he reached up to tap his earwire to tell Taz, then hesitated. Would she take him seriously, or would she be like most of the unit and their boss and call him deluded? He made himself touch his earwire and subvocalize anyway. *"Otak's nose says this corridor has traces of explosives. Likely Kem-X."*

Time stood still until she replied.

"Acknowledged. Give Otak an extra treat for me. I'll do chem scans along with the rest so we can report it. Let's free our targets and jet out."

Relief gave him back his ability to breathe. *"Good. Yes. Right."* Apparently, it also made him sound like a fluffhead.

He turned to take Otak back to his crate when movement caught his eye. Jhidelle's big puffy coat was squirming. Extending his talent told him why.

Giving Jhidelle a raised eyebrow, he pointed to her middle. "Perhaps you should open your coat so your animals can get some fresh air."

She froze, then shook her head. Finally, her expression fell, and she opened her coat. In a cleverly crafted vest with pouches, she carried two small animals. "Father doesn't like them, but I couldn't leave them behind." She pointed to a red-furred face with ears twice as big. "This is Farenoso. He's a Fennec fox." She stroked the brown, large-eyed creature. "This is Tzima. She's a kinkajou."

He couldn't very well fault her for something he would have done as a kid. Actually, considering the crates in the back and the rat nestled against his chest, something he still did. Which made him realize Jhidelle and he might have more in common than he thought. Reaching out to her pets confirmed his suspicion. She was an animal-affinity minder. In their minds, he felt her presence as a kind of extra energy.

While it was unlikely the girl had bad intentions, he kicked himself for not realizing the reason for his own team's heightened interest in her. A higher-level talent could override his connection to his animals. He'd done his best to train them to resist and escape, but they could still be forced to do things against their will.

Taz swore. "*I lost my connection to Hatya. How about you?*"

Returning to the front console, he checked the readout. "*I still have thin band. Considering how thick the denscrete is above us, I bet I'll lose all comms when I go farther down the hallway and out of bounce range.*"

Taz growled. "*This is ridiculous. As soon as we get back, I'm upgrading my suit comms out of my own savings. GSAR Tech Sec will have to catch me.*"

They wouldn't. While the Tech Security division was notorious for confiscating unauthorized tech, it was also the most understaffed and under-funded division in GSAR.

"*I'll send Hatya a ping with our plans, with a status check in thirty.*"

"*Copy. I'll scout for our target.*" She snorted. "*At least our earwires still work down here.*" She took off with a distance-eating stride.

He sent the comms packet and nudged the airsled forward to follow.

Taz was already activating the first storage unit's wallcomp by the time he caught up with her.

The overhead lighting flickered twice, then went out. The residual glow from light-ringed doors and the wallcomps died a moment later.

Their only illumination in the hallway came from the airsled and Taz's suit.

5

Salamaray Citizen Activity Center, Perlarossa • GDAT 3242.334

Taz used to think being trapped in a cave two kilometers below ground was the worst rescue environment, but this basement was making her rethink that. She uttered a vile curse.

"*Copy that,*" replied Rylando dryly. "*Otak is still alerting on explosives. Can't think of many benign reasons they'd be here.*"

"*This day keeps getting better, doesn't it?*" Her scans confirmed three lifesigns behind door number 77.

Theoretically, the units should have egress provisions for sticky situations, but with this jinxed building, who knew?

She knocked three times on the heavy door with her fist. No answer, but she wasn't sure she'd hear them through the thick door plates. Just as she was about to deploy her plasma cutter, the lights blinked on. The door and wallcomp lights glowed bright again.

Hurriedly, she retracted her helmet and used her teke to wake the wallcomp display. "Galactic Search and Rescue. Do you need assistance?"

After a long moment, a baritone voice answered. "*Yes. Get us out of here immediately.*" The accent was snooty and the tone sounded entitled.

Great. Her favorite kind of rescue target. "If the door has an emergency-exit bar or wheel, please try it now." She kept her tone professional. "It might be on the door or in the frame."

After several moments of silence, the voice was back. "*It still doesn't work.*" Accusation accompanied the condescension.

Another, tenor-range voice added, "*We've tried everything we can think of. The access biometrics aren't working for anything, not even lights. We think the lock is jammed. Or corrupted. When the earthquake started, mine was the only door open, so we all sheltered in here. The door locked before we could stop it.*"

"Okay. I'll try something out here. Please watch the comps and locks and tell me if anything changes." It sometimes helped stressed-out victims to give them something to do.

No way was she wire-jacking her suit into an untrusted wallcomp. She used her implant controller to ping the building's AI. Miraculously, it responded and accepted her series of access override codes.

Twenty seconds later, the light-ring displayed rainbow colors and emitted a short, cheerful tune. The multi-layered door plates irised open.

She stepped back. "Please come out now while we still have power."

A sharply pretty young man in tall boots and a stylish corporate kilt under a flowing, layered tunic exited first. A substantial utility pouch hung from his low-slung belt, and he wore a gray hard-shell backpack. His flawless white skin spoke of regular body-shop visits.

On his heels came an older-looking, more distinguished executive-type man wearing an expensive, notice-my-success grey suit and an equally expensive cross-slung, overstuffed messenger bag. His carefully waved bright yellow hair matched the hue of his padded collar and his boots. Someone should have told him to avoid that color altogether.

The third person stood half again as tall as either man and wore solid black that clung to chiseled muscles.

Prodded by instinct Taz had learned to listen to, she had her suit scan the open storage unit while she asked their names.

The young-looking, pretty man hesitated, then pointed to himself. "I am Bagutar Po." His accent hinted at Mandarin as a primary language. He tilted his head toward the others. "She's Pelvannor. I don't know him."

The executive man smiled nervously. "I'm Xolor Stramlo. What are the odds that Mr. Po and his bodyguard would also be in the facility so early? Very lucky, *ja?*"

It wasn't Taz's business that both Po and Stramlo were mixing truth and lies, but it made her want to get out all the faster.

Pelvannor, who wore a heavy-looking utilitarian backpack, watched both men closely, with occasional assessing glances toward Taz and the now-grounded airsled. Her silver eyebrows and very short dusting of silver hair stood out against her cool brown skin. The bodyguard part was likely the truth, considering Taz's sifter sense told her the woman was a ramper, a minder who could augment her body's strength and speed using her talent.

Stramlo's smile faded to a disapproving frown. "What's that dog doing here?"

Moyo, wearing her official yellow and red GSAR harness and multi-pocketed utility vest, padded toward the men. She unexpectedly swerved and approached Pelvannor. The woman's watchful expression didn't change, but Taz saw the subtle outstretch of fingers toward the dog. Moyo saw it, too, and sidled closer.

Rylando appeared in the airsled's open doorway. "She's doing her job, checking for people who need help." He used the determinedly patient tone he reserved for children throwing tantrums.

Taz struggled to keep a smile off her face.

Po sneered. "We're fine, and will be leav..." His words trailed off as he looked down the hall. "What did you do to the lift?"

Blame-finders like Po weren't worth arguing with. "Grounded. We can take you up in the airsled."

"No." Po turned and reseated the pack on his shoulders. "We'll take the lift at the other end."

"That whole end of the building is a no-go," said Rylando. He pointed a thumb back to the open shaft. "You're welcome to climb the service ladder if you don't want to ride with us." He held out his arm and keyed his percomp. "Just state your names again and tell us for the record you're refusing our help, and we'll be on our way."

After a long moment, Po's chin jutted out imperiously. "We will ride." He waved limp fingers toward Stramlo. "Perhaps you should seal your storage unit."

"My what?" Stramlo blinked. "Oh, yes, of course. Can't be too careful these days." He crossed to the wallcomp and entered two codes and a biometric. The door iris closed. "There. All set." He slapped his hands together like he'd performed a difficult feat of manual labor.

Moyo trotted to the airsled and jumped in.

Rylando's tone sounded in her earwire. *"I need your help rearranging the crates."*

Taz didn't like leaving her suit with strangers, but the sooner they got it done, the sooner they could leave. She retracted the armor and stepped down.

Stramlo glanced at the clock display on the wall, then frowned and raised his arm to look at the elegant bracelet-style percomp on his wrist. "The display is slow by seven minutes and nineteen seconds."

Po rolled his eyes as she walked by.

As she approached the airsled, Taz heard Rylando tell his passenger to stand outside for a minute.

The girl stepped down, clutching her coat, shuffling away from the airsled. She peeked warily at the adults from around the edge of her hood.

Taz turned to look and caught surprise and consternation on Stramlo's face. Po's nostrils twitched and his jaw tightened.

Stramlo glanced uneasily toward Po, then focused his gaze on his daughter and swallowed. "Jhidelle. I was worried about you."

A blind mole rat could have seen that he wasn't in the least pleased to see her.

"*Hallo, Vater.*" Her subdued greeting to her father sounded very polite. A tiny ginger-colored head with ears big enough to fly with appeared between the lapels of her coat. "I'm sorry I disobeyed you." Without taking her eyes off her father, she gently coaxed the little animal back inside her coat.

Taz grabbed the rail and swung up into the airsled, pretending she hadn't sensed all the lies. Get the lifesigns out and move on.

Inside the airsled, Rylando was encouraging Shen into Moyo's crate. "Even if I put all the animals in Moyo's crate, and abandon the empties, it's still not enough room for four humans."

"I can carry the empty crates." She touched her earwire and subvocalized her next words. "*The adults are spiky. I don't trust them. It's not a happy family reunion.*"

He touched his earlier. "*Agreed, but we can't leave them. Otak says the storage unit reeks of explosives. So do the adults, but that could be because they were in the storage unit for so long.*"

She released Moyo's large crate from its holdfasts and put it in the doorway. "*How did Otak get close enough... Oh, I get it. You put him in Moyo's saddlebags. Clever.*" She blew out a frustrated breath. "*Not enough evidence to Section 79-A the adults. But I don't want to leave the kid with them.*"

"*Yeah, they haven't threatened our safety, and whatever twist they're perpetrating, law enforcement isn't our job.*" He stood with his hands on his hips, frowning at the crates as he spoke out loud. "Damnit. We're going to have to make two trips."

A solution occurred to her, but he probably wouldn't go for it, since it meant being separated from his animals. "If you keep Mariposa and Otak with you, I could carry two crates with the rest of your team." She pointed a thumb toward the door. "You fly our targets up. I'll take the ladder."

Instead of shutting her down, his eyes narrowed in thought. "They mass almost two hundred kilos with their crates. Can you handle that?"

"My suit can carry twice that. Size and weight distribution will be a problem, though. Could we put Moyo in Shen's crate, and the rest in Lerox's?"

The corner of his mouth quirked. "They won't like it, but they'll put up with it if I reward them later."

Warmed by his trust, she held four fingers over her heart. "Your team is safe with me."

He stilled and met her eyes, his expression serious. "I know. You're the best rescuer Unit 1051 has ever had."

Taz's heart skipped a beat. She turned away quickly before she did something stupid, like reach out to him. Desperate for distraction, she hoisted Moyo's empty crate. "I can strap this to the airsled's roof if we leave both sets of doors open a crack." She didn't dare look at him again until her stupid heart faced reality for once. His words were a frickin' job performance review, not a declaration of passionate love.

"That would be good. Big crates are expensive." His voice sounded matter of fact, so she must not have given her turmoil away.

It only took a couple of minutes to pull out one of the sled's many straps and secure the sturdy crate to the roof. It made the airsled look like a frontier planet's rural transport kludge, but it didn't have to stay there for long.

Getting the hooks set on her suit to carry the crates full of animals was easy. Getting the humans and their apparently priceless luggage into the airsled took all her diplomatic skill.

Stramlo refused to stand anywhere near where the animal crates had been. Po commandeered the jump seat, meaning Jhidelle had to cram herself up front between the vehicle's wall and the hot and vibrating sensor column, and avoid Rylando's elbow. When the doors opened again, tall Pelvannor would be lucky if she didn't pop out like a grav ball in play.

With a final sensor check, Taz rose slowly to standing height. "You are very good beasties," she told her passengers. She raised her camera post so she could see behind her over the top of the smaller crate. After two practice steps and one adjustment, she pinged Rylando. *"Mechanized autocab for rescue team Canis Gulo Felis is green-go. Lead on, illustrious Field Commander, sir."*

"Watch it," he said with a growl, *"or I'll promote you to field commander, too."*

Taz chuckled. *"Oh, no, sir! Anything but that, sir!"*

With a reverberating whine, the airsled lifted sluggishly, then rotated and floated toward the shaft. She followed, trying to walk with a smooth gait.

The airsled floated into the shaft, then slowly rose. She gave it a few extra seconds, then extended her grab bars to the ladder and let them hold her weight while she stepped onto the closest rung.

Above her, the airsled's lights illuminated the shaft. Her own lights let her see the wide doubled rungs as she climbed. Scanning each one briefly slowed her down, but she couldn't afford carelessness. Counting her progress up the rungs helped her manage her impatience.

On her fourteenth step, her suit's sensory interface reported rising vibrations coming from the rungs. Dust arose.

She swore and pinged Rylando. *"Aftershock."*

"I'll speed up top and come–"

A bone-rattling thump came from above. Falling dust and jagged pieces of heavy blue denscrete accompanied the second and third thumps.

Quelling the instinct to hunch her head and shoulders, she swung herself and her cargo sideways to make them as small a target as possible.

Above her, the airsled stalled. The hatch cover for the left coil turned an ominous pink.

More thumps. Moyo's empty crate shifted, the strap straining. When it snapped, the crate fell off the airsled and smashed onto the lift below. Helplessly, Taz watched the coil's hatch door turn lava red. The airsled tilted to one side and started to sink.

6

Salamaray Citizen Activity Center, Perlarossa • GDAT 3242.334

"Hang on!" Rylando shouted as he braced himself against his standing frame and fought the controls. "I'm opening the side door. Dump everything you're carrying, or we won't make it to the top."

In the display for his monitoring cameras, he saw Pelvannor use the grab bar to lever herself, muscles bulging with effort, into a quasi-standing position.

More debris from the top of the shaft rained down. Tilting the airsled again failed to dislodge the heavy section of denscrete that clung to its roof. Alerts flashed and pinged about too much weight. The overheating coil wouldn't last.

On the display, Pelvannor unslung her duffle bag and heaved it with amazing accuracy through the door opening opposite her. The airsled rose. How much had that bag weighed?

Po, instantly outraged, called her the Mandarin equivalent of shit for brains.

Rylando righted the airsled and put every kilo of command he had into his voice. "Dump your luggage, now! We'll get it later." He opened the door next to Pelvannor wide enough to push things out.

Wide-eyed, Stramlo clutched his bag even tighter.

Po unhooked the web and stood. Instead of removing his backpack, he produced a beamer and aimed it at Jhidelle's head. "You! Girl! Out!"

Rylando only had time to subvocalize the word "*trouble*" to Taz before Po's gaze swung to Stramlo. "Pull her out and hand her to Pelvannor. She's leaving, alive or dead."

Astonishingly, Stramlo only hesitated a moment before doing as he was told. Not even Jhidelle's expression of shocked betrayal stopped him.

Rylando sent the airsled as close as he dared to the service ladder wall. Kicking himself for not thinking of it sooner, he touched the control to mirror the audio and video feeds from his tech. If Po killed them all, the recordings would help see justice done.

Pelvannor hooked one leg around a holdfast bar, then lifted Jhidelle like she weighed nothing and held her out to the ladder rungs.

Rylando watched his exterior camera display to make sure the girl grabbed on tight. A small brown shadow appeared on Jhidelle's shoulder and jumped onto the airsled's roof. Only Pelvannor could have seen it, and she was already turning back to face Po.

Rylando didn't have time to think about it as the airsled rose again. With all the dust in the air, he couldn't tell if the aftershock was over or not.

Po turned his beamer on Rylando. "You, Mr. Gee-Sar man. Tell your partner everything's good if she leaves us alone, then strip off your earwire and toss it to Pelvannor." Po's lip curled. "Get us free and you can chat all you want after we're gone."

Rylando reluctantly touched his earwire, spoke the required words out loud, then pulled it off. If he'd been smarter, he'd have been subvocalizing to Taz this whole time. He'd been so focused on the rescue and worrying about her and his team that he'd missed all the signs of trouble.

He tossed it awkwardly toward Pelvannor, who snatched it out of the air with blinding speed and tossed it to the back. It landed somewhere behind the stationary equipment lockers.

Po shook his head and spoke a sneering insult in Mandarin. Stramlo winced. Pelvannor's expression didn't change.

Only half the top scanners and none of the external comms survived the rain of rubble. Thankfully, the bottom camera eyes survived, allowing him to see Taz connect with Jhidelle and web the girl to the front of her mech suit.

Finally, the lift lobby came into view. He turned into the opening as soon as they cleared the floor height.

Debris on the floor began dancing. The lift opening visibly swayed and warped. In front of him, a blue section of denscrete crashed down to block the hallway exit.

Rylando spun the airsled right to avoid the sudden obstacle, only to find the other hallway already fully blocked from a cave-in.

The tortured left coil flatlined. The best he could do was ground the sled and hope the lobby ceiling held.

A tremendous, deafening crack made him hunch involuntarily. Mariposa clung to his shoulder with her sharp owl claws.

The airsled's functioning camera eyes recorded the collapse of an enormous block of denscrete that wedged itself into the lift shaft like a cork, blocking the entire opening.

Po shoved Pelvannor aside and climbed out the still-open side door.

A moment later, he jumped back in, rage distorting his face. He pointed the beamer square at Rylando's chest.

"Get us the fuck out of here right fucking now!"

Taz wished her mech suit had Jumper drugs to manage her runaway adrenaline and nausea. Above her, violence spiked strong enough to wake her sifter talent. The wobbling airsled nearly rammed the side wall, and suddenly, Jhidelle was left clinging to the service ladder.

Rylando's irritating habit of forgetting to maintain a live comms connection left her ready to bite him. Or at least ask Shen to do it. Everything was as far from "fine" as it could get. As soon as she rescued the girl, she bloody well would not be "leaving them alone."

After strapping Jhidelle to her suit like she was a casualty, Taz had intended to go up. The shower of debris from the largest aftershock yet changed her mind. That, and her scans warning of the imminent failure of the pins holding the shaft's capstone.

Climbing down took all her concentration. The crates on her back couldn't take much abuse. Squashing live rescue targets was considered bad form. Groaning from above overloaded her audio and triggered her noise-canceling implants. Dust swirled everywhere, impairing visibility and making Jhidelle and the animals cough. Inside her suit, all she could smell was her own sour sweat.

The pivot-swing back into the basement hallway wasn't pretty. The last ladder rung gave way. She stumbled forward, then scrambled to keep her footing on the slick floor as the aftershock finally dissipated.

Anger at herself for not listening to her instincts about the targets warred with terror that her failures might have gotten Rylando hurt or killed. He wasn't answering any of her pings.

The basement seemed to weather the aftershocks better than the shaft. As soon as she got well past the dust, almost to the cursed storage unit where the trouble began, she stopped. Freeing Jhidelle took just a few moments, giving Taz the chance to retract her armor and step out of her suit.

Taz took a long moment to put her chaotic feelings in a box to sort later. "First off, are you hurt?"

"No," said Jhidelle. She opened her coat and looked down at a creature she was carrying in a sling. A tiny orange-and-white foxlike head sported ears big enough to fly with. "Farenoso is okay, too."

Truth, according to Taz's sifter talent.

"Okay, tell me what happened up there."

"The airsled was too heavy and they didn't want to let go of their bags. Po made me get off. He threatened to shoot me if my father didn't hand me off to the woman Pelvannor so she could shove me out." Despair laced her tone. "My father had no choice."

"Holy chaos, what is in those bags?" She should have scanned them when she had the chance, regardless of GSAR privacy regulations.

"I don't know." Her shoulders hunched tighter. "I came here to save him, but I just made things worse."

Taz kept a lock on her temper as she caught the girl's eye. "Save him from what?"

"Po. Pelvannor." She pointed up. "All I could do was send Tzima back to the airsled to look after him."

Now Taz was confused. "Who is Tzima?"

"My kinkajou. She's very good at jumping and good at getting into things. I can see through her eyes. Hear through her ears."

It took Taz a second to realize what that meant. "You're an animal-affinity minder, like Rylando." When Jhidelle nodded, Taz continued. "Let's go back to the saving part."

"Father brought me to Salamaray to do some shopping. In the middle of the night, four people broke into our condotel. Po and Pelvannor took my father. The other two stayed with me to hold me hostage." She frowned. "They took my percomp and comms, locked me in my bedroom with water and a mealpack, and told me to keep quiet. They didn't know I had my pets with me. Farenoso is a fennec fox. He can hear a whisper from a kilometer away." The fox looked up at Jhidelle's chin when he heard his name. "The two who stayed didn't even check my room before they locked me up, and they complained about everything. Having to guard a stupid kid instead of going to the CAC with Po, who had instead taken stupid-as-stardust Pelvannor. What they'd do with their share. What Po would do to my father if he didn't cooperate. What they'd do to me."

"I see. What did they want your father to do?"

"Help them steal from the basement storage units. That's how I knew where to go." She blew out a sigh. "I couldn't let them use me as leverage, so I escaped out the window and came here. I thought if my father saw I was free, he could get away. The earthquake changed everything."

The girl's story sounded like a tri-D adventure thriller plot, but Taz's talent said she was telling the truth as she knew it.

Half the rescuers in her unit wouldn't have been so resourceful. "How old are you again?" asked Taz.

"Almost sixteen." Subtle annoyance threaded the words, like she had to answer that question a lot.

"But why your father, particularly?"

"I haven't figured that part out." Jhidelle shook her head, frustration evident. "He's a design engineer for asteroid mines, not a thief."

Taz rolled her shoulders back and took a deep, calming breath. "Why didn't you tell us this immediately?"

Jhidelle shrugged sheepishly. "I was afraid you'd wait for law enforcement instead of helping my father. Po and Pelvannor would have killed him to hide their crimes." Abject remorse settled on her face. "I'm sorry I got your partner in trouble. I messed up."

"Yeah, kid, you did." Taz waited until Jhidelle looked up. "I did, too. So let's figure out how to fix it."

Her eyes widened. "You're not mad?"

"Oh, I'm mad as fire. We're stuck down here because of those assholes." Taz pointed toward storage unit 79. "Makes me want to find out what was in there that Po wanted so bad."

Jhidelle's eyes widened, then darted to the animal crates that were still strapped to Taz's mech suit. "Could Farenoso and I say hello to your animals?"

"They're Subcaptain Delroinn's, not mine." Taz hesitated. "Have you been around other animal-affinity minders before?"

Jhidelle nodded. "My father is gone a lot. When I'm not taking classes, I volunteer for an animal-rescue group. Several of us are minders. All my pets are rescues."

"First, promise me you won't order his animals around, or try to bond with them." Rylando would never trust her again if the girl hurt his team.

"Yes, Subcaptain, I promise." Jhidelle's sincerity rang as true as her other statements.

"Call me Taz. Come on, I'll make introductions. You can entertain them while I pop that misbegotten door."

She spoke Jhidelle's name warmly and patted the girl's shoulder to show the animals that she wasn't a threat. Even the cats seemed interested in checking her out.

Unsurprisingly, the building's AI was back to monosyllabic insensibility, but she had a GSAR mech suit with customized capabilities all its own.

Two minutes later, the ring-light flashed and the door irised open.

"How did you do that?" asked Jhidelle.

"Telekinesis," lied Taz.

GSAR's best-kept secret was the existence of their vast hypercubes of access codes. GSAR strictly monitored and reviewed each use to deter rescuers from abusing them for personal motives. Rescuers kept the secret because no one wanted to be held hostage and forced to open every lock in the galaxy.

Taz stood at the threshold for a brief look into the room. One empty set of shelves and dust. No sign of the explosives that Otak had alerted Rylando to. Kem-X packages had to be bigger than a backpack to work, and they were too easy to get to be worth threatening a child's life over.

The dust caught her attention again. A bloom came from the doorway where it had undoubtedly blown in over the threshold.

Oddly, another bloom came from the back corner of the unit, beyond the shelves. Now that she was looking for it, she saw the shadow of another doorway and what might be a powered lift ladder.

Damnit, why wasn't Rylando answering her pings? Had Po and Pelvannor gotten away yet? And what about Stramlo? Her stomach roiled with images of Rylando injured and without her or any of his team to help him.

"Subcap... er, Taz?"

"Yes?" Taz turned to look at Jhidelle, who had pushed her dusty, torn coat off her shoulders, probably because the hallway was hot and stuffy. She looked nothing like her father, but that meant nothing. Considering what body shops could do these days, no one with funds had to keep the appearance they were born with or aged into.

"I can still connect with Tzima from here. I asked her to hide and listen. Her eyes are bad, but her hearing is good. Po is yelling at everyone."

Taz made herself ask the bad-news question. "Can you tell if anyone is hurt?"

"No, but Po's giving them orders. 'Stramlo, sit. Pelvannor, search the sled. Gee-Sar man, stay where you are.' That sort of thing. I think they're trapped in the lift lobby."

Taz double-checked her comms, but nothing from Rylando. She hooked her thumbs into her utility belt and drummed her fingers on it, thinking hard. Finally, she focused on Jhidelle.

"You're old enough to have a vote in this. The storage unit has a power ladder that leads up. If we're lucky, it's an emergency exit to the first floor, or at least to someplace that has working comms. On the other hand, it would likely be safer to stay here and wait to be rescued. This is where our pilot, Captain Wa'ara, will look first."

Jhidelle glanced down the hall toward the shaft, then at the suit, before returning her gaze to Taz. "I vote for the ladder. If we get out, we can get help. Down here, we're not helping anyone."

An almost-sixteen-year-old's sense of adventure wasn't always supported by good judgment, but Taz hoped an almost-thirty-nine-year-old's experience could keep them both out of trouble.

"Okay, the ladder it is. Let's wedge those shelves in the doorway so it doesn't stick again."

Jhidelle pulled her coat back on. "I can do it while you get into your mech suit."

Taz checked that the crates were still secure and thanked the animals for their patience. They'd be happy to be reunited with Rylando. Not that she could ever tell him, but she would, too. She wanted to see him safe and smiling again.

Taz's suit and crates were a tight fit in the power ladder's tube. She hugged the stepped rungs and rode them up, with Jhidelle right below her.

The end of the tube was too short to be the main-floor level. Instead, the access way opened into a darkened room.

Stepping into it tripped motion sensors and triggered a small circle of overhead lights.

"What is this place?" Jhidelle looked down at her little fox. "Yes, baby, I know it's cold in here." She pulled her coat tighter.

Whatever it was, Taz's comms were still blocked. Damnit.

The scans from her suit were so unexpected that she ran them a second time to be sure. "I've only seen training holos of these. It's a galactic hypercube node."

Jhidelle walked to the edge of the darkness. "Like a comms node?" More lights flicked on. Three-meter-tall equipment stacks looked like rows of tall buildings in a planned corporate district. The room had a quiet underlying hum of chilled air circulation.

"No, a data storage node. It's a redundancy relay for the galactic net. It has direct comms with the planet's net and the solar system's comms nodes." Taz frowned. "Or it did, except the other end of the building collapsed and took the comms with it. Probably why the stacks are quiet now."

"Why would they put a node in Salamaray?" Jhidelle's tone suggested she didn't think much of the town.

"Who knows?" A slow-blink floor light caught Taz's eye. She stepped sideways and crouched to get a better angle.

Scans confirmed her visual. Now she knew where the scent of explosives came from. Without even trying, she saw three more of them spaced at regular intervals. She had a twisted feeling in the pit of her stomach that those were the leading edge of the meteor storm.

7

Salamaray Citizen Activity Center, Perlarossa • GDAT 3242.334

S weat trickled down the back of Rylando's neck as he sent soothing thoughts to Otak, still hiding in his pouch, and to Mariposa, perched on the far side of the airsled's roof. He sensed the girl's kinkajou—it miraculously survived the landing—but he couldn't tell where it was.

No circulation made the lobby's air smell stale and increasingly hot. The heavy, indestructible GSAR uniform and the warm rat on his chest weren't helping.

Stramlo, perched nearby on a chunk of denscrete, hugged his messenger bag like a shield. He twitched with each noise, whether from the ruined lobby or from Po swearing.

Rylando was better at projecting calm for the sake of his animals, but not so good at stopping himself from worrying about them or Stramlo's daughter. Or Taz. So far, he'd not been able to make mental contact with his team and had no way to talk to his partner. The overheated lift coil cooked the airsled's comms when it died.

The room's emergency lights were plenty bright enough to illuminate the depth of their predicament. All the ceiling decorations and a third of the roof supports now littered the floor. The beat-up airsled sat in the middle of the lobby. At least the final lurch had shed the heavy piece of denscrete that had weighed it down. More caved-in rubble from the building's roof layer blocked both ends of the lift lobby. The corner of a giant block of denscrete protruded from the lift shaft behind him to his left. That entire wall bulged out from the pressure.

Pelvannor stood in the open doorway of the airsled, alternating between holding the beamer on the prisoners as ordered, and following Po's subsequent orders to lift or move things as he pawed through the sled's contents. So far, they'd found and unloaded two bins of food and water, medical supplies, water-protection suits, climbing gear, and one box of spare parts.

Rylando had already told them the airsled's only useful tools for freeing them from the lobby cave-in were shovels and pry bars, but it had been a waste of breath.

Po appeared in the doorway, brandishing a wand-like tool with the yellow and red GSAR logo. "What's this?"

"A spectrum analyzer for materials composition." He winced when Po carelessly tossed it onto the parts box on the floor. Taz had spent five days repairing and customizing it to work better than the original version.

Otak once again alerted him to the explosives scent. Unfortunately, Rylando couldn't give the rat the usual food reward. A thought of praise would have to do.

It didn't take an astro-engineer to figure out that the source was Stramlo's messenger bag. Too small to be a regular Kem-X packet, but maybe samples? No clue why he'd been keeping it in his storage unit.

Po's hard-shell backpack, which he still wore, must have high-value items, or he'd have given it up. Pelvannor's heavy bag had probably held valuables, too, which explained why he'd yelled at her when she'd tossed it out of the airsled.

He still couldn't rule out the possibility that Stramlo and Po had more than just bad luck in common.

Movement caught his eye. Tzima, Jhidelle's kinkajou, was now on top of the airsled. He was glad he'd managed to open a vent for her so she could slip inside the airsled's cab, but now she was an added worry.

He cautiously reached out with his talent. Instead of encountering the animal's mind, he felt the presence of another, stronger directive, directing her gaze. Jhidelle must be connected to the animal's senses. The best he could do was ask Tzima to hide and hope the girl would take the hint. Po was the type to break or kill things to take out his frustrations.

Rylando wished he was a stronger minder, like Jhidelle apparently was. He'd developed training techniques to compensate, but they were no help now that he needed to connect with his own animals. To find out if Taz was okay. He'd been a rock-brain for not being more wary or paying attention to her instincts. If they lived through this, he planned to tell Captain Bhayrip he'd ordered her into this mess. Otherwise, they'd both get demoted for going in understaffed and getting caught in criminal games.

After two more "what's this" queries, Po jumped out of the airsled and stood with his hands on his hips, glaring at Rylando. "We need your partner in her mech suit. Get her up here, now."

Rylando stopped himself from rolling his eyes, but just barely. "I'm not a telepath. Neither is she. The airsled's comms are still as dead as the lift coil. I'll need my earwire."

Po turned his glare on Pelvannor. "You're the *báichī* who threw it away instead of keeping it. Find it!"

Even though stoic Pelvannor didn't react to Po's insults, Rylando felt a moment of sympathy for her. She had an even worse boss than he did, and that was saying something.

Po's perpetually outraged attitude reminded Rylando of his

favorite fantasy adventure serial, where the emperor's evil daughter could never understand why the universe didn't dance at her command. Supporting characters who told her as much often had tragically short lives.

After a few moments, Pelvannor came back and handed Po the earwire. He examined it, then tossed it to Rylando. "Route the audio through your percomp. Call your partner. No subvocalizing."

Rylando adhered it to his jaw and tapped to connect, then spoke aloud. "Subcaptain, give me a sitrep, please." He hated hearing his own amplified voice.

Taz didn't answer. Hatya wouldn't unless she thought he was talking to her. It wasn't yet time for check-in.

After several long moments, he tried again. He shook his head. "I can send a ping–"

Po interrupted. "Try again!" His face flushed in anger.

Rylando kept a tight rein on his temper. "The subfloor is incalloy and denscrete. It's probably blocking the signal." Rylando didn't mention the possibility that Taz couldn't answer because she was hurt or worse. Stramlo was barely hanging on as it was. Hearing his daughter might be in trouble might push him over the edge.

Po stomped his foot. "Goddamnit!" The next thing Rylando knew, Po was aiming a stunner at his throat. "I fucking hate liars!"

Pain filled Rylando's world. He scraped off the super-heated earwire as he fell to his knees, jerking like a stranded fish. Grimly, he rode out the agony, knowing if he collapsed, he might crush Otak. Knowing the rat might not survive the stunner spillover.

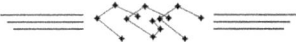

Taz ran a brief scan to confirm that the Kem-X package she was looking at was the same as the last fourteen.

At least now, the thick walls and armored floor made sense. So did forcing Stramlo, who likely had explosives experience from his mining engineering job, to help destroy the node. What still didn't make sense was why.

Galactic civilization lived and died by data. The Concordance's net boasted multitudes of ways to keep and recover data on its five-hundred-plus member planets. Millions of deep-space comms relayed it across civilization. Even newly opened frontier planets had three or four hypercube nodes. Long-settled planets had dozens. Destroying just one made no sense.

Perhaps the act itself was the message. Revenge against the town, or against the famous politician who'd called it home, or a grievance with the galaxy.

Right now, she had more immediate problems. She fast-walked back to where she'd left Jhidelle and the animals in their crates.

No way to phrase it diplomatically. "I think the whole facility is wired with explosives."

Jhidelle sat huddled in her coat between the crates. Her eyes rounded. "What are you going to do?"

Taz stepped out of her suit and crouched down to face the girl. This conversation was too important to have barriers between them. "That depends somewhat on you." She pointed a thumb over her shoulder toward the rows of equipment. "In the good-news column, the timers are powered, but they aren't counting down. The packets all look uniform and straightforward, meaning they can be disarmed. In the bad-news column, if the spacing and placement hold true, there's enough Kem-X to launch the entire town into orbit along with the building. Also, just because the timers aren't running now doesn't mean someone can't change that."

Jhidelle's expression darkened. "Someone like Po." Her eyebrows lifted in realization. "That's why he wanted my father."

"Probably." Taz was glad not to have to broach that subject. "Time isn't our friend right now. Our choices aren't good, either." She held up her thumb. "Option A, we go back to the lift shaft and wait to be rescued. Captain Wa'ara will start searching for us there."

Moyo suddenly stood up in her crate and started whimpering. One of the cats yowled. Shen stood, ears pivoting, nose working.

Even as Taz was about to ask, Jhidelle's eyes jittered momentarily. "They think Subcaptain Delroinn is hurt."

Taz shoved her feelings in a box. "How bad?"

"Give me a minute." The girl closed her eyes. "Tzima's vision is bad, but I think Po is holding something like it's a hand weapon. My father is sitting on something. The Subcaptain is on his knees, bent over, hugging himself, shaking his head like he has water in his ears. Po is saying 'another lie, and I'll stun you again.'" She opened her eyes, her expression a mixture of concern and anger.

"Po is an asshole." Taz spat. "Stunners hurt like fire, but they're not lethal. It'll disrupt Delroinn's minder talent for a bit." She pointed to the crates. "Could you help his team understand that he's not hurt bad but can't talk to them right now?"

Taz could see Jhidelle's success when the animals began to quiet down.

Determination settled on the girl's face. "What are our other options besides waiting for your pilot?"

"Option B is to look for another way out of here. We're lucky this facility doesn't extend into the other section of the building that collapsed." Taz blew out a loud breath. "Or the riskiest of all, and against every GSAR regulation, plus your father would probably kill me if he knew what I was thinking, Option C. Locate and disarm the Kem-X packets in here, *then* take option A or B."

Jhidelle's eyebrows furrowed. "How is disarming the packets riskier than hoping we get rescued? They'd still be there."

"Because I'll need Delroinn's team to find them all. I don't speak dog, cat, or weasel, so I'll need your talent to ask them to help. I have explosives training and my suit has good scanners, but if some of those packets are custom, I'll be out of my depth. If I screw up, we could get hurt. If I *really* screw up, there won't be enough of any of us to even make into memory diamonds."

Jhidelle's head tilted with a puzzled air. "You could've chosen for both of us. I'm just a *Kinder*."

"Yeah, but you're a smart kid, and whatever we choose will be a lot easier if you're on board." Taz smiled wryly. "Besides, I've always hated being treated like I'm not in the room when important decisions are made about me."

Jhidelle put her hand on the crate that held most of the animals. "Then I vote Option C. I want to help. Your team wants to help. Shen especially. She worries about you."

Taz snorted with laughter. "That dog worries about everyone." She rose to her feet, glad to get off the bone-chilling floor. "Let's release the team, and I'll tell you what I need."

GSAR would bust her to no-ranker if they ever found out what she was about to do, or that she involved a child to help. But she was more worried about the explosives than her career. Neither Rylando or Jhidelle's father would make it out in time if Po and Pelvannor got free and started the countdown.

Rylando counted his breaths and throttled his temper hard. He abhorred violence, except when it came to threats to his animals. Hatya had stopped him from beating to a pulp the sick twist who had hurt Moyo. The stunner could have killed Otak. As it was, the rat seemed as groggy as Rylando. While still bent over, he reached a surreptitious hand into the pouch to give Otak a reassuring stroke.

He supposed it was lucky that the stunner was low power and that the flexin-armor layer of his uniform deflected some of the energy. He'd been stunned before and knew what to expect. The involuntary muscle twitches would subside in about fifteen minutes, and his talent would return soon after.

"Call your partner." The look on Po's face said he enjoyed seeing others in pain.

Rylando sat back on his heels. He pointed to the earwire and turned his face to the side with the burn mark seared into his skin.

"Can't. You just fried the earwire." Speaking irritated his throat and made him cough.

Po snarled and aimed the stunner again.

"Enough," said Pelvannor. Her tone and expression held a hint of thunder.

Po glanced at her. After a long moment, he made an inarticulate growl and shoved the stunner back under his multi-layered tunic. "Fine. Get the farking shovels out. We'll dig."

That turned out to mean that Po sat and held the beamer while Pelvannor, Stramlo, and Rylando did the digging. At least Po took Rylando's advice and let him use the materials scanner to determine that the wider side would be easier to dig through. Stramlo only gave Rylando his messenger bag to store on the floor of the airsled because Po threatened to shoot him if he didn't.

On one of the trips to the airsled, Rylando surreptitiously let Otak out of the chest pocket. If Pelvannor noticed the giant rat scuttling into the back, she said nothing.

Unfortunately, digging stirred up more dust, causing them all to cough and sneeze. Every muscle hurt as he cleared debris from around a larger chunk of denscrete, but it helped get his circulation going after the stunner jolt.

Pelvannor's prodigious strength made her fast and effective, but she paid a price by inhaling more of the dust. A nasty coughing fit caused her to stumble as she levered out a large hunk. It narrowly missed Stramlo's foot, causing him to drop his shovel and lurch away.

Rylando turned to Po. "We're using up oxygen. If it drops below twenty percent, none of us will be digging for long. The airsled has oxy meters and filter masks that'll keep the pulverized denscrete out of our lungs. If the pipe excavator is intact, we can use it to drill through the rubble and get some fresh air in here."

Po drew breath to speak but coughed instead. After recovering, he waved loose fingers. "Fine. Pelvannor, go with him. Don't let him touch anything. Make him show you what to do."

Inside the cramped airsled, Rylando pointed to an oval case

attached to the bottom back wall. "That's the excavator. Lock needs my biometrics."

Pelvannor nodded.

He sank carefully to his bruised knees, then put his palms on the handles and turned them. The door sprang up, revealing the long, rifle-like rock cutter with the pipe printer attached.

"Give it to me," ordered Pelvannor.

He released it from the holdfasts and did as she asked. "The controls are power, speed, and pipe diameter." Nodding toward the tank at the bottom, he added, "That's the substrate. Don't make the pipe diameter too wide or you won't have enough to make it to the other side of the cave-in."

She coughed as she examined the controls. "Show me the masks."

He closed the case, then shifted his position so he could move the two bins of parts and open the slim cabinet built into the wall of the airsled. "The ones on top are oxy concentrators with a simple eye shield. The middle ones have concentrators and better filters, but cover most of your face. Without earwires, we'll have to shout." He pointed his chin to the bottom set. "Those are for the animals."

A frown flitted across her face as she eyed the masks.

Rylando wished he could read people as effectively as Taz could. He couldn't guess what Pelvannor was thinking.

He dropped his head and turned it side to side to stretch his aching neck. A familiar shape in one of the parts bins caught his eye. He slid himself back farther, then pulled the parts bins back, as if giving her more room to maneuver.

As she set the cutter down, he pulled the bin even closer and palmed an earwire, then rubbed his hand down his thigh to help slide the earwire up his sleeve. The magic trick he'd learned as a child had turned out to be surprisingly useful in his adult life.

Pelvannor grabbed four of the better-filtered masks and handed one to him.

After he took it, he held it up by the bottom. "It seals better if you tilt it up from your chin, then pull the web over your head." He flexed his wrist to demonstrate the motion. "Lift it up if you're going to sneeze. It's hard to get snot off the faceplate."

She put hers on as instructed, then turned to pick up the cutter.

He used both hands to place his mask so he could slip the earwire onto his face and tap it for always-on. The mask covered it as he stretched the web up and over. The burned spot on his face felt like a bee sting.

When she gestured for him to follow, he rose to his feet and meekly complied.

Interestingly, Pelvannor didn't provide wearing instructions when she handed the mask to Po and said nothing when he put it on wrong. Equally interestingly, Stramlo pulled his mask on with professional ease, barely disarranging his perfect wavy hair.

A tone sounded in his earwire. "*Silver Team, report now, or I'm dumping my passengers and coming after you.*" Hatya's welcome voice sounded professionally calm but held a thread of worry.

Rylando bent over slowly to pick up a shovel and subvocalized as fast as he could. "*Protocol TX Delta. Lift lobby, both exits blocked. Four lifesigns including me. Two hostages, including me. Taz last seen headed toward the deep basement with another lifesign and most of my team. Building unstable.*"

He walked to the rubble pile and started digging again. Every time he turned his back on Po and Pelvannor, he subvocalized more details to Hatya.

"*Ah, hell, Rylando, you two have been having fun without me. I'm five minutes from the ERC. After that, I'm bringing the shuttle for scans. Keep talking when you can.*"

A hand waved in front of his face. When he looked up, masked Stramlo leaned close and shouted. "Po wants you."

Rylando dropped the shovel and crossed to where irritable Po stood, awkwardly holding the cutter. Pelvannor was back to her stoic self.

Po thrust the cutter into Rylando's arms. "Drill the goddamn air pipe."

Unsurprisingly, Pelvannor followed to watch him closely as he used the cutter's densometer to zero in on a thin spot, then set the tripod legs and turned on the cutter. As the debris lasers burned through the rubble, the printer extruded pipe into the deepening hole. Five minutes later, the lasers hit open air and shut down. He extruded the pipe several centimeters longer before turning off the printer and powering down the cutter.

As he folded the tripod legs, he realized they'd still be sucking increasingly stale air if Taz hadn't salvaged the cutter from the regular military trash heap for repair. She'd even cleverly etched the GSAR logo over the cutter's serial number in case someone asked. When, not if, he saw her again, he'd thank her.

Po eyed Rylando with suspicion. "Why didn't you tell us it had a laser? We could have been cutting our way out."

Unexpectedly, Stramlo answered. "It's not a beam, it's a pinpoint array. It'd take half a day to cut enough holes to make a one-meter slice."

Po threw his hands up and stomped toward his perch. "Fine. Get back to digging."

Rylando got Pelvannor's attention, then pointed first to the cutter, then to the airsled. When she nodded, he carried it back inside and stowed it in its case.

He took the opportunity to subvocalize to Hatya. "*If you have a choice, get Taz out first. Being trapped underground will be hard on her. And if there really are explosives, she's in danger.*"

"*Working on it. I know she's important to you.*"

Hatya's half-teasing lilt gave him an out, but the words cut through his defenses. He couldn't lie to himself any longer. "*Yes, she is.*"

Shen sat down in front of the sixty-fourth Kem-X packet and barked twice, then barked twice again.

"Good job," said Taz as she approached. She and the dog had worked out a steady rhythm, marching up and down the aisles, decommissioning every timer. Seventy-five minutes later, per her suit's chronometer, here they were.

"Jhidelle," she said, letting her suit do the amplifying. "Last one. Any outliers?"

"Moyo and Lerox say no." Between the dog's fantastic nose and the weasel's fearless sense of curiosity, they would have uncovered anything interesting, especially with Jhidelle guiding them. "The cats found a door. It's marked exit, but it's heavy and coded."

Taz's audio sensors identified the girl's location as near the northwest corner. "On my way."

She disabled the last timer, scanned it to be sure, then turned to Shen. "Find Moyo."

Shen yipped twice, then turned to trot down the aisle. On impulse, Taz picked up the now-harmless Kem-X packet, then followed.

While she'd been working, she'd been pondering several questions. First, if her military-grade comms were blocked, how did Po and Pelvannor expect to get through with just commercial comms to trigger the timers? Second, if they'd known what type and how many Kem-X packets to get, why had they needed to kidnap Stramlo?

When she reached the corner, all the animals were there. The crates, too, because Jhidelle had dragged them down from the other entrance and opened their doors.

Taz set down the packet and stepped out of her suit. Overusing her teke talent to speed up the timer decomms left her ears ringing like bells.

The chilly air of the facility momentarily felt good on her sweat-soaked skin as she turned to face them with a tired grin. "Good job, all of you." Shen's and Moyo's tails wagged. The cats' ears pricked forward. Lerox chose that moment to lick his butt.

Taz laughed. "Is anyone thirsty?" She patted her thigh pocket. "I have extra water pouches and a collapsible bowl."

Jhidelle's eyes drifted a bit. "No, they're good." She pointed to the packet. "What's that for?"

"Evidence." That sounded better than muttering about instinct and curiosity. "Let's take a look at the door."

The substantial metal slab looked more like it led to a vault, similar to the one that was now a storeroom in the financial firm on the first floor. Still, the door and jamb had the standard bright colors and the word "exit" printed in a dozen languages. It also had a formidable code lock on the wall. Whoever designed the exit had evidently decided security was more important than safety.

"I need my suit for the scans. If the exit is blocked above us, we'll have to go back to the lower basement. Either way, we need to crate the team. It's the only way I can protect them." She snapped her fingers. "Before I forget. Is your father a telekinetic minder?"

Her eyes widened in surprise. "No. Why?"

Taz shook her head. "Nothing, just a passing thought." She climbed back in her suit to check the architectural records and run scans while she poked at the door controls with her GSAR magic.

After three long minutes, the lock begrudgingly accepted her codes. The door slowly irised open to reveal a small anteroom with a standard-sized lift at the end.

"Okay," said Taz. "If I'm guessing correctly where we are, and the lift takes us up instead of down, and the building above is still standing, and the architectural records are correct, we'll be in a space labeled 'Recycling Overflow.'"

"That's a lot of 'ifs.'"

Taz paused. "Want to go back down instead?"

"No." Jhidelle motioned Moyo toward the crate. "The animals don't, either."

As Taz hooked the crates to her suit again, she hoped the undisturbed dust in the anteroom and the wallcomp for the lift meant Po and Pelvannor hadn't lined the lift shaft with explosives.

8

Salamaray Citizen Activity Center, Perlarossa • GDAT 3242.334

"No," shouted Rylando so Po could hear him through the mask, "I can't make my owl crawl through the air pipe to scope out the other side. She's too big."

Po's expression soured again. Watching the rest of them work had apparently been boring enough to inspire a series of harebrained ideas. It never seemed to occur to him that they'd get out faster if he helped with the digging.

Or maybe it had. Rylando was rather certain that Po intended to shoot him, and maybe Stramlo, to give Po and Pelvannor time to escape.

They'd gouged out enough material that they should break through to the other side any minute. It would have been sooner if they hadn't been forced to detour around a two-meter decorative block of denscrete.

Hatya's tone sounded in his earwire. "*Good news, bad news, and really bad news.*"

Rylando grabbed the handle for the nearly full bin of tailings—Stramlo's word—and pulled it out of the work area. "*Go.*"

"*Good news. Two lifesigns and five animal signs just showed up on my scanners. They're together. Still no comms, but I'm about to deploy a relay to see if I can fix that.*"

He worked his way over the rubble to the dump pile. The bin's poor wheels would never be the same. "*Copy.*" The hope that he'd be seeing his team and Taz again before the day was done made it easier to breathe.

"*Bad news. The building is cracked all over. Whoever manufactured the denscrete did a shit job, and it aged badly. Fucking settlement company.*"

Upending the bin made dust rise to temporarily envelope him. "*Not surprised.*"

"*Really bad news. Bhayrip and the entire unit are back.*"

Rylando froze in surprise. "*Why? What happened?*"

"*Bhayrip has been trying to reach Silver Team for the last hour, but he couldn't get through until the town got your borrowed uplink hub working. You are ordered to get your asses off the planet immediately and report to the space station right now. Even if you have to leave equipment behind. He can't order me to do anything, but he made a strong request. He ignored questions, so I asked my Jumper buddy T'lem. The CPS is recalling all GSAR units across the galaxy. Officially, it's a reorganization. Bhayrip probably wants you up there because the unit has two days to be in transit to the big military base on Lan Dalishi Epsilon for reassignment.*"

It took him two tries to pick up the bin's handle. He'd been expecting something like that for a multitude of ten-days, but the reality was still a shock. "*What about you?*"

"*Separate, sealed orders from Jumper Command. Not reading them until I'm sure you and Taz are safe. Speaking of which, I'm going to chat with the ERC, seeing as how his regular job is the regional law enforcement chief. Back online in five.*"

"Daylight!" shouted Stramlo.

Rylando pulled the empty bin carefully back to the dig. Worrying about impending disasters would have to wait. First, he had to deal with the one in progress.

Time to cinch up his rescuer harness and get everyone out safely.

Taz's nose was running like a faucet by the time the doors to the Recycling Overflow room opened. More blowback from overusing her talent. And fucking annoying while stuck in a mech suit.

The room's emergency lights revealed what looked like a landfill moon's worth of broken and discarded tech, all covered with thick layers of undisturbed dust. In any other circumstance, she'd be tagging the veritable gold mine of contents for emergency requisition and evacuation to her tech repair lab.

"Stay put while I check." Taz carefully pushed aside a stack of overflowing bins as she ran scans and tried comms again.

Rylando's tone sounded. *"This is a prerecorded ping. Get a sitrep from Hatya. Use the band and access codes I'm about to give you. They're for Shen's controller. She can help you."*

Tears of relief threatened when she heard his voice, crushing all the dire images her vivid imagination had been plaguing her with. Then his words sank in as she listened to the long strings of numbers and symbols.

"Taz," asked Jhidelle, "want me to find out what Tzima is hearing? She's a lot closer now."

"Yes, please." Taz pinged Hatya.

"Taz, welcome back. You and the doggos safe?" Hatya's obvious concern renewed the threat of tears. Damnit, she didn't have time for wellsprings of emotion.

The scans came back with mixed results. *"Yes and no."* She sent them to Hatya, then sent every other scan she'd taken that day for good measure. *"We're in a stable area, but the rest of the building is an accident waiting to happen."*

"Copy that. I'm sending you a map of the safest route out. But you need to know some things first."

"Taz?" Jhidelle asked. "Tzima hears digging and muffled voices in front of the airsled." The girl stepped into the room and promptly sneezed.

"Thank you, Jhidelle. I'm getting comms again. We're getting out now. Cover your mouth and nose with the hem of your tunic and follow me." Taz knew the words sounded abrupt, but she was juggling too many priorities at once.

Once she sent codes to open the far door, Taz pushed aside equipment to clear their path. *"Okay, Hatya, what do I need to know?"*

After listening to the bad news and orders from Bhayrip, she thanked Hatya, then described her plan to get Jhidelle to safety. She couldn't involve Hatya in phase two of her plan, where she went back for Rylando instead of obeying the immediate recall order.

"I sent you a route to the lift lobby." Hatya knew her too well. *"See you there."*

Taz turned to Jhidelle. "How about I carry you and we see how fast my suit can run?"

Captain Hatya Wa'ara was not a happy Jumper. Life was an ever-unfolding adventure, but hers had taken a sharp vector change into the stinky offal pit of secrets and twisty politics.

Circling west of the ruined Citizen Activity Center, she looked for a good place to land the shuttle. Few buildings had survived the raw destructive power of tectonic-plate upheaval, but a cluster of tall trees stood huddled together like a herd of green sheep. That would do.

She wished she hadn't read the separate orders she and the regular military pilots had received. She especially wished she hadn't opened the orders for Jumper eyes only.

Regular pilots were instructed to get all GSAR personnel to the designated military base, even if it took commandeering a commercial freighter and to do so. The orders said to take all the equipment they could ship and leave the rest for the next squad. Space Div and the CPS outright threatened to charge the regular pilots with dereliction if they left even one GSAR staffer behind.

The top-secret orders from CPS Jumper Command, however, took the prize. After everyone left, Jumpers were to disable or destroy the GSAR equipment and resources, then hunt down and forcibly detain any GSAR staffers who evaded the recall order. Lethal force was authorized if the staffer resisted.

If nothing else, the orders confirmed that the rumors were all too true about how the recent base shutdowns had caused Minder Corps staff to go absent in droves. And apparently, the lesson the CPS's dung-eating dunderhead leaders took from that debacle was to give GSAR employees even less notice so they wouldn't have time to disappear. Fark!

The grove of trees was a tight fit, but the shuttle would be safer under trees that had survived instead of out in the open.

This would be her last mission on active duty. She'd pulled every dodge and twist to hide the fact that the fucking incurable waster's disease had caught up with her early. Active Jumpers were supposed to be immune, but not her. The very next Jumper medic who examined her would decommission her on the spot.

Until an hour ago, she hadn't been ready to leave the Corps she loved. But she hadn't ever signed up to be a corporate fixer or a farking bounty hunter. She growled low in her throat. CPS High Command could suck flux. Jumper Command, too.

Ignoring the constant pain in her hip as beneath a Jumper's notice, she strapped herself into the ship-loader assist frame and picked up the bag of goodies she'd gathered. Before she fell out of line for the last time, she had one final mission.

Jumpers never left teammates behind.

Rylando shoveled with renewed effort, working off his feelings and glad the mask made it harder for the others to read his expression. Hatya's brief message said Taz was alive and well, and they'd both see him soon.

He was late in telling Taz so many things he should have, and now the reorganization threw any future into a chaotic maelstrom. If he survived Po's plans.

Thanks to his recovered talent and Mariposa's superior owl senses, he hadn't needed to be anywhere near to overhear Po's quiet orders. The moment the opening was wide enough, Pelvannor was supposed to shoot Rylando to disable him, grab Stramlo, and follow Po out to finish the job—whatever that was.

From Hatya's annoyingly breezy comment, he'd bet it had something to do with the basement data center filled with explosives that Taz had "taken care of."

"Hello." The rich alto voice he'd know anywhere sounded muffled but close. "Subcaptain Correa from Galactic Search and Rescue. Do you need assistance?"

Po stood up. His startled expression morphed into craftiness.

Pointing the stunner at Rylando, he pointed toward the almost-excavated exit. "Tell her 'yes,' and to hurry, because Stramlo is bleeding."

Rylando lifted his mask up long enough to shout, "Good to hear you again, Subcaptain. Yes, we need assistance. Three plus me. One is bleeding."

"Copy." Her tone was the model of professionalism. "In that case, I'll clear the exit fast. Please step as far away as you can."

Po frowned and motioned them all back.

Rylando moved with alacrity. He knew what Taz's suit could do when she was motivated.

Stramlo crossed toward the airsled, but Pelvannor herded him toward Po instead.

Rylando edged farther back and left. Reaching out with his talent, he discovered his whole team was just on the other side. He sent them a warm greeting, then subvocalized a warning to Taz. "*Po has a stunner. Pelvannor has the beamer.*"

"*Copy. Bang-flash in three.*"

Even though he expected it, the bright explosive boom made his shoulders hunch. Stramlo crouched and covered his head. Po stumbled back and would have fallen over the block he'd been sitting on if Pelvannor hadn't grabbed his arm and pulled him upright.

A blinding searchlight strobed through the now-wide gap, highlighting the new swirls of dust.

Stramlo launched himself toward the airsled and grabbed his messenger bag to sling across his shoulder.

Po snarled curses in Mandarin and pointed the stunner at Stramlo. "Set them now."

Stramlo shook his head. "We're too close."

"We'll be free in minutes. Pelvannor, motivate him." The beam from Pelvannor's weapon was close enough to char Stramlo's pant leg. "The next one makes your kid an orphan."

Rylando sent a request to Moyo. A loud, chill-raising howl echoed in the room, startling Po.

A moment later, a large, back-lit form appeared in the new opening. Hatya stepped into the room wearing the ship-loader assist frame over her Jumper uniform. Her loose, wild hair went perfectly with the berserker-crazy smile on her face. "Oh, target practice! Can I play?" Twin beamer arrays rose over her shoulders.

Pelvannor lowered her weapon.

Quicker than Rylando had thought possible, Po closed the distance and caught Stramlo by the neck, stunner pressed hard into the man's temple. "Sure, right after Engineer Stramlo here does what I told him. I mean, what's the point of using professionals if they aren't going to do their fucking jobs? And you know what? I hate this fucking mask." He pulled the mask off, half-strangling Stramlo in the crook of his elbow as he did so.

"*Rylando*," said Taz in his earwire. "*Po's a low-level ramper and a haze of violence. Pelvannor's a ramper, but she's calm. She has a soft spot for animals. Moyo and Shen are armored up. Might distract her.*"

"*Okay*," he subvocalized. Sending a prayer to the universe to protect them, he asked both dogs to come to him. Rescue work sometimes meant hard choices — and trusting his partner's judgment.

Moments later, Shen trotted in and made a beeline for him. Moyo followed more sedately, looking more like a working hellhound in her black GSAR protective vest and helmet.

Pelvannor's eyes flickered to the dogs, lingering longer on Moyo.

Rylando asked Moyo to see if the woman wanted a friend. Hopefully, the dog had forgotten her long-ago military training that told her to bite and shake people holding weapons.

"Tell you what," said Po conversationally. "Since we all want out of this goddamn cave, Engineer Stramlo, Pelvannor, and I are going for a stroll." He shoved the man forward into a stumbling walk, keeping the chokehold tight. "Give us a few minutes to get out of the building by ourselves and no one will get hurt."

"*He's lying*," said Taz with certainty.

"Pelvannor!" yelled Po. "Leave the stinking dog alone and come do what Zumu told you. Protect my ass."

Moyo's magic had been working on Pelvannor, but now she stepped around the dog and followed Po and his prisoner.

"*Let them go*," said Taz. "*More options out here.*"

Hatya hesitated, then stepped farther into the dusty lobby to get out of the way.

Though Pelvannor only glanced once at Hatya, the hand holding the beamer tightened as she passed by.

The second they were out of sight, Rylando asked the dogs to follow as he crossed to Hatya. "What's the plan?"

Hatya smiled. "Our plan is to let them self-rescue their merry way out of the building." She tilted her head toward the exit. "Yanoshi's plan is to detain and restrain them for ques–"

Taz's voice interrupted. "*Frelling hell. Po just stunned Pelvannor, grabbed the beamer, and took off dragging Stramlo away from the exit.*"

"I can handle Pelvannor," said Hatya.

Taz swore. "*I'm going after Stramlo. I don't want to have to explain to his kid how he died.*"

Rylando blew out a frustrated breath. "*I'm sending Moyo and Shen out. Wait for me.*" He patted both dogs and shared an image. "Find Taz," he told them.

As he strode toward the battered and begrimed airsled, he stripped off his mask and hooked it to his belt. Raising his talent, he asked Otak and Mariposa to meet him. The little owl swooped off the top and landed on his shoulder pad. Otak soon appeared in the open doorway, nose working and whiskers quivering. Rylando quickly scooped the rat up and into his chest pocket. "You've both been very brave. Triple treats when we get back."

More carefully this time, he extended his mental invitation to the little kinkajou and held out his forearm as a perch. After a few hesitant steps, the little animal made an astonishing leap from the far corner of the sled onto his arm, then ran up to sit on his other shoulder and cling to his collar. He sensed Jhidelle's presence encouraging the animal to trust him.

He stepped up into the sled and grabbed the face masks for the animals and the last filter mask. On his way out, he picked up the medical kit and carried it by the strap.

When he joined Hatya at the exit, he handed her the filter mask. "Just in case. The dust is bad."

Hatya took it and led the way out.

Taz tried to split her focus as she tracked Po on her scanner while watching Moyo and Shen greet Lerox and the cats in their shared crate.

Hatya emerged from the lift lobby and went straight to Pelvannor's unconscious form.

One of the knots in Taz's stomach untwisted when she saw Rylando, a little worse for wear, emerge and cross to her. Mariposa and the kinkajou riding on his shoulders gave his GSAR uniform an eccentric flair.

His eyes flicked to the new dents and scratches on her suit before meeting her gaze. "You okay?"

"Green go. My suit took the damage. You?"

He touched the swollen red mark on the side of his face. "Nothing a burn patch and a couple of bruise washers can't fix." His head circled in a quick neck stretch. That familiar gesture told her he'd been under a lot of stress.

Hatya used the ship-loader assist frame's forks to lift Pelvannor. "Want me to take the kid's pet to her?"

Rylando nodded and walked closer to her, arm extended up to Hatya's shoulder height. "Go on. She's only scary on the outside."

The little brown creature obligingly crawled onto Hatya's shoulder and burrowed itself under her hair and wrapped its long tail around her neck.

A delighted smile lit Hatya's face. "Don't tell any other Jumpers about this, or I'll never live it down." She turned to leave. "Keep in touch."

A pang of loss went through Taz. She'd probably never see either Hatya or Rylando again after the GSAR reorganization.

Rylando squared his shoulders. "Where is Po taking Stramlo?"

She ordered herself to focus on the here and now. "Probably closer to the hypercube facility below. I'm guessing he needs Stramlo, or at least his biometrics, to operate the detonator." She pointed to his team. "Want me to carry the crate, or are they walking with us?"

He looked at them for a long moment. "Shen and Moyo want to walk. Lerox and the cats will ride."

"Copy that." She sank to one knee to give him easier access to the back of her suit. "Hook it up."

He rapped his knuckles twice on her shoulder plate when he was done. "Thank you for not asking me to leave them."

The implications of his words sank in as she rose to her feet. "Captain Bhayrip is a platinum-plated asshole." Jutting her chin forward unrepentantly, she added, "And I'll say it again for the official record if you want, Field Commander, sir."

Hands on his hips, he gave her a mock glare. "Just for that, I'm promoting you to Field Co-Commander as of right now. Let's go after those lifesigns."

Amusement relaxed some of her tension as she turned toward and started on the path Po had taken. "The scanners say they're still on the move." She held out her arm to show him the holo map and the realtime scanner trace.

Rylando walked beside her. "I'm assuming the detonator won't work." His tone held a note of uncertainty.

"I disabled the timers." She'd wait to tell him how many there had been. He might not appreciate how she'd used his team to help. "Damn, I wish we had our flying camera set."

"We have the next best thing." Mariposa launched herself from his shoulder and flew ahead of them. He slid the medical pack around so he could wear it as a backpack. "Po sure was talkative all of a sudden."

Taz appreciated his circumspect phrasing. "I asked the ERC if they had any sifters who might help make him more tractable." She'd gotten the idea from the instructor they'd rescued that morning. "Probably needed more time."

She glanced at Rylando but couldn't tell if he was upset. GSAR rescuers weren't supposed to use their talents that way. Asking a civilian to do it was a gray area headed toward black.

"Oh, so that's how you knew he was lying. And that he's a ramper."

Oops. That had been her. "Sifter talents are interesting, aren't they?"

"Yeah, they're ace. Wish I knew..." His feet slowed. "Mariposa found them. Po isn't dragging Stramlo anymore, but he's still holding the beamer on him. They're stopping. Po is telling Stramlo to set the countdown. Stramlo is shaking his head."

Taz held up her scanning holo map again. "They're in this short hallway. If I distract Po, you and the dogs can streak by and pull Stramlo around the corner."

He stopped and frowned at her. "He's fast. Your suit is not beamer proof."

She slowed and turned to face him as she walked backward. "Yeah, but it's beamer-resistant." When his frown deepened, she stopped. "I think this ends in tragedy if we wait for law enforcement. But I know it's stretching 'rescue' to the breaking point, and maybe I'm thinking with adrenalin instead of brain cells. Your call, Subcaptain. What do you want to do?"

Emotions flickered across his face too fast for her to interpret. "I want you safe." He blew out a heavy breath. "But we're in the rescue business, and I can't think of a better way to save Stramlo."

Of course her stupid heart would pick that completely inappropriate moment to urge her to ask him what else he wanted, and tell him what she wanted, too. She shook it off. "Ready-set, then. You might need room to run. Scans aren't definitive. Can Mariposa tell us if that far hall is clear?"

He snorted. "Only if Po is blind to an owl flying past him."

"Good point. Okay, new gambit. I'll cover our retreat while you jet out with our prize."

Hatya's tone sounded in her earwire. *"You GSAR people sure have interesting conversations. If Po needs to hear an explosion, we can give him one."*

Taz had forgotten Rylando's earwire was on broadcast. She hoped she hadn't said anything that required an apology later. "I'll keep that in mind."

"Out of time," said Rylando. "Stramlo's opening his bag."

This would probably top her list of career-ending maneuvers, but she had to try. "Green go." As she walked, she deployed her suit's helmet. Better a communication barrier than a beamer to the face.

She rounded the corner into a long hallway that her scanner told her made a U-turn at the end. Deliberately clomping so her footsteps would echo, she let her suit amplify her voice. "Hello. Galactic Search and Rescue. Do you need assistance?"

"Yeah, sure. This building stinks." shouted Po. Her suit's audio easily picked up his hissed whisper to Stramlo. "Send the code now or I'm telling them you self-terminated."

Taz increased her volume. "How about you, Engineer Stramlo?"

In her earwire, she heard Rylando tell Hatya to ready her explosion.

"Er," replied Stramlo. "Yes. I'd very much like to leave."

"*Now,*" said Rylando.

A second later, the floor vibrated with a satisfying whump. Taz eyed the ceiling, hoping her scans were right about it holding in this part of the building.

She added concern to her voice. "Might be an aftershock. Everyone all right?"

"Help! Get us out of here." Stramlo sounded panicked.

"Almost there." With one backward glance to make sure Rylando and the animals were ready, she turned the corner at the end of the hall. "There you are. No need for the weapon, sir. The path is clear from here to the exit."

"Of course." Po looked considerably more relaxed than before as he pocketed the beamer. "Let's go."

Stramlo, clutching a thick, dull-gray tablet to his chest. He lurched forward and picked up speed, almost running toward her.

Po scooped up Stramlo's fallen bag and followed at a more leisurely pace.

Taz fired up her sifter talent and tried to get a reading on Po. No violence haze for now. She really needed to learn how to use her talent better.

Stramlo rounded the corner, then stumbled to a halt when he saw Rylando and the dogs. "Where is my daughter?"

Rylando motioned him forward. "I'll take you to her." He turned to lead with a brisk walk that Stramlo emulated.

Taz tracked Po, timing her move so she stepped in front of him at the last second. He bounced back off her suit. "Sorry, sir." She grabbed both of his upper arms to steady him, then let go. She started a countdown on her display. *15, 14...*

"Ow!" He grabbed his left arm and rubbed it. "What was that?"

She stepped back. "My apologies, sir. I must have grabbed you too hard. It's sometimes a problem with mechanized suits." *...9, 8...*

"Something poked me!" He glared suspiciously at her hand. The activation of his ramper talent felt like pinpricks on her sifter senses.

She raised her hands in front of her chest, one slightly higher and in front of the other, facing her gloved palms toward him. "Do you see anything that could have done that?" *...6, 5, 4...*

He looked, then shook his head, then again. His ramper talent blazed as his hands reached for his pockets.

Taz grabbed his arms, harder this time, pinching into his biceps. "Careful, there, sir. Looks like you're feeling dizzy." With the drug she gave him, he should have been halfway to oblivion by now, not still standing. Damnit.

He snarled and pulled back with a jerk, freeing his arms. Before she could react, he jumped and launched himself off her chest, sending her back a step as he flipped in the air. By the time he landed, his hand held the beamer. "Step out of your suit or you're dead. And so are those stinking animals on your fucking back." A cruel smile played across his lips. "Maybe I'll shoot them first."

The anger she'd been bottling up all day broke through her controls. "Thank you for saying that, sir. Per Regulation 79-A"—she grabbed his neck with her teke talent—"I get to leave your worthless waste of perfectly good carbon and water right here." She tightened the pressure on his throat. "Be a bloody fucking shame if something catastrophic was about to happen to this building, say, in the basement." She took satisfaction in seeing the panic in his eyes as he lost consciousness. When she released his neck, he collapsed to the floor. Finally!

Rylando spoke through her earwire. *"Make sure he's really down before you transport him. He's a twisty little shit."* His voice took on a teasing note. *"And if I'm ever foolish enough to make you mad, oh respected Field Co-Commander, please consider this an advance apology. Sir."*

She took a deep breath and let it out slowly, imagining she was exhaling the anger out with the air. "Noted, Field Co-Commander."

Chaos, but she was going to miss him. "See you in ten."

9

Rylando stood at the top of the shuttle's ramp, watching the sturdy maple trees and admiring the red half-moon shaped seed pods. Their distinctive leaves danced in the hot summer afternoon breeze and cast dappled shadows. It had been more than a decade since he'd even been stationed on a planet, much less on a base with natural greenery. The unpredictable air currents that tickled the bare skin of his bare chest reminded him how much he'd gone without over the years.

The usual adrenaline drop-off effect at the end of a rescue he could handle. He didn't know how to handle the end of friendships. Of partnerships. Maybe of his career.

He had zero doubts that the CPS would be willing to sacrifice the entire GSAR branch to keep the galactic peace. Or more likely, to keep their budget from bleeding out. But he couldn't imagine what other use the regular CPS Minder Corps had for trained and experienced rescuers, much less a mid-level animal-affinity minder with a knack for training animals and their human handlers.

Moyo pushed her big head into his hand and drooled on his shorts. Which reminded him that if GSAR dissolved, he'd have to do something about his team. GSAR rules would no longer protect them from being separated. The regular military hated animals on their bases, stations, and ships. He rubbed Moyo's ears and raised his talent to check on the well fed, sleepy animals who were resting in their nest or surface of choice. Even Shen dozed. "We'll manage."

"Manage what?" asked Taz.

He turned around to look at her. The first thing they'd done when Hatya sent them to wait in the shuttle was grab quick water-based showers from the shuttle's full tank. Her sleeveless top and exercise pants highlighted her sexy curves and muscular strength. With a colorful towel wrapped around her head and piled high, she looked like a pre-flight Egyptian queen.

"Just wondering about the future." He patted Moyo's rump and gave her permission to investigate the interesting smells under the trees. She gleefully bounded down the ramp like a puppy.

"Me, too," she said. "Any predictions?"

He sighed. "The CPS won't know what to do with any of us, but they won't let us go, either." Shen's brindle-coated form caught his eye. "We're kind of like her. The controller gives her enhanced abilities to work with humans, but it's wasted on owners who just want a pet." He looked back at Taz. "Were you able to connect with her using the codes I sent?"

"No." Her lips tightened. "I didn't want to form a bond with her, then be forced to abandon her a few days later. It seems bloody unlikely that we'll be assigned to the same unit again. I'm going to miss your team a lot."

"They'll miss you, too." He'd wasted so much time pushing her away instead of inviting her closer. And now it was too late to change that.

Her gaze dropped to her toes. "If it's none of my business, just say so, but do you have an emergency-shelter plan for your team? In case the CPS forces you to retire them?" She rocked back and forward on her heels and gave him a sideways look. "I don't have much in savings, but I'd help you pay for long-term boarding. They saved a lot of lives today."

The usual evasions stuck in his throat. She deserved to know the truth. "I know a place. All I have to do is get them there. It's a charity for animals that GSAR thinks are missing in action."

"Oh?" Her eyes widened in dawning comprehension. "Oh." The corners of her mouth tilted upward. "Very clever. Much better than letting GSAR bureaucrats decide what to do with 'retired' animals."

Before he lost his courage, he added, "It's my life-after-GSAR plan, too. They're a privately funded sanctuary on a donated chunk of land. They can use my talents. Maybe you could come visit, after we both term out."

She stilled, then studied his face, her expression serious. "Do you like me? I mean, not just professionally?"

"Yes." He tightened his fists in his pockets. "To be honest, I'm crazy about you. I dream about you. Very nonprofessional, nova-hot dreams." The air froze in his chest as he waited for her reaction.

"Oh." She blew out a loud breath. "I dream about you, too. Especially when you're gone. You make me laugh. You make me feel safe." She opened her mouth to speak, then stopped herself and shook her head. "And don't we have the lousiest damn timing in the universe?"

A rueful chuckle escaped him. "Yeah, we do."

She put her fists on her hips and looked down. "In the spirit of full disclosure, I'm no prize. I have a history of epically bad choices in lovers. The last one set me up as the scapegoat for a massive heist. It made me so mad that I put in for a transfer to Unit 1051, then sent the damning evidence to everyone in his command structure right before the ship went transit. When he finally gets out of military detention, he might want to settle the score." She ended with a forceful sigh.

Since she'd been so candid, he could be no less. "I'm no prize, either. I nearly killed a previous teammate when I discovered he'd been torturing Moyo for weeks. Hatya had to pull me off him. The only reason I'm not in long-term military detention with your ex is because I gave the asshole a concussion that erased his memory of that afternoon. He had a long record of instigating violence, and Hatya swore on her oath that I'd acted in self-defense." He wasn't proud of what he'd done, but knew he'd do it again in a nanosecond.

"Sounds like we both have a temper when provoked. I knew there was a reason I liked you right from the start." She held out her hands to him. "When does your contract terminate?"

He took her hands and stepped closer. "Three years, two days. What about yours?" She edged closer, only centimeters away.

Her warm breath on his chest raised goosebumps. "Almost the same. A little under three years."

"That seems like forever right now." She looked up at him with her gorgeous emerald green eyes. "In the meantime, would you be interested in a kiss?"

"Hell, yes." He slowly lowered his mouth to hers, savoring the anticipation.

A loud series of tones sounded in the shuttle. *"Damnit, Silver Team, would one of you put on your damn earwire? I'm at the edge of the grove. I'll be peeved if one of you shoots me."*

Taz pulled back from him with a laugh. "See what I mean about the lousiest timing ever?" She fished in her pocket. "Maybe we can revisit this later."

"I'd like that." He kept his smile, but he could already feel her slipping away. Crossing to the worktable where he'd left his clothes, he put on his earwire, then pulled on his pants over his shorts. Pain hollowed his chest and made the air seem too thin to breathe.

A minute later, Hatya walked up the ramp, still wearing the ship-loader assist frame. Her hair was back to its more normal top braids. Moyo followed her into the shuttle and headed toward the back.

Hatya gave them a weary smile as she stepped out of the frame, then lifted it like it weighed one kilo instead of fifty and pushed it into the shuttle's holdfasts. "I'm planting my ass in the pilot seat. We need to talk."

Taz followed Hatya up front. Unease tightened his shoulders. He grabbed his boots and tunic, then joined them.

"I'll cut to the core. Your orders from Bhayrip are to get to the space station. Regular pilot orders are to make sure you get there by any means necessary. After you all transit out to the reassignment base, Jumpers have secret orders to secure or space any GSAR equipment left behind. Which tells me GSAR is being zeroed." She pulled a water pouch from the floor bin and took a long draught.

The ice of adrenaline seeped into Rylando's lungs, stealing his breath. He'd thought he'd have more time to make arrangements for his team.

"This debacle is a colossal cluster, so I have a proposition for you. I take you and the animals to this continent's commercial spaceport. I'll use my Jumper credentials to arrange commercial transport for *my family*, since military ships won't let you bring your menagerie of household pets. You pick the destination. You're on your own after that. The town gets what's left of your gear. Yanoshi gets your airsled for his farm and the chance to screw the CPS by confirming my story that you died when more of the CAC's first floor collapsed. Which it did, by the way. Oh, and seeing as how it houses a previously unsuspected galactic node that you miraculously saved with your last brave act, the town will probably build a memorial to GSAR. If Bhayrip gives me shit about any of this, I'll remind him he sent two humans and a few animals on a high-profile rescue instead of the full team he promised. But he won't have time to investigate."

The possibilities intrigued Rylando, but he saw multiple problems to solve. "How much trouble will you be in for doing this?"

"Little to none. Bhayrip's world is crashing. My nearest chain of command is five transit days away and has no idea what I do. Besides, with GSAR zeroed, I'm out of a job. I'm retiring."

Taz cleared her throat. "Not to be ungrateful or anything, but why are you doing this?"

"Told ya, this is a cluster." Her chin jutted out pugnaciously.

Taz raised a skeptical eyebrow as she met and held Hatya's gaze.

Hatya fought it for a second, then made a sour face. "Okay, fine. Bhayrip is going to force Unit 1051 to leave *all* the animals behind as one final 'fuck you' to Rylando. No way am I destroying good and loyal dogs because the CPS wants a clean slate."

Taz shook her head in shocked disgust, then looked away, blinking fast. "Damnit." The word sounded watery.

Rylando wished he could say Bhayrip's revenge and the CPS's orders surprised him, but he'd spent too many years in Unit 1051. "We'll need funds. If you declare us dead, they'll freeze our accounts. My family doesn't need the money, so my estate and the on-duty death payout are willed to charity."

"Mine, too," said Taz. "I don't have much cash, but GSAR will owe my estate for two thousand-plus hours' worth of leave along with the death payout. It all goes to a search-and-rescue charity. My family refuses to admit to having any minders in their gene pool, so they don't need my money, either."

An idea bubbled up into Rylando's thoughts. "I remember a story where the character embezzled from herself by creating bogus certified debts. If we make backdated debts to Hatya for buying something, or maybe losing a bet, she could file claims against our estates and send us the proceeds." He looked to Hatya. "That is, if you're willing. It'll probably be a bureaucratic pain in the ass."

"Sure, why not? Retirees have all the time in the galaxy on their hands. Better make a few of those debts to my brother, though. Wouldn't want a CPS payout officer getting any sharp ideas. You'll have to keep in touch and tell me where you each end up." She cast glances at them both. "So, are we doing this?"

"Yes," said Taz. Her jaw tightened.

He nodded. "Yes."

"Good." Hatya made shooing motions with her hands. "Go

arrange your pets for a fast trip to the spaceport. Pack everything from the shuttle you think you'll need or could sell. If Bhayrip asks, I'll tell him I got a head start on decommissioning GSAR equipment." She turned away to trigger the controls to retract the ramp.

Taz tilted her head in tacit invitation. He nodded and followed her to the back of the shuttle. In the confines of the storage area, she reeled him in for a long embrace that he hadn't known he'd needed. Their bodies fit together like perfect puzzle pieces. He longed to melt into her warmth.

She loosened her hold to look up at him with a serious expression. "That place you invited me to visit. Can they take you now? Would they want someone like me?"

"Yes, and yes," he said. "They don't know it yet, but they desperately need a telekinetic tech genius."

"Good to know." Her head drifted back to his shoulder. "This is all... a lot to take in."

He nuzzled his nose into her hair and took in the intriguing scent of her. "Second thoughts?"

"No. Naughty thoughts, though. And again, my timing is lousy. Would it scare you if I told you I love you?"

"No. Do you?"

"Yes. I fought it from practically the first day I met you, but your animal magnetism was just too much for me." She lifted her head to give him an impish grin. "Field Co-Commander, sir."

He palmed the side of her face. "I love you, too, Field Co-Commander. Shocking breach of protocol, I know."

"Kiss me again, and I'll forgive you."

He did just that, with a hopeful promise of a lot more to come.

Paz de Lune Animal Sanctuary, Verderi Kashtar • GDAT 3243.094

"Valtrova, open front door." Taz voiced the command so Shen, the shepherd at her side, would know her wish was being granted.

The Russian-named house computer opened the floral-decorated interleaved sections to reveal the wide entryway.

Shen bolted through them and launched from the front steps into the small expanse of green beyond, sliding a bit on the rain-slick grass. She danced in a circle, barking in excitement.

Taz followed more sedately, amused by the silly dog who loved to bite raindrops. She cradled a warm mug against her chest and savored the subtly fruity whiff of hot morning kaff that tickled her nose. Her loose, drapey tunic and pants fluttered a little in the chilly morning breeze. The cold textured plascrete under her feet made her wish she'd stopped to put on slippers and a scarf over her head. When she'd cut her hair asymmetrically short to change her look, she hadn't anticipated that her ears and neck would miss the insulation.

The covered front porch bumped out into a shallow half-circle on this side of the house, with a blue-tinted glass railing. In the summer, she hoped it would be a nice place to sit with Rylando, soaking in the sunlight.

He called their sprawling home a modest ranch. Her childhood in a crowded city and career on military bases had never involved any living space so spacious and open. For just two humans and their pets, they had a dozen rooms with windows everywhere, even the roof.

Out in the grass, Shen crouched and barked twice, tail wagging.

Taz didn't need to access the dog's controller to know what she wanted. "No, it's too wet for me to play right now."

Contentment filled her as her gaze drifted to the low shrubs and narrow trees beyond the grass where Shen cavorted. The previous owner installed them as a living privacy screen between the neighboring houses in the enclave. Rylando liked the illusion of living in a wilderness clearing. She liked knowing they were still part of a community.

After the recall, their shorthand for the CPS's precipitous dissolution of the Galactic Search and Rescue division, the journey from Perlarossa to Verderi Kashtar had been more stressful than a rescue. Hatya's connections got them temporary travel identities, the kind celebrities used, and her Jumper credentials got them passage on a large, slow interstellar passenger liner.

But the "family stateroom" that she and Rylando shared with six "household pets" had been no bigger than their rescue airsled. And the trip itself had taken twenty-two long interstellar transit days to reach their destination.

On the ship, they kept to themselves. At first, they'd just needed the sleep. Then news of the recall exploded across the newstrends and that was all anyone wanted to talk about. Rylando had to maintain near-constant contact with the animals to keep them calm in their cages, meaning he overused his talent and paid for it with insomnia.

She fended off the hospitality stewards who wanted them out of the room and buying souvenirs. She also arranged room service for their prepaid meals and finagled items for the more exotic dietary needs of the animals.

Trending rumors said several thousand GSAR fugitives were on the run. Her and Rylando's reported deaths should have kept them off the wanted list, but if the rescue business taught her nothing else, it was that mitigation measures worked better when taken before the potential disaster. After her own improvised haircut and makeover, she pried Rylando out of their stateroom long enough to visit the ship's body parlor and change his look enough to fool casual AI surveillance.

When they finally arrived at the animal sanctuary, physically flatlined and emotionally exhausted, their new life truly began.

From Rylando's descriptions, she'd imagined the sanctuary facility would be a frontier-style slab building with space for a small population of animals and volunteer keepers. To be fair, his memories were fifteen years old. His contribution to the organization at the time had been a large swathe of rural land on the nothing-special planet of Verderi Kashtar, acquired from a complicated, multi-property real estate swap of inherited family land on other planets.

The actual Paz de Lune Animal Sanctuary and Rehabilitation Research Center now occupied nearly ninety square kilometers of rural land, with five major buildings, a veterinary hospital that put big city human medical centers to shame, dozens of staff, hundreds of animals, and enough territory to create habitats for all. Most of the staff and residents were minders, and easily half were GSAR or Minder Corps veterans.

Rylando was in heaven. The sanctuary was more than an hour's flitter flight to the nearest city. He was surrounded by nature and animals who loved him, had non-recycled air to breathe, and a lake big enough to swim in. And best of all, no disasters.

The no-disasters part suited her just fine, but she'd needed a few ten-days to appreciate the other aspects. She was still unaccustomed to sleeping in, though a nova-hot sexy lover in her bed gave her every incentive. In a way, she was like Shen, still needing things to do with her time, and having to learn how to play. It helped that Paz de Lune really did value her tech skills and welcomed her telekinetic talent. And that she'd fallen deeply in love with Rylando.

Shen shook herself like a wooly weasel, then trotted up onto the porch to sit in front of Taz, watching her expectantly.

"Yes, Captain Shen?" This time, she connected to the dog's controller. Per Rylando, Shen had decided on her own that Taz was clearly in need of shepherding. Taz was enjoying learning to be a good partner.

See...Rylando.

Taz nodded. "Yes, let's do that. I bet he hasn't checked messages."

Her hand was halfway to her ear before she caught herself. Civilians didn't wear earwires at home. They talked in person.

She reentered the warm house with Shen at her heels. The doors irised closed behind them. The dog veered straight for the built-in solardry unit next to the coat rack and barked the two-one-two pattern Rylando had taught her. Contained jets of warm, dry air coaxed the water out of her wet fur.

Taz dropped her mug off in the kitchen, then walked with the damp-smelling dog to the largest room at the far end of the house. It stood nearly two levels tall, with a domed ceiling full of octagonal window ports that concentrated or generated daylight as needed to keep the room warm, bright, and airy. Rylando designed it as a playroom room for his team... er, pets, and she'd put her construction experience to use and helped build it for him.

He sat in the center of the room, cross-legged on the floor, with gaily colored Moyo sprawled to his right, gently snoring. Rylando's back rested against the heavy crescent-shaped padded bench. The blue-green color complemented the fading blue tint to his skin, the remnants of the hasty cosmetic job from the passenger liner's body parlor. His lap held a blanket filled with six roly-poly feline kittens.

They snuggled against a custom-printed, fur-covered pouch that delivered temperature-regulated formulated milk.

He looked up at her with a grin. "The new pouch you designed is a hit. They're all eating today."

"That's great." She basked in the warmth that flooded her from his smile, unabashedly admiring the smooth planes of his muscled bare chest. "If you don't mind my asking, can you feel the kittens with your talent when they're this young?"

The orphaned litter of starving babies had kept her and Rylando up at all hours for days. He'd insisted on taking most of the shifts, so he was tired but full of heart-melting smiles. This was his element, helping animals thrive.

"Sort of." He twitched a shoulder. "They're like little sparks of potential. Once they start recognizing and interacting with each other, they'll start recognizing me, too." His finger delicately brushed along the top of the darkest kitten's head. "They'll know our scents a lot sooner. The dogs' scents, too."

Taz laughed. "They're going to be very confused kittens, thinking they have four mothers." When neither she nor Rylando could tend the kittens, Shen or Moyo stayed with them and patiently let them snuggle up against their warm bellies.

"They'll be fine. Domestic cats are amazingly adaptable creatures."

She pointed toward the media wall. "We got news from Hatya. Want me to queue it up for you, or just tell you the highlights?"

"Highlights. I'll listen after I feed the rest of the menagerie." He gave her a shy smile. "I like the sound of your voice."

"Thank you." Subtle pleasure stole over her, making her want to curl up in his lap with the kittens. He always seemed to know the right thing to say.

"Let's see. First, the CPS held an emergency mass sale of GSAR's non-military ships and equipment. Maybe they needed the funds? Anyway, Hatya and her brother bought six of the better transit ships and a bunch of shuttles to start an interstellar transport outfit. They're hiring ex-Jumper buddies as pilots."

Rylando smiled. "How fitting. I'll put in a word with the office. Paz de Lune will be needing a trustworthy shipping company more than ever." He pulled a damp textured cloth from the small bucket on the floor to his right. "I got a casual ping yesterday from a rescuer I went to vet-med training with, asking about job leads. The sanctuary replied with the usual 'no one here by that name' notice, but sent the link to their position list. If the query is legit, we might have more new residents on the way."

"This would be a great place for them." She sighed. "Chaos, but I hope we can someday go back to assuming old friends just want to reconnect, not betray us to the CPS. Buying a new set of permanent identities and running again would totally tank."

"Yeah, it would. I don't hold it against them, though. The CPS can exert tremendous pressure when it wants something." He lifted the dark-furred kitten to gently wipe its butt, like the mother cat would have done, then put it in the heated nesting crate to his right. "I'm glad the sanctuary asks for background checks on all new residents, regardless. Some people shouldn't be allowed anywhere near animals."

"Like Bhayrip." It still outraged her that their asshole former captain would have killed Rylando's team out of spite. She hoped his next post made him the local commanding officer over the bots on a hazardous landfill moon.

"What else did Hatya say?" The snowy-white kitten squawked and squirmed when he lifted it from his lap.

"She misses Moyo." Taz glanced down at Shen, still standing by her side. "I was thinking maybe you could source a trained military dog for her like Shen. Someone to travel the galaxy with her. A Jumper might be too proud to accept help from people, but I bet she would from a dog."

His eyes crinkled as a smile widened his face. "What a great idea." He deftly wiped the white kitten's butt and put it in the nest. "I don't know how she got the CPS to pay out our supposed debts so fast, or we'd still be staying in the sanctuary's guest suite. We owe her."

"That we do. Let's see, what else? Oh, yeah, she found out why that jerk Po wanted to blow up the galactic node data center on Perlarossa. Turns out they'd already secretly destroyed all the others across the planet. Some twist about deleting the last authoritative archive of land ownership records so his family could scam a bigger percentage of the RSI settlement. And Stramlo wasn't as innocent as he claimed. He sold Po the explosives and the instructions. Po wanted insurance, so he kidnapped Stramlo and Jhidelle. Even with the scans and Kem-X packet I saved as evidence, Po's family matriarch got him and the bodyguard acquitted. Stramlo got sentenced for indenture, but he disappeared himself and his bank accounts, abandoning Jhidelle. I guess he'd already showed her how little he valued her when he let Po shove her out of your airsled to lighten the load."

"Still a rough ride for a kid." Rylando frowned. "I hope she finds a better family of her own."

"She's smart and resilient. She'll be okay. Besides, she'll inherit Stramlo's fraction of the RSI settlement, plus an extra decimal for her part in saving the planet's last node. I'm glad our last mission had no casualties."

"I can't say I'm missing the rescue business these days." He put the last kitten in the box.

"You and me both. I like that the only disasters we have to respond to now are when the cats tease Moyo into chasing them across the furniture." She waved toward the wall's clock display. "Do you have time for us to try breakfast? Or should I grab something for me and Shen at the community kitchen?"

He set the milk pouch aside, then rose to his feet. "I've got rounds this morning. Let's save our science experiments for the evening meal."

Neither of them knew anything about cooking, but they were

having fun learning. In the win column, they hadn't yet set the house on fire.

She laughed. "Deal." Crossing to him, she plied him with a lingering kiss so she'd remember the taste of him for hours. "Love you."

His arms tightened in a momentary bear hug, then freed her. "Love you, too. Take your flitter. It's warmer."

At the door, Shen vocalized a soft yip.

Taz laughed. "Coming, Captain Shen. You're a much better captain than we had before."

Rylando watched the love of his life leave the room, suppressing the urge to follow her just like Shen. He had an advantage in that as long as he was physically close enough to the dog, he could find out how Taz was doing without having to ping her more than once or twice a day. If he pinged her as often as he thought about her, she'd never get anything done.

He'd used up all his luck for a lifetime when she'd agreed to give up her career and bind her star with his. With each new passing day, he was discovering how deep her compassion went. Probably made her so good with people. Made her so good for him.

He wanted—no, needed—to be as good for her. Share his feelings with her, not just with the animals. Talk to her. Tell her how much he admired and appreciated her. Build a strong family together, since her own biological relatives had pushed her out the airlock for the unforgivable sin of being a minder.

"Mealtime," he announced, and sent a brief nudge to the daylight-active animals. He'd kept his unusual team together for now, but he knew it would change with time and looked forward to it. After one more check on the kittens, he crossed to the room's food prep station and began pulling out containers.

Thanks to Hatya's crafty efforts, he and Taz both ended up with more funds than they'd anticipated. The room addition had been his idea, and Taz had readily agreed. She handled all the details that would have driven him to distraction. He was learning to be more careful in what he asked for because she loved making things happen for him. He never wanted to take advantage of her.

Taking a veterinary behaviorist job with the sanctuary and living in a private nature preserve settled his restlessness, but had the opposite effect on Taz. Complaining wasn't her style, but he noticed how much she looked forward to working with people, or even just socializing. Since she'd given up everything— even her customized GSAR mech-suit— to disappear quietly into the countryside with him, the least he could do was go with her on more trips to the city. Besides, during their first visit a couple of ten-days ago to try out her newly acquired flitter, she'd followed her sharp ears to the alley that had six orphaned kittens, so cities had good things, too.

If he was honest, Moyo the soft-hearted hellhound needed more interaction with people, too. She'd make a fantastic therapy dog for rehab treatment centers.

He couldn't give up Moyo right away, though. Her comforting love and protectiveness had done wonders for the residual post-stress trauma that afflicted Taz and him both. His nightmares had mostly faded, and only really loud unexpected sounds triggered Taz's hypervigilance response. Since they couldn't trust unknown minder specialists to be mucking about in their heads, they'd have to use Moyo's brand of therapy for a while longer. Better their unorthodox treatment method than hoping for the nonexistent mercies of the CPS.

Two cats materialized on the countertop as if by teleportation. Devious Deimos had learned to broadcast hunger pangs to him as she paced with excitement. Punctilious Phobos sat and hurriedly licked his foreleg in an emergency grooming session.

After Rylando pushed a bowl in front of each cat, he set bowls in front of Moyo and Lerox, then set the mix of vegetables and protein cubes in front of Otak's den. The rat liked to nibble throughout the day rather than inhale it. He'd feed the snoozing owl later that day around sunset.

When his veterinary rounds were done for the morning, he planned to take Moyo and Lerox out for a ramble near the start of the red-colored canyons. The river that fed his beloved lake came from there. Hellhounds liked the exercise, and exploration was in the big weasel's DNA. Maybe his, too.

Then he'd have the luxury of a whole evening with Taz. He looked forward to it. Every hour they spent together strengthened their heart connection. No life was perfect, but theirs was damned close.

He couldn't wait to see what their future together would bring.

ABOUT THE BOOK

Thanks for reading *The Galactic Pets Collection*. Each of these stories debuted in the limited-edition Pets in Space® anthologies.

The stories are set in the Central Galactic Concordance universe. They're side trips from the big damn story arc that's going on. They're also a chance to explore aspects of my future universe that are usually in the background. Plus, my cats are thrilled when I include pets in stories.

If you love space opera, adventure, and romance, check out OVERLOAD FLUX. Two misfits have secrets they must keep. But if they expose the secrets of a corrupt pharma corp, they may end up dead.

When the cure for a deadly disease is stolen, two misfits are all that stands between greed and intergalactic tragedy.

Luka Foxe can't let anyone know about his secret mental abilities. Debilitated by their influence when faced with violence, the brilliant forensic investigator now only takes assignments involving theft. But when he has to hunt down a hijacked vaccine for a galaxy-wide pandemic, the tragic first clue is his best friend's brutal murder.

Nightshift guard Mairwen Morganthur knows she must keep a low profile. The product of illegal genetic alteration, she's a lethal weapon with no social graces. But when she's tasked to protect a detective with frightening intuition, she finds herself falling for him even though he could expose her.

Racing to recover the cure for a galaxy-wide pandemic, Luka is surprised by his developing feelings for the capable-but-mysterious guard. And Mairwen may have to risk everything by revealing her identity, with deadly mercenaries hot on their tail.

Can the unlikely pair survive an interplanetary conspiracy long enough to save lives and find love?

Overload Flux is the first novel in the sweeping Central Galactic Concordance space opera series. If you like haunted characters, compelling mysteries, and interstellar romance, then you'll enjoy Carol Van Natta's epic tale.

**Buy Overload Flux to uncover
cosmic corruption today!**

Author.CarolVanNatta.com/OF

*

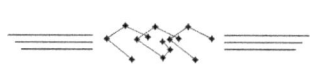

ABOUT THE AUTHOR

Carol Van Natta is a USA TODAY bestselling science fiction and fantasy author. Works include the award-winning Central Galactic Concordance space opera series and the Ice Age Shifters® paranormal romance series. In addition, she edits the Pets in Space science fiction romance anthology.

She shares her Colorado home with just the right number of eccentric cats. Connect with her on the web at Author. CarolVanNatta.com.